Praise for the Novels of Kate Saunders

Bachelor Boys

"An unusually witty and intelligent romance."

—*The Boston Globe*

"A funny, touching, and sweet story about love, family, and keeping promises."

—*Booklist*

"Witty banter and spirited characters propel this lighthearted novel."

—*Publishers Weekly*

"Saunders is a witty writer with a talent for creating quick-moving plots and striking the right balance between comfort and surprise. And, unlike many of her chick-lit colleagues, she has a well-honed sense of life's rhythms....The book is sweet and satisfying reading, made all the stronger because its characters all seem to live in apartments they can actually afford."

—*Chicago Sun-Times*

"A radiant romantic comedy about the ties that bind us. It is both humorous and heartfelt, with colorful characters and poignant moments that stick with you for a long time."

—Emily Giffin

"*Bachelor Boys* is about going next door to find family, about keeping promises, and about how people live forever in the hearts of those who love them. Kate Saunders has written a wonderful novel filled with the real and magical power of love."

—Luanne Rice

The Marrying Game

"Such wit, such charm, such intelligence, and what I loved most is that although in some ways it's a very serious book, it gave me that money-can't-buy serene glow that everything was going to be okay....A gloriously buoyant, uplifting book."

—Marian Keyes

"A whimsical and witty comedy of manners."

—*Kirkus Reviews*

"An absolute delight!"

—Susan Isaacs

"Once every three or four years, I find a novel that so enchants me, I make the following claim: I couldn't put it down if the curtains were on fire! ... *The Marrying Game* has unexpected depth, perfect characterization, and holding power that will make a rainy Saturday afternoon seem a gift from heaven. This is simply literate fiction of the highest order."

—Victoria Skurnick, editor in chief,
The Book-of-the-Month Club

BACHELOR BOYS

Also by Kate Saunders

The Marrying Game

BACHELOR BOYS

Kate Saunders

St. Martin's Griffin

New York

www.stmartins.com

Library of Congress Cataloging-in-Publication Data

Saunders, Kate.
    Bachelor Boys / Kate Saunders.
        p. cm.
    ISBN-13: 978-0-312-33941-8
    ISBN-10: 0-312-33941-0

    1. Parent and adult child—Fiction. 2. Terminally ill parents—Fiction.
3. Female friendship—Fiction. 4. London (England)—Fiction. 5. Mothers and sons—Fiction. 6. Mate selection—Fiction. 7. Brothers—Fiction. I. Title.

PR6069.A915B33 2005
823'.914—dc22

                                                                    2004061904

First published in United Kingdom by Century

First St. Martin's Griffin Edition: July 2006

10 9 8 7 6 5 4 3 2 1

FOR RUSSELL

Acknowledgments

Many people have helped me with the writing of this novel, in many ways. Russell Celyn Jones, Amanda Craig, Joanna Briscoe, Charlotte Mendelsohn, Bill Saunders, Charlotte Saunders and Louisa Saunders have listened and advised most kindly. Felix Wells, as always, has helped simply by being lovely (and putting up with his mother's unlovely moods).

And I know I have been inspired by the lives and deaths of my parents, Basil and Betty Saunders.

They beckon to me from the other bank.
I hear them call, "See where the stream path is!
Crossing is not as hard as you might think."

—CHARLES CAUSLEY, "EDEN ROCK"

BACHELOR BOYS

CHAPTER ONE

I was in the middle of cutting down a dotty and rambling piece about the Golden Age of Crime Fiction when Phoebe rang.

"Cassie, darling. I know how busy you are, so I won't keep you."

Her voice was soft and fresh, with a faint Edinburgh accent like the scent of heather. It was the voice of gentleness and safety and I unconsciously curled up in it, ripping off my glasses and stretching out in my office chair.

"That's okay, we're not particularly busy."

"The thing is," Phoebe said, "I've been thinking about something. And I really need your advice."

"Mine?"

"It's in your area of expertise."

"You mean books." I was the editor of *The Cavendish Quarterly*, London's most respectable literary magazine, and Phoebe often asked me to recommend books for various friends (in vain did I hint that this was not, in fact, a normal part of my job description).

"Not this time," Phoebe said. "I can't tell you over the phone, because you'll laugh."

I said, "You've had one of your ideas."

This was not a question. Phoebe was famous for having ideas.

"Well, yes," she said, with that familiar air of being awed by her own brilliance. "It's a wonderful idea, but I don't see how it can be done without you."

"As long as it doesn't involve dressing up as a squirrel," I said.

At the other end of the phone, Phoebe giggled. Ten years before, in my student days, she had persuaded me to hand out leaflets dressed as a red squirrel. This ghastly experience had left deep scars on my psyche, and I never let her forget it.

"Nothing like that," she assured me. "This is a totally different sort of idea. I can't wait to tell you—could you possibly come tonight?"

I made a quick calculation. It would mean putting off Matthew, which he wouldn't like. But he would understand. He knew that any summons from Phoebe was sacred. She was the nearest thing I had to a mother.

"Of course," I said. "I'd love to."

"I'll make some supper. I've got some lovely fresh tagliatelli."

"Can I bring anything?"

"No, my darling, just yourself," Phoebe said tenderly. "It'll only be the two of us. This isn't something I can talk about in front of the boys."

I might have guessed it would be about the boys. For as long as I had known her, Phoebe had been cockeyed about those boys of hers. In every other department she was perfectly rational, but where the boys were concerned, she could talk herself into anything. I loved her all the more for this large blind spot.

"You're being very mysterious," I said. "What's going on?"

"Wait and see." Her voice was light and teasing, which I took as a good sign. "And Cassie, if you happen to run into Fritz or Ben, you mustn't say a word about any of this. I mean, you can say you're coming to supper, but that's all."

"Okay, my lips are sealed. See you tonight."

The call ended with me holding up the receiver so that Betsy could shout greetings from the other side of the office. Betsy Salmon was my deputy editor, but I had been at school with her four daughters, and she had known Phoebe since the boys were babies—she had once smacked Fritz at a birthday party, for persecuting the conjuror.

As soon as the phone was down, Betsy asked, "Well? How do you think she is?"

"Fine. Tired, obviously." I was sharp. I hated talking about Phoebe's health.

"And how are the boys?"

"She didn't say, so I assume they're fine." I knew it was mean to be

2

sharp with Betsy, when she was so unfailingly kind. I stretched and rolled my chair back. "I heard Shay and Puffin sloping off to the pub just now," I said. "So let's declare an official lunch break."

"Oh, good idea," Betsy said. "Just what we need to turn morning into afternoon." She bent down to the tartan shopping bag she used as a briefcase and pulled out a Tupperware box, a Thermos flask and some rainbow-colored knitting. Her oldest daughter had baby triplets, and Betsy snatched her knitting whenever her hands came free.

I dug in my briefcase for the cheese baguette I had bought on the way in, now squashed under Volume Three of a biography of Lord Beaconsfield. While I ate, I watched Betsy lapping at her vegetable soup between stitches, and thought what a comfortable presence she was to have nearby. She had long gray hair, which she bolted into a bun with a hideous leather slide, and she was usually dressed in a washed-out needlecord sack. She had been holding the *Quarterly* together since the Repeal of the Corn Laws, and I knew that I'd have been lost without her. It was odd how quickly I'd got used to working a few feet away from my classmate Sally Salmon's mum.

"You know," I said, "we really ought to stop calling them 'boys.' They're grown men now, even if poor Phoebe can't see it."

"Of course. Fritz must be thirty-one—the same age as you and Sally," Betsy said thoughtfully. "And I know Ben's the same age as Jonah, because Phoebe and I used to meet at the baby clinic." Jonah was (and is) Betsy's only son, then living in the attic of his parents' home. Sally called him "Mrs. Rochester." "It's so hard to remember sometimes how grown-up you all are these days."

Betsy and Phoebe had matching blind spots. I frankly wondered sometimes why women bothered with sons. The boys I had grown up with, in our segment of middle-class London, were a disappointing crew. Betsy's Jonah was only too typical. He had two degrees (one more and he could have sung as a group), but he had never had a proper job. Betsy's daughters said he spent his entire life eating, smoking and running up phone bills. And there were so many like him—hearty young men who had never broken an honest bead of sweat in their lives, and who cheerfully assumed the world owed them a living.

My female friends and I were always trying to solve the mystery

3

of what had gone wrong with the middle-class boys of our generation. We were all educated up to the nines, but the paths of the two sexes seemed to have divided somewhere in the late teens. Us girls were high achievers—ravenously ambitious, and obsessed with success. We set our sights as high as possible, and went for our goals like starving tigresses fighting over meat.

Take me. At the age of thirty-one, I was turning round a threadbare old warhorse of a literary magazine. True, my only qualifications for the job had been a spell in publishing, a longer spell with a national newspaper and ridiculous amounts of chutzpah. But I was slowly inching up the circulation. I was often to be heard on radio book programs, and seen on television. I had helped to judge several literary prizes. I don't like boasting, but I was proud of the things I had achieved because I had to work so hard for them. And I applied this relentless work ethic to all areas of my life. My natural state, I often think, is chaos. Left to myself, I create mess and clutter—far more than a normal, tidy person. A normal person can brush her hair and wash her face and look passable. I knew that more effort was required of me. I put incredible amounts of work into being as perfect as I could. The point is not that I'm clever or talented. The key word here is "work."

My achievements were only average when set against those of my (female) friends and acquaintances. All Betsy's daughters were hugely successful—one was in banking, Sally was a barrister, one produced award-winning documentaries and the one with triplets was (appropriately) an obstetrician. Still in the same neighborhood, my old form prefect had been short-listed for the Turner Prize and the girl who shared my flute lessons had made a fortune from mail-order fashion. I could go on.

Where, meanwhile, were the boys who had grown up beside us? My female friends and I often sighed over the dreadful shortage of proper men. We had to cast our nets far and wide, because there was nothing worth catching at home. In the bee community, all those useless drones would have been stung to death years ago. In the human community they toiled not, neither did they spin, and they clung to their family homes like ornamental plasterwork. Their aging parents were resigned to buying economy sizes and paying drug fines until the crack of doom. I only hoped those without daughters were saving for their funerals—if they left it to their sons, they'd be buried in wheelie-bins.

Not that the mothers would admit to any of this. Betsy, Phoebe and the whole regiment of genteel mums with useless sons all delighted in finding ingenious excuses for their boys' chronic idleness. Jonah, for example, claimed to be writing poetry. Not one jot or tittle of poetry ever issued from his attic, and his sisters regarded him as a waste of food, but his doting old mum maintained that he was "sensitive." This was a popular, almost standard excuse among the doting mums.

"Sensitive—phooey," my friend Hazel (youngest-ever editor of a glossy magazine) would say. "Lazy, more like. Why can't gorgeous, successful women like us find decent male counterparts?"

"Just solvent and self-supporting, that's all I ask," my best friend Annabel (merchant banking) would sigh wistfully. "Why can't I ever fall in love with a guy who has a job?"

"Or even a guy who does housework sometimes," my friend Claudette would add. Claudette was a doctor. We didn't think she had much right to complain, since she was safely married to another doctor, and her brother had regular work, albeit as a nightclub bouncer. But Claudette said her brother was only employed as a bouncer because he was six foot four and black, and they would fire him as soon as they found out how lazy he was.

Hazel would sometimes murmur, "Still, he's awfully good-looking."

And Claudette would firmly say, "Don't even think about it. You didn't do all that grafting to support a man who was chucked out of Cambridge for sleeping all day."

"Yes, but when he's got himself together—"

"*All day,* Haze. Never forget that. Dearly as I love him, I wouldn't wish him on my worst enemy."

I was aware that I was one of the lucky ones. I was madly in love with Matthew, who was pursuing a glittering career in corporate law with the single-minded intensity of a woman. This was because he had been brought up far, far away from middle-class, woolly-liberal north London, and was therefore able to think about more than recreational drugs and the club scene.

Matthew Jeremy Peale had been brought up in Cheadle by wealthy Tory parents with no books. He had attended a respectable but unglamorous public school, from which he was never once suspended. He had a serious character, and serious tastes. I had always dreamed of a boyfriend who could sit through heavy culture without flinching, and Matthew had delighted me by booking us a holiday in Salzburg, for the festival. Yes, my girlfriends teased me horribly about this (Hazel kept e-mailing me with sarky suggestions about bikinis), but I felt there was something heroic about a man who could take that much pure Mozart and class it as leisure. If that was his definition of leisure, how tough did that make him at work?

Besides, when my friends protested that Matthew was "dull," I felt they were missing the whole point of our relationship. Matthew was the first man I'd ever been out with who liked "dull" culture as much as I did. Yes, I have peculiar tastes. I'm a highbrow—out and proud. And Matthew's brow was even higher. The hardest plays, the most fatiguing operas, the obscurest chamber concerts were nothing to him. Sometimes, he even made me feel shallow. I found this a mighty turn-on.

I had met Matthew about two years before, at a dinner party given by an old publishing colleague. He had come straight from his office. He wore a crisp gray suit and striped (not remotely gaudy) silk tie. He was fair-haired, with blunt, strong features and what I can only describe as an air of clean certainty. There was a calmness to his confidence, an earnestness to his interest, which I found incredibly attractive. I had dreamed of a man like this for years, and Matthew slotted neatly into the space I had made for him.

I didn't see much of him for the first year or so. His firm moved him to New York, and we kept up a rather glamorous and very expensive transatlantic affair. At the time I am writing of, he had been back in London for about six months. We planned to move in together, when the time was right. We were still working through the practicalities. But his prolonged absence had definitely made my heart fonder, and I freely admit that I adored him. Yes, he had his flaws. Knowing about them made me love him more.

I swallowed the last of my mangled baguette, and punched Matthew's direct line into the phone. I knew I would get him. He only went out to lunch if there was money involved.

"Cassie!" He sounded pleased. "Hi, darling. How's it going?"

"Darling," I plunged straight in, "I'm really sorry, but I'll have to put you off for tonight. Phoebe wants to see me."

Matthew's voice was immediately full of concern. "Is she all right?"

"Oh yes, she just wants to talk to me about something—lord knows what."

"Well, of course you must go."

"Oh, Matthew, you are nice. I hate standing you up. Can you come round tomorrow instead?"

"I've got a better offer for tomorrow," Matthew said cheerfully. "You're going to love this. I've managed to blag a box at the Coliseum— that new production of *The Flying Dutchman*."

"Oh, how amazing!"

He chuckled down the phone. "I knew you'd be thrilled. The tickets are like gold dust."

"God, yes!"

"I'll meet you in the foyer at six forty-five tomorrow, and we'll have a bottle of champagne. As it's a box, we can take it in with us."

"Heavenly!"

You will have noticed, as Matthew did not, the slightly forced quality of my interjections. Yes, I was interested in the hot new production of *The Flying Dutchman* at the English National Opera. But my overwhelming reaction was disappointment. Matthew and I hadn't had an evening at home together for nearly three weeks. He preferred going out to staying in. He was forever getting tickets to operas and concerts, saying his job made him hungry for the higher culture. I was tough enough to take any amount of culture on the chin, but I did absolutely love it when Matthew just came round to my place for dinner. On these occasions, I would cook one of the elegant little dishes taught to me by Phoebe. Matthew would arrive with his briefcase, a bottle of wine and a clean shirt for the next day. This last item was an unofficial guarantee that we would have sex and sleep together afterward.

I thought of the four lamb chops sitting in my fridge. I had bought

7

them for Matthew. Now that I was seeing Phoebe, he would not come round to dinner and there would be no sex. And now that we were going to the opera I wouldn't get any sex tomorrow, either. After the opera, Matthew preferred to go home alone, because he always seemed to have meetings at the crack of dawn. I was a little hurt that he had not thought of this while congratulating himself over the tickets. When would we have sex again? Never, at this rate.

"He's got tickets for *The Flying Dutchman* tomorrow," I told Betsy, testing the sound of it.

"Hmmm. That's nice." Betsy guessed how I felt, but was too kind to challenge me.

"It's had stunning reviews—Annabel's been, and she said it was mind-blowing."

"Wonderful," Betsy said, exuding benevolent skepticism.

I was talking myself into the right frame of mind. "I'm so lucky to have a man who actually likes going out and seeing something worthwhile. I can't stand too many evenings in."

"All the same," Betsy said, "it wouldn't do young Matthew any harm to slow down a bit. Is this his idea of fun, or is he trying to prove something?"

"Some people actually enjoy opera, Betsy, strange as it may seem."

"But how do you know he's enjoying himself? I mean, a night at the opera isn't exactly letting your hair down."

"He says it relaxes him," I said.

"Funny notion of relaxation. He'll never unwind properly until he stops thinking about work all the time."

It was never any use trying to make Betsy understand the inner workings of the ambitious male. "He can't stop thinking about work till he's a partner."

Betsy drained the last of her soup and began a new row of knitting. "Has he said any more about getting engaged?"

No. He had not. I was not going to admit this to Betsy, when I could hardly admit it to myself. "We talk about it from time to time," I said. "The time's not right at the moment. We both have too much to do first."

She looked at me solemnly over her glasses. "You know, by the time I was your age, I'd been married for six years and I had three children."

"Yes, I know. But a little thing called feminism came along, just in time to save women like me from the same ghastly fate."

"Cassie, one of the few advantages of being an old bag is that you know what's really important. I don't like to see you throwing so much of your energy into your career. What's the point of being the most successful person in the world if you don't have a life outside the office?"

She didn't expect an answer to this question, but it hung in the air like the aftertaste of cheese. The embarrassing fact was that I longed, longed, longed to marry Matthew. Somewhere inside this single-minded career woman there apparently lurked a frilly creature with no ambition beyond being loved. When my work became too stressful, I often escaped into a furtive little fantasy about jacking it all in, moving to a leafy suburb and raising a family.

I didn't feel I'd ever had a real family of my own. My childhood had left me with a permanent ache of outrage. On paper, I was fortunate. My parents were both psychiatrists (my father wrote fashionable books, my mother had a reputation for treating the criminally insane) and we lived in a handsome Georgian house in Hampstead.

But it was a house without warmth. My parents—mainly my father, I think—liked white walls and blond wood, and modernist sculptures that bristled with barbed wire. Nothing in the place acknowledged the existence of a child. My tasteful educational toys were confined to my bare and drafty playroom. My parents worked all hours: my father in a rented office and my mother in her locked wards. The business of bringing me up was left to a series of foreign au pairs.

My parents were chilly people. I have no memory of caresses or playfulness. I was trained to keep quiet and not bump into the expensive, scary furniture. My father is a dry, unexpressive, critical man. My mother was, at that time, silent and impossibly distant. I grew up under the distinct impression that my father was in charge, and my mother was his resentful prisoner. Her baffling relationship with him surrounded her like a fog, leaving little room for me. They divorced when I was in my teens, and I felt nothing except a mild relief. I was glad to leave our petrified house, and move to a less pretentious but more comfortable flat near the railway in Gospel Oak. Without my father, I could draw a proper breath.

I found I could live quite easily with my mother's gloom. You can ignore gloom.

Later, I came to a better understanding of the sadness that lay between my parents, without coming near to guessing what caused it. As I grew up, Phoebe urged me to keep in touch with my mother. Mainly to please Phoebe, I called her about once a week. It was hard work. Ruth, my mother, had absolutely no gift for light conversation. We were distantly courteous, and I couldn't help thinking of Winnie-the-Pooh trying to cheer up Eeyore.

I couldn't mention Winnie-the-Pooh to my father. He banned the book during my childhood, on the grounds that it was "elitist and anthropomorphic." Yes, he was a barrel of laughs. We met then as we do now. He takes me out to lunch at Simpson's in the Strand, twice a year, Christmas and birthday. He used to express a tepid interest in my career. I used to enjoy listing my various academic and professional triumphs, until I realized he was only showing the interest he would have shown to one of his patients. I'd spent my whole life trying to impress him, but it was a waste of time. I don't think he ever wanted children. What freakish spasm of heat warmed me into being? I have no memory of a single sexual frisson between him and my mother.

All the warmth and love in my childhood (and my access to the unsuitable works of A. A. Milne, E. Nesbit and C. S. Lewis) came from the house next door. My parents were insular and never fraternized with the neighbors, but as soon as I was aware of a longing for anything, I longed for the next-door garden like the banished Peri at the gates of Paradise.

The home of the Darling family vibrated with noise and heaved with chaos. I used to sit in our bay window in the mornings, hungrily watching the drama of Jimmy Darling leaving for work. Jimmy was a handsome, rosy, boisterous man, with a loud and tuneful voice (we often heard him singing through the wall) and a jubilant laugh. He was a venereologist at the Royal Free Hospital. He would come bursting out of his front door scattering papers, shouting over his shoulder to his wife and their two little sons. Sometimes he would swear because he had forgotten something, and dash back inside. Sometimes he would run back to give his wife and the boys one more bear hug. Although he was very busy, and although my parents had only spoken to him to complain about a tree house he had built, Jimmy never forgot to wave to the solitary little girl in the window. He was the kindest man I have ever known.

And I adored his wife, who used to give me the sweetest smiles and hellos when we met in the street. What can I say about Phoebe Darling? The greatest writers have a hard time describing real goodness, so I have to fall back on lukewarm clichés—"sweet," "warm"—which can never convey the pure essence of Phoebe. I can't write about the scent of a rose.

In those days, she must have been at the height of her special brand of loveliness. She was slight and dark and softly spoken, and her brown velvet eyes brimmed with watchful humor. I was interested to see how often Jimmy kissed her lips and swept her into his arms. Both parents practically worshipped their two dark-eyed sons. The fortunate Darling boys were hugged and squeezed and kissed and thrown into the air. Slight as she was, Phoebe carried Ben on her hip until he was at least four.

The day the barrier between the gardens came down is seared into my memory. I was four years old. A photograph of the time shows the little girl I was: tiny and defensive, with anxious brown eyes under a fringe of wispy brown curls. This is the child who pulled a kitchen chair into her paved back garden, one glorious summer afternoon.

I stood on the chair, gazing into the leafy well of the garden next door. That garden was my theater, and the show that day was particularly good. They had a paddling pool. Four-year-old Frederick and three-year-old Benedict were stark naked, splashing and fighting like a pair of noisy puppies. Both had Phoebe's beautiful dark eyes. Little Ben had ringlets, and behaved (his brother would claim later) in an offensively ringletty manner—he sucked his thumb and was given to weeping big, photogenic tears.

Frederick (equally pretty, but an unmistakable little devil) looked up at the top of the fence, and saw my earnest face through the clematis. He stared. I stared back, in a vacant way, as if watching television.

Then he startled me by asking, "What's your name?"

He had noticed me, as so few people did. I was not invisible. "Cassie," I whispered.

"My name's Frederick. That's Ben. That's our mummy."

Phoebe, coming out of the back door with a tray of orange squash, walked across the lawn toward me. She wore a striped Breton shirt, and denim shorts that showed endless bare brown legs. Her long, glossy black plait lay over one shoulder.

"Her name's Cassie," Frederick informed her.

"Hello, Cassie. I'm Phoebe."

Feebee. I turned the funny name over in my mind, liking it.

Phoebe put her tray down on the grass. She poured orange squash from a glass jug into a plastic beaker. She handed this libation through the clematis like Hebe dispensing nectar. I was not allowed orange squash at my house, and I sipped it reverently, amazed by the violent golden sweetness that flooded my tongue.

"Thank you," I whispered, daring to hand back the drained beaker.

"Would you like to play in our pool?"

Of course I wanted to, but I shook my head. I didn't have the language to explain that I wasn't strong enough to break through the screen into Paradise. I couldn't imagine what would happen to me if I did. I was beyond shy. Suddenly feeling exposed, I jumped off the chair and dragged it back to the house. I was partly sorry and partly glad that I had ended the conversation.

I was reckoning without Phoebe. A short time later she appeared at the front door, clutching a German phrasebook. Haltingly, she told Gudrun (the au pair of the moment and a nice girl, if dim) that I would be next door until six. She held out her hand to me. I slipped my sharp little paw into her soft, cool palm. We walked next door and I became part of the beautiful picture. Dazzled, I sank down on the tattered lawn—still watching, but from a better seat.

Phoebe gently persuaded me out of my dress and into the cool silver water. I felt the delight of it like an internal explosion, and Phoebe giggled at the look on my face. The two boys soon forgot I was a novelty, and threw open their game to include me. Frederick appeared to be loud and rough, and I was a little wary of him. But he was also kind, and he let me sit in the deep end of the pool where the lawn sloped. The game was that Benedict and I were daffodil bulbs and Frederick was growing us. He watered our heads with his red plastic watering can. We all thought this was hilarious.

Time sprouted wings. The sunlight danced on the leaves, beads of water dried on my warm skin. Phoebe sat cross-legged on the grass, watching us. Every so often she darted into the kitchen and emerged with more squash, or slices of apple. The grand finale, as I still remember, was a chocolate biscuit of astounding deliciousness.

Jimmy came home. The boys flung their wet bodies at him, soaking his shirt. I wondered if he would be cross. He laughed and tickled Ben's tummy. He hurled Frederick back into the pool with a tremendous splash. He landed a hard kiss on Phoebe's mouth.

She loosened his tie, saying he looked hot. "Look who's here," she said, nodding toward me.

He smiled down at me. "So you've enticed Rapunzel out of her tower."

"She's not called Rapunzel," Frederick said. "Her name's Cassie. And guess what—she's never seen anyone's willy before."

This was true—I forgot to mention the interest we expressed in each other's privates. Once my initial shyness had worn off, I wanted to know everything.

Jimmy said something like, "I wish I could say the same—I've been eyeballing willies all day."

Phoebe laughed, and said, "Don't, darling—what if she repeats it? They won't let her come back."

"Well, we can't have that," Jimmy said. "It's taken us too long to get to know Cassie. We want her to come back very soon. Don't we, monkeys?"

"Yes," Frederick said firmly. "I like her, and I like her bottom."

That was the start of my acceptance into the Darling family. Ben and Frederick became my first proper friends. We played and fought and giggled, through long summer days that seemed to have no beginning and no end. Gudrun and Phoebe found that they could pass me to and fro over the garden wall through a hole in the trellis. I was automatically included in any treats that were going on. As the year moved on, I joined them at the pantomime and the zoo, Madame Tussaud's, the Tower, and all the other attractions enjoyed by well-off London children. Phoebe threw in educational outings, as a sop to my parents, and I have happy memories of strolling round the National Gallery and the Wallace Collection, where men in peaked caps told Frederick off for sliding across the parquet and strumming the radiators.

Jimmy very quickly forgot there had ever been a time without me. I got my full share of hurling and tickling and hair-ruffling. He was a warm-blooded, passionate man who loved the company of children. He was given to shouting, but I was never scared when Jimmy shouted at me. It was all part of the package, as harmless and exhilarating as a stiff breeze. It meant I belonged.

Frederick (to my own father's icy irritation) liked to throw clods of soil at our windows to bring me out. Ben called to me over the wall every time Phoebe made a batch of cakes. Once, when I was for some reason unavailable, he kindly posted a chocolate brownie through our front door. The three of us were a team. I look back now, and it pierces me to think how sweet Phoebe was, opening her arms and her heart to the prickly little animal I must have been.

My parents did not approve of the Darlings. Nothing was said, so I can only guess at the reasons for this. I think it was something to do with control. My father feared chaos, and had trained my mother to avoid emotional actings-out that might be dangerous. But they put up with the amount of time I spent next door. In fact, they were relieved to have me off their hands when Gudrun was otherwise engaged. They often implied that the responsibility of a child was painful, and that the Darlings were somehow too crude to mind about it.

This was how it went on for the next few years. The Darlings and I went to different schools, but kept up the easy, informal shuttling between the two houses. Our two sets of parents managed a distant cordiality. Every Christmas, the Darlings invited my parents over for a drink (and what a pair of ghouls they looked amidst the tinselly clutter). One day, however, the relationship shifted into a different gear.

It was a desolate afternoon in February, just before my seventh birthday. I arrived home to find an empty house. I had been driven home by the mother of a schoolmate, who roared off the minute I climbed out of her car. It dawned on me gradually that nobody was coming out to receive me. Not Gudrun, not my mother, not my father. The house was blind and shuttered, cold as a tomb. I remember ringing the bell for ages, and hearing its forlorn echo through the empty rooms.

I wasn't exactly afraid. I was mainly anxious about doing the right thing, whatever that might be. I wasn't surprised. A kind of fog settled around me, as I accepted what seemed to be the completion of a long process. They had finally made me disappear. There was nothing to do except sit on the doorstep and wait for something to happen, so this was what I did.

Phoebe found me when she came home with the boys, twenty minutes or so later. I was shivering stoically and doing my French homework. I was taken aback by her concern, and startled by her indignation. She smiled, to show it wasn't me she was cross with.

"Oh dear," she said. "There's been some silly mix-up. Come and have tea with us, and we'll sort it out."

I was happy at once. I loved having tea with the Darlings, and wasn't normally allowed to do it on a school night. I wasn't allowed television on a school night, either—which may have been good for my burgeoning intellect, but made me an outcast in the playground. My father had drawn up all these rules. He was an authentic lentil-scoffing, humorless middle-class killjoy. At the Darlings' I could expect forbidden foods like fish fingers and Penguin biscuits, forbidden books about animals who talked and wore tweed, and incredibly forbidden American cartoons. I trotted into the warmth behind Ben, feeling that things were looking up.

The boys and I sat round the kitchen table in the basement, all horribly overexcited by the novelty of the situation. I can see us now—Frederick and Benedict in their gray prep-school jerseys, me in my blue pinafore, all three of us singing loud enough to make the crockery rattle. The inimitable Frederick had learned a new song. The words were simply "willy-bum" in various combinations, sung to the tune of the William Tell overture (try it at home—willy-bum, willy-bum, willy-bum-bum-BUM!). Benedict, a musical child, soon found that the words went to many other tunes. How little it takes to make children happy. The joke seemed exquisite to us, and infinite. Odd that I should associate this sense of timeless happiness with the day I was abandoned by my parents.

Because this was, essentially, what they did. The details didn't emerge until Gudrun returned the following day, from an unauthorized jaunt in Wales with her boyfriend. It seemed that my parents—not bothering to wonder where Gudrun was—had left her a note on the hall table, to the effect that they had gone to a conference in Vienna.

On that first evening, they might as well have fled to Samarkand for all anyone knew of their whereabouts. The house remained dark and empty, and Phoebe became increasingly worried. "You'll have to stay here tonight," she said, almost to herself. "And Jimmy can drop you at school in the morning."

The boys and I thought this sounded terrific. We ate ginger biscuits and watched *Star Trek,* and I felt this was really living.

Jimmy came home when it was dark. The boys hurled themselves at him, giving him the news headlines and singing the willy-bum song.

"Hello," Jimmy said, a small boy under each arm, "it's Cassie—what are you doing here, my lovely?"

Phoebe pulled him away to the other end of the long open-plan kitchen. I heard her telling him, in a low, stricken voice, what had happened. I had apparently been deserted with only the clothes I stood up in. What on earth should they do?

Jimmy said, "That pair of—" followed by a string of strange words which I didn't understand then, but can now imagine. I saw, in all its glory, Jimmy's intense dislike of my father, his polar opposite. Jimmy despised my parents for forgetting their only child, and almost hated them for making Phoebe cry. I saw her sobbing into his shoulder, deeply hurt that there should be such cold hearts in the world.

We—the boys and I—might have started to be frightened. Jimmy, however, had a talent for making everything all right. He poured Phoebe a glass of red wine and led a rousing chorus of the willy-bum song. He made me giggle by suggesting silly things—tea towels, cushion covers— I'd have to wear in bed because I didn't have my nightie. In the end I wore a pair of Ben's pajamas, and Jimmy gave all three of us piggybacks upstairs.

I never found out exactly what happened between my parents and the Darlings. When Gudrun came back and the note from my parents was found, Jimmy pounced on the contact phone number and gave my father a dressing-down that nearly melted the receiver. The upshot of it all was that the shamefaced Gudrun was only allowed to bring round a bundle of my belongings. Jimmy refused to hand me over until I was claimed by a parent. In the meantime, I was to stay with the Darlings, in the blessed land of sweets and television. Even better—it was arranged that Phoebe would give me tea and supervise my homework *every day.*

Now I really was part of the family. The arrangement continued until my parents' divorce. It was the best thing that ever happened to me, as I often told Phoebe. She shared Jimmy's dislike of my father, but she staunchly maintained a bridge between me and my mother, when the whole relationship might have been lost forever. That's just one of the things I owe to her.

The boys quickly accepted the relationship. Frederick, who was a tease, nicknamed me "Grimble," after the boy in Clement Freud's story whose unreliable parents go to Peru without telling him. I didn't like the nickname, but was honored by Frederick's attention. He was our leader, though I was closer at that time to Ben. When Frederick wasn't around, Ben and I were free to live up to our ringlets with teddy bears' picnics and other harmless, girly pursuits. We had a pointless game called "Cotton Houses," which involved nothing more than sitting against a wall with our duffel coats on backward and the hoods over our faces.

I'm beating back a whole flock of memories that rise up whenever I remember my peculiar, borrowed childhood. The past becomes more important every day. You have to store up every moment and treasure it, as we all learned six years ago, when Jimmy died. It was liver cancer, and it wore him out in a matter of months.

They never accepted living without him. Phoebe, though sweet and humorous as ever, carried a spike of anguish in her heart. In my sadder moments, I used to think this anguish was slowly killing her. But let's call things by their right names. Phoebe was dying of leukemia.

When I left work that evening, I hurried along Piccadilly toward the tube station thinking about anything that would distract me from the arctic waste that was the future. She was going out so gently that it was still possible to carry on, if you pretended time had stopped.

CHAPTER TWO

It was a lovely spring evening. I emerged from the tube into a shimmering, opalescent light that made the bricks of the old houses look as soft as velvet. I thought, as I had often thought, that Hampstead had the air of being a secret village, in another dimension to the rest of London. Perhaps everyone feels this way about the place where they grew up. Hampstead Village was both reassuring and mysterious. The square, old-fashioned lampposts, glowing pale and eerie on the edges of the wild Heath, have always made me think vaguely of Narnia.

I went into the off-license to buy a bottle of wine for Phoebe, and then my footsteps turned automatically toward the street where I had once lived. I could pass my old house without a pang, but I couldn't approach the Darlings' without a warm, homecoming glow. This was still where my triumphs mattered most, and my failures least. The big rectangular windows were golden in the blue dusk. For a moment, as I ran up the steps, I thought of those windows with their lights extinguished, and my throat contracted with fear.

Phoebe's bones felt hard and sharp under her jersey. She was wearing the cashmere polo neck of deep, dark Christmas red that I had bought her just before Jimmy died. Her eyes were huge above the soft collar, and her face seemed to have shrunk. But her smell was just the same. Perfumes didn't really register with Phoebe. She carried her own scent, a mixture of sponge cake and tea rose.

"Cassie—oh, how lovely. I was praying you'd bring wine."

She didn't want to be asked how she was. She wanted me to fall into exactly the old relationship, so that was what I did. "All right," I said, "let's have it. Why the dramatic summons?"

"Food first," Phoebe said. She was excited, and rather pleased with herself. I heard Jimmy saying, "Watch her, Cass—I can feel one of her daft ideas coming on." He and I never stopped teasing her about her ideas. After Jimmy died, it was left to me to talk her out of starting impractical businesses and unlikely charities. What would it be this time? I didn't care. I hadn't seen Phoebe so animated for months.

"The boys are out," she said. "Which explains the deathly hush below."

Before Jimmy died, the basement had been made into a flat for the two boys. Phoebe's double drawing room had had a new kitchen installed at one end. I put down my briefcase and tried to be useful. The round table was already beautifully laid. There was a bouquet of salad, and a bowl of ruddy nectarines. I opened the bottle I had bought and poured us each a glass. Phoebe sipped hers absently, intent on stirring a small saucepan on the hob. She was most herself when preparing food, which she did exquisitely.

"Ben's at the Festival Hall," she told me, over her shoulder. "He somehow got his hands on a ticket for Alfred Brendel, lucky boy. And Fritz has gone to Sheffield, to see a friend—well, you remember Toby Clifton, don't you? He's in *Macbeth* at the Crucible, playing Donalbain." (It was odd to remember how long Phoebe and Jimmy had resisted calling their Frederick "Fritz," when the nickname had been set in cement for at least fifteen years.) "I'm glad he's got a decent part at last."

"Donalbain is not a decent part," I couldn't help saying. "It's about the smallest part you can have in *Macbeth,* without being billed as a piece of furniture. You don't have to talk up the achievement of everyone else's sons."

Phoebe smiled, suddenly looking years younger. "I might have known you wouldn't be impressed."

"It's not bad for a boy, I suppose. At least he's in gainful employment."

"He's got a good leg in tights," Phoebe said, draining pasta over the sink. "Perhaps it'll lead to something."

The tagliatelli was fresh, and cooked to perfection. Phoebe served it with a creamy mushroom sauce. I ate with gusto, to draw attention (hers and mine) from the fact that Phoebe hardly ate at all. The fork looked enormous in her hand. Afterward, she made a pot of tea and we moved to the deep sofas beside the log fire. The scents of woodsmoke, food and Phoebe mingled deliciously.

She said, "I asked you here because I need your help."

"You know I'll do anything."

"It's not something I can talk about in front of the boys. You see, it's about the future."

"Oh." I had that contraction in my throat again. Phoebe had never spoken to me directly about the approaching change.

"Not in a nasty way, darling," she added gently. "The first thing you have to understand is that I'm fairly reconciled to dying. I'd rather not, but everyone has to do it some time. And you know I can never be happy in the old way. Not without Jimmy."

"I know."

"I'm not exactly religious," she went on, "but I've been thinking a lot about what I should expect, after all the dying business. And I can't help being absolutely sure that there'll be a way of being with Jimmy. I couldn't tell you how or why I'm so sure, but I do have this strange confidence. I think I might almost be looking forward to it."

You'd think I'd cry, wouldn't you? Even with a lead weight on my chest, however, I didn't. I was beginning to discover that when things are really bad, you don't.

Phoebe poured tea, and pushed a plate of homemade macaroons toward me. To please her, and to show her that I was still her Sensible Girl, I put one in my mouth. It was ash against my tongue.

"But of course, I'm worried," Phoebe said. "I'm getting more and more worried about the boys."

"Why? What's the matter with them?"

"Oh, nothing—I didn't mean—it's just that I'm so worried about leaving them. Who on earth will look after them? How will they cope? I suppose what I mean is, who will love them?"

I was sturdy, swallowing fear. "I think it's safe to say they'll never be short of love. Half the women in London are in love with them."

"It's not just the love," Phoebe said, fixing me with her earnest brown eyes. "Who will buy their food? Take care of their washing? If they stay in this house, they'll never be able to run it properly. They have no idea what things cost. They're not ready to be orphans. I can't throw the two of them straight into the world."

"Do you want me to talk to them, or something? Assist their stormy passage into real life?"

"It suddenly came to me this morning," Phoebe said, "so I rang you straight away. We have to find wives for Fritz and Ben. If I know they're safely settled and cared for, I can die in peace."

I was deeply moved—moved beyond tears, to the very core of my bones. This mother's heart would burn with love long after the body around it had turned to dust.

But I was also slightly irritated. "So you want me to provide the wives?"

"Well, since you're always telling me your women friends can never find nice men, I thought—"

"Phoebe, my girlfriends are brilliant, beautiful and successful. Yes, a surprising number of them are single—but they're not desperate. Not one of them deserves to be lumbered with your layabout sons."

Phoebe was still smiling. She never minded my criticism of her adored ones, because she simply didn't believe I meant it. "You said yourself, hundreds of girls fall in love with them."

"Yes—floozies and slappers and aging rock chicks."

"All we'd have to do is find some nice girls, with a proper sense of responsibility."

"Why can't Fritz and Ben learn responsibility for themselves?"

"That's what you always say," Phoebe said calmly, "and you know they never will. I can't possibly leave them until I've seen them settled. Why are you laughing?"

"You're like someone in a Victorian novel, fretting over unmarried daughters. I could just about take your plan seriously if Fritz and Ben were a pair of eighteen-year-old girls."

"Come on, Cassie." Phoebe was impatient and eager. "Will you help me or not?"

I loved her so much for her blind love. Though the idea of tracking down solvent wives for the boys was ludicrous, I couldn't refuse. I would do anything for Phoebe.

Almost anything, I should say. "Of course I'll help you," I said. "But

21

before we start, I must make one thing very clear. I know what you're thinking, and the answer is no."

Her eyes widened innocently. "What? What are you talking about?"

"You're hoping I'll marry one of them myself."

Phoebe laughed, not at all guilty. "Why not? You've loved them both since you were tiny."

"They're like my brothers."

"Not any more. It wouldn't take much for you to fall for one of them properly."

"Sorry, but I would have done it by now."

"I'd be so happy to know they were with you!"

"I couldn't marry both of them, anyway," I pointed out. "Why don't you advertise for a nanny?"

Her optimism wavered. I softened my tone. "Sorry, but I'm spoken for."

"Matthew." Phoebe had met Matthew several times. I had taken him to Sunday lunch at the Darlings', on a day when I knew there would other people present to take some of the blame for the inevitable smoking and swearing.

"Yes," I said.

"So you think Matthew is the one."

Hadn't I told her this? "Yes," I said again.

"I didn't realize he'd proposed."

"Well, not proposed exactly. Not in so many words." This was a sore point. Matthew talked about marriage, but very distantly. It always seemed to be part of his ongoing fantasy about picking up a tip from a client, making a huge killing on the market and retiring at thirty-five. He had said he loved me, but not often—not nearly as often as I wanted to hear it. And he had never said, in so many words, that it was actually me he wanted to marry.

"So you're not engaged yet?" (She was as bad as Betsy—this obsession with having it all official.)

"Not officially," I said. "We haven't set a date."

"Oh well," Phoebe said. "I'm a bit disappointed for the boys, but Matthew struck me as terribly nice. His lovely begonia is still a mass of blossoms."

I laughed at that. I liked the way Phoebe coupled people with the plants they gave her.

And as soon as I had laughed, I could have cried. Matthew had to ask me soon. I wanted Phoebe to see us married.

Phoebe's mind had moved back to the "problem" of her boys. She reached for a notebook and pen on the little table beside her. "I thought we'd start by making a list of all their best qualities."

"Their selling points," I suggested, trying to keep a straight face. This wasn't going to be a long list, so the new notebook was a bit superfluous. Oh God, had she bought it specially, thinking it would make us more businesslike? Jimmy would have howled.

"That's right," Phoebe said happily.

"Okay." I realized she was waiting for me to say something. "Shall we start with Fritz?"

"Good idea—I knew I was right to enlist you." Beaming, Phoebe scribbled in her notebook, muttering the words as she went. "Frederick James Darling—widely known as Fritz—age thirty-one—professional actor."

Her pen hovered. She was quiet. Unkindly, I didn't fill in the silence. I wanted her to see that there was precious little left to say, as far as selling points were concerned.

"Lovely singing voice," she added.

Another stretch of silence.

"Absolutely sweet to his mother."

I let out a snort of laughter. "What a catch!"

Phoebe asked, "Don't I make him sound good enough?"

"If anything," I said, "you're talking him up too much. 'Professional actor' might make some poor girl think he's had a decent job."

Her candid brown eyes were reproachful. "We won't get very far if you can't be positive."

"Sorry. You know Fritz and I have a habit of sniping at each other. I'll start being very polite to him."

"Oh no, you mustn't do that," Phoebe cried, "or he'll guess we're up to something, and the whole plan will be ruined!"

I took a moment to process this, and another moment to cast around for the right argument. "Phoebe, the boys have to know about the plan."

She was shocked. "Certainly not! That would spoil everything."

"But of course they have to know," I said. I saw that I had hit one of the submerged rocks of obstinacy in her gentle character, and made my voice firmer. "We'll never marry them off unless they cooperate."

"But darling," Phoebe begged, "if we go and tell them, it will all be so cold and unromantic! It might make them self-conscious. They might not show their natural selves."

"We don't want them to show their natural selves. We want them to pretend they're normal."

Phoebe giggled. "Seriously—"

"I'm being very serious. Will you at least consider telling the boys what we're up to?"

"I'll think about it," she said. I knew she wouldn't. Her romantic mind was made up. "Now let's do a bit about Ben." She turned a page of her notebook. "That really should be easy. Benedict Henry Darling—age twenty-nine—professional concert pianist."

How Phoebe liked that word "professional," and how very inappropriate it was. Much as I loved Fritz and Ben, I was tempted to snatch the notebook and set the record straight. Fritz was an unemployed actor, and absolutely sex-mad. Ben was an unemployed musician, a bit of a mummy's boy and also sex-mad. Both were best known down at the dole office in Camden Town. As far as I could see, both passed their days in idyllic idleness. How on earth was I supposed to find respectable girl-friends for these two lotus-eaters?

Phoebe gazed pensively into the fire. "I wonder if we should put about Fritz being a doctor?"

"You could say he *qualified* as a doctor," I said. "But that was only be-cause Jimmy would've mashed him if he hadn't. He's never actually per-formed as a doctor—unless you count doing locum work in Cornwall so he can go surfing. I think you should leave it out altogether."

"Do you?"

I reached for another macaroon, able to appreciate it now that I was in a state of irritation. "Look, before we go any further, what about their current love lives? Haven't they already got girlfriends?"

A thoughtful line indented Phoebe's brow. "To be honest, I'm not quite sure. They're both rather secretive about who they're seeing. I think

Fritz still goes out with Madeleine from time to time—but she's married to someone else, and doesn't show any sign of leaving her husband. So that means he's technically free."

I was sorry to broach this painful subject, but it had to be done. "And what about Ben? Is he still entangled with that old bag?"

She sighed. "If you mean Lavinia Appleton, he does see her sometimes. But I really don't think it's anything more than friendship."

"Hmmm. I bet it was Lavinia who got him that ticket for Alfred Brendel."

"Well, yes, it was—but her husband hates music, and—"

"Face it, Phoebe," I said, "they're a pair of disasters."

She smiled suddenly. "I left something out. We should have put it first—they're both gorgeously handsome. You're not going to argue with that, I hope?"

No. It was as true as taxes. Phoebe's boys were, indeed, gorgeously handsome. It was the greatest (perhaps the only) point in their favor. I knew that several of my female friends would be quite happy to overlook all the other stuff on the strength of it.

Ben was tall, pale and dreamy. He had Phoebe's troubling dark eyes, and used to drift into the dole office in a green velvet jacket, like Percy Shelley. He was romantic and soulful, and still relied quite heavily on his flowing dark ringlets to keep him in free concert tickets.

Fritz was darker. He had Jimmy's beautiful voice, and a high color beneath clear olive skin. His black eyes snapped like firecrackers. He had immense energy, and rather scary charm. I had once seen him in evening dress (for the party after his girlfriend's wedding), and thought he looked like an old-fashioned picture of the devil.

But all my female friends swore they wanted more than good looks in a man. And the biggest talking-up campaign in the world couldn't make Fritz and Ben into anything but expensive luxuries. Ben was a wonderful musician, who studied at the Royal Academy of Music. He was, however, too "sensitive" to perform or to teach. Mostly he sat at home, driving the neighbors crazy by playing loud Scriabin in the small hours, on the grand piano his parents had bought him for his twenty-first birthday.

As for Fritz, he was the very worst sort of unemployed actor. Being handsome should have guaranteed him some sort of a career, but he was dreadfully pretentious, perhaps to mask his glaring lack of talent. We had been at Oxford together, and I had watched him being talentless in several college productions. His Iago was particularly wince-making. He spent the whole time facing upstage and muttering with his hands in his pockets. He was a perfectly good medical student, so what on earth had made him give up medicine? What wicked charlatan had persuaded him to act for his living?

But I knew I was being too hard on him. I should be honest. The fact is, all through my teens and early twenties, I had a major crush on Fritz. He played a starring role in my dreams for years. I don't mean only the sexy dreams—I mean fantasies about impressing people. Fritz was always present, being impressed and later declaring undying love, in every one of my dreams of future glory. In those dreams I accepted the Booker Prize, the editorship of the *Guardian* and the school cup for growing candytuft before large crowds that inevitably contained my father and Fritz.

Deep in my memory lay our one, solitary encounter. It was never mentioned by either of us, and I suspected Fritz had forgotten. Why shouldn't he forget? It belonged to another era. We had just finished our A levels, and the Darlings—typically—threw a party. I remember feeling tipsy and euphoric and unusually bold. I was outside, in the warm summer garden, beside the climbing frame. Fritz appeared out of the dusk, and silently stood beside me. I remember feeling slightly sick with nerves, wondering if he could see my pulse hammering in my neck. We had a long, breathless moment of staring at each other, as if seeing for the first time, then Fritz took my face between his hot hands and kissed me, and when his tongue slid into my mouth I nearly passed out. I don't know what might have happened, if dear Ben had not suddenly erupted into the garden at the head of a conga line.

That was the end of my kiss. At the time, I was sure there would be another. We promised each other that we would meet at Oxford. But then Fritz went off backpacking in Italy, I went to New York for a tense few weeks with my father, and by the time we actually got to Oxford at the end of the summer, we had missed the moment. Fritz was a theater star and sex symbol, and I was an obscure, earnest student of literature. No matter how hard I tried to impress him (for example, by constantly mentioning the campaigning magazine I had started, to keep my college women-only), he would only see me as little Grimble from next door. I'd assumed I'd be running into him constantly, but I was lucky to get even a sight of him. Sometimes he'd shout to me from across the road. Occasionally, he would buy me and Annabel a drink (or, less occasionally, allow us to buy him one).

Frankly, I was miffed. My wounded pride healed any damage done to my heart. I do remember how galling it was to meet Fritz around the town with one stunning girlfriend after another. I never stood a chance. I was sensible enough to acknowledge this before I made a fool of myself. I hate looking like a fool.

Sitting with Phoebe that evening, I pitied my younger self for being dazzled by appearances. Fritz had met Matthew, and called him "Mooseface," but this was grossly unfair. Matthew was simply a different style of man. And anyway, handsome is as handsome does. The old crush could still make my pulse miss a beat, but I dismissed it as mere chemistry.

My feelings for Matthew went so much deeper, I told myself. If there were more men like Matthew, my lovely female friends would not be singing "Dinner for One, Please James." I decided that there was only one way to proceed with Phoebe's plan. I had to make Matthew my template for the new, marriageable Darlings.

CHAPTER THREE

It won't be easy," Betsy said next morning. "Finding the girls might take months, and then you'll have to persuade them to get married. But you can't ignore a dying wish, can you? Maybe you should pay a couple of girls to pretend?"

I laughed. "I'll hold that idea in reserve, but I don't think we'll need it. Fritz and Ben aren't that bad."

"Oh, no." Betsy handed me a mug of tea, brewed in her steamy glory-hole beside the filing cabinet. "Don't get me wrong, I think they're both lovely. I only meant that girls seem to expect so much these days. My generation wasn't so fussy."

"Sally had a huge crush on Ben when we were at school," I said, suddenly remembering. "I don't suppose she'd consider—"

"Certainly not," Betsy said promptly. "You leave my daughters out of it. I can't afford any more idle men in my family."

"Fair enough," I said. Betsy is married to a good-hearted but incredibly unsuccessful novelist. In between dropping babies, she'd spent her entire married life working to support this man. I felt she had suffered enough.

"But I'll help in any other way I can," she assured me. "I'm fond of Phoebe. And if there are any spare candidates left over, you can always send them to Jonah. He hasn't had a girlfriend for ages. He's starting to go bald, so he can't afford to hang about. Have you come up with any suitable names?"

"Not yet."

"Well, let me know when you do." Betsy slotted her reading glasses back on her nose, and turned her attention back to laying out the children's page on the computer.

I stared anxiously at the unfinished article on my own screen. I had lied to Betsy. Of course I had thought of suitable brides for Fritz and Ben. The problem was that they were my dearest friends. I had tried to think of women I didn't like, because it seemed cruel to throw my eligible friends away on the Brothers Darling. But I really did love them, and I wanted them to have the nicest possible wives. In the end, I decided that forgetting all scruples and going for the best was my only chance of success.

Naturally, the first person I thought of was Annabel. But was any man good enough for her?

Annabel Levett is my best friend. We've known each other since we were six. I sat next to her throughout my school career, from infants' playground to sixth-form common room. We went to the same Oxford college. Every right-thinking woman has a best friend like Annabel—someone who miraculously combines being uncannily similar to her, and wildly different. Annabel and I were busy people, but we managed to meet at least once a week. At work we bombarded each other with e-mails. We talked constantly on the phone. The pity of it is that there will never be a man I get on with so beautifully. I can't remember how it felt not to know her.

Annabel is tall and willowy, with unfairly luscious breasts and long, straight blond hair. (Am I envious? Always—a best friend must be slightly enviable.) She has a guileless, dimpled smile and great trusting blue eyes. Part of her brain is excellent. She got a first in PPE, and a job in a merchant bank, and was constantly being promoted.

Sadly, however, the part of Annabel's brain that concerns the opposite sex is scrambled egg. Men can do anything with her. Here is an example of Annabel's silliness regarding men.

When we were eighteen, she fell madly in love with a very nasty unwashed poet (poets are scum, by the way; this is the first piece of wisdom I shall impart to my daughters). This nasty poet had a nasty flat in Holloway. One morning, he lifted his head off the pillow to remark that he fancied a kipper. He then rolled over and went back to sleep.

Annabel longed to satisfy her beloved's craving, but there wasn't a penny in the house. So she went out into the streets and begged the money from passersby. Let's have that again, in italics. *She begged to get kippers for her boyfriend.*

She had a charming but unreliable father, and I think this is what made her such a half-wit about romance. When I felt she was getting too silly, I used to say, in a warning voice, "Begging for kippers!"—this being our code for stupid things you do to make a man like you.

Annabel's professional success had a terrible effect on her romantic life. At the time of Phoebe's idea she was head of arbitrage and earned a fortune, but she hadn't had a single boyfriend since her last-but-one promotion. Matthew said men were put off when a woman was too high-flying. In vain did I protest that out of office hours Annabel was a dippy blonde who begged for kippers. Matthew said this was canceled out by the ball-breaking salary. The poor thing spent every waking moment that did not involve arbitrage (sorry, but I've never found out exactly what this is) yearning for romance.

The great question was, could I bring myself to push her toward the Darlings? I realized at once—practically before the great idea was out of Phoebe's mouth—that Annabel would be a perfect mate for Fritz. She was just his type: pretty and daffy, and irresistibly drawn to scoundrels. Her inner fragility might bring out Fritz's protective side, I thought, assuming he had one. I absolutely knew that they would fancy one another, if I threw them together in the right way.

How did I know this? Well, I've sworn to be honest. Fritz and Annabel had, of course, met many times over the years. As my official best friend, she was quite a teatime fixture chez Darling. But I had put a lot of energy into keeping the two of them apart, making sure I stood between them like a kind of Chinese wall, diverting any dangerous throbs of attraction. I told myself it was to protect Annabel from the inevitable broken heart, but of course there was jealousy involved too. I still fancied Fritz myself in those days, and felt that if he were allowed to fall for Annabel, I wouldn't be able to bear it.

Things were different now, however. I was in love with Matthew, and Fritz needed a bride. Phoebe was extremely fond of Annabel, and would love to have her as a daughter-in-law. I had to work through my own mental block, and push her into Fritz's arms. How was this to be done? I wasn't quite ready to work out the details, but I had my first candidate. Fritz was as good as married. Now I just had to dream up someone for Ben.

The names of various solvent young women floated about in my head for the rest of the day. I even wondered if a certain glamorous lady novelist, whose book we were featuring as Paperback of the Month, happened to be single. I fretted over the problem through most of the new production of *The Flying Dutchman*, which Matthew and I saw that evening. I didn't confide in Matthew, because he did not approve of Fritz and Ben. Or rather (as I told myself), he didn't understand them. I'd done my best, at that one Sunday lunch, to keep them off politics and sex. Matthew knew I was fond of them, and had kindly refrained from giving me his opinion in Technicolor, but I sensed words like "work-shy" and "immature" floating in the ether, just waiting to be uttered. I could guess what he would think of my determination to marry them off to unsuspecting young females.

The great Wagnerian chords swirled around us. Matthew leaned forward in his plush chair, frowning with concentration. I watched his blunt, fair, honest-looking profile, and felt fortunate. From time to time, he reached unseeingly for my thigh and gave it a warm squeeze. After the opera, to my delight, he escorted me home in a taxi. His early meeting had been canceled, opening an unexpected window for sexual activity. Without a clean shirt to his name, the reckless devil stayed the night. We had glorious sex, and I fell asleep blissfully curled against his back. This was the real, essential point of existence, I thought, as I drifted off. Sod the career. Having a warm back to curl against was the only kind of success that mattered.

The following day was the day the magazine went to press. Our cramped Edwardian offices in Dover Street were a comparative hive of activity, and I was annoyed when my friend Honor Chappell called "for a chat." She never knew when to shut up.

"I've finished my book," she announced.

"Good for you," I said. "Shall we get together? It's been ages."

Honor started talking about how long her book was, the problems she was having with the index and the amount of illustrations her publisher would allow. I carried on fiddling with the layout on my screen with the receiver tucked into my shoulder. I remembered that it was months since I had seen her—she had been working on her book at one of the big universities up north.

And then I remembered that Honor was single. Incredibly, famously single. Good grief, why hadn't I thought of her sooner?

I got to know Honor at college. She was a brilliant, earnest, rather awe-inspiring person; your classic manless egghead. She had never been seen with a boyfriend in any shape or form (though she gave me to understand there had been a sort of romance in the sixth form of her school in Harrogate). Her chronically single state had nothing to do with her appearance. When you looked past her terrible haircut and unflattering specs, there was something almost beautiful about her large, open features and wide gray eyes.

Annabel used to say Honor's problem was that she was too clever, and didn't know how to hide it. We take it as one of the elementary rules of romance that men tend to steer clear of clever women. Honor's degree was one of the best in the whole university. She lectured on modern history at University College London, and her book was a weighty tome about nineteenth-century socialism. If men were not similar geniuses, Honor frightened them off. And if they were geniuses, they were either too competitive, or bonkers.

She further reduced her chances, I thought, by having terrible taste in men. Honor tended to get soppy about anemic Victorian pretty-boys. But couldn't Ben Darling do the soulful expression and cascading curls? And wouldn't Honor be the perfect woman for Ben? He liked women who were strong and protective and told him what to do. He had been gadding around with the old bag Lavinia Appleton (forty-seven, married, rich, with a passion for both music and management) for far too long.

"I feel as if I've been in prison," Honor was saying dismally. "Shut in a library for months, miles from all my friends. I'd really love to see you, Cassie. Maybe we could meet for dinner?"

My great mind was working fast—think now and pay later, I told myself. "Actually, Matthew and I were planning to take Phoebe out to dinner this weekend. There's a terrific little French place in Flask Walk."

"How is Phoebe?" Honor asked.

This was not the time to talk about Phoebe's illness. "Amazingly well," I said robustly. "And I know she'd like to see you again." I began to improvise wildly. "She said so, just the other day. Why don't you come with us? Then you could meet Matthew."

Honor had never laid eyes on my future husband, and I knew she was curious.

For the first time, her gloomy voice took on a lighter note. "That would be lovely. I need a bit of relaxation—and I only feel I can relax when I'm out with other women, or men who are safely spoken for. Well, you know me. I usually make a mess of any situation with romantic overtones."

"Goodness, you won't have to worry about that!" I lied artfully. "It'll be just the four of us."

I must admit, Honor can be rather downbeat. She sighed, in a way that usually heralded a long moan about the awfulness of the opposite sex. "I've given up romance," she told me dolefully (I couldn't help thinking that Honor giving up romance was the same as me giving up hang-gliding). "I don't think the kind of relationship I want exists. The men I meet are so tedious and scruffy. Where has the poetry gone? Was there ever any?"

Thank God I didn't have time for all twenty-five verses of this familiar dirge. I rang off, promising to call her with the details later.

Then, still clutching the phone, I punched in Phoebe's number. "We have liftoff. Clear your diary for this Friday. Got a pen? Here are your instructions."

I'd already worked it out. Matthew was to meet us at the restaurant. Honor and I would have a drink with Phoebe first. Phoebe must produce at least one clean son, ready to impress Honor with his sensitivity, intellect and general handsomeness. Could she manage that?

"Of course—don't make difficulties. Honor's a delightful girl." Phoebe had been very tired recently, and I rejoiced to hear the energy in her gleeful voice. I knew she would save every scrap of strength for this dinner, and relish every moment of it. "I'll simply encourage the boys to be themselves. When she sees them in their natural habitat, she won't be able to resist."

Afterward, when I had replaced the receiver, I caught Betsy staring at me gravely above her glasses "Honor Chappell? Is that the academic with the crew cut?"

"It's not a crew cut," I said, already defensive.

"Hmmm. I hope you know what you're doing. My Jonah would run a mile."

"I'm not trying to attract your Jonah. Fritz and Ben aren't threatened by women like Honor. And all they have to do is meet her—I want this first encounter to be as casual as possible."

"Well, I suppose it might work," Betsy said. "As long as nobody tells them to 'be themselves.' "

On Friday evening I made my preparations as if I were about to be parachuted into occupied France. Matthew was to come to my flat in Chalk Farm after dinner. This meant changing the sheets, placing white wine in the fridge and putting the croissants I had bought at Fortnum's in the bread bin. I still felt it was vital to make the maximum effort. Matthew, though he never criticized or complained directly, had standards. I had heard indignant speeches about women who were "slipshod." A hint was enough. I was not going to allow any kind of slipshoddery to spoil my chance of married bliss. I fully intended to run our entire marriage along these perfectionist lines. The harder I worked for Matthew, the more I loved him. To do him justice, I don't think Matthew realized how hard I slaved. I think he assumed I was just like that naturally.

I plucked my eyebrows. I washed and dried my hair, and put on my short dress of softly draped dark blue velvet. I then drove to Tufnell Park, in my freshly vacuumed Fiat, hoping Honor had made a similar effort. I was a little disappointed when she emerged from her front door wearing a denim skirt and apparently carrying a fishing bag.

But why would she make an effort? As far as Honor was concerned, she was going out for a quiet dinner with friends. She was simply being herself. Why did people always tell you to Be Yourself? It was starting to seem like very bad advice.

"You look nice," Honor said, fumbling in her bag for an evil-smelling cough sweet. "Having someone to notice must make all the difference. Like one?" She held out the sweets.

"No thanks."

"I seem to have had this cold for months. I think it's a reaction to the central heating in the library. I told the chief librarian he ought to test the place for Sick Building Syndrome."

Oh dear, was she going to be stuck in this drippy mood for the whole evening? By the time we got to the restaurant it would be too late. She had to lighten up before she met the boys.

"I like your hair," I said. "I'm glad you're letting it grow." (I didn't and I wasn't, but it was a good opportunity to drop a hint about the crew cut). "It suits you."

"Does it? I haven't had time to go to the hairdresser's. I've already had to snip away at the fringe myself."

"I know a fantastic hairdresser," I said. "He'd make you look stunning."

At last she smiled, and her well-hidden charm poured through the crack in the clouds. "I knew it. You think I've let myself go—and you're absolutely right. I'll obviously make an effort if there's the remotest chance of meeting someone. I need hardly tell you that my love life is the Gobi Desert."

"You don't know when you'll meet someone," I said. "Cupid could strike at any hour."

This cheered her up. The mildness of the spring evening, and the grace of the old houses in the last of the thin sunlight, further mellowed her. We reached Phoebe's, and I allowed my spirits to rise. The house, as always, looked charming.

Phoebe opened the front door. The impression could not have been lovelier. I can see her now. She wore a white silk shirt, with a collar that covered the new lines and puckers in her throat. She was very thin, but her face was full of vitality. There was music in the house—cascades of notes rising and falling like flocks of birds. The scents of woodsmoke and cedar embraced us.

"Honor, I'm so glad you could come. It's been too long." Phoebe kissed Honor. I shot her a small eye-signal not to overdo the warmth. She ignored it. "Come into the drawing room. We've just opened a heavenly bottle of Pouilly."

I understood her air of satisfaction when we went into the drawing room. It couldn't have been more perfect. The music danced and curvetted around us. In the corner beside the window, Ben was playing the Victorian harp that had once belonged to Phoebe's grandmother.

Honor was—no other word will do—gobsmacked. Even I was nearly smitten. Ben's dark eyes were serious in his pale, poetic face. His long fingers coaxed waterfalls of music from the harp strings. A pale shaft of dying sunlight fell across his raven hair. He was Honor's dream made flesh.

We stood, the three of us, listening to the music. The last chord bled away into silence. Ben's hand hovered above the strings. He bowed his head.

"Thank you, darling." Phoebe leaned forward to kiss him. "That was wonderful."

Ben looked up. He blinked at us, and smiled as if waking from a trance. "Hi, Cassie." He tilted the harp upright and came over to kiss my cheek. I hugged him. Ben—my oldest friend, companion of my Cotton House days—was the brother I loved best. I had never fancied him, which might have been why.

"I don't think you've met Honor Chappell," I said. "We're taking her out celebrating, because she's just finished a book."

"Have you? Well done." Ben smiled and shook her hand charmingly. He was always charming, but I was sure he liked Honor. "Is it a novel?"

Poor Honor gaped when their flesh touched, and struggled to speak normally. "No, it's history. It's about the birth of British socialism."

"Honor teaches at UCL," I said.

"That sounds fascinating," Ben said, smiling down into Honor's face. "A history is far better than a novel. Everyone's writing novels these days, aren't they? Even footballers and people. But I'd like to see David Beckham writing a history of socialism."

Ben was rather given to rambling. I decided to divert him, before he rambled off on a discourse about suitable books for footballers. "Your playing was terrific, by the way."

"Oh, yes," Honor blurted out, too loudly. "Yes, it was—you have such a—"

Phoebe came to the rescue. "He might be doing a recital at Kenwood House this June, in the Orangery. But it won't be the harp—he really plays the piano."

We sat down around the fireplace, and Ben poured us all glasses of wine. He perched on the fender, and he and Honor talked about Beethoven's late sonatas. Honor was nervous and deferential. They agreed that the late sonatas were "difficult," and that Beethoven's rhythms "anticipated syncopation."

"I'm sure Ben is the ideal person to play them," Phoebe said, passing round olives. "He's late for everything."

Ben inched a little closer to Honor. He was gazing at her intently. "I heard Alfred Brendel playing them on Wednesday."

"Brendel," murmured Honor, as if saying "Amen." "That must have been an experience."

"Stupendous. An absolute revelation."

"I tried to get a ticket, but it was sold out. He always is."

"Do you go to a lot of concerts?" Ben asked.

"Oh, yes, as many as I can. But I hate going on my own."

"Awful, isn't it?" Ben agreed. He smiled. "Tell you what, if you ever find yourself with a spare ticket, do feel free to give me a call."

"Really?" Honor breathed. "What kind of concert do you prefer?" Her wan library complexion had the faintest haze of pink, and her large gray eyes were radiant.

"I should think I'd love whatever you chose," Ben said. "We seem to have so many tastes in common."

I was indignant. Ben had sniffed out Honor as a source of free concert tickets. He craved any kind of live music, and relied on five or six besotted females to pay for the seats—there was one woman he kept specially for the Proms, for instance. In return, the ticket buyers would get his company and (sometimes) the honor of buying him dinner. They waited for a little spark of romance, and they waited in vain. Ben talked feelingly to them about his bowel complaints, and said it was great to go out with a woman just as "mates." Jimmy used to call these unfortunates the Foolish Virgins. I wasn't going to let poor Honor join their ranks.

"Perhaps you should choose the music, Ben," I suggested suavely. "You could buy the tickets and give one to Honor. I'm sure she trusts your taste."

"Oh, yes, absolutely," Honor faltered. She glanced at me rather reproachfully—I suspect she wouldn't have minded being one of the Foolish Virgins.

Ben stood up abruptly, with an air of wounded dignity. He knew he had been rumbled. "Lovely to meet you, Honor. I'd better be off now. I only came up to get the washing."

"Darling, why don't you come out to dinner with us?" Phoebe asked. She was smiling. She thought everything was going famously. "I'm sure the restaurant wouldn't mind."

"Thanks, but I said I'd go round to Vinnie's."

"Vinnie" was Mrs. Appleton. She was a good flautist, and liked to play duets with Ben when her husband was away. I didn't like to think of someone with that much lipstick smearing it all over a flute, like greasy raspberry jam. In my marrow I was convinced that poetic, soulful Ben was sleeping with that painted old baggage. If Phoebe ever suspected such a thing, she would be devastated. I was annoyed with Ben, and frankly disappointed that my first attempt at matchmaking had failed.

Ben sloped off to the utility room at the back of the house, behind the kitchen. Honor's face had a kind of dazed, radioactive glow. "This is such a beautiful room."

Phoebe beamed. "How nice of you. Yes, I love this room. It catches the evening light, and on summer days the window at the back is full of birdsong."

"How long have you lived in this house? Did you have to do a lot to it when you bought it?"

"We moved in when I was pregnant with Fritz," Phoebe said. "We could only afford it because it was in a bit of a state. It took every penny we had in the world, but we just fell in love with it. We think it was built in . . ." and she launched into the history of the house. Honor listened intently.

Ben was heard emerging from the utility room.

Phoebe leaped up—one of those flashes of her old, quicksilver energy. "Honor, do let me show you round the house. We'll start in the basement—Ben, would you mind?"

"Yes, I'd love to see it," Honor said.

Ben, weighed down by a plastic laundry basket, halted at the door to the basement. "It's not terribly clean, I'm afraid," he said.

This was a dreadful, dreadful idea. Horrified, I tried to catch Phoebe's eye. She did not look at me. I suspected she was ignoring me on purpose. She simply didn't believe anyone could get a bad impression of her beloved boys.

Ben led the way down the narrow flight of stairs. I stuck closely behind him, possibly with a mad idea of throwing myself in front of Honor before she saw anything too degraded. I kept trying to shoot Phoebe warning glances over my shoulder.

Ben turned round and caught one of these. "What's the matter, Cass?" he asked innocently. "Why're you making faces at me? Oops—" A pair of blue underpants slid off the top of the basket and flopped to the floor. "Get my knickers, would you? Thanks."

"I haven't been down here for ages," Phoebe told Honor.

"You should have given us a bit of notice," Ben said.

"Oh, darling, Honor won't expect it to be immaculate."

Ben opened the door at the bottom of the stairs.

A disgruntled voice said, "Where the fuck have you been? I need my clothes!"

"Oh, how nice," Phoebe said. "Fritz is here." Absolutely pushing me aside (she still had moments of surprising toughness, for all her frailty), she showed Honor into the basement flat.

I hadn't seen the place for years, and I couldn't help gasping. Neither could Honor. Once, this had been a perfectly respectable kitchen-cum-sitting-room, with a glass door leading to the pretty, overgrown garden. It was now the headquarters of the Untidy Society. The floor, the sofa and the table were strewn with sheet upon sheet of music, which Ben had marked with his complicated system of arrows and scribbles. On top of the music lay Fritz's weights, hundreds of dirty mugs (the only visible crockery), and parts of a bicycle. The overflowing bin was surrounded by squashed lager cans and crumpled takeaway cartons.

And on the sofa, among the festoons of sheet music, Fritz reclined stark naked.

"Good God," he said. He whipped a cushion over his privates and burst out laughing. "My darling Grimble—forgive me if I don't get up. Mum, have you gone mad?"

"I'll fetch you a dressing gown," Phoebe said, shaking with laughter. "Honor, I'm so sorry—I should have warned them. Fritz, this is Cassie's friend Honor Chappell."

"How do you do, Honor," Fritz said. "I'm so sorry about this. I expect I know you, don't I?"

"I was Cassie's flatmate at Oxford," Honor said stiffly.

"Oh God, yes, of course. Sorry. How are you?"

"Fine."

"Mum, for pity's sake, find something to cover my blushes."

Phoebe, helpless with giggles, vanished into Fritz's bedroom. The giggles ended suddenly, on a gasp of horror.

"It's not awfully tidy at the moment," Fritz explained, smiling at Honor in a friendly way. "Look, I really am very sorry about this." He made a minute adjustment to the cushion. "The fact is, we totally ran out of clean clothes. Don't you hate it when that happens?"

Honor, obviously embarrassed, fixed her angry gaze on the floor.

I looked at Fritz. How could Honor not look at Fritz? His body, as befitted someone who spent several hours every day running on the Heath, was taut and muscular. He had a gorgeous washboard stomach and (it had just been possible to see, before the descent of the cushion) a huge cock. He was incredible, and of course I fancied him. But it meant nothing, I told myself—mere chemistry because Fritz was pumping out pheromones right under my nose. Pull yourself together.

"Fritz, really!" Phoebe said, stepping back into the room with a black toweling robe over one arm. "I've never seen such a mess. You can't expect Mrs. Wong to clean down here unless you tidy it first." She threw the robe across Fritz.

"That's mine!" complained Ben.

"It was the only thing I could find."

Fritz leaped up from the sofa and extinguished his splendid body under the robe. He rummaged through the washing basket, impatiently throwing aside unwanted socks and shirts.

"Don't just chuck it all on the floor!" Ben protested.

"I'm in a tearing hurry, dear boy. Madeleine expected me an hour ago."

"Well, you should do the washing when it's your fucking turn, shouldn't you? You're the one who let it all pile up."

"Boys!" Phoebe protested. "For goodness' sake, stop squabbling. What will Honor think?"

One glance was enough to show me what Honor thought. Her pale mouth was tight with disapproval.

"Phoebe," I said, "we really ought to go. I don't want to keep Matthew waiting."

Phoebe had not registered Honor's sudden and drastic freezing over. She touched Ben's arm. "Can't you change your mind about dinner?"

"I'm not eating dinner at the moment," Ben said solemnly. "I'm detoxing."

Phoebe was mildly alarmed. Ben's delicate stomach was an historic cause of worry. "It's never healthy to miss dinner, darling."

"Vinnie says I need to clear my system," he said. "I have to eat raw vegetables for ten days, and I've still got six days to go."

Ben was a hypochondriac. While Fritz went on his daily runs to Highgate and back, Ben fought a succession of mysterious illnesses. I suspected that Mrs. Appleton had won him through their shared obsession with his health. We all knew there was never the slightest thing wrong with him. Fritz, who had trained as a doctor, treated his brother's ailments with cheerful contempt.

By this point I already knew all was lost, and had started laughing. I decided I had better step in before it got any worse.

"Come on, Phoebe. We should get going."

Fritz threw an arm around his mother's fragile shoulders and kissed her forehead. "Don't stay out too late, all right? If you get exhausted, I'll never speak to you again."

"I'll be careful." Phoebe's pride in him was so transparent that for a moment it burned away the bad impression of loucheness and disorder. Sometimes, Fritz was uncannily like Jimmy.

"Cassie, please make sure she has something to eat," Fritz said. "You know how silly she can be."

"You can't expect me to have supper if you don't," Ben said, dropping a kiss on the other side of Phoebe's head. "Do you think she should have a glass of wine? It won't clash with the drugs, will it?"

Fritz said, "Not at all. I think she should drink as much as possible."

"Red wine," Ben said, with a knowledgeable air. "It's full of antioxidants. And you should also try to have some fresh spinach, for the iron."

"Don't listen to him," Fritz told Phoebe. "Have anything you fancy—but bear in mind that I shall be returning at eleven. And if I don't find you here, I shall march up to the restaurant and drag you out by your hair."

Phoebe kissed them both and promised to treat herself "like a piece of crystal."

"Lalique," Ben said. "Only more precious."

We left the boys robing themselves in fresh jeans and shirts, for their reprehensible nights out with their married women. I couldn't help being annoyed at the way they had ruined Honor's fleeting good impression—but neither could I help being softened by their love for Phoebe.

Honor was quiet during the walk to the restaurant. Up to a point, I sympathized. She had been through quite an emotional shock, especially when you considered that she had spent the past few months shut up in a library with a lot of Victorian socialists. She had glimpsed the man of her dreams, only to watch him crumbling into exactly the kind of spoiled, scruffy wastrel she loathed. She was far too polite to hint at any of this in front of Phoebe.

Fortunately, Phoebe was still convinced that the encounter had been a triumph. She was at her happiest, thrilled to be alive and energetic and out on a sweet spring evening. She seemed to know everyone in Hampstead, and we exchanged greetings with half the neighborhood before we reached Flask Walk.

Matthew was waiting for us at a crisply draped table in the corner, reading the *Financial Times* folded very small. He kissed Phoebe (he treated her with a rather heavy chivalry that made me intensely proud of him) and shook hands with Honor. He delighted me by giving me a heartier kiss than usual, and muttering, "You're absolutely gorgeous!"

It was a magical dinner, entirely because of Phoebe. Everything pleased her. The setting was charming, the wine Matthew selected was nectar. She was touched that the owners of the restaurant remembered her, and almost too honored when the chef made her a special omelette that wasn't on the menu. He came out briefly and mentioned that he knew Fritz. I suspected that Fritz had told him about Phoebe's illness. He was treating her like the Queen.

Phoebe ate most of the omelette and a few leaves of salad. The candles flickering on the table obliterated the new lines on her face, and made her eyes sparkle. I nudged Matthew's foot under the table, suddenly filled with happiness because it was so easy to pretend there was no such thing as the future.

She made Matthew and Honor talk about themselves, in a far livelier and more interesting way than usual. I don't think I had ever seen Matthew so relaxed—he was even making jokes about his clients. Phoebe had a knack for presenting people to themselves in their best light.

The four of us laughed and talked and ate. Phoebe naturally moved on to the subject of the boys, and her anecdotes about them were so funny that Honor's disgust turned to amusement. We vied to cap each other's stories, and it was only afterward that I reflected this might not have been a very good idea. Everything we said seemed to highlight the boys' least admirable qualities—their naughtiness, their fondness for partying, their brushes with the law. Phoebe assumed that their innate loveliness was obvious to everyone.

I had said I would drive home, but I was having such a good time that I drank too much. Matthew said he would drive, and frisked me for my keys. We were to drop Phoebe off first, then Honor.

As soon as we had waved Phoebe into her front door, Honor let out a long sigh.

"What an adorable woman! How did her sons turn out so awful? It's enough to put you off having children. I was so sorry for her. I didn't know where to look." And she launched into a description of her meeting with Fritz and Ben.

I was very annoyed with the Darlings for being so oafish in front of a potential bride, but I found myself irritated by Honor's self-righteousness. I had enjoyed laughing over the old stories with Phoebe, and remembering why I was so fond of the boys next door. They might have been oafs, I thought, but they were very kind and entertaining oafs. Nobody in the world could make me laugh like the Darlings.

Honor didn't see the funny side of anything. Dull old poop, I thought. No wonder she couldn't get laid.

And how could she possibly overlook the sheer gorgeousness of Fritz's naked body? Too sozzled to feel guilty, I closed my eyes to conjure it up again. I had shown Honor a body to die for, and all she could think about was the untidiness. It was great that Matthew was making such an effort to be nice to her, but I wished he would stop agreeing with her, and adding his own criticisms of the Fritz-and-Ben lifestyle.

"God knows why they think the world owes them a living," he said.

43

"And it's rather appalling that they've let their flat get into such a state. Don't they care about the house?"

One thing was abundantly clear. We had a serious problem with presentation. Fritz and Ben had to be in on this whole matchmaking plan, or it was doomed.

CHAPTER FOUR

Next morning, while Matthew was out at the gym, I took the step of calling the boys—without Phoebe's knowledge—for an emergency meeting.

I got Fritz's voice on the answering machine. "Hi. You've reached the residence of Fritz and Ben Darling. Leave a message and we'll call you back."

I left a message. "Hi, it's Cassie. Could one of you ring me? It's important. Thanks."

There was no reply that day. Perhaps it was just as well, since I was on boyfriend duty and very busy. Matthew's weekends were as labor-intensive as his working week. We read quantities of huge newspapers, drank coffee and bought organic brie at Villandry, saw a depressing foreign film, had sex three times, and shopped at Heal's for a desk lamp. In between, I left three more messages for the Darlings.

By Monday morning, my office seemed an oasis of peace. I'd had a wonderful weekend with Matthew, I told myself—but I did notice that I was looking forward to wearing jeans and eating a pizza on the sofa. We had an editorial meeting about the next issue. I persuaded an eminent old author to write our main article, and left three more messages for Fritz and Ben. Didn't they ever return calls? I was beginning to be irked by the intractability of the entire project.

On Tuesday, I left three more messages, of escalating sharpness.

"Look, will one of you lazy bastards just ring me?"

On Wednesday, I decided I had to call Phoebe.

"I had such a marvelous time on Friday," she said happily. "Honor's a fascinating girl, don't you think? And Matthew's such a nice man when you draw him out. I can see exactly why you love him."

"I need to speak to one of your sons," I said.

"Which one?"

"Either. I've left about a million messages."

Phoebe chuckled. "Aren't they dreadful? I'll put a note through the door. What shall I say it's about?"

"Oh, nothing—I mean, I can't really explain." I couldn't bring myself to tell Phoebe that I was about to break my promise and admit them into their mother's plan. "Beg them to ring me. Give them my work number if you have to."

On Wednesday, I met Annabel for supper. We went to our usual cheerful Italian place in Camden Town, to eat serious portions of spaghetti carbonara and drink a bottle of red wine. We never brought our boyfriends here. We wanted to wear comfortable clothes and no lipstick.

Annabel looked beautiful in her tight black jersey and prim gray skirt, and the waiters were all over her (waiters and policemen always love Annabel). She was in no mood to appreciate it, however. Her latest crush—a senior colleague at the bank—had done what they all seemed to do, and waltzed off with some bimbo from a catering firm.

"It's only one date," I said, trying to be encouraging. "He'll get tired of her as soon as he realizes how thick she is."

Annabel shook her glossy blonde head disconsolately. "She's not thick. She has a degree in Russian. I know what will happen. I've seen it a hundred times. He'll fall in love with her, and they'll have a lovely posh wedding and three children. It's not fair. Why did I waste my time taking exams? I should have done directors' lunches."

"Come on, woman. Pull yourself together. You're successful and brilliant. You're the head of arbitrage, for heaven's sake."

She was mildly reproachful. "You don't have the slightest idea what I do."

I pretended I hadn't heard, in case she started explaining. "There are loads of men out there who actively like a successful woman," I said, knowing this wasn't true.

"I really thought Miles was one of them. I wish I'd known not to be

46

clever in front of him. Perhaps I'll be more helpless next time I'm alone with him."

"Spare a kipper, guv!"

Annabel relaxed into a laugh. "You can afford to be politically correct, because you've got Matthew. Where is he tonight, by the way?"

"Dinner with clients—the poor man has been working far too hard lately. I think there's some sort of important job, which has implications for his partnership. It means I'm seeing a lot less of him."

Annabel said, "Poor you."

"Don't be too sorry for me. You know how his ruthless ambition turns me on." Under the table, my mobile phone bleeped in my handbag. "Sorry," I said. We usually switched our phones off when we met, but I was still chasing those boys.

It was Phoebe. "I've got Fritz," she said. "I'm actually holding his arm so he can't get away. Talk to Cassie, darling."

Fritz took the phone. "Okay, Grimble, here I am."

"At last—do you know how many messages I've left?"

"Yes, and I'm sorry. But I've been going through a spot of emotional turbulence."

I longed to know if this had anything to do with Madeleine, but could hardly bring her up when Phoebe and Annabel were listening at either end. "I really don't want to nag," I said, "but it is actually rather important."

"What is? Why can't you just tell me now?"

Once again, I had to be careful. "I can't do it over the phone. I thought you and Ben could come over for dinner."

"Dinner? Is that all? You're overloading my answering service for the sake of one of your hideous dinner parties?" Fritz was allowed to say my dinner parties were hideous. The three he had attended (in Oxford, New York and London) had been, despite my best efforts, tense combinations of boredom and bad food. The art of entertaining has to be learned, like everything else, and I had never studied it properly.

"It's not a dinner party," I assured him. "But I need to talk to you. It's urgent. And if you kiss me off, I'll tell Phoebe."

"Three-line whip, eh? Okay—but it'll have to be next week. Can't do the weekend."

"Whatever. Name a day."

"Tuesday."

"Tuesday it is," I said briskly. "My place, eight o'clock—and that means real eight o'clock, Fritz. Not ten."

"All right, all right. Eight sharp."

"I'll provide food and wine. You bring your brother."

"Yes, O Queen. Can I go now?"

"Thanks, Fritz. You won't regret this." It was done. The opening moves could now be planned.

They were late for dinner. I knew they would be. I had made careful preparations for their inevitable lateness. I went to Fortnum's at lunchtime and bought an immense jar of French cassoulet, which could be left in a warm oven for hours. I poured myself a glass of red wine. I settled into *EastEnders*. Fritz and Ben would not find me weeping with rage because the dinner had burned to pumice stone. I was planning to be extremely calm and businesslike.

By the time the bell rang at nine o'clock, I was seething—but it was impossible to stay angry with them for long. I burst out laughing as soon as I opened the door. Fritz was holding a large box of apple doughnuts and a bottle of wine. Ben was carrying a wooden chair they had found in a nearby skip. The chair was excellent—just what I needed—and both Darlings knew my ancient weakness for doughnuts. I kissed them both, then poured us all large glasses of wine. It was difficult to be businesslike. Having Fritz and Ben round was always such a lot of fun—and for some reason, the three of us hadn't met up like this for ages.

"Sorry we're late," Fritz said. "It's entirely my fault."

He was wearing very tattered, faded jeans and an ancient leather jacket. Ben was wearing a builder's donkey jacket, and his hair was hidden under a woolly hat like a condom. Neither had shaved for several days. This sort of thing could not be allowed to continue. They looked rather gorgeous in this state, but that wasn't the point. Although decent women might look at them, they wouldn't be thinking of marriage.

"We can eat whenever," I said. "It's cassoulet."

Ben held out a plastic bag full of bean sprouts. "I'll only be eating this, if you don't mind."

I said fine, as long as he didn't suddenly change his mind later and eat all the doughnuts. I knew Ben.

Fritz was looking round my sitting room with alert interest. "This is very smart. I like all the cushions and lamps. I suppose you did it for the Moose. Where is he, by the way?"

"This is just the three of us. I can't talk about this with anyone else."

"Talk about what?" Fritz flung himself across my sofa. "Let's have it, Grimble. You're being mighty mysterious."

"I'd rather not have wine," Ben said seriously. "Do you have any mineral water?"

Fritz and I ignored him.

"Thanks for coming," I said. "I know you're only here because Phoebe begged."

They both laughed.

"She said that if we didn't come she wouldn't have the car mended," Ben said.

"All right." It could not be put off any longer. "Let's sit down." I sat in the armchair. Ben, after a fight with Fritz's feet, took the other end of the sofa. "Phoebe doesn't know I'm telling you this," I said. "But basically, she's asked me to find wives for you."

And I outlined the idea. After a stunned moment or two, they caught each other's eye and burst into roars of laughter.

"You'll have to clean up your act," Ben said, punching Fritz.

"Me?" yelled Fritz. "What about you? You'll have to wash your prepuce."

He said the last word in such a silly voice that I started laughing too. "Seriously," I said. "If we're going to do this thing properly, we ought to talk a bit about where we go next." I stood up. "We can do it over dinner."

"Hold it," Fritz said. He was no longer laughing. He swung himself into an upright position, and his black eyes snapped at me belligerently. "This has stopped being amusing. It's getting surreal."

"Yeah," said Ben. "Totally surreal. I feel Salvador Dali's about to walk in with an enormous fish."

Fritz and I shot him impatient looks. His rambling tendency was getting in the way of the argument, as it had often done in the past.

"Let me get this straight, dear Grimble," Fritz said. "You've actually promised our mother you'll find wives for us?"

"I obviously didn't promise. I just wanted to help."

"You just wanted to muck about with our sex lives."

"I did not!"

"Women always try to change you," Ben said, off on one of his diversions. "And when they find they can't, you have to go through the unutterable hurt of knowing they don't like you as you are. Every woman I've ever loved has hurt me."

"Look, you're both single," I said. "All I'm asking you to do is spend some time with a few of my friends."

"I've seen all your friends," Fritz said, "and I don't fancy any of them. They all seem to wear thick glasses and cut their hair with hedge-trimmers."

"You know that's not fair!" I cried, as if Fritz and I were six years old again and having one of our fights over the swing.

"He means that Honor chick from the other night," Ben said helpfully. "As a matter of fact, I rather liked her. But that doesn't mean I want to marry her."

"Thank you," Fritz said. "We'll find our own wives."

"When you've finished mucking about with other people's," I said.

Ben was injured. "What's that supposed to mean? If you're talking about Vinnie, you've got it wrong. It's nothing more than a close friendship, okay?"

Fritz scowled. "Why are our private lives suddenly your business?"

"There's nothing particularly private about your private life, Fritz. The whole of north London seems to know about you and Madeleine."

"So what if they do? Her husband hasn't found out yet."

"You're a bloody disgrace," I snapped. "You think you can just carry on forever, doing whatever the hell you like—behaving as if you were still at college, as if responsibility was something for suckers—"

"And you've decided it's time to turn me into a clone of Mister Dullard, the lawyer who books you for sex three weeks in advance."

At this point, I'm afraid I lost it. The crack about Matthew was the last straw. I hadn't felt such volcanic fury with Fritz since I was ten.

"This is for Phoebe!" I yelled at him. "Someone has to help her, when

50

you won't lift a finger! Don't you get it? Your dying mother is worrying about who will take care of you when she's gone! For once in your life, can't you do something to make her happy?"

Then it hit me, as if for the first time, that one day we would have to face a world without Phoebe. Suddenly I was sobbing. I couldn't stop myself. The sobs tore out of me like spirits being exorcised. I felt the chill of the hateful new world in which I would no longer be able to pick up the phone and hear Phoebe's gentle voice.

The boys and I had never discussed Phoebe's approaching death. Now that I had ripped down the barrier, the whole tone of the evening changed. I saw, through my frightened and involuntary tears, their shocked faces.

"Oh God," I gasped, "I'm so sorry—so sorry—"

"Don't, Grimble," Fritz said. "Don't, darling." At once, he was gentle. He put his arms round me, and I howled into his shoulder. It was very like being held by Jimmy, which made me sob harder at first.

"I'm sorry—I didn't mean—I'm sorry—"

"Stop being sorry," Fritz said. I felt his hand, large and warm, stroking the back of my head. "You have to cry about it—that's all you can do. There isn't anything else. We found that out when Dad died. So you cry as much as you want, honey."

"Mum doesn't really want wives for us," Ben said sadly. "She just wants our hearts not to be broken." A tear slid down his face. "And they're broken already. Losing Dad was bad enough, but I don't know how any of us can live without Mum."

"Don't you start," Fritz said. "We can't all cry, or we'll never bloody stop. I think we should have a nice cup of tea. Fancy a cup of tea, Cass?"

I was trying to pull myself together, deeply ashamed of my outburst. But the boys seemed to want to carry on comforting me. Perhaps I was helping them express something. Fritz released me with a friendly kiss and went into my tiny kitchen. Ben sat me down beside him on the sofa. Solemnly, he took off his donkey jacket and spread it across our legs.

"There you are, Cass," he said, "all safe in our little Cotton House."

Fritz came in, with three mugs of tea on a tray. It was highly characteristic tea, thick and red and searing hot. I found myself wondering how long it was since I had tasted this late-night beverage. Spending time with the Darlings was forcing me to confront a version of myself that I had forgotten. I was remembering now why I had enjoyed being that slightly scruffy, hedonistic person. Little by little, the world became normal again. I felt peaceful, and deeply fond of my two old friends. At that moment, I made a conscious decision to be as tough as possible about the future— for their sakes as well as Phoebe's.

I untangled myself from Ben's jacket and went into the kitchen, to scrub my tear-boggled face with a tea towel and dish up the cassoulet. We were all ravenous. Ben forgot about Mrs. Appleton's healthy bean sprouts and ate two helpings. More wine was opened. More tea was made. We talked about Phoebe, and how hard we all found it to even think about saying good-bye.

"It's worse because we sort of know what to expect," Ben said. "It doesn't seem five minutes since we were going through all this with Dad."

"It's odd, how much of it feels the same," Fritz said thoughtfully. "The routine of it all, I mean—the medicines, the tests, the endless and ultimately futile visits to consultants. The fantastic thing about Dad was that he wouldn't take any bullshit."

"He had to know as much as possible," Ben said. "He wanted to feel he was in control. He was only thinking about Mum, and making it easier for her. And now she can only think about us."

"She's sorry for us," Fritz said. "I can't stand that. I wish I knew how to stop her worrying about us."

The brothers exchanged brief, private looks of understanding. I felt foolish. I don't think I had fully realized, until now, that Jimmy's death was the point at which their lives left the rails. I remembered now how unearthly the silence had seemed, when that lively presence was extinguished. I also remembered (how could I have forgotten?) the heroic way the boys had played down their own grief, to comfort Phoebe.

"We'll do anything in the world for her, you know that," Fritz said quietly. "And if she wants us to get a couple of wives—we'll bloody well do it, okay? Find me someone Phoebe likes, and I'll do my level best to fall madly in love with her."

"Me too," Ben said. "Open up your address book and do your worst."

They were listening. Now I had come to the hard part. "It won't be that terrible," I assured them. "But there are a few little changes we have to make first."

"Here we go," Fritz said. "Extensive washing of prepuces."

"Yes," I said, "appearance is the first area. You should probably get yourselves some new clothes. And maybe haircuts. And you both have to shave more." I hurried on nervously. "You're both great-looking, but the kind of women I bring in are not going to appreciate guys dressed for the dole office."

Ben asked plaintively, "You mean we have to wear *suits*?"

"Sometimes," I admitted. "Mostly, it's just a question of looking sharper and tidier, and wearing stuff that isn't riddled with holes."

"But we're poor. We can't afford new stuff."

"Phoebe will bankroll you," I said.

Fritz was grinning, enjoying my effort to be tactful. "And will new threads and a shave be enough, or is there more?"

"Of course there's more, Fritz." Bugger tact. This was the time to let them have it between the eyes. "You have to do something about that disgusting flat, in case someone sees it. When was the last time Mrs. Wong cleaned it?"

Fritz chuckled. "Christmas. She says she won't go in any more."

"You two have to clean that basement until it's in a fit state for the cleaner."

They both laughed. Ben said, "It's mainly him. You wouldn't believe what a slob he is. It'd be in an even worse state if I didn't vacuum round his legs occasionally."

Fritz said, "Benedict, you wound me. Who cleaned the microwave only last week?"

I had been working my way up to the first bombshell, and it could be avoided no longer.

"And the most important thing you have to do," I said, "if this scheme has any chance at all, is get proper jobs."

There was a stunned silence. I had uttered the unutterable.

Fritz scowled. "Proper jobs? What the hell does that mean? You know perfectly well why I'm not working at the moment. I'm an actor. I can't conjure an acting job out of nowhere."

"I'm a musician," Ben said, stubborn as a child. "I need time to develop my performing style and work on my repertoire. I can't just write to the Wigmore Hall asking for a gig."

"No," I said boldly, "but there's nothing to stop you teaching, is there?"

"Teaching? Come on."

"Why not? You could put an ad in the *Ham and High*. And I bet Phoebe will know someone who wants lessons. As for you, Fritz," I was taking my life in my hands here, "you have to stop turning things down."

This was dangerous territory, and we all knew it. Fritz had turned down several acting jobs he considered beneath him, including an advertisement for lager that might have brought in good money.

His scowl reappeared. "I haven't got an agent any more."

The last agent had chucked Fritz off her books for walking out of an episode of *The Bill*.

I said, "You'll have to find another one."

"How, for fuck's sake? Do you have any idea how hard it is?"

They were both angry with me. It was one thing to criticize their appearances and sex lives, but quite another to expose their professional inadequacies. I gave a sigh that was half a groan. "Look, I'm sorry. But I had to say it."

"As a matter of fact," Fritz said coldly, "there is another agent who's interested."

"Great!"

"She needs to see my work before she decides."

"Oh."

At last he gave me a rusty, reluctant smile. "This friend of mine from RADA is directing a fringe production, and he wants me in it. There's no money, but it should be a good enough showcase. I'd better give him a call, and offer myself up as a sacrifice."

"That's brilliant," I said warmly. "What's the play?"

"Dunno. But he said it would be a great part."

"Wonderful. I can bring eligible young ladies to see you. There's a certain type of posh girl who loves hanging round a fringe theater—well, I daresay you know that." I was being as positive as I could—though when it came to the point, forcing these two between the jaws of Real

Life felt strangely sad. "Even if you don't earn pots of money, you have to be seen to be doing something. Doing nothing is the biggest turnoff. I want to tell my friends you're ambitious and hard-working, and focused on your future careers, and—"

"Whoa, Grimble, steady on," Fritz said. "Your nose is growing."

"I'm not lying," I said firmly. "I'm only exaggerating a little." I looked at them both keenly, to make sure I had their full attention. "The thing is, I know dozens of women who'd fall in love with you—but only if I have your full cooperation. You have to be with me one hundred percent."

The boys looked at each other cautiously.

"I'll think about it," Fritz said.

"You said you would a second ago," I reminded him.

"That was before I heard the terms."

"Maybe settling down isn't such a bad idea," Ben mused. "Is that doctor friend of yours still free?"

"Claudette? No." I shot Fritz a meaningful look. "She's married."

This, of course, was my preparation for the second bombshell. I didn't think I had to say it aloud—they both had at least a basic grasp of the Bleeding Obvious. Before I let any friend of mine near them, Fritz and Ben needed to scrub their current love lives with Dettox.

Fritz sighed. "Here we go again. That's the problem you can't get over, isn't it? Naughty Fritz and his married strumpet."

"Well, I'm sorry," I said, exasperated, "but I can't do a thing with you until you get rid of that dreary Madeleine."

Unexpectedly, Fritz chuckled, a little savagely. "I don't know why I'm telling you this, when my sex life is absolutely and totally none of your business—but I have a feeling Madeleine will soon be going to Potters Bar."

"Oh," I said, tactfully trying not to sound too thrilled. "Going to Potters Bar" was our old teenage slang for being dumped.

"I'll give you the green light when she gets there."

"Fair enough." I was longing to interrogate him, but had the sense to keep my mouth shut. He was scowling. I knew him well enough, however, to see that he was inwardly smarting. Fritz drove all hurts deep within himself.

"And possibly," he went on, "Ben might think about Old Mother Appleton."

Ben was instantly defensive. "What's that supposed to mean?"

"Only that Potters Bar is lovely at this time of year."

"I wish people wouldn't get the wrong idea about Vinnie. It's a purely spiritual relationship."

"If I have to be a proper bachelor, so do you," Fritz said. He was serious, but I was sure he was enjoying himself—he loathed Mrs. Appleton. "You don't count as a bachelor while you're hanging out with her."

"Look, for the last time, it's a purely—"

"Rubbish," Fritz said cheerfully. "If she hasn't got into your trousers yet, it's only a matter of time. You won't hang on to your virtue for much longer. And if I have to give up my girlfriend, you have to do the same."

Ben was scowling. In his ringletty days he would have pouted. "But she's not my—"

"Fine. I'm not giving up mine unless you give up yours." Fritz folded his arms.

"Yours is different," Ben muttered. "I don't have sex with Vinnie, all right? But I suppose I'll stop seeing her if you stop seeing Madeleine."

Fritz grinned at me. I could see that he was starting to like the idea of interviewing a succession of hopeful young ladies.

"Okay, Grimble—we'll get single, then you can get busy." He threw back his head and put on his Olivier voice. "Cry havoc, and let loose the dogs of marriage!"

CHAPTER FIVE

A surprisingly short time after this, Fritz sent me an e-mail at work.

Re: Single Gents R Us
We've done it. Come round with a list of gorgeous girls.

Betsy, reading over my shoulder, snorted scornfully. "Not sobbing and broken-hearted, then—just clamoring for more girls."

"He's only joking," I protested. "Misery makes him brutal."

"Was he serious about that married woman? Surely not!"

"More serious than he let on. I wonder what happened?" I was burning with curiosity. The chaotic Darlings had managed to shed two unwanted women in a matter of days. I couldn't even begin to imagine how they had done it.

Betsy was in a cynical mood. "He obviously thinks he's doing womankind a huge favor. You'd better get in quick, or they'll be snapped up by another pair of unsuitables."

How right she was. The minute it got out that Fritz and Ben had come free, unsuitables would flock to them like iron filings to a pair of well-hung magnets.

I pressed "Reply," and wrote:

See you tonight @ 7:30. Cassie.

Truthfully, I was glad of an excuse to see Phoebe and the boys. I needed distraction and reassurance, because something was wrong between me and Matthew. Though we were as civilized as ever on the surface, some kind of worm was eating at us. At the time, I couldn't be clearer than that. I didn't even have a fully formed suspicion, let alone proof. All I had was the vaguest sense that the emotional temperature around Matthew had changed—and that could have meant anything, from born-again Christianity to piles. But (like Miss Clavell in the storybook) I simply knew Something Was Not Right. I couldn't go any further than that. I was too scared. A nerve had been exposed. It wasn't hurting yet, but I knew the lightest touch would be agony.

Matthew had called hurriedly from work to cancel our date. We were supposed to be going to a tough concert (Hindemith), which I was rather glad to get out of, but it was a bad omen all the same. Matthew almost never chickened out of an event when he had already paid for the tickets. Yet this was the third time in two weeks. I knew that he really was working incredibly hard. But I was frightened. If I'd been alone, with nothing to do, I might have cried.

Betsy, who had heard the whole call, said, "By the way, I forgot to ask about Matthew. What's the problem this time?"

I forced my voice into breeziness. "Another dinner with clients."

"Oh. Well, at least you'll be able to finish up some work. He's not the only busy person in the world."

"Actually," I said, "I'm matchmaking this evening. If Fritz and Ben really have dumped their girlfriends, I need to be ready with suitable names. I don't know where I'm going to find the time."

Betsy was right about us being busy. The centenary of the magazine was looming, and we were working flat out on plans for a special double issue. We had a wild hope that this might hike up our sagging sales, and possibly provide us with a few readers below retirement age. And we were eking out a tiny budget, assisted only by Puffin (our twenty-four-year-old office slave, an amiable and extremely cheap upper-class twit) and Shay (part-time contributing editor; highly talented but we got him cheap because of the drinking).

I was writing a long article about the minor Edwardian novelist who had founded the magazine. One of his novels had recently been televised, complete with lush nude scenes, and I was wondering if I dared to give scores of elderly readers heart failure by putting bare tits from the series on the cover. On a more exalted note, I had persuaded the Poet Laureate, two eminent British novelists and one distinguished American to contribute essays and reviews. I was preparing to be interviewed on several radio arts programs, and possibly *Newsnight*, about the past century from a *Cavendish Quarterly* point of view (strangely quiet, in case you're interested). Work is a great distraction when there's something you don't want to think about.

"So how will you get them together?" Betsy asked.

"Sorry?"

"The Darlings and their brides. How will you engineer the meeting?"

"God, I don't know," I said. "Where did you meet David?"

"At a poetry reading," Betsy said. "In Camberwell."

"Oh." This was a bit of a nonstarter.

Betsy sighed. "He looked just like Jonah does now—without the ponytail, obviously. But sometimes, when I catch him in the half-light, in his duffel coat . . ." She sighed again. "Where did you meet Matthew?"

"At a dinner party." I allowed myself a pang of nostalgia; remembering how my knees had weakened at the first sight of his sharp, square shoulders. "I thought a dinner party might be the best way to launch Fritz and Ben."

"Hmmmm." Betsy was doubtful. "It's an awful lot of work, though. What does Matthew think?"

"He'll be all for it," I said. "He loves dinner parties. He's been on at me to hone my entertaining skills. Dinner parties are important for future partnerships, apparently."

"What does he think of your matchmaking plans?"

"I haven't told him."

"Why not? Surely a male point of view would be useful?"

"Not Matthew's. He can't stand the Darlings."

"Oh. Won't that be awkward? I mean, how will you get them round the same table?"

I had thought about this. "Fritz and Ben are the only single men we know who aren't gay, prematurely bald or barmy. Matthew wants to 'network' with his female colleagues, and they're all single."

"So?"

"If we invite single women to dinner, we have to invite single men to go with them, like potatoes with meat," I said patiently. "This has been the law of the dinner party since Plato's *Symposium,* and Matthew always respects a law."

"Well, I wish you luck," Betsy said kindly. "And before I forget, there's a huge mistake in this month's crossword."

"Who's on?" I stepped back into the neutral professional zone.

"Argonaut."

"Oh God. Isn't he dead yet?"

Betsy chuckled. "Do you want me to phone the silly old codger, or shall I just have him humanely put down?"

We laughed so much at this that we decided to take a tea break. Then we composed insulting speeches for poor Argonaut's funeral, and laughed more. This sort of thing is what makes office life bearable. Shay and Puffin squeezed into the room to join us, bringing chocolate biscuits. Shay was a bloated, dark-haired Belfast man, who looked a decade older than his forty-eight years, and who couldn't come to work until he had stopped shaking. Puffin was a skinny pipsqueak with mad yellow hair and hilarious upper-class vowels. They were both delightful, and Betsy and I loved the days when they came into the office. I'm afraid it made us both dress slightly better than usual.

The tea break had stretched to forty crumby and convivial minutes, and Puffin was in the middle of teaching Betsy to dance the Gay Gordons, when there was a scuffle at the outer office door. We all dashed back to our desks, giggling like guilty third-formers. We were at the top of six flights of stairs, and when someone called unexpectedly, it was usually the dull and stingy old man who owned the magazine.

But our visitor was Ben Darling, alight with energy, despite the mountain of stairs—and smiling so that he looked, for a moment, remarkably like Phoebe. He swept me up into his arms.

"Cassie, I've come to take you out to lunch."

"What are you doing? Put me down—this is terrible for the editor's dignity." Laughing, I struggled free. "I'm penniless till the end of the month, so you'll have to take someone else."

"No, Cass, honestly—this time I'm actually paying." I hadn't seen Ben this pleased with himself for ages. "I've reserved a table for us at a very nice Italian place round the corner. It's to thank you because you made me get a job."

"What? What's this?" I was bewildered. "A job?"

"I know you thought I should give piano lessons, because you and Fritz think I'm a bit of a loser—"

"Ben! That's not true!" (It was a bit.)

"But I thought I'd do better with some session work. So I called all my old contacts, and struck gold. A tenor from college is adding *Pagliacci* to his repertoire, and his regular accompanist's having a baby. So I'm taking over. Don't you think that's a reason to celebrate?"

"It's wonderful," I said carefully. "But didn't you say—I mean, I saw you more as a soloist."

"Did you? I see myself as a musician, pure and simple. And Neil and I make tremendous music together."

I saw that Ben was on his dignity and beginning to be pompous. "It's fantastic," I said warmly. "Phoebe must be thrilled."

Ben grinned. "That's putting it mildly. You'd think I'd won a Nobel prize or something. I'm playing for him at a recital next month, and I know she'll move heaven and earth to come to it."

"Ben, this is incredibly fabulous. Where's the recital? What's he singing?"

"Shut up, you two," Betsy said, opening her flask of soup. She had recovered from her astonishment that any contemporary of Jonah should find paid employment. "Go away out to lunch. You can't do your gossiping here."

Ben gave her one of his radiant smiles. "Thanks, Mrs. Salmon." (I was amused that he thought Jonah's mum must be in charge of the rest of us.) "I won't get her drunk."

And so I found myself following Ben down the six flights of stairs and out into the sunshine, suddenly feeling foolishly optimistic. Ben, when he was truly happy, had Phoebe's gift for diffusing happiness. He was smiling and shining, and effortlessly beautiful. I checked my pulse, and was amazed that I still didn't fancy him.

He had found a pleasant Italian restaurant, tucked away into an ob-

61

scure side street, far from the ruinously posh haunts of Piccadilly. We sat at a table in the window, watching the occasional passersby and drinking light, sharp white wine.

"It really is fantastic about your job," I said, feeling I hadn't lavished quite enough praise. "It sounds as if you might even enjoy it, too."

Ben, whose ethereal and supposedly ailing form contained a stomach like an incinerator, snatched yet another slice of bread.

"I know I said I wanted to be a soloist," he said, "but I'm not competitive enough. And it's lonely up there, anyway."

"Tell me about your tenor," I said. "Is he single?"

"I think so," Ben said. "But he's rather fat and he has red hair, so don't get your hopes up. Neil's beauty is in his voice."

"Is he good?"

Ben nodded seriously. "He's got what they call a 'silver' voice—very flexible and sweet. His agent's trying to push him into opera, but I don't think his heart's in it. He prefers recitals."

"What's the money like?"

He laughed. "I knew you'd ask that. The rehearsal rate isn't great—but there's a chance of a lot more if I do the concerts."

"Wow, you'll be on a concert platform. Do you realize, you just made yourself about a hundred times more eligible."

Our food arrived at the table, and Ben muffled himself in lasagne.

I picked at a risotto. It was sticky, and I never felt hungry when worrying about Matthew. "Fritz sent me an e-mail this morning," I said. "Is it true? Has he really disentangled himself from Madeleine?"

"Yes," Ben said, through a mouthful of pasta. He put down his fork and looked at me seriously. "Look, when you come round tonight, don't mention the bruise on his face."

"Bloody hell, are you saying Madeleine hit him?" I was partly horrified, partly intrigued. Why on earth had Fritz involved himself with this harpy?

"She threw a brass candlestick at him. It could have killed him, so we decided not to tell Mum."

"She thinks he walked into a door," I guessed.

Ben smiled ruefully. "That's the sort of thing."

"She dented his head because she couldn't dent his heart."

"He's not good at showing emotion, that's all." Ben, who had endured a lifetime of teasing and bullying from his firecracker brother, always had to defend him. "He buries it, and you have to guess how he feels."

"His e-mail seemed quite jaunty."

"Don't be too hard on him. He's not as tough as he makes out. He doesn't show it, but he's having a rough time at the moment. What with Mum."

"So are you," I said.

"Yes, but I think it's harder for Fritz. He takes on all the responsibility, you know—he doesn't let me do nearly enough for her. It's as if he has to take Dad's place."

I put down my fork. My throat had closed. "How is she?" It was time for the question that always had to be asked.

"Very cheerful," Ben said. "Very busy pretending not to be ill. But she's started the new course of chemo, and even she has to admit she's exhausted. She doesn't even argue when Fritz orders her to lie down."

"Oh God, that's a bad sign."

"Fritz says we have to let her do it her way," Ben said. "She has to rest every afternoon—but I go upstairs to play for her, and we all have to pretend she's just listening to me practicing."

I swallowed several times and took a sip of water, wondering at that moment if I would ever be able to eat again. I did my best to keep my voice light, for the sake of my old Cotton House companion. "I'm sure it does her good, though. You know how she loves to hear you play."

Ben smiled. "I'll never have a better audience."

"Fritz said you were both single," I said. "Does that mean you've done something about Mrs. Appleton?"

"Is that what he told you?" Ben was nettled. Points of color appeared in his pale cheeks. "I didn't do anything, actually. It's just that our understanding has—changed."

"Oh?"

"She—she wanted to sleep with me," Ben muttered crossly. "I had to tell her we didn't have that kind of relationship. Not on my side, anyway. I thought it was purely friendship, you know. In the platonic sense. A meeting of minds."

I had to bite the inside of my cheeks not to laugh at this. Good grief,

I had done Ben a terrible injustice. Incredibly, he had been telling the truth about his relationship with the aging music lover.

I asked, "Was she angry when you turned her down?"

"Furious," Ben said morosely, wincing over the memory. I didn't expect him to elaborate, and was all ready to change the subject, but he was in confessional mood. "I was round at her place, and we were literally in the middle of a Haydn flute sonata, and all of a sudden she was trying to snog me and get her hand down my jeans. I barely got out of there alive."

"Poor you." I reached across the table to squeeze his hand.

"So you see, I certainly wasn't having sex with Vinnie. God, no. I haven't had any sex since I split up with Karen."

"Karen? Did I ever meet her?"

"No. It didn't last long enough." Ben sighed heavily, and took a huge mouthful of lasagne. "You know me, Cass. I never can make these things last. I'm still looking for the right person. I'm not like Fritz. He dumps his women, and I get dumped."

"That's not entirely true," I couldn't help saying. "They only dump you because they can't get any sort of commitment out of you and you never pay for anything. That's why Phoebe's so particularly anxious to see you settled."

"I'd love to be settled," Ben said seriously. "I need to fall in love properly. Especially now."

"Leave it to me," I said, determined to be as bullish as possible. "I'm coming round tonight with a list of hand-picked brides."

He smiled wryly. "I don't know. I don't seem to have Fritz's pulling power."

"Nonsense—you've been beating them off with a stick since you were twelve. Quite frankly, now you've got a job, you're more marriageable than that brother of yours."

"You reckon?" Ben brightened. "That'd be one in the eye for him, wouldn't it? If I got there first for once."

A waiter removed our plates—mine still full, Ben's wiped clean—and Ben cheerfully ordered cheesecake for pudding.

Before it arrived, he suddenly pointed to the door of the restaurant. "Hey—look who it is!"

I glanced over my shoulder at the tall, striking dark-haired woman. "Do you know her?"

"Not as well as you do," Ben said. "Don't you recognize her? It's your friend Honor. The one who was going to buy me concert tickets, until you ruined it."

"What?" I swiveled round in my chair to take a closer look.

Yes, it was Honor Chappell. But what had she done to herself? The terrible mousy crew cut had been replaced by a neat cap of dark hair that showed off an unexpectedly well-shaped head and the luminosity of those great gray eyes. She had also visited a decent clothes shop—possibly for the first time in her life—and was wearing a gorgeous dark red linen jacket. Designer glasses had replaced the unflattering specs.

I was vindicated. The egghead was beautiful. Cinderella had emerged from her dusty library. There had to be a man in the picture, and I was desperate to hear the details. Within seconds, I had mentally composed e-mails to Annabel and Hazel.

"Honor!" I waved her over excitedly. "How are you? Your hair's wonderful!"

When Honor saw us, she flushed almost as red as her jacket. "Cassie—hello—what are you doing here?"

"I work in Dover Street."

"Oh God—of course."

"You remember Ben," I said happily. "Come and join us."

"Oh no, I'm not exactly—I can't—actually, I'm meeting my publisher."

I couldn't think why she was so flustered. "Do you have time for a glass of wine?"

"I'd love to, but I really can't." Honor stiffly shook hands with Ben. "Nice to see you."

"Hope it goes well," I offered.

"Thanks." She scuttled to the back of the restaurant. An elderly man in a corduroy suit (academic publishers are not known for their elegance) rose to meet her.

"She looks great," Ben said.

"I told you, didn't I? But I think you're probably too late." I was laughing softly. "Honor only gets into a state like that when she's in *lurve*.

Now I'm totally intrigued. Maybe she's seeing some famous married novelist, and knew I'd recognize him."

"I should have listened to you," Ben said, attacking the large wedge of cheesecake that had just arrived. "Next time you chuck a girl at me, I'll pay more attention. Fritz might think he can do it without you—but I obviously need all the help I can get."

On the packed Northern Line, standing all the way up to Hampstead, I mentally ran through my select list of suitable females. Honor Chappell appeared to be spoken for, but you never knew, and I didn't want to cross her off entirely. And there was always Annabel, whom I considered my Star Buy. The Darlings had known her for years, but I was sure she could be presented to them in a new way, like a secretary in an old film who suddenly takes off her glasses ("Why, Miss Levett—you're lovely!"). Hazel was another obvious winner.

Hazel Flynn, as I believe I've mentioned, was the youngest-ever editor of a glossy magazine. I'd met her at college. For the first five minutes, I thought she was ghastly—loud, brassy and assertive, with tons too much makeup. And then I noticed the bank of steady warmth behind her swaggering confidence, and the intelligence of her raucous humor. In a matter of days she had become one of my essential friends. Hazel had a deep, sexy northern drawl and a pneumatic figure, and was always knee-deep in boyfriends.

These days, she was sleeker and more angular, an immaculate assisted blonde in conspicuous designer clothes. She was still surrounded by men, but none of them had stuck for more than a few months. She was devoted to her job, and besides this, Annabel and I thought she had dreadful taste in boyfriends. The worst of it was, you couldn't pin it down to just one taste—she had been through every type of dreadful boyfriend, from a dreadful titled guy at one end of the scale to a dreadful street busker at the other. She was constantly lamenting her single state, and she had fancied Fritz from afar at Oxford. She was a fabulous candidate.

Annabel and Hazel were my top girls, but I also had two of Matthew's female colleagues up my sleeve, and a couple of excellent names from my old school. The Darling boys would soon see that I meant business. In fact, I was so sure of my success that I was even slightly worried about being beaten to the altar by one of my friends.

As I approached the Darlings' house the sound of the piano poured from the open drawing room window. I halted on the pavement for a moment. Ben was playing one of Phoebe's favorite Chopin ballades. God, he was good. The woman across the road, listening as she pruned her roses in the front garden, gave me a friendly wave.

Fritz opened the door of the basement. He was wearing shorts and a vest. His muscles were magnificent, and gleamed with sweat. He had been working out with his weights in the back garden. There was an angry bluish bruise on his cheekbone, which I tried hard not to stare at. Good God, Madeleine must be insane—he was so well rid of her.

"Thanks for coming," he said. "Ben will be down in a minute."

"He took me out to lunch today. I daresay he told you."

"Oh, yes. Great about his job, isn't it?"

"Wonderful."

"Fancy a beer?"

"No thanks. I brought some wine." I held out the bottle, which I had picked up on the way. Fritz took it. I followed him into the sitting room, feeling a little awkward to be alone with his sweating, gleaming, half-naked body. He searched among the clutter on the kitchen counter for the corkscrew. The flat was as chaotic as ever, but I was heartened to notice certain small signs that tidying had taken place. Ben's sheet music had been bundled into one heap. The bicycle parts had gone. There were fewer mugs, and they were all clean.

"I heard about Mrs. Appleton," I said, mainly to make conversation. "Poor Ben."

Fritz chuckled, a little savagely. "We live and we learn. Another time, he'll know not to form a beautiful friendship with someone, unless he's prepared to have his cock felt."

I couldn't help laughing. "Oh, harsh but fair."

"I expect he told you about my little fracas with Madeleine."

"Yes."

"The official story is that I whacked myself with one of my weights, okay? Mum will have a fit if she hears the truth."

"You can trust me," I assured him. I longed to offer him comfort.

He was bristling at me, to show he didn't want it. He opened the wine and poured some into a cleanish glass. "She lost her temper. She wasn't really trying to kill me, as Ben would have you believe."

"Congratulations, anyway," I said. I suddenly realized why I felt shy—this was the first time in untold years that I had seen Fritz truly single. In the normal way of things, he never jumped until there was someone to catch his fall.

He handed me the glass and opened the fridge for a beer, releasing a smell like an invalid's belch. "Mum's pleased," he said. "That's the main thing. She wants to see you later, by the way."

"Phoebe doesn't know why I'm here, does she? You and Ben aren't supposed to know about the matchmaking."

"Relax. We'll tell her you just happened to be passing." Fritz led me through the glass door, out to the leafy garden. We sat down at the weathered wooden table among the tubs of flowers.

"Yes, it's great about the job," he murmured, almost to himself. "Ben needs something to take his mind off it all." He shot me a calculating look. "I know he's a silly arse sometimes, and that whole thing with Mrs. A was laughable. But don't give him too much of a hard time about it, will you?"

"Of course not." I was startled to hear this, from Fritz of all people.

"I have to bite my tongue, but I'm making a huge effort not to tease him. He takes things badly. I worry about what'll happen when we lose Mum. He's not as tough as I am."

We sat in silence for a few minutes, listening to birdsong and Chopin, and soft, indistinct conversation from the garden next door. I found myself watching Fritz with real and surprising tenderness. I was deeply touched that both brothers had asked me not to be too hard on the other—as if I ever could be.

The Chopin stopped. The window directly above us opened, and Ben's head appeared. "Hi, Cassie. I'll be right down."

This pulled Fritz out of his pensive mood. He smiled at me. "I hope you've come prepared."

"I certainly have."

"Do bear in mind, dear Grimble, that being unattached hasn't made either of us one whit less fussy."

"Only the best, I swear."

Ben's Doc Martens could be heard pounding down the stairs. He opened the fridge (muttering, "Phew, what died in here?") and emerged into the garden clutching a beer. He sat down, with a look of expectancy.

We were ready to begin. I nodded up at the window. "Phoebe won't hear us, will she?"

"Not unless we start shouting," Fritz said. "Come on, Cass—what've you got for us? When do we get to meet them?"

"Well . . ." Facing them both, I suddenly felt foolish. "I thought I'd start by having a dinner party."

Both Darlings groaned.

"Oh God, hours of ennui," Fritz said. "Can I wear my Walkman?"

"Don't be so rude."

He raised his eyebrows at me. "Darling, I'm joking. Lighten up. If you want us to come to one of your dinners, of course we'll do it."

I hadn't expected them to love the idea (I knew it wasn't ideal), but I had to be firm. "Sorry, but there aren't really any other options. Unless you can think of something better."

"I can," Ben said. "You should have a cocktail party. You know— wine and nuts and things on sticks, which are far less work than a whole dinner. You could invite all the girls on your list, then we could meet them all in one go. It would be a huge time-saver. We could size up the whole lot in about ten minutes and reject the ones we don't like."

"What a sensible notion," Fritz said, a glint of humor in his wicked black eyes. "We could call that the first heat, and save the dinner for the second heat. The girls who get through to the third heat would get one-to-one dinners and an experimental snog."

"And full sex could be the semi-finals," Ben suggested. "What? What's so funny?"

Fritz erupted into a great shout of laughter, uncannily like one of Jimmy's howls. "You arse, you can't put them through a cattle market!"

"Why not?"

I was also laughing. "Shall we get them to parade in evening wear or swimsuits?"

"Oh, I see," Ben said, a little huffily. "You think they might find it a bit humiliating."

"I fear Cass is right," Fritz said. "A dinner party is probably the only sensible option. And it's nice of her to suggest it—last time she invited me to dinner, I accidentally broke the bathroom blind."

I laughed harder, pushing away the memory of that dismal evening, back in the days before I met Matthew and discovered perfection. "It'll all be different this time. You only did it because you were drunk. And you were only drunk because I imagined I could cook a leg of lamb. This time I won't choose something that's still pink at ten thirty."

"All right. And I'll go easy on the wine."

"It mustn't be too formal, though," Ben said. "I don't feel we're at our best in a formal setting."

I had to remove Ben's prejudice about formality. "Yes, but the first impression has to be stunning—glossy and sexy and upmarket and generally grown-up."

My tumult of words made Fritz laugh again—I was glad to see that he had cheered up enormously, but worried that he was not taking the matchmaking seriously. "Okay, we get the idea."

"Before we set a date, we ought to think about the first two candidates. Annabel Levett is single at the moment."

There was a dispiriting silence, during which Fritz and Ben stared at me with stony faces.

"Annabel?" Ben obviously thought I was mad.

Fritz asked, "What—as in your fat little friend who cries when she sees a spider?"

I couldn't let them dismiss Annabel. "She's thirty-one now, and she hasn't been fat since she was fifteen. She's beautiful."

"So why is she single? What's the matter with her?"

"Nothing!" I had to breathe hard not to snap this.

Ben was frowning thoughtfully. "No, she really is great-looking these days—I've seen her more recently than you have. She's lovely, actually."

I smiled at him gratefully. "You'd like her to come to the dinner, wouldn't you?"

"Oh," Ben said, "I always like to see her. But I don't want to marry her or anything."

"Why not, for God's sake?" This time, it definitely came out as a snap.

"How can you know you don't want to marry her until you've spent some proper time with her?"

Ben was shaking his lustrous head. "Sorry. We go back too far. Fancying Annabel would just be weird and slightly pervy. Like fancying you."

"Hang on," Fritz said. "There's nothing pervy about fancying Cassie. I quite fancy her."

"Pervert," Ben said.

"She's not our biological sister. It's perfectly all right for us to notice that she's really pretty." He gave me an affectionate version of his wolfish grin.

I was unprepared for the warm rush of blood I felt when Fritz said I was pretty. I hurried on light-headedly. "Ben, won't you let me invite Annabel for you? Just so you can see her properly?"

"Maybe when I've seen all the others."

Fritz emptied his can of beer. "That's settled, then—Annabel's on the reserve list. Who's next?"

This wasn't going as smoothly as I had planned. If Annabel wasn't good enough for them, who would be?

I had carried my briefcase out into the garden. I extracted a copy of Hazel's magazine, folded open at the shot of its foxy young editor.

"Hazel Flynn," I said. "Fritz, you probably met her at Oxford when her hair was a different color."

This was better. The boys passed the magazine between them, each taking several long looks. It was a wonderful photograph—Hazel had been immaculately made up, and was the epitome of slinky.

"The hair used to be red," Fritz said, staring at her. "I think she made a pass at me at some ball or other, but I was too smashed to do anything about it. And I always felt it was rather a shame." He handed back the magazine. "Okay."

"May I invite her, then?"

"Absolutely. Great pair of legs on her."

"Don't assume she's automatically yours," Ben said crossly. "She might prefer me."

I hissed, "Don't start fighting! Do you want Phoebe to hear us? Hazel won't be the only woman there."

Ben was poised on the brink of a sulk. "What else have you got, then?"

"A couple of Matthew's colleagues—"

"Lawyers, eh?" Fritz said. "Count me out. Ben can have the lady mooses."

"Fritz, will you shut up? Their names are Elspeth and Rose, and they're both brilliant."

Ben asked, "How pretty are they?"

Fritz added, "On a scale of one to ten."

I ignored his insolence. "Elspeth's tall and pale—very slender and elegant—with dark hair." (I didn't add that she wore scarlet lipstick and bore a strong resemblance to the wicked queen in "Snow White".) "And Rose is short and a tad plump, but very pretty and amazingly nice."

"We'll take Elspeth," Fritz said. "She piques my interest. What do you say, Ben?"

"Actually, before you make up my mind for me," Ben said crossly, "I think we should try the plump one. They usually have far better breasts than skinny girls."

I had known before I started that the selection process would be distasteful, but this was getting too rank for words—the feminist in me, bound and gagged, writhed in outrage.

I said, "You're not getting near either of them unless you show some respect."

They both murmured, "Sorry," unconvincingly.

"These are all—every single one—totally gorgeous women," I said. "But this can't just be about superficial sex appeal. We're playing for much higher stakes."

"True love begins in the gonads," Fritz said. "This is how it works for us, so pay attention." He leaned across the table, more than half serious. "You see a girl, and suddenly you'll die if you don't get her straight into bed. You do it, and you immediately want more. You want to stay inside her forever. And then you notice how much you like her, and how everything's great when you're with her. And then you're in love."

His eyes were as black and gleaming as the top of new Marmite, and when he uttered the word "love," with intense and almost aggressive energy, I felt a sudden, embarrassing blush of heat between my legs.

Ben nodded agreement. "It can happen amazingly fast."

"My point is, dear Grimble, that sexual attraction is how it starts. So if you're throwing us a lot of moose-faced high achievers with lovely natures, we're all wasting our time."

"Dear Fritz, would I ever be so foolish?" The blush had cooled, and I was myself again. "I never forget how fussy you are. You're the man who turned down a Page Three girl because her ankles were too thick."

"Such a waste," Ben said, chuckling. "Mum really liked her, too."

"I only fall in love with beautiful women," Fritz said.

This was true. All Fritz's girlfriends had been beauties. Thinking about it gave me a feeling of inadequacy, mingled with vague disappointment. It was just as well, I thought, that I'd given up fancying Fritz. I'm not at all bad looking, but his women were way out of my league.

I stood up. "You'll just have to trust me. I'll give you plenty of warning about the dinner—but don't wait to buy those suits. And Fritz, please don't mess it all up on purpose. I'm putting a lot of work into this."

"I promise you perfect behavior. I won't get drunk. I'll be interested in anecdotes about corporate law. If I have to talk about politics, I'll remember to say 'Conservative' instead of 'scum.'"

I snorted with laughter. "Come on, for the last time, Matthew only voted for them once."

Fritz could be evil sometimes. He knew I was sensitive about this. The fact was, I wasn't sure about Matthew's politics. One or two things he had muttered while reading the papers had made me wince. I didn't dig deeper for fear of what I might find.

But I wasn't going to let Fritz annoy me. We had done well. I kissed them both, and went up the basement staircase to Phoebe's part of the house ("The Mainland," as Jimmy used to call it). I stood in the hall, listening to the silence. A solid bar of evening sunlight lay across one wall, glinting on the gilt picture frames. The air was full of golden specks of dust, swirling with hypnotic slowness.

"Hi—it's me," I called softly.

"Oh darling, how lovely." Phoebe's voice was as warm and youthful as ever, so that it was a slight shock to find her stretched out on the sofa, covered with the old bluebell quilt her mother had made. There was a small table beside her, crowded with sinister brown bottles, tissues, glasses, paperbacks—a collection you only see at the bedsides of invalids. I think this was the first time I had ever seen Phoebe looking like an ill person. She lay in a cradle of cushions, with the phone at the ends of her fingers. I kissed her forehead. Her skin felt as frail as tissue paper.

She sat herself up, however, with reassuring briskness. "Isn't it wonderful about Fritz and Madeleine?"

We laughed together gleefully, like Dastardly and Muttley, and my spirits rose.

"My matchmaking is going extremely well," I told her. "We have a scheduled dinner party at my house, which will include two very eligible young ladies."

I described Hazel and Elspeth. Phoebe wanted every detail, and was disappointed that I only had a photograph of Hazel.

"But I'm sure they're both lovely. Let's do them a stupendously romantic dinner. Something so meltingly delicious that they can't help losing their hearts."

"All well and good," I said, "but I have to cook it, don't forget."

"Can't I—"

"Phoebe, don't be insane. If Fritz finds you doing a single thing for this dinner, he'll kill me."

She smiled, not convinced—but not arguing either, because she was so proud of Fritz and the care he took of her. "All right, I won't cook anything. But I can lend you the damask cloth and the napkins."

"Oh, I've got a tablecloth."

"That checked thing?" Phoebe shook her head sorrowfully. "That won't do at all. You'll need the candelabra, too. It looks magnificent, and it hides the brown stain in the middle of the cloth."

"It all sounds a bit grand, and my flat's a hovel."

"Everything looks better by candlelight," Phoebe said confidently.

"I suppose so. Should I have flowers? Or is that too la-di-da?"

"Definitely flowers," Phoebe said firmly. "And that's something you must allow me to help with. I mean it—whatever Fritz says. You're a disaster with flowers."

"I know." My lopsided arrangements were famously inept. I had to admit, it was a huge relief to me that Phoebe was up to giving advice. I needed it, and I needed the comforting sense that she was still there.

With a shaking hand, she reached for a glass of water and took a careful sip. "Darling, would you get me down some books? I need inspiration. And let's have a cup of tea."

Phoebe kept a precious library of cookery books on a shelf in the kitchen. I handed her Elizabeth David, Jane Grigson and a venerable Marguerite Patten whose pages were spotted and stuck together. Purring with contentment, she flipped through these while I made a pot of Earl Grey. For the next half-hour, we drank tea and talked about food.

"You're much better than you think, you know," Phoebe said. "You have the makings of a really fine cook—all you lack is the confidence."

The last rays of the setting sun poured through the kitchen window. Phoebe shaded her face with a hand that was almost transparent.

I asked, "Shall I pull the blind down?"

"Oh, no, darling. Thank you. I like to feel it. Don't you love this glorious weather? One beautiful day after another!"

And I couldn't help thinking that these sunny days, and the flowers she loved, were coming back in their best clothes to delight her one more time.

No, I couldn't bear this—the sense of approaching grief that would swell my heart until it burst out of my chest. I focused determinedly on a wicker basket, resting on the floor beside the sofa. I saw that it was crammed with bottles and jars, each one neatly labeled in Phoebe's jagged handwriting.

She saw me looking at it. "That's for my cousin Molly," she said. "She's coming for the weekend."

"From Edinburgh?"

"Yes, isn't it nice of her? I can't wait to catch up." Phoebe was animated. Catching up with the doings of other people was meat and drink to her. Her curiosity was as endless as her sympathy. "I packed the basket this morning, while I was feeling lively. I wanted to send her back with a few of the things she likes."

I pulled the basket across the floor toward me, knowing she wanted it admired. "Don't tell me—marmalade."

We both smiled. Phoebe's marmalade had a cult following.

"They all seem to like it," she said.

"That's because it's the best marmalade in the world. I think Matthew fell in love with me on the strength of your marmalade."

"Did he? You must take some home with you—they're at the bottom of the pantry. Perhaps I'll leave you the recipe in my will."

"Thanks," I said, deliberately echoing her lightness of tone.

"I'm giving Molly my recipe for damson chutney. She was always mad about it." Phoebe smiled to herself, as if satisfied, and I suddenly saw what she was doing. Why hadn't I seen it before? Fritz and Ben often complained that their mother wouldn't stop exhausting herself by inviting legions of friends and relations to stay with her. But these were her good-byes. No one left her empty-handed—there was always some kind of gift or keepsake.

Again, you wonder why I didn't burst into tears. It was only possible to be brave because I was doing it for Phoebe. My job was to keep up the pretense that normal life went on. I knew that Phoebe noticed my efforts, and appreciated them. She wanted to be in the world, and of the world, for as long as possible.

But the sorrow lay on my heart like a slab of stone and I couldn't always work round it. I went home that night in a taxi, laden with three jars of marmalade, a cardboard box containing a large and rather tarnished silver candelabra, a damask tablecloth scented with lavender and a bunch of late tulips from the garden.

My poky, cluttered flat seemed particularly empty and forlorn. Matthew was out with his clients. Loneliness washed over me. I put my head down on the kitchen table, beside Phoebe's jars of marmalade, and cried.

CHAPTER SIX

Matthew loved dinner parties, which made it all the more strange that he was so difficult about mine—and that was before I had mentioned that I was inviting the Darlings.

He put his reservations in the form of a polite cross-examination. "You think you should hold it here?"

"Well, yes. Where else would I hold it?"

We were in my flat. He had at last made it round for one of our intimate evenings. I had made a huge effort not to be slipshod, but I was on edge. Matthew only wanted to talk about the "impossible" hours he was working, and he appeared not to have brought a clean shirt.

"And where would you put everyone?"

"The big table in here. It'll easily take six."

"You don't think we'd be rather a tight fit?"

"No."

I spoke confidently, to overcome my own doubts. True, my flat wasn't exactly the ideal setting for a romantic dinner party. I'd bought the place five years ago, with money grudgingly coughed up by my father. It was a small upper maisonette in Chalk Farm, filled with dilapidated cast-off furniture. I had applied one coat of paint upon moving in, and done nothing since. There were far too many books and not enough chairs.

But I knew I could easily bring it up to scratch. My books and papers could be moved to the tiny second bedroom. I could deploy lamps and cushions to mask any shabbiness. And Matthew had never minded my place before.

"I see," he said. He sighed to himself. "It might be fun, I suppose. Who were you thinking of asking?"

"I thought Hazel Flynn."

"Ah, yes." Matthew had met Hazel, and liked her. "But not if she brings that ghastly man who plays his sax on the tube."

"Actually, she's single at the moment," I said artlessly.

"Thank God for that."

"And I wondered about Elspeth Dunbar. I liked her so much when we met."

"Elspeth?" For the first time, Matthew showed some animation. He even smiled. "That's a great idea. I'd love to socialize with her more, but it's difficult when she's on her own."

"Ask her when she's free."

"She's always free." Matthew paused, and I could see that he was checking the idea for flaws. With professional contacts, every detail had to be perfect. "You'll need to find some men, though—we can't just fill the table up with girls. Do you happen to know two single men?"

This was my cue. "Fritz and Ben Darling."

"Oh."

"They're both single at the moment, and they both love being charming over a dinner table."

"Do they?"

I was annoyed that I had stooped to lying, and so soon. "Look, they're both perfectly presentable. And if we're going to ask Elspeth and Hazel, we need two presentable bachelors. It's either the Darlings or Steve and Gavin." Steve and Gavin were cousins of Matthew's, perennially single and both hideous.

Matthew chuckled savagely. "Point taken."

"Come on," I said, "I thought you'd be pleased. You said you wanted us to entertain more. As a couple."

"Oh, yes." He sighed again, and looked at me with sudden kindness. "You're awfully nice to do this, darling. I'm sorry I'm a bit distracted. Blame it on the job."

I nestled into his shoulder. "Okay."

"I might as well sleep in that bloody office."

"Never mind," I murmured. "Soon it'll be summer, and we'll be in glamorous Salzburg, wallowing in unlimited sex and Mozart."

Matthew laughed too heartily at this, and his next utterance didn't quite answer me, as if the record had jumped forward. He didn't want to talk about our holiday.

"You're sweet to be so understanding, Cassie. Be patient with me. I'm having to put my entire outside life on hold." He paused. "For instance, I won't be able to make it up to Cheadle next weekend."

"We'll do it another time, when you're not so frantic." I spoke lightly, hiding my dismay. Weeks ago—months ago—he'd decided to introduce me to his parents. I had assumed this visit would be the precursor of his formal proposal. But Matthew hadn't mentioned it for ages, and now he was telling me it was off. And I was suddenly sure that the proposal was never going to happen.

Matthew had stopped wanting to marry me. When had this happened? And why? I couldn't do anything about it now, but suddenly knew that the icy wind of change had blown a frost over all my dreams. I had been holding myself together with a vision of our sheltered future. I didn't realize, until now, how I'd been counting on it. The thought of facing life without this happy vision was frightening. My fear made me stubborn. I would ignore my instincts. I was going to cling to Matthew until he blew me off with dynamite.

Beside me on the sofa, Matthew withdrew his warm body. He stretched and yawned.

"I think I'd better get home," he said. "I've got a conference call at practically dawn."

I wasn't at all surprised that he was leaving. He hadn't brought a clean shirt. He'd never intended to stay.

"Of course, darling. You need a good night's sleep," I said tenderly.

It's not only the guilty party who has to tell lies.

Next day, ignoring the birds of ill omen that were hovering over my romantic life, I invited Hazel to my dinner party. She e-mailed back within half an hour.

Matthew e-mailed later, to tell me that Elspeth would be delighted to accept. My dinner party was on, which meant that I could proceed to the next stage—clothes. I took it for granted that neither Fritz nor Ben had the slightest notion of how much work needed to be done in this department.

Shay and Puffin were in the office that day. During the tea break, I asked them for sartorial advice. True, Shay mostly shambled about in various musty garments covered with stains, and Puffin tended to sport shapeless upper-class things made of cavalry twill, but I trusted them to know more about the philosophy of men's clothes than I did. (I'd meant to ask Matthew, but didn't have the nerve when I'd just puffed the Darlings as perfect dinner guests.)

Shay asked, "What do they normally wear?"

"Jeans, and variations thereon." I was prompt. "T-shirts and sportswear. Fritz has some flashy shirts, and Ben has a rather seedy velvet jacket."

"Flashy and seedy," Shay mused. "Not good words, if you're trying to set them up with nice girls. Any suits?"

I had to think about this one. "I'm not sure. I seem to remember that they appeared in quite decent suits for their dad's funeral. But that was six years ago."

There was a silence, as everyone in the office, including me, thought of how the boys would need new funeral suits only too soon.

"A suit without a tie's a good bet for an informal dinner," Puffin offered. "How much money do they have?"

I didn't know. Later, when I was supposed to be adding a dash of sparkle to my piece about the magazine's founder (like trying to add blood to a turnip—the man and the article were both deadly), I rang Phoebe.

"Give me your bank details," she said. "I'll pay some money into your account."

"Mine? Why not theirs? Don't you trust them?"

"Oh, of course. But if I give the check to Fritz, it'll all be swallowed up by his overdraft. And you know Ben's talent for losing things—he's had so many passports, I'm sure the authorities must think he's an international con artist. I'm afraid you'll have to go shopping with them and do the actual paying for things on your card."

"Hmm. They're not going to like that."

"I'll beg. That usually works as a last resort."

She must have begged hard, because Fritz called that afternoon, to book me for shopping on Saturday.

"I'm rehearsing in the morning," he told me, "but it's right in the West End. You and Ben can meet me afterward."

"So this fringe thing of yours is really going ahead?"

"Certainly."

"And what's the play?"

Fritz sighed heavily. "Not chosen yet. We're still at the stage of chucking beanbags at each other. I just hope to God it's something that makes me look good—I've already written a groveling note to that agent. She's a terrifying old lesbian, but maybe it's time I got an agent who doesn't fancy me."

"She's only interested in your talent, then?"

I heard Fritz chuckle. "My last agent is her worst enemy. She'll do anything to put one over her."

"Fair enough. See you on Saturday, then."

"Okay—but I'm warning you now, Grimble, you'd better behave yourself."

"What's that supposed to mean?"

"Don't try to dress us up like Matthew. We're far too young and sexy."

I pondered this later. Naturally, I had been using Matthew as my model. But when it came to the point, I simply couldn't see Fritz or Ben in Matthew's boxy gray suits, cautious ties or tasteful chinos. Oh God, where did young, sexy men buy their clothes? I seemed to have lost the language of the young and sexy. Were my own understated clothes as dull as Matthew's? Why was I dressing as if middle-aged? Bloody hell, I was only thirty-one. Youth couldn't be over yet. I had decided that Matthew and I made the Darlings seem shallow and immature. I realized now that actually, Ben and Fritz made me and my boyfriend look like a pair of boring old gits.

Deep down, beneath all the accumulated layers of respectability and achievement, something inside me was protesting.

Ben had started working with his Welsh tenor, and was inclined to be superior about Fritz's unpaid fringe production.

"You know why this director wants Fritz so much?"

"I expect he fancies him," I said resignedly.

"Oh—did he tell you that?"

"He didn't have to. In the professional theater, men get treated just like women do everywhere else. And if Fritz was a girl, he'd have blond hair and gigantic boobs."

"Wow," Ben said. "What would I have?"

We were making our way down the side street off Tottenham Court Road where Fritz was rehearsing. It was another radiant day—Phoebe's weather. I studied the flat, grimed façades of the houses anxiously. They all seemed to belong to wholesale dress companies.

"I think I'd be a brunette," Ben said. "My boobs would probably be rather small, but I like to imagine they'd be firm. Pert."

"Ben, what on earth are you talking about?"

"If I was a girl."

"Oh." I decided not to respond, to discourage him from going off on one of his riffs. "This seems to be it."

There was a large, dingy hall down some steep, dingy steps. A notice stuck to the scuffed wooden swing door said, QUIET! REHEARSAL IN PROGRESS! Ben and I crept in respectfully. Somehow, the notice made us creep elaborately, as if we had been instructed to act it out.

But when we tiptoed into the hall, we found that the company had finished for the day. Ten or so people were bunched around a trestle table, all shouting at once. Propped against the wall behind them was a blackboard, upon which was written, EMOTE/REPRESS. A skinny young man, in sweatpants and a singlet, was handing out cups of Starbucks coffee.

Everyone wore sweatpants and singlets, as if heaving coals or training for a marathon. Ten resounding RADA-trained voices bounced off the bare walls. The noise was extraordinary. Nobody turned round, or even noticed us.

Fritz stood a little apart from the others, staring moodily at the blackboard. He was the only person not talking.

"Cassie? Oh my God, it is! Cassie Shaw!"

I turned to see an absolutely stunning woman coming toward me. She had masses of gleaming black hair, legs up to her chin and magnificent, gravity-defying breasts.

"Oh shit," I whispered. "Felicity Peason."

I had not laid eyes on this goddess since we were at school. Peason was our Class Bitch (every class has one, it's almost an official position). Beautiful, cruel, power-mad Felicity Peason had blighted my school career for a decade. Annabel and I had hated her with a passion. Only recently, we'd wondered if we could ever hate anyone that much again.

Poor Annabel suffered more than I did. Being tall and soft and dreamy made her particularly teasable, and Peason's bitching had given her intense pain. When we were eight, Annabel and I heard that if you buried a person's name, that person died. So (kindly helped by Jimmy) we buried Peason's name in the tomato patch—not really believing it would work, but enjoying the thrill of revenge. Despite the inevitable disappointment of finding her alive and well the next day, Annabel said it had felt nearly as good as committing a genuine murder.

Now, as Peason shimmied toward me, I wondered if she would remember the time I decked her. It happened when we were thirteen. Peason had jeered at the huge sanitary pads Annabel's mother had made her wear, and Annabel had wept. Annabel often wept, but perhaps this was the proverbial last straw. I grabbed my school rucksack and whacked Peason's head with such force that she fell down on a desk and broke it. I don't know why I didn't get into more trouble. Peason made an incredible fuss, but I only got detention, and the supervising teacher gave me a biscuit. I suspect the teachers didn't much like Peason either.

"Poison" Peason had left school at sixteen, to be a model in Paris. She had been quite successful at one time. Her father was rich, so I assumed she had stopped modeling before she degenerated into catalog work. Until this moment, it had not occurred to me to connect her to the theater, but I could see that acting was probably the logical next move for a woman like her. She was still fabulous looking. I was sure she was still thick, lazy and morally bankrupt, but these qualities seldom stand in the way of a successful career on the stage.

She kissed my cheek. "This is so amazing! How long has it been?

You're like a ghost from another life! I try not to think about that time—but it's actually lovely to see you!"

I was ashamed of myself for automatically hating her. Come on, how old was I? If I had changed since school, why shouldn't Peason?

"And you're Fritz's brother, aren't you?" She directed a scorching smile at Ben, who beamed as if he'd been given chocolate.

"Ben," he told her breasts. "Hi."

Peason said, "I'd forgotten you lived next door to Fritz, until your name came up in our memory session." She gave my arm a playful squeeze. "He says you and Annabel Levett tried to kill me."

"Sorry," I said.

"Oh, don't. I was a terrible bitch. There was so much tension at home, you see—so much that was unspoken. I'd love to explain it properly sometime. We should have lunch."

"Mmmm, great." Telling myself that Peason had changed, I tried to dredge up some enthusiasm. "That would be fascinating."

"But it'll have to be after we open." She turned her lustrous dark eyes to Ben, becoming slightly more animated. "We're going to be digging very deep. This is going to be an amazing piece of theater. I couldn't be more excited." Her smile widened as Fritz came up to us. "This has been an incredible morning, hasn't it?"

"Incredible," Fritz said. His brow was dark. "C'mon. Let's get out of this wank-fest."

Without taking leave of the other actors, or checking that Ben and I were following, he sprinted out into the sanity of the street. Ben and I had to trot to keep up with him.

"Fritz, you know who that was!" I said breathlessly. "You didn't tell me you were working with Felicity Peason!"

"No. Why should I?"

"Because she's THE Felicity Peason. Old Poison, from school."

"Oh, right."

Ben asked, "Why was this morning so incredible?"

"I can't imagine. I thought it was a monumental waste of time."

"Do you mean the emoting-and-repressing lesson?"

"Look, watch it, Ben—okay? I've got to work with those tossers for the next six weeks. I'm not in the mood to joke about it."

"I am," Ben said cheerfully.

Fritz's scowl faded. He smiled at me. "Sorry, Cass. I need a couple of minutes to get my temper back. It's been a very depressing morning."

"Please try to cheer up, Fritz. We won't get a thing done if you're in one of your moods."

"Sorry, all right? I've got low blood sugar, and I was too hacked off with the emoting and repressing to get any coffee."

I decided we all needed some coffee. We went into one of the many interchangeable coffee places, and I bought huge cappuccinos and a heap of chocolate croissants. Ben had eaten one of these before we even sat down.

"Is it really that bad?" I asked Fritz.

He laughed briefly. "Terrible. I'm praying it improves when we start blocking the actual play."

"Does that mean the play has finally been chosen?"

"It was nothing to do with me—but yes. God help us all. It's got disaster written all over it. No wonder we're not being paid for it. We don't deserve to be paid."

"Oh well," Ben said cheerily. "It keeps you off the streets. Anyone want that last croissant?"

Fritz picked the croissant off the plate and firmly rammed it into his brother's mouth.

Ben let out a muffled roar of protest, but spoiled the impact by starting to wolf down the croissant. Fritz reached into his rucksack, pulled out a paperback French's edition and threw it down on the table.

"Here it is. We open in three weeks. Don't you dare laugh."

I was too puzzled to laugh. "This? You're not serious!"

He frowned. "Oh hell, yes. We're all so incredibly serious, we're about to disappear up our own bums."

Ben pulled the book toward him to read the play's title. "*Rookery Nook*. By Ben Travers. Pretty heavy stuff, I suppose—like that Strindberg thingy you did at college."

"It's a classic comedy," I said carefully, feeling for the positive spin. "A farce—from the 1920s, I think. Well, that could be extremely—"

"Have you seen it?" Fritz demanded.

"Yes, actually." A couple of years ago I had seen *Rookery Nook* performed by my mother's patients in a secure mental hospital. I could only recall that though the farce itself had been amusing, it had been difficult to forget that the juvenile lead had once chopped his wife into tiny pieces. "Do you know what part you'll be playing yet?"

"Not yet." He was grim. "All I know is, we won't be playing it as a comedy. Apparently, it's about an obsessive relationship between a mad German and his nubile stepdaughter."

"Oh." I didn't recall anything like this—perhaps it was a good choice for my mother's patients after all.

Fortunately, my bewilderment made Fritz laugh. "It might get me a new agent, but it'll never get me a wife. We'd better keep prospective brides well away."

He cheered up properly after this, and Ben forgave him for the croissant incident (as I think I've said, Ben was of a forgiving habit where his brother was concerned). The three of us—guided by me—headed down Oxford Street toward Liberty.

"I'm not saying we have to buy everything there," I told them. "But it's a good place to start. I thought we could work our way down Bond Street, toward Armani."

Ben gave a plaintive bleat. "That'll take ages!"

"Ben, we can't just nip into Mister Byright. Phoebe expects us to spend all that money she paid into my account."

Fritz asked, "Are these the places Matthew gets his gear?"

"Yes. You're going to learn to appreciate things like tailoring and design."

He was smiling, but there was a combative gleam in his eye I didn't like. "Will we be allowed to express opinions of our own?"

"Certainly not." The silken labels in Matthew's clothes had told me all I needed to know about understated male elegance. I led them into the men's department at Liberty like Queen Boudicca, wishing I'd worn higher heels to emphasize my authority. Ben was (as it says on shampoo bottles) fairly soft and easy to manage. But I sensed rebellion brewing in Fritz, and prayed he would not make trouble. People never really change, and Fritz had always been famously naughty in shops. When he was four, he suddenly bolted in the middle of a shoe-fitting at Selfridges (wearing one Start-Rite sandal and one welly) and caused £15 worth of damage in Glass and Crystal before Phoebe caught up with him. Three years later he was chucked out of Habitat for spitting on pillows. Phoebe said there was obviously something about shops that awoke a strange primeval psychosis in Fritz.

At the beginning he was obedient. He got through trying on two (extremely elegant) gray suits with nothing worse than an expression of festering boredom. When I handed him the third suit, he growled, "Gay."

"Fritz, this will not make you look gay!" I pleaded. My jollying-along smile was starting to hurt. "It'll make you look smart, that's all. Go and try it on."

I turned my attention back to Ben, who was proving difficult to fit. All the trousers seemed to be too short in the leg or too large at the waist, or both.

"Either they fall down, or they make me look like Tintin," Ben complained. "It's all right for Fritz—he's the same shape as those plastic blokes in the window."

A patient young man was assisting us. He assured Ben that the shop would be happy to make any alterations.

Fritz suddenly burst out of the changing room, his hair artfully tousled over his forehead. "Darlings!" he cried. He slung the jacket of the suit over one shoulder and pouted.

Oh hell—he was right. The suit made him look as gay as Ascot Week. Of course, I was laughing. So was the shop assistant. We should never have encouraged him. From that moment, Fritz turned the trying-on into a cabaret, assuming a new persona for every outfit—the mincing queen morphed into a barrow boy, then a naff estate agent, then a very thick toff. The climax came when he emerged from the changing room with his hair soberly parted on one side, irritably looking at his watch in a perfect imitation of Matthew.

"Okay, I've got the point," I said, when the three of us were outside Liberty. "I know nothing about men's clothes. When we get to Emporio Armani—"

"Oh, I don't think we'll bother with Armani," Fritz said.

"Not Armani?" I was mystified, to the point of being worried.

"It's a question of image," Ben explained, kindly but firmly. "You're trying to impose something that's just not us. You might as well give up and let Fritz handle it. He'll be impossible until you do."

I looked at Fritz. He did his Matthew imitation again (adding some very good business with an imaginary handkerchief) and I found myself laughing with almost savage intensity.

What was happening to me? Matthew—the man I loved and longed to marry—had been my idea of a perfectly dressed man. Yet here I was, absolutely howling when Fritz sent up his perfect style (his impression of Matthew taking off his trousers nearly changed my blood group; you had to be there). I wondered what made laughing at Matthew feel like laughing at the government.

"I give up," I said. "Do it your own way."

Fritz gave a theatrical sigh of relief and hailed a taxi. We went to Paul Smith in Covent Garden.

"This was on my list," I said defensively. "We would have got here eventually."

"Oh, I daresay," Ben said, making for a pile of gorgeously colored shirts. "After you'd made us try on even more golf sweaters and safari suits."

He, Fritz and the (formidably trendy) male shop assistant all roared with laughter.

"That's not fair! I was showing you perfectly lovely clothes—you just think being clean and tidy makes you look gay—"

"Off you go, Grimble." Fritz turned me round and gave me a firm push. "Bugger off and look at the girls' stuff."

Public argument is undignified. I retreated into the women's section before he threw me out.

Huh. Of course I'd thought of Paul Smith. It was just that Matthew disapproved of the clothes. He thought they were too noticeable. But I wanted Fritz and Ben to be noticed. And I saw that Fritz had far more definite ideas about style than I had assumed. It was possible that he had far more actual style than I did.

I couldn't decide whether the fabrics in the women's collection were fabulous or rather alarming. In the end, because I was waiting for such ages, it was impossible not to try on a few things. I was skint—editors of literary quarterlies are not high earners—but a couple of the suits were irresistible.

When Fritz and Ben did finally come to collect me, they were amused to find me so cozily entrenched in the shop that one of the girls had popped out to get me a doughnut.

"Just like a woman," Ben said. "I thought you were only shopping for us."

Fritz said, "Hurry up—we're done. The suits will be ready on Tuesday. There's a whole heap of other stuff to lug home, and a gigantic sum of money to hand over."

Ben asked, "Will Mum mind that we got socks and pants as well? Our knickers are in absolute rags."

"It's all the wear and tear," Fritz said, giving the pretty salesgirl a friendly smile that made her giggle. "Frankly, the pants haven't been built that can stand the strain." He put his hands in his pockets and looked at me, narrowing his eyes. "Not that suit, darling. Far too old for you."

I told him I wasn't listening. "It's total heaven. Men know nothing about women's fashions."

"Maybe not," Ben said, "but we know what makes a woman look foxy. And that suit makes me think of Mrs. Hutchings."

"It does not!" Mrs. Hutchings was our old piano teacher, and anyone who has ever had piano lessons will know how deep this cut (it is a curious fact that an attractive piano teacher is as rare a sight as an ugly fireman).

"This is more you," Fritz said. He leaned across me to pluck a silk shirt off the rail behind me. "Yes, you should definitely get this—don't you think, Ben?"

"Yes," Ben said. It was his decided tone that made me look at the shirt (I will never wear anything that can be described as a "blouse") properly. It was made of silk, in a penetrating shade of aquamarine, intriguingly flecked with orange—mouthwatering, but I'd never have considered it for myself in a hundred years. I did try it on, however, and was startled to see that Fritz knew what suited me better than I did myself. In some way that I couldn't define, the cut and color of the shirt made it a statement of freedom, style, youth—basically, it looked tremendous. In the mirror of that changing room, I saw a version of myself that I had been working at repressing since I met Matthew. Why had I done this? No wonder Matthew was being distant. It wasn't just that I looked younger and prettier in this Paul Smith shirt. For once, despite my shrimpy dimensions and tidy-proof clump of hair, I looked sexy. Matthew would go wild, I thought. Matthew wasn't very gifted at foreplay, and I loved the rare occasions when he got too excited to bother with all that painstaking twiddling. Once (tipsy after a particularly good Mahler's Fifth at the Festival Hall) he didn't even wait until we got through my front door, but had his way with me on the stairs. It hadn't happened for ages. My stomach fluttered with anticipation (I don't know how else to describe that frisson of sex that feels like fearless fear). I was seeing Matthew that very evening, for a quiet dinner at the Camden Brasserie. I bought the shirt.

I came down to earth a little when I saw the size of the bill. We all winced as my credit card went over the polished counter. Fritz aggravated my guilt by refusing to tell me anything about the suits they had bought. These had now been spirited away for alteration, but he wouldn't even point out the similar ones on the rails, or describe the cut and color. He said I would simply have to wait until they arrived on my doorstep for the dinner party, now just one week away. I decided not to interrogate him. The suits were all terrific, anyway. They couldn't possibly come out of Paul Smith looking bad, and Phoebe would be in ecstasy—she wouldn't give a damn about the expense.

In high spirits (because there are few things as exhilarating as spending money you haven't got) we reeled out into Floral Street with our boxes and bags, and launched ourselves at the nearest bar. The sunny afternoon was fading into warm evening. We sat out on the Piazza, idly watching the clusters of people around the shops and cafés.

Fritz ordered designer beers all round, and we drank to the success of my dinner.

I said I shouldn't be drinking.

"Because you're meeting Matthew," Fritz said.

"Yes. He doesn't like it when I roll in reeking of booze."

Fritz was eyeing me thoughtfully. I was wearing the new shirt with my jeans. He gave me a slow smile.

"Matthew's going to love you in that," he said.

Matthew didn't say anything about the shirt until I mentioned it. Then he said, "Actually, I'm not too mad about it. It's a bit—well—hippyish."

I spent the rest of the meal trying not to be depressed. Across the room, I had to look at my hippyish reflection in the big mirror. Not that

90

Matthew was in a bad mood, however. Yes, he was distant and abstracted—melancholy in a rather grand way, extremely kind when he noticed me properly. I remember that I was angry with him, but that I nevertheless worked incredibly hard to liven him up (I wonder if men realize how much women jolly them along—I sometimes think they'd all be in locked wards if not for us).

We chatted about the lighter sides of our respective jobs (I'll spare you), and shared a taxi back to my flat. Matthew carried in his briefcase (he'd come from work) and the Mulberry overnight bag containing the chinos, polo shirts and deck shoes he wore out of office hours. Yes, he was staying the night. The flat was particularly non-slipshod. I had dusted, vacuumed, changed the sheets and scrubbed the bath early that morning. We drank peppermint tea and went to bed.

Sex occurred.

I fell asleep, clinging to Matthew's warm bare back, telling myself that the bad dream would soon pass.

Early on Sunday morning, we were woken up by a terrific rumbling crash—almost like an explosion. It came from the sitting room, and was followed by an eerie silence. Matthew—stark naked—ran in first.

"Shit!"

I was right behind him, owlish and giddy with sleep. "Oh shit," I echoed.

My sitting room ceiling had fallen down. The room was filled with a brown haze of ancient plaster dust. Every surface was thickly covered with huge jagged lumps of plaster, and inches of this sticky, clinging dust. It grabbed at our throats and plugged our nostrils. Coughing angrily, Matthew wrenched up the window so fast he snapped the sash cord.

As the first shock subsided, I became aware that Matthew was muttering to himself, "Shit, shit, fuck, oh fuck, shit, fucking hell," and this from a man who never swore.

I stared dazedly up at the place where the bulging old ceiling had been. It was a mess of filthy wooden lathes. This was going to cost me a fortune.

Matthew had left his briefcase on the sofa. Frantically, he tried to beat off the thick carapace of dark red plaster dust. He struggled to open the dust-choked lock. The case came open, and he gave a great groan (a little like the groan when he came, only more passionate). All the vital papers inside the briefcase were entombed in dust. He began to pick them out one by one, moaning piteously.

I stuck a dusty Yellow Pages into the window to keep it open. "Darling, I'm sorry," I found myself rasping—though it did occur to me to wonder why I felt the need to apologize. Oh God, this was a nightmare. This was slipshoddery run mad.

"For God's sake!" Matthew had found his Mulberry overnight bag, similarly interred. He tried the zip. It was stuck. We were both wheezing by now, and weeping as dust seeped into our eyelids. We were naked, like two ancient Britons freshly daubed with woad.

"This is the last fucking straw!" Matthew shouted.

He had never shouted at me. I stared at him, horrified, waiting for him to return to his proper self.

"You live in shit, Cassie—did you know that? Not this flat, but your entire bloody life—I might have known my stuff wouldn't be safe here! You don't care, do you? Because you surround yourself with people who don't give a shit! You can't get away from it—it's in your background, the types you know, types who think it's FUNNY to give a shit. Well, I've done enough—I'm not taking this."

He went into the bedroom. I stumbled after him. The dust had spread like a disease. A film of dirt lay across the duvet cover. My dressing table was like Miss Havisham's. A filthy fog hung over everything. Matthew, shaking with anger, dived for his office clothes from the day before. He pulled on the trousers and shirt, snatched the jacket and tie, grabbed his bags and walked out without another word. I stood, shocked and shivering, watching the storm of dust he had raised when he slammed my front door.

I was crying—a sort of dusty snivel.

Shouldn't Matthew (my lover, lest we forget) have tried to help me, or at least offered a word of sympathy? Wasn't my dust-covered computer a more serious casualty than his suit or his briefcase? Shouldn't he have asked me home with him, instead of leaving me in a flat that was plainly uninhabitable?

I put on my white dressing gown, now khaki with dust. Lumps of plaster dug into my bare feet. My bathroom and kitchen were coated with dust. So were the tins in the cupboard, the vacuum cleaner, everything. I would never clean this up. And my boyfriend had blamed me and left me. Dust thou art, to dust thou wilt return. I made myself a dust-tasting cup of tea, and called Phoebe.

I ought to have worried about waking her, but this disaster had wiped out any awareness of her mortality. She had become eternal again—the one vital, unfailing source of comfort.

Her calm voice crooned through my sobs. "Darling, it's going to be all right—no, of course it's not a disaster—oh, my darling, this is no time to worry about a silly dinner party! I'm just thankful you weren't underneath—you could have been hurt! And how beastly of Matthew. No, of course you can't stay in that mess—you must come straight round here. Yes, that's an order. I'll send Fritz to fetch you."

It was a huge relief to let myself be soothed and taken care of. I was thirty-one years old, but Phoebe's comforting was as steady and all-knowing as it had been when I was six, and I had sobbed in her arms because Felicity Peason hadn't invited me to her birthday party.

Phoebe could still make everything all right. Meekly following her instructions, I put down the phone, washed off the worst streaks of dust in the shower, and dug out a pair of old jeans that had escaped the worst.

The doorbell rang before I could find any passable socks. I ran barefoot down to the street door, and found both Fritz and Ben. Fritz was carrying several rolls of black plastic bags and a large bucket filled with packets of sugar soap. Ben's arms were full of J-cloths and drums of Ajax. Both brothers had mops slung over their shoulders like rifles. Ben wore a bucket on his head. For the first time since the start of this nightmare, I broke out into a smile.

"We're the cavalry," Ben said. "Lead us to the injuns."

I began, "Guys, you didn't have to—"

"Yes we did," Fritz said. "We're under orders. If you try to stop us, I'm afraid we'll have to tie you to a chair."

I blew my nose resoundingly, leading the way up the stairs through the dusty haze (it was everywhere—I'd have to write a cringing note to the woman who lived underneath me). "Be prepared. It's awful. You can't possibly clean it up, because nobody can."

I wish Matthew had been there, to see the reactions of Fritz and Ben when they saw the mess. After a minute of startled silence, they started laughing.

That was all it took to put the world right. Before I knew it, I was laughing too. Matthew's rage suddenly seemed absurd. I realized that he had not been angry about his damaged possessions, but about his damaged dignity. A memory flashed back at me, of his willy bobbing about while he wrestled with his briefcase—well, dignity and nudity aren't often seen together. And it is dreadfully undignified to be an angry nude person. Poor Matthew, this would probably haunt his dreams for years.

"I think the Moose was a bit of a shit, running out on you like that," Ben said warmly. "Next time I see him, I've a good mind to get Fritz to hit him."

"Seriously," I said, "you can't do anything about this. It'll take hours."

"Heavens, this is nothing," Fritz said. "I can't think why you're making such a fuss. So go away and leave us to it."

"Oh no, don't be silly." I was feeling a little ashamed of my hysteria, which had mostly been a reaction to Matthew's outburst. "I'll start putting the biggest lumps in black bags, and sweeping up the worst—"

"Grimble, shut up." Fritz put his hands on my shoulders and gently pulled me round to face him. "Get out of this flat and drive straight round to Mum's. She's waiting for you."

For a second I could have cried again. After Matthew's unkindness this was bliss. Why didn't I just let them look after me? I pulled myself together, found socks and car keys, and fled gratefully into the fresh air.

Phoebe had made a pot of coffee. A jug of hot milk steamed beside it. There were warm brioches wrapped in a napkin. My domestic catastrophe had poured energy into her, summoning her old self from the shadows.

I can't describe the deliciousness of that coffee. I drank two large cups and gave Phoebe the whole story. This was the first time I had admitted to her that Matthew wasn't perfect. She showed no surprise, only concern—which took the form of endless pots of homemade jam lining up beside my plate.

"He was cross, that's all," she said thoughtfully. "Men do get cross about things like this—remember Jimmy, when the pipes burst?"

I tore a hollow in a brioche and filled it with apricot jam. "He said I lived in shit. And I honestly don't, Phoebe. He knows how hard I work at having a nice, normal, hygienic house. I've always been determined not to be some seedy old Boho like Ruth."

"Darling, your flat isn't at all seedy. It's charming."

"He looked at me as if he really disliked me. It felt horrible."

Phoebe said, "Perhaps you'd better not marry him."

But I couldn't face any more destruction. I couldn't face losing my last refuge, that blissful dream of secure married life. "Oh no, it's only a row. Everyone has them. I wondered what it would be like to row with Matthew."

Phoebe raised her eyebrows. "Don't tell me that was your first."

"Yes," I said, "I suppose it was." I racked my brains, but really couldn't remember anything worse than a little sarkiness on my side, a little tetchiness on his. These highly controlled exchanges could not be called rows. Until today, we had existed in a state of calm and temperate reason.

Phoebe reached across the table to squeeze my hand. "Don't worry, my lamb. I think it'll all blow over. As soon he's washed the dust out of his creases, Matthew will see the funny side."

"What's so funny anyway?" I was despondent. Matthew wasn't big on humor.

"It's the nudity, I'm afraid," Phoebe said apologetically. "Have another brioche. More important, he'll realize he owes you an apology."

"He does, doesn't he?"

My uncertainty made Phoebe roll her eyes. "Listen to yourself. Of course he does. It wasn't your fault that the ceiling came down on his briefcase."

I laughed, beginning to feel positively cheerful. "I'm the one who's going to suffer most. I have to pay for a new ceiling, and my flat looks like downtown Pompeii. I'll have to cancel that dinner party."

"Not necessarily," Phoebe said. She smiled mysteriously, and I saw that she had had one of her brilliant ideas.

"Well, where else can I hold it? Matthew lives in a loft, and it's so incredibly clean that I'd be too nervous to cook properly. And before you say anything," I added firmly, "I'd rather not hold my dinner party here. An eligible bachelor never lives with his mum."

"No, not here." Phoebe was delighted by her own cunning. "Downstairs."

"The basement?" This was a good one. "Phoebe, have you gone mad?"

"Don't be silly, darling—it's a perfectly lovely flat. And it's their territory. Fritz and Ben would be the hosts." Phoebe's dark eyes were full of vitality in her worn face. She was excited. "That's far more romantic—two elegant young bachelors, entertaining in their Hampstead pad!" Bless her, she was more than half serious. "What? What's so funny?"

For the second time that day I was helpless with laughter. "Which one's James Bond?"

"Actually, I've always thought Fritz would make a marvelous James Bond. Yes, you can laugh, Miss Cassie, but stranger things have happened. Sean Connery was plucked from obscurity."

"Oh, Phoebe, I do love you!"

She stopped being dignified and started giggling. "I've had another idea—I'll pretend I'm not their mother and dress up as a foreign cook. I'd so love to be a fly on the wall."

I sighed. I could see that the idea had taken hold. She wouldn't be talked out of it, so I might as well give in gracefully. "I suppose it could be done," I said reluctantly. "But you'd have to find an industrial cleaner. The place is in such a state."

"I'll tell the boys they're doing it for you," Phoebe said. "I'll say you had nowhere to hold your party. They'll agree because they're so kind-hearted."

And so fond of you, I thought; they'd do anything to please you.

I spent the rest of that Sunday morning with Phoebe. I went out for a heap of papers, and we read them in the garden. Fritz and Ben returned just as I was putting the finishing touches (under Phoebe's instructions) to a summery salad of tomato and basil. They were hot and tired, and clouds of brown dust puffed out of their clothes whenever they moved. I provided them with cold beers, almost incoherent with gratitude.

"We filled loads of black bags," Ben said. "You'd never think one ceiling had so much plaster in it."

"I'm afraid your vacuum cleaner gave up the ghost," Fritz said. "The place is far from perfect—but you can probably sleep there tonight."

I was waiting for the right moment to introduce Phoebe's mad idea, but she told them immediately.

"Poor Cassie can't hold her dinner party there now. We thought we'd move it to your basement."

I half expected them to be annoyed, but Fritz only laughed. "Good grief, did you hear that, Ben? Our very first dinner party."

"I'd be really grateful," I said humbly. "I'll do the cooking, obviously. I'll also help with the cleaning and fumigating—it's the least I can do, after you've spent a Sunday morning bagging up my ceiling."

Ben was solemn. "She can't hold it at her place, Fritz—her sitting room looks terrible. She'll never get it fixed in a week."

I was still addressing Fritz. "We'll find a time next week to really clean the hell out of your place."

"It's all settled then," Phoebe said contentedly.

"Not quite," Fritz said. "If we're putting up with this monumental intrusion, it has to be our show."

"Your show?" I couldn't help sounding doubtful—Fritz and Ben hadn't done any kind of entertaining in their lives, unless you counted certain rowdy gatherings after the pubs had shut. "What about the cooking? Elspeth and Hazel will expect more than pizza."

"You can help, obviously," Fritz said. "But we're in charge. We choose the food, we choose the wine, we decide what we wear. The evening will have our stamp upon it—the dinner party reinvented."

It was late in the afternoon by the time I got up the courage to go home. Outside my house I found a large, dusty heap of black binbags and the mangled corpse of my vacuum cleaner. I also found Matthew's Saab, with Matthew sitting in it. He leaped out as soon as he saw me. He had rehearsed his speech.

"Cassie, I'm so sorry about this morning. I don't know what possessed me. I've been under incredible stress at work, but I know that's not an excuse. I behaved like a shit."

He hugged me hard, squeezing my rib cage. The relief of being held by him made my eyes sting. I wiped the scattering of hot tears discreetly on his shoulder.

"I was really nasty to you," Matthew said. "As soon as I cooled off, I hated myself. I've been sitting in the car for more than an hour, wondering what I'd do if you didn't come back. Ignore the million messages I left on your phone."

"We were both in shock." I was eager to make excuses for him.

To give him his due, Matthew wasn't having any of this. He shook his head solemnly. "No, my response was totally self-centered. I ought to have seen how much worse it was for you. I've been doing some hard thinking, and—we need to talk."

I was a little wary, as I always am when people say "we need to talk." It invariably means "I need to mention things you don't want to hear." But Matthew was being gentle and kind, and wrapping me in the affection I longed for. This blast of warmth reminded me how cold he had been lately. I had a blind eagerness to be part of a cozy couple again.

"Come on in," I said. "Let's take a look at the damage."

Matthew nodded toward the cairn of black bags beside the gate. "You didn't do all this on your own?"

"Oh, no—Fritz and Ben handled everything."

"That was nice of them." Matthew winced slightly as he said this—it must have been galling to acknowledge the Darlings' unexpected moral superiority. Clearly, Matthew's self-image had suffered a blow. His fit of temper appeared to have shocked him more than it had shocked me. He held my hand all the way up the stairs, and insisted on going into my flat first, presumably to protect me from any more collapsing ceilings.

The sitting room was bad. I stepped through the door and let out a moan. The fallen ceiling resembled a plowed field of raw soil, lowering over my furniture in a way that made it look particularly shabby and defeated. The air was still a fine haze of dust. Every surface had a transparent film of the stuff.

But the lumps and boulders had gone. No wonder the vacuum cleaner had died—Fritz and Ben had worked like furies, sweeping every inch of my dreadful, treacherous flat. They had dusted and polished the television. There was a note stuck to the screen—"This works." They had driven the dust from the shelves, the tops of the books, the lampshades and the sofa. I let out a shaky sigh, suddenly calm because the day's crisis was over.

"You poor darling," Matthew said. From the pocket of his immaculate chinos he pulled a piece of paper. "This is a list of local plasterers, by the way."

"Really?" I was genuinely impressed. "How on earth did you get that? Are you a Freemason or something?"

He put his arms around me again. "I called Talking Pages while I was waiting in the car."

"You're so efficient."

He was very serious. "Cassie, I've been asking myself a lot of questions. I've been looking at what we've built together. I've been quite distant with you recently, haven't I?"

"Yes."

"What we've made is too good to throw away. I realized this morning that I don't want to lose you."

I put my arms round his neck and buried my face in his shoulder. "I don't want to be lost. Please don't lose me." I had never begged for his love so blatantly.

He kissed me, and we made love on the sofa with something like the old passion, raising clouds around us.

CHAPTER SEVEN

The following Wednesday was set aside for Hampstead's biggest clean-up since they renovated the town hall. This was the only day I could carve out of a schedule packed with Matthew, the magazine and a volatile Polish plasterer. Somehow, by burning midnight oil (and surreptitiously catching up on sleep during a Palestrina concert at St. John's, Smith Square), I managed to take the afternoon off. I arrived in a taxi, laden with every cleaning product in existence, down to a fierce foam that claimed to act like napalm on carpet stains.

I found a scene of seething chaos. Ben and Fritz had been hard at work since early morning. The French windows stood open, and various shabby articles of furniture had been turned out into the sunny garden. Cupboards were open, spewing out the boxes and bags of ancient junk stored there since the boys moved in. Ben was outside, his long hair bundled into a ponytail, scrubbing the big table. Fritz was washing down the walls with sugar soap. A bulky, sweating stranger with red hair was kneeling in front of the oven, chipping at the crusted gunk with a knife.

Ben leaped in and flung a friendly arm around the stranger. "Cassie, this is Neil Evans—my tenor." As if he kept a tenor as a pet.

Neil had a ruddy complexion. His permanent blush deepened when he stood up to shake my hand. He was a shy man, with a soft Welsh voice. "Hi. Ben's told me loads about you."

I looked round forlornly. "I don't know where to start. How on earth are we going to be ready for Saturday?"

Neil said, "It's not as bad as it looks."

"Has anyone tackled the bathroom?"

"We saved it for you, darling." Fritz pointed to one of the black bags silting up the narrow hall. "I've cleared out Ben's stash of useless folk remedies. Now it's ready for a good scrubber."

"The penalty for being late," I said. "Neil, it's tremendously nice of you to help—but how on earth did you get roped in?"

Puffing slightly, Neil dropped back to his knees. "I don't know. Ben was going on about it, and the next thing I knew, I was buying Brillo."

I could have told him that I understood. The Darlings had an extraordinary talent for drawing people into their orbit, and mesmerizing them into doing menial things (those of a literary bent might like to remember Tom Sawyer whitewashing the fence).

"It happened yesterday evening," Ben told me. "We were rehearsing for Neil's *Pagliacci* at the Harrogate Festival, and the subject of housework just came up."

"So it was off with the motley, and on with the apron," Fritz said. "I must say, for a rising young tenor, you know a hell of a lot about cleaning."

The rising young tenor shrugged. "You can thank my mum for that. Her kitchen's like an operating theater."

I gathered up my carrier bag of products and put my head round the bathroom door. "Oh, dear God!" No, I won't describe it. I rolled up my sleeves, removed my jewelry and began with a large can of foaming Harpic.

Neil, once he had finished the oven, joined me. "The foam won't take all that off, you know. It needs some old-fashioned elbow grease."

"The Camden Sainsbury's was out of elbow grease, unfortunately."

He smiled shyly, not at all annoyed by my sarcasm. "Here, I'll give you a hand. You do the bath and the sink. I'm bigger than you, and a gentleman, so I'll take on the toilet."

It was impossible not to get friendly—even intimate—with Neil while we were bumping against each other in that awful bathroom. I found him a gentle and genial character, disarmingly modest about his burgeoning career. In between answering my nosy questions about recitals and recordings, he stuck his red head out of the bathroom door to shout suggestions to Fritz and Ben: "Fritz, you want to mop those tiles with the stuff in the red bottle, man. It brings them up lovely."

I couldn't help getting caught up in his enthusiasm. In a surprisingly short time, the bathroom was white again, the medicine cabinet polished, the scarred cork tiles spotless. Neil then helped Fritz to rehang the sitting room curtains, while I wiped down shelves. Ben ferried bags and boxes of rubbish out the front gate—a rubbish-collecting firm was to remove them tomorrow morning. As the three of us got dirtier, the flat got cleaner. Little by little, the lineaments of civilization were restored. Holding the dinner party here no longer seemed foolhardy.

Fritz found his CD of the twenty best garage anthems and put it on. We danced as we worked—yes, including the rising young classical tenor, who wasn't as groove-proof as one might think.

By about six o'clock, after extensive work with two vacuum cleaners, damp cloths and dusters, Fritz decided it was time to bring in the furniture. While Ben and Neil finished waxing the floorboards, Fritz and I went into the garden armed with a squash racquet and a large spatula, to beat out the dust. This was invigorating, filthy work. We pounded the clouds of centuries out of the sofa and rugs. Then we flopped down on the sofa to rest. I was sweating and gasping. Unlike Fritz, I was woefully out of condition.

"I've invited Neil to the dinner," Fritz said.

"Oh."

"Is that a problem?"

"No, of course not. He's lovely, and he's done all this work." I paused, to stop myself being the kind of prat who whines about having her table "put out." I wouldn't be petty. Neil was more than presentable. "Is he bringing someone? You know, does he have a girlfriend?"

"No. He's apparently rather diffident with girls. I thought you could find another girl for him."

I let out a laugh that was half a groan. "Oh yes, just like that. As if I had a stash of them in my airing cupboard."

"I'd like to make it worth his while," Fritz said. "The fact is, Neil's offered to do the cooking. He's marvelous at it, apparently."

"Oh, I see—that's why you're suddenly so desperate to accommodate him. I might have known."

Fritz nudged me with his bare tanned arm. "He fancies you."

"Who—Neil? Get off."

"No, really. Perhaps you don't know how foxy you look in those jeans. He's been brick red ever since you arrived."

"Isn't he always that color?"

He was laughing softly. "You could do a lot worse. Neil will be famous one day."

"I don't go for fat blokes with red hair."

"Sorry—I assumed you weren't fussy."

"What?"

"You manage to endure moose-faced blokes with eighties hair."

"Fritz, I'm aware that you don't like Matthew—all right?"

He sighed. I felt his warm body stretching on the cushions beside me. "Only because he's wrong for you."

"How do you know? I think he's perfect for me."

"I don't know what you're trying to do to yourself," Fritz said. "Why do you want to be somebody else?"

I looked at him, not sure I'd heard him properly. I was surprised that my strivings to be somebody else were obvious enough for him to notice. He was smiling, but I felt he was serious.

I said, "What do you mean?" Knowing exactly what he meant.

"I get the sense that you're acting out a role," Fritz said. "You're like a transvestite, buying stuff for his female persona."

"Thank you. Please don't overwhelm me with compliments."

"Darling, I'm trying to be nice."

"Really? You said I was like a transvestite."

He smiled, and said, "Okay, I put that really badly. What I mean is, the natural Cassie is perfectly sweet and lovely, and I don't understand why you work so hard to hide her."

"I don't think I'm trying to hide anything. Isn't it natural to try to improve on nature?" I suddenly wanted Fritz to understand that I was only doing it because I had lost the genuine me. I wasn't even sure of my own tastes any more.

Phoebe tapped on the kitchen window upstairs, and the moment vanished like a bubble bursting. Fritz and I waved.

"I said we'd have tea with her when she woke up," Fritz said. He glanced at his watch. "She slept for a long time."

I hoped this was good. I hadn't the heart to ask. We dragged the sofa back indoors, and the four of us climbed to the sunlit uplands of Phoebe's domain. It was obvious that Phoebe felt well rested. She had set out the tea service, put several sorts of chocolate biscuits on plates and made tomato sandwiches. She laughed over our dirtiness, and made Ben sit on the *Guardian*.

We were all parched and ravenous, and we fell on the tea as if we had just come off the Raft of the Medusa. Phoebe replenished the biscuits and kept the tea flowing. She was in her element—so transparently delighted to be entertaining that Fritz did not tell her off for overdoing it.

Phoebe already adored Neil, and not only because he had provided paid work for her less-effective son. They fell to discussing food. I noticed that his face did not turn magenta when she spoke to him. People were never shy with her for long.

Incredibly, it seemed that the eligible young bachelors really were going to throw their first posh dinner party. I was relieved, but also a little anxious that so much of the business had been taken out of my hands. I was still the senior consultant, however, and there were still details that needed attention.

I looked at Fritz and Ben, trying to picture them in sharp suits instead of sweats and T-shirts.

"Forgive me if this is a silly question," I said, "but the two of you are going to shave before this dinner, aren't you?" Both handsome faces were pebbledashed with stubble. I felt it gave out totally the wrong message.

Ben sighed, his mouth crammed with biscuit. "You don't trust us at all, do you? You think we're going to whip out our knobs between courses and show you up."

"And are you planning to get haircuts?" I took it for granted that Ben would be cutting his long hair.

"What's wrong with my hair?" He was wounded.

I placed a soothing hand on his arm. "Ben, you'd look so fantastic with shorter hair. Only wizened old rock stars have long hair these days."

"That's not true, actually."

"All right, and motorcycle messengers—but nobody else."

You'd think I was Delilah, telling Samson he'd look great with a Number One. Ben's eyes widened with horror (twenty years ago, they would have brimmed with tears). "I like it, actually. If you want to cut it off, you'll have to chloroform me first."

Fritz said, "Good idea. A whiff of chloroform might stop you talking bollocks."

"I mean it, Cass," Ben said. "I'm not cutting my hair."

"Oh, darling, I'm so glad!" Phoebe had caught the end of this. "I love your hair. Every mother secretly dreams of having a son who looks like Little Lord Fauntleroy."

She meant it—the irony had never entered Phoebe's soul.

Ben did not have the grace to look embarrassed. He only smirked at me, knowing he had won the hair argument.

"You keep forgetting, dear Grimble," Fritz said, "that you have surrendered control to us. This is our gig. If Ben wants to look like a big wendy, that's his business."

Ben would not rise. "You're eaten up with jealousy. You can't bear to admit that I've got better hair than you."

"No you haven't."

"Yes I have. Yours is coarse."

"Coarse!"

"Stop it, boys," Phoebe cut in, mild but firm. "Neil and Cassie don't want to witness one of your silly arguments."

"I appeal to you," Fritz said. "Is my hair coarse?"

"Stop it, both of you." Phoebe gave Ben a biscuit, momentarily forgetting that he was no longer six years old (when we were children, Ben would do anything for a biscuit). "Go and play the piano. Neil says he'll sing for me."

Ben and Neil went to the grand piano, their dirt and dishevelment making incongruous reflections in the depths of its polished lid. Then Ben began to play, and I forgot everything else—as people generally did when Ben played, if they had even the smallest liking for music. Neil sang the old Scottish songs that Phoebe loved, and he was a revelation. His stout body swelled and firmed before us, and out poured a glorious voice. If you have ever heard a trained singer in a small room, you'll know how the sound flattens you like a gale.

Phoebe's eyes were stars of bliss. The beautiful tenor voice sang "Bonnie Mary of Argyll," "Auld Robin Grey" and the "The Land of the

105

Leal." These were the songs Phoebe had warbled around the house when we were little. I had ordered myself not to come over sentimental, but by the last verse of "The Land of the Leal" I had a lump in my throat the size of a cricket ball.

To finish the concert, Neil sang "Aye Waukin'-O." He throttled back his voice to almost a murmur. A single tear fell from Phoebe's eye and slid down the ladder of lines on her cheek. At the end of the song, she wiped it away and smiled at Fritz. "I used to sing that to you when you were teething."

Fritz reached across the table and picked up his mother's hand with great gentleness, as if holding a butterfly. For a long moment they smiled into each other's eyes, and Fritz gave her a look that made me catch my breath. How would it feel, I wondered, to be on the receiving end of such fathomless love?

CHAPTER EIGHT

We had a terrible time keeping Phoebe away from the dinner party.

"I know I can't actually be there, but I don't see what's wrong with me simply staying upstairs," she said wistfully. "It's not as if I'll interfere."

"Phoebe, you're dying to interfere. Why don't you just admit it?"

"All right, all right." Phoebe's voice was airy and unrepentant. "I admit that I probably wouldn't be able to resist dropping hints about marriage. But what if I promised not to say a single word?"

She had taken to calling me at work, hoping I would be easier to get round than the boys. But I was under strict instructions from Fritz not to relent.

"Don't be silly," I said.

"Well then, what if I made everyone tea and coffee?"

"They're trying to come across as debonair young bachelors. You don't see James Bond's mum suddenly popping in with a tray of tea and biscuits."

"Poor Mrs. Bond died in a freak mountaineering accident," Phoebe said, as if she were a friend of the family. "But if she'd lived, I bet she'd have taken a good look at the sort of girls her son was seeing."

I refused to be led up one of her conversational garden paths. "Phoebe, listen to me. If you hang about at that dinner, Hazel and Elspeth will run a mile from the boys."

"I don't see why. You could all come upstairs for a drink first. I could make some of those little cheese canapés." Her voice was as soft as ever, but I could hear the undertow of obstinacy.

"Fritz says you're not allowed to cook."

"Oh darling, canapés aren't proper cooking. You just fold a little grated cheese into the pastry, and—"

"Phoebe, stop it." This was the very day before the dinner party, and I had to be firm. "There mustn't be the smallest whiff of apron-string. Fritz got you a lovely invitation from the Cohens, so don't disappoint them."

When I put the phone down, Betsy said, "You're quite right, she'll be better off out of it. That way she won't be too horrified if it all goes pear-shaped."

"Rubbish, it'll be fine." I was determined to be cheerful. Matthew had spent three whole evenings with me that week, and was staying for another weekend (despite the unlovely appearance of my newly plastered ceiling). I would be attending the dinner party as one half of an established couple. This went a long way toward covering my doubts. "That flat is so clean, it squeaks. The boys aren't even wearing shoes until Sunday morning. Nothing's going to go remotely pear-shaped. Unless the ceiling crashes down on us."

Betsy laughed, saying lightning never struck twice, and wasn't it time for a nice cup of tea? She was also very cheerful today. The reason was that Jonah had got himself a job. Yes, that shy denizen of the attic had emerged into the sunlight, to work as a park-keeper on Hampstead Heath. The way his mother was acting, you'd think he'd been made head of ICI. Despite her concern for the momentous dinner, Betsy couldn't keep off the subject.

"Jonah's job will probably only last till the end of the summer." She handed me a slice of the chocolate cake she had made to celebrate (Betsy reacted to any kind of upheaval by staying up late and making cakes). "But he gets his own hut—one of the nice ones beside the pond."

"That'll look good on his CV," I said, with my mouth full. "Job With Own Hut."

"I gave him an electric kettle, as a hut-warming present." Betsy sat down, absently adding a few stitches to the tiny scarlet hat she was knitting. "I should probably give him an alarm clock, too. He's always been dreadful at getting up."

"He'll learn," I said brutally. "Shades of the prison house begin to close about the growing Jonah—and not before time. Everyone else has to do it."

"The girls never seemed to have any trouble," Betsy mused. "I think women must have a natural talent for getting up early."

There was no point in arguing with this, or even noticing it. I finished my cake and turned my attention back to trimming down a long and winding article about John Ruskin. I'd barely made a dent in it before my phone rang again.

It was Hazel. Her voice was grim. "I can't make it tomorrow. You'll have to send my apologies."

"Oh no!" This was a terrible blow. I'd practically designed her wedding dress, and now she couldn't come.

"My dad's had a heart attack."

"Oh God." I immediately felt guilty—good grief, what kind of heartless person was I turning into? "Hazel, I'm so sorry."

"Mum says he's all right," Hazel said. "She says there can't be much wrong with him—he's already complaining about the hospital food, apparently. But they want me to go up there right away."

"Yes, of course."

"I wish I could get out of it—well, you know what I think of Dad. He's a manipulative old git, and I wouldn't put it past him to be doing this on purpose."

Hazel knew she could say things like this to me. One of the first bonds between us had been the discovery that we both had fathers we disliked.

I did my best to be bracing. "You'll feel better once you've done it."

"I suppose so. It's a bugger getting away from work. Sorry about your dinner party."

It was awful to hear the anxiety and helplessness in Hazel's voice. She had dropped the broad accent and reverted to northern middle-class, a sure sign that she felt her family was catching up with her. She usually tried to hide any hint that she was the kind of Northern Babe who had once owned a pony.

"Don't be silly," I said, as warmly as I could. "Forget the dinner. I hope your dad's all right. Call me any time if you need to talk."

"Thanks."

"I mean it. Really any time, day or night."

When I hung up, Betsy was hovering sympathetically with another slice of cake. "Oh dear, poor Hazel. And poor you—what'll you do about tomorrow?"

There was only one thing to do. I flipped my diary to Annabel's work number (I didn't know it by heart because we had a pact never to phone each other at the office, for fear of never shutting up).

"Annabel Levett."

She answered in her brisk and unrecognizable office voice, which threw me off balance for a moment. "Annabel? Sorry, but this is an emergency—" I gabbled out a begging invitation.

"You knew I'd be free." She was reproachful.

"I hoped you would be. Please come."

"I'm free in theory, but I've sort of decided not to go out any more until I've lost half a stone. I can't risk meeting men when I'm so fat."

"Oh God! We've had this conversation a squillion times! You are not fat. And it'll be quite safe. The only men present will be Matthew, Fritz and Ben, and Ben's tenor—who really is fat. And he has red hair. You won't want him to fancy you."

"Well . . ." Annabel's voice was more cheerful. "In that case, it sounds rather fun."

"You're coming? Thanks so much. It's their basement, eight thirty. Bless you."

"It's years since we had one of our sessions with the Darlings." She giggled suddenly. "Will you be serving Fritzy-Witzys?"

I laughed. A "Fritzy-Witzy" was a nasty cocktail of orange juice, tonic water and cough medicine, invented by Fritz when one of our basement sessions had run dry. "Certainly not. It'll be far too posh."

"Tell them I'll lay in a case of Actifed Chesty anyway."

Annabel rang off before I could explain that this was not a normal basement entertainment. We were not planning to eat takeway Chinese and get hammered, as in the olden days. Still, I knew I could trust her to behave beautifully. I rang the boys to break the news about the change in the table plan.

Ben answered, and was philosophical. "Never mind, it'll be lovely to see Annabel. She's one less girl I have to make an effort for."

"I just hope nothing else goes wrong," I said. "One of you had better be fixed by the end of the evening, or I'm turning in my Matchmaker's badge."

Matthew was trying very hard, but he couldn't hide the fact that he was miserable. I had never seen him so spiritless and gloomy. He met my bright remarks with shrugs and sighs, until I asked him point-blank what the matter was.

He was startled that I had noticed anything was wrong. "Sorry, Cassie. I've been having a hellish time lately."

"At work?"

"Of course at work. Where else?"

"Can't you leave it behind sometimes?"

"Sorry," he said again. He made a visible effort to pull himself together. "You look lovely, by the way."

"Thanks."

He had spent the previous night and most of that day catching up with work. He had come round to my house straight from the office. We were to drive up to Hampstead in my car. I was wearing a superb black dress from Emporio Armani (no, I couldn't afford it) and lethal new shoes that made me walk as if I'd just had a visit from the footbinder. The dress was a deliberate attempt to look a little less boring. When I held my stomach in and made my mirror face, I was positively gorgeous—but I was aware that I had contravened several of Matthew's rules regarding tartiness. Why hadn't he noticed that I was way over my lipstick allowance? He hadn't even disputed my hemline, or the amount of exposed bosom. And he had always taken meticulous interest in my appearance.

"You need to relax," I told him, as I hobbled down the stairs. "You don't have to carry your work around with you all the time."

"It's very tense at the moment," Matthew said. "Frankly, I'm wishing you hadn't asked Elspeth Dunbar this evening."

"Why?"

"I need her on my side—she could seriously scupper my chances of a partnership."

"Darling, everything will be fine. She can't possibly have a bad time."

"Well, I hope not." He was morose. "She's so straitlaced. She's got this lifeboat collecting box on her desk, and if you swear in front of her, she makes you put money in it."

I wished he'd told me that before I invited the woman—Fritz and Ben, even on their best behavior, blithely peppered their speech with rude words. I decided to warn them, before they ended up bankrolling the first-ever north London lifeboat.

"Don't worry," I said robustly. "She must let her hair down sometimes."

We climbed into my car. I slipped off my killer shoes (the relief!) and pushed my feet into the old trainers I kept for driving. Matthew sat rigidly beside me, cradling two expensive bottles of wine in his arms.

My car wouldn't start. I did all the things you do (checking batteries and petrol, fiddling with the choke), while Matthew sat like a disapproving Easter Island statue.

"I knew I should have brought my car," he said.

"And a very merry Christmas to you too," I muttered crossly.

"What?"

I could not allow myself to be irritated with Matthew, or where would it all end? "Nothing," I hissed, through clenched teeth. "We'd better call a cab."

It was Saturday, and there was not a cab to be had in under an hour—I tried six numbers, and got the same answer every time. Matthew remained eerily silent.

"We might as well take the tube," I said eventually. "It's only two stops."

Matthew sighed heavily. He got out of my car. In barbed silence, we trudged toward Chalk Farm station. Only when we were sitting in the carriage did I realize that I was still wearing my old trainers.

Hell and damnation. My wondrous shoes were in the car. The trainers were absurd with my skinny calves. I looked as if I had been drawn by Dr. Seuss.

We arrived at the basement nearly an hour late. Fritz opened the door, holding a glass of champagne. "Here she is, late for her own party." He leaned forward to drop a kiss on my cheek. "Love the shoes, Grimble. Did you jog here?"

I was confused, and a little alarmed. Fritz looked almost criminally handsome. His gleaming hair had been cut. He had shaved. The new Paul Smith suit was frighteningly trendy, and with a checked pattern loud as a foghorn. It wasn't what I would have chosen for him, but that was the whole point. He was being himself. He was elegant and flamboyant and incredibly sexy.

The basement flat had undergone a similar transformation. I even thought Phoebe might have overdone it slightly—I recognized a lamp and two Persian rugs from the poor short-sighted woman's bedroom. The dining table was set with Phoebe's creamy damask cloth. Fritz had rejected the candelabra, and the brown stain was covered instead with a glass vase of lilies. In the kitchen section of the room, Neil bobbed between various seething pans. He blushed and smiled at me through wreaths of fragrant steam.

Ben completed this perfect installation. I finally admitted that I had been wrong about his hair. The famous Fauntleroy ringlets looked fabulous with the lethally sharp new charcoal suit, and had to be an asset.

Naturally, I was far too much of a lady to make any of these observations out loud. I pretended the Darlings lived like this all the time.

Elspeth Dunbar was sitting stiffly on the sofa, holding but not drinking a glass of champagne. She had left off the scarlet lipstick, and I was a tad disappointed by the flatness and squareness of her face without it. Her silk dress softened the angles of her bony figure, but the print made her look too pale, and her rigid shyness lay over the room like lead.

We shook hands, claiming to be delighted to see each other again. Elspeth volunteered absolutely nothing, and answered my polite questions in monosyllables. She kissed Matthew, which made him smile for the first (and last) time that evening. The presence of a senior colleague galvanized him into something like geniality. He sat himself at her side, and they exchanged a few cautious off-duty jokes about their office.

Annabel leaped out of her chair to hug me. "Where have you been? You look . . ." her eyes traveled down to my feet, "lovely."

"I know, I'm wearing trainers, but it's a long story." I slipped them off, and my expensive frock reasserted itself. I raised a refined little laugh with the story of the car. Matthew collapsed back into gloom the moment Elspeth's attention veered away from him. He stared into the middle distance, gulping champagne like a sleepwalker. What was the matter with him? Why couldn't he make an effort? Did he think this sort of thing came naturally to the rest of us?

I was glad to see Annabel. She was at her absolute best, I decided—the less she tried, the prettier she looked. She was squeezed into a tight black skirt and white blouse. Her guileless face was made up in the polite, nonthreatening way necessary for bosomy blondes who work in male-dominated offices. Her long fair hair was all over the place. She has a way of making demure clothes look luscious, and both Darlings unconsciously addressed all remarks to her cleavage. She was relaxed, and giggly with champagne.

She said, "It's a good thing I've postponed my diet. Neil's cooking is making my stomach rumble. I don't think I'll ever be thin."

It would have been lovely to sink into gossip with Annabel, but I was not here to enjoy myself. I made another attempt to pull Matthew into the conversation. I can't remember exactly what I said—some inanity about buying tickets for Neil's next recital.

Matthew jumped as if I had applied a cattle prod to his privates. "Yes," he said. "Yes indeed." He squared his shoulders, and blurted, "Sorry—have to make a phone call."

He hurried out into the street, digging his mobile from his pocket.

"Work," I told everyone. "Honestly, they never leave him alone."

"Well, that's work for you," Ben said. "Neil's just the same—an absolute slave driver. Doesn't know the meaning of relaxation."

"Don't listen to him," Neil said. "He's just lazy." He watched Ben with an amused affection that made me see what a nice man he was. No wonder Phoebe adored him.

Elspeth's flat voice fell into the silence. "I've always thought classical music must be a very demanding career."

Ben feels sorry for shy people, and this made him very kind to Elspeth. He topped up her glass, and he and Neil managed to pull the poor creature into a three-way conversation about music. She glanced from

Neil to Ben, and her square face softened. I stopped worrying about Matthew. Had we found a match for Ben? Was it really going to be this easy? What would Phoebe think? I tried a mental snapshot of Elspeth as a bride. If she could be persuaded into a different shade of lipstick, she and Ben would make a magnificent couple. Mrs. Elspeth Darling. *My husband's a musician—my husband's a pianist—my husband accompanies Neil Evans, the rising young tenor.* Yes, it could work.

And there wasn't much chance of any other wedding, such as mine. My social smile was making my cheeks ache. Prince William would propose to me before Matthew did.

"I think we ought to sit down," Neil said. He began to place the first courses on the table—individual cheese and spinach soufflés, beautifully puffy and brown.

"Neil," Fritz said, "you're a fucking diamond."

I glanced at Elspeth, to see if the offensive word had offended her. No collecting box was forthcoming. She only smiled at Neil and said, "This looks delicious."

We sat down.

"Don't wait for Matthew," I said.

At this moment Matthew returned. He was pale and agitated. "Cassie, I'm so sorry about this, but I've got to leave."

"What?" I didn't even try to hide my dismay.

"Something's come up, that's all, and I absolutely have to fix it."

"But it's Saturday night! Couldn't it wait till Monday?"

"No. I have to leave. Sorry."

Fritz said, "Don't let us keep you."

A frisson of dislike passed between them.

Very much on his dignity, Matthew kissed me, promised to phone me later, and made his exit.

I bowed my head over my plate, feeling that the corners of my mouth were stapled to my ears. I couldn't lose that awful bright smile. I felt it made my mortification grotesque.

"Well, I'm glad I don't have a job like that," Ben said. "It's a shame he had to make that call before he had any food. Would anyone mind if I ate his starter?" He scooped it off the plate without waiting for a reply.

I noticed that Fritz was looking at me thoughtfully.

"Let's hope Elspeth doesn't have to do a runner too," Ben said cheerfully, through a mouthful of cheese and spinach. "I mean, you're Matthew's colleague, aren't you?"

Elspeth said, "Yes. We've just finished working on a case together. I can't imagine what that phone call was about."

"Wow. Maybe he's been fired." Ben favored me with one of his beaming, tactless smiles. I smiled back, longing to Sellotape his mouth shut. "That would explain why he looked so freaked just now. Either that or he's having an affair and he was phoning his mistress."

"Ben," Fritz said gently, "shut up."

"Why should I? Shut up yourself."

"You're spraying Elspeth with spinach."

"Oops. So sorry." Ben scrubbed at his mouth with one of Phoebe's damask napkins. "Neil, you've given me green teeth—the classic dating disaster. It's a good thing I'm not trying to pull."

I ate a forkful of soufflé. I didn't want it, but it would give my mouth something to do besides smiling. Of course Matthew wasn't having an affair. How absurd. I wasn't even going to think about it. God, Ben could be insensitive.

Kindly, as Jimmy would have done, Fritz changed the subject. He began telling us about his "experimental" production of *Rookery Nook*.

"Annabel, you know one of the cast," I said.

"Do I?" Annabel's cheeks were becomingly tinged with pink. She was staring at Fritz.

"I told you," I said. "He's working with Poison Peason."

"Oh, of course—poor you. Is she still an unspeakable cow?"

"I'd say so," Fritz said. "She bores us all to tears."

"I expect you fancy her," Annabel said innocently.

He leaned closer to her, smiling. "Not my type, darling. Too demanding. And anyway, I prefer blondes." I noticed, with a slight quickening of the pulse, that he could not keep his eyes off her. He was pouring himself into that wide blue gaze. And Annabel had that beatific glazed expression she got whenever sexual infatuation reared its goofy head at her. All her old fancying of Fritz came rushing back, with horns on.

The evening was spiked with sex. I thought of Matthew, and felt intense loneliness and deep yearning. I needed love before I disappeared.

I refilled my glass (noting, in my self-pity, that no one had thought to do it for me), and resolutely tuned in to the other end of the table. Neil and Ben were entertaining Elspeth with stories about their college days— rather tame stories, I thought; but Elspeth seemed to love them. She was smiling.

Neil dished up noisettes of lamb on a bed of flageolet beans (the man was a truly fantastic cook). Fritz kept the wine flowing. He continued to focus most of his attention on Annabel. He wasn't flirting with her. What Fritz did was too intense and electric to be called flirting.

I had a bleak moment of isolation. I was miserable because Matthew didn't want to marry me, and also because I didn't want Fritz to fancy Annabel. Yes, of course, obviously, this was because I fancied Fritz myself. He was still—in a purely physical sense—the most attractive man I had ever seen. I told myself that the strong aura of sex around him was distorting the atmosphere. I reminded myself that I was in love with someone else. It was up to me to ignore the chemical disturbance. After all, wasn't this exactly what I'd wanted? Being jealous of Annabel felt all wrong.

I noticed that Ben was quiet, and also watching Fritz and Annabel. The rest of us were becoming increasingly invisible.

Out in the street, a car door slammed. Above us, we heard the front door opening and closing.

"Oh, is that Phoebe?" Annabel asked. "How lovely!"

At last Fritz tore his eyes away from Annabel. He looked at his watch. "Half past ten—and I told the Cohens to keep her till eleven, at least."

He and Ben were laughing softly. Ben said, "I give her ten minutes."

"She'll never wait that long," Fritz said. "She's only looking round for an excuse."

For the first time that evening, I felt a surge of optimism. The house only seemed right when Phoebe was in it. And despite all the lectures I had given her about snooping, I longed to see her.

Light, hesitant steps were heard on the basement stairs. There was a soft knock, and Phoebe's head appeared round the door. As the boys had predicted, no power on earth could have kept her away. I had the usual moment of shock that she had become so much smaller all over—even her head seemed to have shrunk—then rejoiced to see that her dark eyes were lamps of energy. Curiosity might have killed the cat, but it was the breath of life to Phoebe.

"Ignore this woman," Fritz told us. "She's just an old family retainer. She doesn't speak a word of English."

"Darling, I'm so sorry to interrupt," Phoebe said, smiling round at us all. "I know I promised not to bother you, but I can't get the hot tap upstairs to turn off."

We were laughing now. What could we do? Phoebe had achieved her ambition and become part of the evening. She gazed around at us with gentle triumph.

Annabel leaped out of her chair to embrace her. It was a while since they had met, and I could see that Annabel was shocked by the change in her. But the way she covered it made me suddenly remember all my fondness for her. Without being told, she was treating Phoebe as we all did, pretending nothing was wrong.

"Well, doesn't this look nice?" Phoebe said, as if she hadn't set the table with her own hands that afternoon. "You must be Elspeth. How lovely to meet you. I'm their mother—I live upstairs, not that we're in each other's pockets. Goodness, no. Sometimes I don't even see them for weeks on end."

"Quite true," Fritz said. "The poor old thing hardly recognizes us these days."

"Well, now that I'm here, I might as well make the coffee. Why don't you all come upstairs?"

Fritz stood up. "You are a very wicked and conniving woman," he told Phoebe severely. "You can't be trusted. Your word is worth nothing."

She knew she had won. "Bring your glasses, everyone. There are some nice little almond biscuits, if anyone's still hungry."

We all rose (unsteadily, in my case), and followed Phoebe's insubstantial figure up the narrow staircase. Ben and I were at the back of the procession, behind Fritz and Annabel. It was impossible not to notice that they were holding hands. Annabel glowed as if she had swallowed the sun. Both Ben and I caught the look Fritz gave her before releasing her hand.

Fritz went over to the sink, to examine the faulty tap. "Well I never—it seems to have cured itself. This kitchen must be a sort of plumbing version of Lourdes."

"Fritz, come and sit down," Phoebe said. "Next to Annabel." She had picked up the signal, as I ought to have known she would.

Fritz might smile at her transparency, but he did not object to sitting on the sofa beside Annabel. I went to the other end of the long room, to help Phoebe with the tea and coffee. It was a good moment for a conference.

"Well?" Phoebe murmured. "How did it go? What's been happening?"

"Fritz and Annabel started hearing heavenly choirs at about half past nine," I said. "And I think we might have found a match for Ben."

"Ben?" Phoebe was puzzled.

"Elspeth really likes him."

"Oh no, darling," Phoebe said indulgently, spooning coffee. "You're quite wrong. Elspeth likes *Neil*."

I looked across the room, to where Neil and Elspeth stood in the curve of the grand piano. Neil had somehow persuaded Matthew's dour colleague to talk animatedly, and to smile. Phoebe was right—Cupid had been doing his stuff. I had been too wrapped up in Matthew and Fritz to notice. Knitting people into pairs was proving unexpectedly difficult.

I whispered, "But he's a fat guy with red hair!"

"Well, someone has to like them best," Phoebe whispered back, "or fat men with red hair would simply become extinct—and I can think of at least three of them."

She slid homemade almond biscuits on to a plate. She put the plate down suddenly and clumsily, bending over the counter, shoulders hunched defensively. I gently pushed her into the nearest chair.

"Don't make a fuss, Cassie. I'm absolutely fine."

"Oh yes. Just rest for a minute." The fiction had to be maintained, and I mustn't show that I was in the least scared by the bluish tinge to her lips. "I'll finish the coffee. Let me make you some chamomile tea."

"That would be lovely." The lamplight made deep shadows in the hollows under her cheekbones. "I think I'd better go upstairs."

Fritz started to his feet.

"No, darling, I'm fine," Phoebe said, staunchly dredging up her normal breezy voice. "Annabel, it's been so wonderful to see you. Make sure you come again very soon."

Annabel stood up, to embrace her. "Try and keep me away."

Phoebe would not let anyone accompany her upstairs. Once she had said her good nights, the dynamics of the room changed. Annabel began talking to Ben.

Fritz walked over to me. "How is she, do you think?"

"Reeling with exhaustion," I said, "but dying to hear every detail. I bet she phones me at dawn."

He smiled, and murmured, "You can tell her one of us is doing very well." He put his mouth close to my ear. "Am I a complete dickhead, Grimble? Why didn't I notice? Has Annabel been this stunning all these years?"

The intimacy of this felt odd and uncomfortable, in a way I couldn't define. "Well, I told you enough times," I whispered back. "Maybe you'll take me seriously now."

"Oh, I always take you seriously. You're a highly serious grown-up person with a boyfriend who works in a suit. Did you tell Mum Matthew walked out on you?"

"He didn't walk out on me. It was work."

"Grimble, let's not have any more truck with Mister Bullshit. Would you like me to punch that dismal moose of yours in any vital region?"

The kettle boiled. I poured hot water over the tea bag—glad to duck away from his ticklish whispering, which was raising bumps on the back of my neck. "No thanks."

"He's cheating on you." Fritz was calm.

"I told you. It was work."

"If you insist. Let me know when you're ready to accept reality."

I wasn't ready to surrender my dreams yet. What did Fritz know, anyway? I busied myself with teas and coffees so that he couldn't say any more.

Neil offered to drive Elspeth home to her Docklands warehouse conversion, alleging it was on his way. Look on the bright side, I thought—this ought to do wonders for Matthew's partnership. The Wicked Queen was exposed as an ordinary female, just as silly about romance as the rest of us. Ben and I waved them off at the front door.

I was about to go back into the sitting room, but Ben stopped me. He put his finger on his lips, and nudged me gently toward the open door.

I saw them reflected in the big gilt mirror over the fireplace. To say that Fritz and Annabel were kissing would be to put it mildly. They were locked together, oblivious to everything except each other. They both looked beautiful, and far beyond the reach of any poor mortal. I turned hot with (I think) embarrassment.

"Phew," I muttered feebly. "No good asking Annabel for a lift, then."

"I'll drive you home," Ben said. He was frowning.

"Are you sure?"

"Come on."

We had to get out before the hormonal storm broke over our heads. I hurried down the basement stairs behind Ben. Annabel let out a moan of rapture, which I tried not to hear.

I stuffed my feet back into the trainers. "I should help you with the clearing up." I had suddenly remembered that I hadn't done a thing for my own dinner party (besides, this would make a fine excuse not to go home, and either find Matthew there or not there; impossible to decide which would be worse). "The table isn't too wrecked, thankfully."

"Leave it," Ben said. He was rummaging about among the dirty pans and plates on the counter. "Fuck, what's he done with the car keys?" He found them in the fruit bowl. "I can't stay here. If Fritz finds me hanging about, he'll strangle me."

"Poor you, that's not fair. You live here too."

"It's all part of our agreement," Ben said crossly. "We have to bugger off if the other one brings someone back for sex. And it's only fair in theory, because he scores far more than I do."

"Yes, but this is Annabel," I pointed out. "She won't mind you being around. She'll positively like it."

"Please, Cass," Ben said. His hand squeezed my arm. "I just can't bear to watch him going through that old routine—not with Annabel."

I was surprised by the anger in his voice. "What do you mean? Why not with Annabel?"

"Because he's not good enough for her. Look, we've both seen how Fritz treats girls." Ben scowled. His jaw hardened. "If he does that to Annabel, I'll have to think seriously about killing him."

CHAPTER NINE

I was sober enough to be apprehensive while Ben drove me home. It had been arranged that Matthew would be staying at my flat over the weekend, but his hasty exit from the dinner party might mean everything had changed. Would I find him waiting for me? Did I want to?

My flat was empty. Tired, drunk and dispirited, I went to bed alone. At some point in the small hours—perhaps three or four in the morning—I woke to the quiet click of my front door. I had given Matthew a key (we had exchanged keys early in our romance), and I think this was the first time he had used it. I made myself as still as possible, pretending to be asleep.

I heard the creak of floorboards as he crept into the bedroom. I heard him breathing above me, and concentrated upon keeping my eyelids relaxed.

He whispered, "Cassie?"

I stayed asleep, and heard his unmistakable sigh of relief.

He seemed to be undressing for ages. Finally, reeking of toothpaste, he rolled into bed beside me. Within minutes, he was out cold. I always knew when he was really asleep. I wonder why men can never tell when women are only pretending. Perhaps it's related to our ability to fake orgasms.

And I don't think men ever weep silently while their girlfriends slumber. I held myself rigid, carefully breathing through my mouth and sniffing in slow motion, with what felt like about a gallon of tears pooling under my cheek. Somehow, without knowing how or why, I had missed the last boat out.

The phone woke me. I opened my swollen eyes. I was alone again. I knew this from the quality of the silence around me, and the empty chill of my bed. This must be Matthew, I decided groggily, calling me with his latest excuse. I snatched the phone. "H'lo?"

"I've woken you up," Phoebe's voice said. "Sorry, darling. Shall I ring a bit later?"

"No, I'm awake now." I struggled into a sitting position. "God, it's half past ten."

Phoebe's soft voice was full of jubilation. "Cassie, it was a triumph. You should be feeling incredibly pleased with yourself. Congratulations."

"What?" I couldn't think of a single reason to feel pleased with myself.

"You did it! You made a match! Fritz took Annabel home last night—and they've only just come back, both absolutely radiant. Isn't it fabulous?"

"Fabulous," I echoed stupidly.

"Didn't I always say you were the perfect woman for the job? Darling, I can't thank you enough. Annabel is one of the sweetest girls in the world, and I know she'll be just perfect for Fritz. You should see them together—she'll make an angel of him."

"Yes, but aren't you going rather fast here?" (One night with Fritz didn't necessarily count for much, though I could hardly put it like this to his mother.) "I mean, do you think it's a genuine match? Isn't it a bit soon to tell?"

"Call it a mother's instinct," Phoebe said, sublimely confident. "I know Fritz. Well done, my clever girl. Now we only have to find someone for Ben."

"This morning?"

"Don't be silly!" Phoebe laughed, then added, "Still, you could call your friend Hazel, couldn't you?

"She's still away," I said.

"As soon as she comes back, then. Look, since you're properly awake now, why don't you meet us up at Kenwood? It's such a glorious morning. The boys and Annabel are taking me for coffee in the garden. Do come, darling."

I didn't think I had the stamina to watch Annabel and Fritz being radiant. "No thanks. I have to get my car fixed. And I'm not sure if Matthew's planned anything."

Phoebe's voice was gentle. "Oh, Matthew's there. How nice."

"He's not here at this precise moment, but I think he's popped out for croissants and a paper. That's our normal Sunday routine."

"I'm glad you're back in your routine. Fritz told me how oddly he behaved last night."

I explained that Matthew was under great pressure at work, almost believing it.

Phoebe was not convinced. I hadn't expected to convince her. She had an emotional sensibility that amounted to second sight, and I daresay she sensed that I was not yet ready to accept defeat.

We rang off, and I swung my legs out of bed. If Matthew was already reading the *Observer* in the queue at the French bakery, I'd better get the coffee started and run a comb through my mad hair. I stumbled out into the sitting room, stuffing my arms into the sleeves of my dressing gown—and stopped short when I saw the sinister thing on the table. It was a bunch of pink roses, still wrapped in Cellophane, hastily stuffed into a jug.

Flowers. Why?

There was a note beside them. "Cassie darling—you are wonderful. Sorry about last night. I have to go back to work. Call you later. Matthew."

He said I was wonderful, but he did not say he loved me. This was not quibbling. Think it through. Anyone can be wonderful.

Coffee for one, then.

I had to get out of the flat. I drank my coffee at the Camden Starbucks, weeping discreetly behind my sunglasses.

There were threads of white in my hair when I arrived at work on Monday. This was because I had spent the rest of that barren Sunday painting the ceiling of my sitting room, but I felt it summed up my general weariness. My e-mail inbox did nothing to lighten me up—one from Annabel, one from Matthew. I opened Annabel's first, as the least dangerous.

Sorry I didn't phone and please don't think I'm a slut for going straight to bed with Fritz—it wasn't like that. When he kissed me, it was like shifting into another dimension—I would have followed him to the ends of the earth. Nobody else existed for us. He is INCREDIBLE in bed!! But it's more than sex. He's so kind and funny—he has a gentle side you'd never imagine. I spent the whole weekend with him. You'll want to know if I'm in love, and the answer is YES. Work seems pointless this morning. Cassie, you were so right to tell me to keep the faith. There IS a right person for everyone—just like you and M— and Fritz is IT. I'd do anything for him.

Good luck to you, I thought sourly; at least you're rich these days—when Fritz fancies a kipper, you won't have to go out begging for it.

In theory I was delighted for her. In practice, I allowed myself a pang or two of deep envy.

Matthew's message was short and to the point.

I'm sure you'll agree we need to talk. 7:30 L'Etoile okay? M.

I sent back an (equally brief) acceptance, with my heart in my shoes. He wanted to meet me in what I privately called his "telling-off" restaurant—a rather starchy French place in Charlotte Street, where he had twice taken me to complain about various aspects of my behavior (oh yes, I had form; my previous offenses were mentioning politics in front of his boss and "going on" about my career in front of men who were less successful). What, exactly, was I supposed to have done wrong this time?

We met straight after work. Matthew was waiting for me, suited and serious, his shining briefcase propped against his chair. I kissed him warmly, hoping I would not allow myself to be manipulated into apologizing.

Matthew said, "Thanks for meeting me like this, Cassie. I know you must be wondering what's going on."

"I do realize you're working very hard," I said carefully. Anyone who has ever gone out with a lawyer will appreciate the cautious nature of my replies.

"Yes, but you must have guessed it's more than that." He neatly quartered his bread roll. "You must have noticed that I'm under a lot of emotional pressure. And I think it's important to level with you." The faintest flush dyed his cheeks. "I know I shouldn't have run out on you on Saturday, and—and I'm sorry." (He didn't sound it.) "But I suddenly couldn't face a night at the same table with Fritz and Ben Darling."

"Oh, come on. They're not that bad."

"It's not only the Darlings. It's all your lifestyle choices."

"Lifestyle choices?" Surely this was a euphemism for sexual irregularity, and I certainly couldn't be accused of that. "What on earth are you talking about?"

Matthew let out one of his patient sighs. "I might have known you'd refuse to understand. Look, we've talked about long-term commitment—marriage, and so forth."

"Yes." I held my breath, feeling that my whole future hung by a glass thread.

"Well, lately—but it's been building for some time—I've felt that I need more space."

"Oh."

"Don't get me wrong, Cass. I do have very deep feelings for you. You're a wonderful person, and you've mostly managed to detach yourself from your background. But I do find your lifestyle a bit—well, a bit static and claustrophobic. You don't move. You don't change. You don't seem to think you have to adapt."

"Oh." (I had got his drift, and I daresay you have too.)

"The same places. The same circle of people."

"You do like some of them. Annabel, Hazel, Honor—"

"Some of them, yes." Matthew was solemn, with an air of keeping calm under pressure. "But I wasn't expecting to spend every spare moment in their pockets."

"All right," I said, with an edge. "We simply won't see anyone you don't like. Write me a list."

He sighed, as if I was being tiresome. "Don't be silly. It's not a ques-

126

tion of personalities. I'm talking about your attitude. The way you arrange your life unilaterally, without any kind of consultation."

"But Matthew, I always consult you first. And the Darlings are like family—they have a claim on me too."

"This isn't about Phoebe," Matthew said. "She's lovely, and I know how much she needs you at the moment—especially when those sons of hers are so useless."

"They are not!" I snapped. I was surprised by the sudden ferocity of my desire to defend them. "Fritz and Ben are totally devoted to Phoebe!"

"It's a general problem about the type of people you choose to socialize with," Matthew went on. "Losers and wasters, and people who think the world owes them a living because they've read a few books. There's more to life than clever-clever chatter."

The unfairness of this took my breath away. I'd been trying very hard not to use long words or gossip about literature in front of Matthew, who had barely scraped through GCSE English. For his sake, I had once pretended not to have an opinion about Jane Austen, in case I unbalanced a particularly bone-headed dinner party (I now think this was as bad as begging for kippers, if not worse).

"We've built up a relationship," Matthew said, "but I'm frankly scared of taking it any further. As I said, I think it's time to give each other more space."

"How much more? Are you handing me my P45?"

He frowned. "Please don't be flippant."

"Sorry, but you can't blame me for wondering." I licked my dry lips. "I was sure you were going to tell me you're seeing someone else."

Matthew sighed again. "And I was sure you'd try to turn this round, forcing me to defend myself so you don't have to take criticism. For God's sake, Cassie—why must everything be so childish?"

"Well, are you?"

"No, as a matter of fact. I thought you knew me better than that."

There was my answer, folks. He was challenging me to call him a liar, knowing I had no proof but my own intuition. I was surer than ever. Very few men in this situation are able to lie convincingly. I considered my options. I could say I didn't believe him—but then a row would be my fault, and I was determined to cling to the high moral ground.

"Sorry," I said again. Here I was, apologizing to my boyfriend because I had made him cheat on me—but there's always a good reason for doing this. I was going to make Matthew pay for the damage to my dignity by being incredibly difficult to get rid of. He would have to spell it out in letters a foot high.

"This isn't about ending it," Matthew said. "I don't want to throw away our relationship. But I do want us to take a step back."

"Meaning what?"

"Don't be offended, Cass. I'm just saying we shouldn't assume we have to spend every single evening together. Especially during the week—staying over with you is all very nice, but it's playing havoc with my work. I know the demands are ridiculous. I sometimes wonder if I'm allowed to have any sort of love life at all."

Resolutely deaf to this final note of pathos, I dredged up an affectionate voice. "Oh darling, you've been so good about staying over with me. We seem to have fallen into the habit of always going to my place. I should be coming to your place sometimes, shouldn't I?"

"Er . . ." He was shifty, and I'm afraid I enjoyed seeing him squirm; we never went to his place because he was paranoid about messing it up. "We certainly shouldn't spend all our free time in your neck of the woods."

"How right you are," I said warmly. "I haven't explored any other necks, have I? I've been selfish. I'll start making a proper effort to fit into your life. Next weekend, I'll stay at your place."

"Er . . ." This wasn't the reaction Matthew had wanted, but he couldn't protest without admitting that he'd been a lying, cheating shit. I often thought I should have been a lawyer.

I couldn't say, however, that I had won this round completely. When I mulled it over at home, in a sickly miasma of ceiling paint, I was depressed. I realized I had given Matthew permission to see me as little as he pleased. My warm, safe future was evaporating before my very eyes.

No, no, NO. It wasn't true. I couldn't let it happen. I wanted to hate Matthew, and I could only love him.

I needed a crisis meeting with Annabel. She was the only person I could expose to the death rattle of my relationship. Unfortunately,

Annabel's brain was out to lunch—the first throes of infatuation made her absolutely gaga. She could not be detached from Fritz, but hovered around him adoringly. Rather surprisingly, Fritz appeared not to mind this besotted clinging. In breaks between rehearsals he would phone Annabel at work and describe, in filthy detail, his sexual plans for the night ahead.

I wish I hadn't had to know about this, but Annabel always sent me an e-mail immediately afterward. Sometimes, I was absolutely faint with envy. Lucky Annabel had a man who loved her and worshipped her body. My body hadn't been worshipped properly for ages. The temple was gathering moss and falling into ruins. When Matthew deigned to spend a night with me, he went about sex as if visiting the gym. Even his orgasms were conscientious. Mine were faked, of course. It's hard to have an orgasm with a man whose mind has left the building.

A woman needs a demanding job at a time like this. Seeing less of Matthew meant I got an amazing amount of work done. Night after night, I would still be hammering at my keyboard when Betsy tore herself away at six. Unable to endure the spinsterish loneliness of my flat, I took to burning midnight oil at the office. Whatever happened in my private life, the double centenary edition of *The Cavendish Quarterly* was going to be a humdinger.

But it was a huge relief when Hazel called. She had returned from the parental home in very low spirits, and she was also trying to bury her feelings under a ton of hard work.

"If I have to spend one more evening in a deserted office I'll go crazy. Let's go out and get disgracefully drunk."

We met in our usual wine bar, halfway between Hazel's office and mine. In days gone by, we had gathered here with Annabel and Claudette, but Claudette was pregnant and Annabel was lost in new love, and neither had time to bond with her female friends. We didn't say anything, but Hazel and I both felt rather left out and sad—two unclaimed women, caning the red wine because there was nobody waiting at home. Somewhere along the line, I thought, we had slipped into the wrong novel. We'd started out in Helen Fielding, and ended up in Anita Brookner.

Hazel was wearing a plain black shift dress with a red cardigan. She had left off her makeup, and wore glasses instead of contact lenses. As a consequence, she looked older and more weathered than her usual glossy self. She wasn't so obsessed with her appearance when she was in red-hot working mode. Work always came first with Hazel—I remembered this from college.

"The ad revenues are down, so we're changing the design again," she told me gloomily, halfway into the first glass of red wine. "Heads are rolling all over the place. At one point, I wondered if I'd still have a job when I got back. How're things over at *Stairlift Monthly*?"

"Never mind me," I said. "I want to hear about you. How was it at home?"

"Hell," Hazel said darkly. "I've been interrogated about every single aspect of my life. Why am I not married? Why is my skirt so short? Why do I disfigure myself with this haircut? I tell you, Cassie—you're lucky to have parents who don't try to control you."

I considered this. My mother had never tried to control me. My father had stopped trying when he stopped giving me money. Their indifference still smarted. I didn't feel lucky.

"Your dad must have been pleased to see you, though," I said.

Hazel laughed bitterly. "Well, you'd think so, wouldn't you? I'd got him a fabulous flower arrangement. It took up the entire backseat of my car."

"That must have cost you a bit."

"Actually, it was a freebie. A tampon company sent it to the office as part of a promotion."

"Oh well. Waste not, want not," I offered. "It's the thought that counts."

"I needn't have bothered. I was hardly through the door before he started saying he was allergic to it. I had to leave the bloody thing out in the corridor."

"Still, if he's up to criticizing you, doesn't that mean he's feeling better?"

Hazel smiled. "My mum said he needed someone to have a go at. She said it perked him up just to see the terrible color I'd dyed my hair."

"You'd think he'd be proud of you."

"But he is, in his way," Hazel said. "He tells everyone about me, apparently—the doctors and nurses certainly seemed to know a lot about my CV." She sighed. "I wish he could express it to me, that's all."

"Is he still in hospital?"

"He came home yesterday—fit as a fucking fiddle and threatening to call the police if I didn't get my rear light fixed—and I took the opportunity to escape back to civilization."

"It sounds as if you've been behaving like a saint," I told her. "You need to do something thoroughly self-indulgent. Such as falling in love." (I was, naturally, thinking about Ben.)

Hazel sighed, and said, "I don't know if I've got it in me any more. Seeing Dad strapped up to a heart monitor—well, it made me think. I know it's a cliché," she added, "but in that situation, you put your life under the microscope. And I didn't much like the look of mine. Thank God he didn't die, because when he does, half my life will become redundant. I won't know how to fall in love."

"What do you mean? Why not?"

"I realized that I've always fallen in love to annoy my dad," she said. "I've been attracted to exactly the type of men he hates—and I was the one who got hurt, so what was the point? I've decided I need to break the habit of a lifetime, and fall for someone kind. How d'you do that, Cassie?" Luckily, she didn't wait for a reply. "Let's have another bottle."

On the other side of the bar, the door suddenly burst open, and five or six noisy people erupted into the room like a flock of starlings. Shouting and laughing, they all squeezed themselves round one tiny table.

"I bet they're actors," Hazel said scornfully. "Look at the way they're all talking into the mirror."

"Oh my God," I said. They were indeed actors, and one of them was Felicity Peason. Sultry and pouting, she sat with her glossy black hair tumbled over one shoulder. Let's be honest, she was breathtaking. Think of a posher and slightly grungier Catherine Zeta Jones.

Hazel, with her professional eye for the glossy, spotted her at once. "What a great-looking woman. Do you know her?"

"Not really," I said. "Not enough to want to talk to her." We were on the other side of the large room, and the actors were far too up themselves to notice us. I would have liked Hazel to stop staring at them. Before I could distract her, however, her beady gaze darted toward the door.

"That's Fritz Darling, isn't it?"

With no idea that I was watching him, Fritz breezed into the bar and joined the crowded table. He sat beside Felicity. Her cold, sulky face was suddenly transformed by a thousand-megawatt smile. She kissed him on the lips.

"Yes, that's Fritz," I managed to say. I hadn't yet told Hazel about Fritz and Annabel—and I couldn't talk about it until I was over the shock.

To do Fritz justice, he had jerked his head away immediately after the treacherous kiss. But it was blatantly obvious that Peason was making a play for him, and equally obvious that he was very powerfully attracted. I remembered Fritz's historic talent for ignoring his better self in the face of sex, for binding and gagging his good shoulder-angel. I was on the other side of the room, but I saw and sensed the electricity between them.

I could not tell Annabel anything, however, on the basis of one kiss. And it was always possible that my envy was warping my perception. Wasn't I making too much of this? Weren't actors constantly slobbering all over each other?

"I haven't seen him since college, but I'd know the bugger anywhere," Hazel said. "He's still gorgeous. You snogged him once, didn't you?"

"Yes, at the party we threw after our A levels."

"So what happened?"

"I don't know," I said, deliberately vague. "As soon as we got to Oxford, we went off in opposite directions."

"What a waste," Hazel said wistfully. "I snogged him once, you know."

"Really?" I decided to pretend not to know.

"I often wonder what would've happened if I'd been sober. I wonder if we'd have gone all the way."

"I'm sure you would," I said.

Hazel grinned at me suddenly. "Tell me something, Cassie. If Fritz is so easy to get into bed, why haven't you ever tried?"

"Oh, I've never wanted to."

"Come on," Hazel said, laughing. "Even lesbians want to sleep with Fritz."

"We were sort of brought up together. Maybe we've known each other too long."

"Hmmm. Remind me to put some money in the blind box."

Across the crowded room, through a forest of heads, I looked at Fritz. He was laughing. Peason leaned against him, seemingly casual. Oh, how I hoped Fritz had acquired enough intelligence to see through her repertoire of smolders and pouts (long hair and generous breasts are essential to carry these off).

"Let's go and find somewhere to eat," I said, standing up quickly with my back to them. "I'm ravenous."

I was not ravenous. I just wanted to get out before Fritz saw me. To be honest, I wasn't thinking of Annabel. I just couldn't bear to meet his dazzled gaze when it was full of someone else.

CHAPTER TEN

For the moment, there was no time for anything except work. My centenary edition went to press, and was printed to (comparatively) huge acclaim. All the broadsheet newspapers suddenly remembered the existence of *The Cavendish Quarterly* and decided it was a national treasure. Phoebe (still rather embarrassingly wedded to scrapbooks of our triumphs) cut out several pictures of me at my desk trying to look intellectual. I appeared on *Late Review,* and was all over Radio Four like a rash.

Even Matthew was impressed, and minded my long words less than usual. He was busy too. We managed sex perhaps four times in as many weeks. One night, he blurted out that he had sold our Salzburg tickets to a colleague—frivolous summer jaunts being out of the question for someone who worked as hard as he did. He was tender because I was good about it, and I was good about it because I was relieved. Cracks were appearing in my culture. A year ago, when Matthew obtained the tickets, I had almost convinced myself that I was delighted. Now I admitted what I had always known: that so many classical music geeks in one place would have driven me over the nearest cliff.

Matthew said, "It's not just my schedule I'm thinking about. I knew you wouldn't want to be away from Phoebe."

He was right, though I couldn't bear to admit that the sand was running through the hourglass. It wasn't that the decline was visible, or shocking. She tired more easily, and now spent most of her day lying on the sofa in the sitting room. I visited her every weekend, and at least two evenings a week. And each time I saw her, she had faded just a little more.

Annabel often joined us when Fritz was rehearsing. Fritz's rehearsals seemed to take place at all sorts of odd hours. The unpaid production had, apparently, taken a turn for the better.

"He just loves rehearsals now," Annabel told us happily. "He can't get enough of them."

Phoebe said, "That's Fritz all over—limitless dedication."

I kept my lingering suspicions to myself. Only a monster would have tarnished the happiness of these two doting females. I had to listen to endless hymns of praise to Fritz. Phoebe made me lift the big photo albums down from the top shelf in the sitting room, so she could show Annabel pictures of Fritz through the ages.

Actually, that evening turned out to be rather fun. The flood of memories made Phoebe lively. She showed us herself as a bride, doe-eyed and impossibly young. Jimmy, we all agreed, was the image of Fritz. Annabel blushed to see how Fritz might look in morning dress.

On the next page, after some winning pictures of a pregnant Phoebe in a Laura Ashley smock, Fritz made his first appearance. I have to report that he was an absolutely adorable baby—fat and twinkly and curly, crowing in the arms of his laughing young mother (if Fritz had known what we were doing, he would have been mortified). A page later he was a grinning toddler, awkwardly holding a very apprehensive-looking baby.

Annabel cried, "Oh, look at Ben! Isn't he beautiful?"

There was a pause in the pictures, while Phoebe listed all the times Fritz had tried to kill or maim his infant brother. I had heard these stories often, and I loved hearing them again. The familiar words were like the sound of the wind in the chimney, or the ticking of a venerable clock. Once upon a time, in the great legend of the past, Jimmy caught Fritz bundling the baby out of the playroom window. In his earliest days Ben had been poisoned with eyedrops, choked with jelly babies and stifled with soft toys.

"And yet," Phoebe said, "in between all that, Fritz absolutely adored him. I offered to tell him a story once, and he wouldn't let me until Ben woke up, so he could hear it too."

"How lovely," Annabel said.

Phoebe giggled. "He spent the next half-hour trying to pinch Ben awake—I had terrible trouble getting that baby enough sleep. Fritz said he was lazy. Look, here they are in the garden. I don't remember when, but Fritz must be in one of his generous moods—he's allowing Ben to wear his pirate hat."

I felt the threat of tears at the back of my throat, like dull thunder. There was something desperately poignant about these remnants of the life before death.

At that moment I loved the Darling boys intensely, as if that could help them when they lost everything. I couldn't bear to be suspicious about Fritz. How dared I judge him, or think at all badly of him, when he was the light of Phoebe's eyes?

Oddly enough, that unpaid fringe production of *Rookery Nook* turned out to be a good career move for Fritz. At some point during rehearsals, the company had decided to reverse the genders of all the roles. Fritz, though appearing and behaving as a man, was actually playing the runaway girl in pajamas, and Felicity Peason was playing the young man who falls in love with her. On paper it was pointless and pretentious, but it played surprisingly well. The farce is great enough to carry a whole stage full of terrible actors—and Fritz, for once, was rather good. I was impressed by the flirtatious and slightly kinky way he acted up to his silk pajamas. Both the *Telegraph* and the *Guardian* mentioned the "elegance" and "intelligence" of Frederick Darling's performance.

The agent who had expressed an interest in Fritz promptly offered to take him on. He didn't have to wait long for gainful employment either. The sex-change *Rookery Nook* caused all kinds of excitement among the executors of the Travers estate, the controversy generated interest, and the production moved triumphantly to the Gielgud Theatre on Shaftesbury Avenue, for a twelve-week run at full West End rates.

But I'm running ahead of myself. Matthew surprised me by agreeing to come to the first night of the unpaid fringe production, though it was a weekday and he didn't like Fritz. I think he was still feeling guilty about Salzburg. He came straight from work, in a pale gray suit from Hackett, clutching his briefcase. I stood guard at his elbow, trying to look as if we belonged together. I was in my jeans and the Paul Smith shirt, so it was tricky.

After the show, which he said he'd enjoyed, Matthew explained that he had to go home, to finish preparing for his early-morning meeting.

"Fuck," I said. "You mean I cleaned that bath for nothing?"

We were in a packed theater bar, and I only said this because I knew he couldn't hear.

"What?"

I raised my voice. "I said, poor you—you'll miss the party."

"Oh, I don't think that'll be quite my sort of thing. I never know what to say to actors."

Once Matthew had pushed himself disdainfully through the shabby crowd, I could let my face relax. I bought myself a large gin and tonic. Fritz and Annabel had driven an exhausted but delighted Phoebe home (Ben was away in Bury St. Edmunds, accompanying Neil at a recital of Schumann *lieder*). While I waited for them to come back, I wove through the forest of braying theatricals, into the comparative peace of the auditorium.

The stage manager and a woman from the cast were lining up bottles of plonk and plastic glasses on the stage, and striking the more delicate pieces of the set. There was to be a traditional first-night party, and I knew what to expect. They would all be aquaplaning with elation, clutching at each other, shrieking company in jokes, and generally ignoring anyone who belonged to the outside world. If Annabel didn't hurry back I'd be stranded here without a soul to talk to.

Peason entered, stage right. She halted under the strongest light to fling her long hair over her shoulder. She was wearing a fabulous dress of heavy scarlet silk. She automatically preened and bridled at the empty seats, then squinted as she saw me.

"Hi, Cassie."

"Hi, Felicity." I took a few steps toward her. "That was marvelous. You were brilliant." (You have to say this, even to actors you hate; it's rather like bowing to the altar in church.)

"I was incredibly nervous," Peason said. "God, I could murder a drink." She took a bottle from the table and sloshed red wine into a plastic glass. The stage was only a few inches higher than the floor. Peason stepped off it, out of the spotlight. "So you really think it went well?"

Her smile was attractive. She had learned to put some warmth in it.

"Beautifully," I said.

"By the way, have you seen Fritz? I've been looking everywhere."

"He's taking Phoebe home."

"Oh." She was put out. "I thought Annabel was dealing with all that."

"Fritz likes to be sure Phoebe's all right."

"Oh shit. What a nuisance." Peason's cold, level gaze locked into mine, and I felt I was looking into the very depths of her black heart. She didn't give a damn about Phoebe, and considered Annabel less than the dust. She hadn't changed one tiny bit, I thought; I was free to dislike her as much as ever.

"You'd think they'd leave him alone on his first night."

"Maybe he doesn't want to be left alone," I said. "Sorry, but you do know that Fritz and Annabel are an item, don't you?"

She laughed theatrically, up and down the scale. "An item! God, how sweet. Are they both coming back for the party, do you know? Or will Annabel stay behind to look after the mother?"

"They're both coming back," I said, teeth gritted.

"Really? I sort of assumed that was what Annabel was *for*. Oh well."

She undulated past me, in a cloud of scent, toward the bar. The moment she opened the door, there were loud cries ("Felicity! Dahling!") from the adoring multitudes waiting behind it.

I sat down on one of the seats, to finish my gin in peace. Peason thought she had won. Did that mean she had already seduced Fritz? No, I couldn't believe that. But she meant to have him, and I didn't trust him to resist. I knew for a fact that he fancied her. During the performance, the whole stage had throbbed to their mutual attraction—and Fritz wasn't that good an actor. Poor Annabel.

I was suddenly incredibly lonely. At least poor Annabel had people around her tonight—my Fritz and my Phoebe. I had no one. If I left the party now, nobody would notice. I wouldn't speak to another living soul until half past nine tomorrow morning when I arrived at the office. I ached for a little love, for warmth, for intimacy. I longed for Matthew. At the beginning, when we were first in love, he used to massage my feet if he thought I looked stressed. I had one of those snapshot memories of looking down at the top of his dark blond head, and loving the way his hair was thinning slightly because I was at that stage of love where your lover's flaws pierce you with their sweetness.

We'd made that agreement about "space." But this was an emergency. I was aching to batter down the wall between us. Perhaps, I thought, he needs to see how much I need him. Perhaps I've been too independent and self-sufficient. Perhaps he was holding back because I hadn't run out far enough to meet him?

I fought my way through the bar and went out into the street. I rang Matthew, and got his answering service. This didn't mean anything, however. He often unplugged the phone when he had a lot of work on. I decided to buy a bottle of wine and take a taxi to his place. Matthew would be surprised to see me—but very pleased, and possibly sexually aroused by my vulnerability. We would make love, and he would whisper (as he had done once before, long ago), "I want to hold you safe with me forever."

Please don't laugh. What followed isn't remotely funny.

Matthew's pristine flat was an island of gracious living in a sea of urban nowhere. I stood on the street of shuttered shops, craning up at the converted warehouse, which had been expensively carved into yuppie apartments. The lights were on in his windows. I dug around in my bag. The keys to Matthew's flat had hung unused on my key ring since he gave them to me. I used the first to let myself into the hall. I took the lift up to the fourth floor.

I had been here before, of course, but not for many months.

On the dim landing, I heard a cry.

I tried to work out which flat it was coming from, and heard another cry. Then a series of them, rather like a seal barking—sort of "Uff! Uff! Uff!"

I listened, and refused to understand. I was as cold as a ghost, as mechanical as a robot. I simply refused to believe it, until the knife had plunged all the way into my guts. I opened Matthew's door and closed it behind me very quietly. Strange as it seems, my main feeling was intense excitement.

The door to the bedroom stood open at the end of the short corridor. "Uff! Uff!" cried the seal.

I crept toward the light, my pulse beating uncomfortably in my throat.

When I saw them, the shock whacked the breath right out of my body, so that I gasped aloud. The terrible picture froze (it's branded on my memory to this day, formal and static, like a Renaissance painting).

A woman was sitting on the flat, white, hard bed. She was naked. Her

139

legs were spread wide, and Matthew was kneeling on the floor vigorously giving her head.

It was Honor Chappell.

Honor Chappell. I had caught my boyfriend giving head to Honor Chappell, of all the people in the world. It took several long seconds for my brain to acknowledge what my eyes were telling me.

The maddest thing of all was that I was almost polite to them. I nearly apologized for intruding. I had an insane desire to make small talk and pour drinks.

Honor looked thunderstruck and (a small consolation to me later) incredibly undignified.

Matthew's head snapped round to look at me. He panted, "Oh shit—"

Without knowing properly what I was doing, I stumbled out of the flat without a word, and down the stone stairs.

"Cassie!" His voice echoed at me from the landing. "Cassie, wait!"

I shouted, "No!" and broke into a run. I didn't know what the hell I was doing, let alone how I felt. I was a seething soup of horror, misery and anger—with the painful seasoning of comedy that goes with loss of dignity on such a scale. I was unsettled by how calm I was. I think I must have been in shock. I should have wrapped myself in blankets and sipped hot sweet tea. Instead, I flagged down a solitary taxi, and told the driver to take me back to the party. I couldn't face my flat. I needed to drink and shout and drown in mindless noise.

I'd only been gone for forty-five minutes. The theater bar was still open. I bought myself another gin and tonic, and dodged through the noisy crowd looking for Fritz and Annabel.

I found Fritz in a corner, with—of course—bloody Felicity Peason smarming all over him. I grabbed at his sleeve. "Where's Annabel?"

"She decided not to come back," Fritz said. "She has a proper job to get to in the morning."

Much as I loved Annabel, this was a relief. I wasn't ready for a post-mortem. I took a large swig of gin, with what I hoped was a devil-may-care swagger. Some of it dribbled down my chin. "By the way, you were terrific. Congratulations."

He was eyeing me curiously. "Are you okay?"

"Yes! Of course! Why shouldn't I be okay?"

"Pardon me, Grimble—I only asked. Would you like another drink to pour down yourself?"

"Gin and tonic, please." I didn't want another drink. I didn't even like gin. I simply wanted to get the job done as quickly as possible.

Fritz gently unwound Peason's arm. "Sorry, I need to get at my wallet." She murmured something into his ear.

He shrugged her off, still eyeing me doubtfully. "Look, you don't drink gin. What's going on?"

"Oh, nothing. I've just split up with Matthew. But I'm fine."

"What? Are you sure?"

I smiled brightly. "Oh yes. Totally fine. It's been on the cards for some time, you see. Though I must say," I added, with a glance around and a social smile, "I wasn't prepared to find him having oral sex with Honor Chappell."

Now I had really startled him. "You—he was doing what?"

"You remember Honor."

"I certainly do. The bird with the crew cut." Fritz was still surprised, but starting to recover. He leaned closer to me, lowering his voice. "What a shit—but that's hardly the point. I'll take you home."

"Home? But I'm fine!"

"Cassie, darling, do stop saying you're fine. You're obviously nothing of the kind, and it's just grotesque."

"I'm not as conventional as you seem to think," I told him airily. "Of course I was shocked, but that's because Matthew said he was working. Actually, I'm finding it amazingly easy to deal with."

"Rubbish. Crap. You're an absolute wreck. You shouldn't be out in public." He put his hands on my shoulders, and looked down into my face with a sort of severe kindness. "Come on. The car's right outside."

I felt that his kindness was dangerous. It would break the glass bubble if I let it, and I wouldn't be able to pretend any more that I wasn't gutted.

"I want to stay!" I protested. It came out as a whimper.

"Oh, let her stay," Peason said, thrusting her vivid face between us and grabbing Fritz's arm. "Don't waste time arguing with her. Come and talk to your potential new agent."

"I don't think I should leave you, Grimble," Fritz said. "I should really be rushing off to smack that git Matthew. Failing that, I should be taking care of you."

"Fritz, honestly—"

"She's fine," Peason interrupted me. "Look at her. She doesn't need taking care of. Come on."

I insisted that I would be all right. I urged Fritz to talk to the agent. He was skeptical, but he allowed Peason to haul him away. I took a deep breath. Now that I didn't have Fritz's sharp eyes on me, I could put up a reasonable show of being tough. I didn't know a soul at the party, but I had learned that shouting "You were brilliant!" made me accepted everywhere. Over the next hour or so I talked to several young actors (two girls, one boy) all about themselves. I must also have talked about myself, because I dimly recall one of the girls assuring me that men only gave head to women they didn't respect.

And then I was seriously drunk, and the demons closed in. I felt despair clutching at me. I saw what I had lost. Without Matthew there was no future. Nothing to hope for, nothing to dream about, nothing to stand between me and the Reaper. I was, I realized, a woman without love. I was a single woman. Nobody would invite me anywhere ever again. I'd always said that the white dress didn't matter to me—but it mattered like hell. Beyond the astonishment of finding Matthew with Honor Chappell, there was only desolation.

I heard the high sawmill tones of Felicity Peason saying, "Take no notice of her, darling—she just caught her boyfriend in bed with someone else."

I moved in a cloud of other people's giggles. My misfortunes were, apparently, hilarious. Gusts of laughter followed me through the crowd.

Fritz introduced me to a rapacious old vampire who turned out to be his new agent.

"Who did you say she was?" the vampire asked. "Editor of what? Oh, books. Well, you'd better take her home—she's as pissed as a lemon."

I was about to protest (as very pissed people do) that I was not pissed. Fritz drew the agent aside, and murmured something into her ear.

"Oh, it was her!" the agent exclaimed. She gave me a look of sympathy. "You poor darling, I know exactly how you feel."

I began to think I might be rather drunk. I was the still center of a whirling maelstrom. Faces loomed at me, chattering things I couldn't hear. I was distantly aware of my own voice shouting for gin.

Jump to the next frame.

Cold air on my hot cheeks. I was outside. Fritz was with me, holding my arm and making some sort of speech to Peason.

". . . and I've no intention of leaving her here, all on her own and smashed."

Peason snapped, "Why can't you put her in a taxi?"

"She can't go back to her place. I'm driving her to Mum's."

"But the table's booked—everyone's waiting—you can't miss this just because Cassie caught her boyfriend muff-diving!"

Fritz propped me up against his car while he opened the door. He said, "For God's sake, it's just an Indian meal. And if I desert Cassie, my mother will murder me."

"What about deserting *me*?"

"Do be reasonable, darling. You are collected and capable. You can find your own way home without ending up in the cells. Cassie can't— look at her, for God's sake."

"Well, what about if you told the taxi driver to take her to your mother's? They're very good, you know. If you give them a big enough tip they take you up the steps and ring the doorbell and everything." (My last sober brain cell wondered how Peason knew this.)

Fritz said, "I'll be a bit late, that's all. Save me a place."

Peason let out a cross gasp. "I can't believe you're doing this! I can't believe you're letting her ruin your first night!"

"Order me a chicken tikka."

Peason muttered something, and flounced back into the theater.

The cool air had revived me. I found I was able to stand up straight. I thought I must be sober.

"This is really nice of you," I told Fritz forlornly. "I was finding the party a bit of a crush. Shall we have dinner somewhere?"

Fritz smiled, looking at me as if seeing me properly for the first time. "Certainly not—I think I'd better take you straight home."

I clutched at his shirt. "I don't want to go home. I'd rather sleep at the office."

"Good grief, Cass—I've never in my life seen you so plastered." He almost lifted me into the car. He leaned over me to fasten my seatbelt. His head was close to mine. I shut my eyes. I was bone tired, and the pain was awful.

"Well, now you know," he said. "Getting drunk doesn't help, does it?"

"No," I said.

"You'll probably feel worse for a while. But it won't last long." His eyes were on the road. His voice was kind. "Honestly, it'll soon start to feel better. Listen to the voice of experience. When you're splitting up with someone you're not really meant to be with, the agony is sharp, but it doesn't last long."

"It's not fair," I said. It came out as a whimper. I was crying. Great sobs shook me. The facts lay in my path like lumps of stone, impossible to bypass or ignore. My hopes were in ruins. "It's not fair!" I sobbed. "Why should Honor get him? She hasn't done any of the work!"

We'd halted at a traffic light. Fritz put his warm hand on my knee. "That Moose is even denser than he looks. Only an idiot would prefer the one with the crew cut."

"She's obviously got something I haven't," I cried out. "Matthew never went down on *me*!"

Fritz turned the car into a side street. He parked under a street lamp and took me in his arms.

It didn't occur to me until much later that he was expected at a first-night dinner. He let me weep into his shoulder as if he had all the time in the world.

Weeping in Fritz's arms is the last thing I remember.

CHAPTER ELEVEN

I was struggling in the jaws of a ferocious hangover. I hadn't felt this dreadful since the aftermath of my finals. Every fiber, every capillary, every tiny muscle I never knew I had sang and vibrated with pain. My blood had turned to iron filings. Opening my swollen, gritty eyes was a tremendous effort, like heaving up two metal shutters.

First, I was aware of a piercing self-pity. Then I registered that I was lying in Phoebe's spare bedroom. Bright daylight hammered at the Habitat curtains, and lay in hard lozenges on the faded rug.

Now I remembered being hauled up the steps by Fritz. I remembered darling Annabel making me herbal tea and unzipping my jeans. And if I'd had a drop of spare moisture in my desert of a body, I would have wept again. How were the mighty fallen. My best friend was now part of a loving couple ("You go out, Fritz—I'll take care of her") and I had been exposed as a beggar for kippers on a vast and unprecedented scale.

I decided sitting up might make me feel better. I was wrong—but once I was upright, I thought I might as well stay like that. The mirror on the dressing table showed me the ruin of my face. Several broad black smudges of eye makeup did not improve its creased puffiness.

Slowly (none of my senses were working properly) I registered the comforting smells of coffee and Phoebe. With a vague idea of casting myself into her arms, I put on a dusty toweling robe which was hanging on the back of the door, and stumbled downstairs.

I found her sitting at the kitchen table. A pot of fresh coffee waited on the counter. She had not felt strong enough to carry it to the table. For once, her physical delicacy didn't seem to matter. Phoebe was calm, radiating compassion, absolutely *there.*

She smiled as the wreck of HMS *Cassie* lurched into the room. "Hello, darling. I thought I heard you. I didn't trust myself to get up the stairs, but I knew you'd smell the coffee." (Yes, I'd woken up and smelled the proverbial coffee at last.) "Now, before you say a word, Fritz has already spoken to Betsy."

I gasped, "Oh God, it's Friday! Oh God—what's the time?"

"I hope you don't mind, but he told her what happened."

The shock of losing control on such a scale had winded me like a kick in the stomach. Dear lord in heaven, I'd forgotten to go to work. I was the woman who had got herself to work through hell and high water, with raging temperatures and on crutches. And I'd bloody well forgotten. I collapsed into a chair.

"I've got to get in," I moaned. "I can't leave Betsy all alone—did you say Fritz told her?"

"Not in detail," Phoebe assured me. "Just that you'd had a bad bust-up with Matthew. He didn't say anything about you getting drunk," she added, "but I'm afraid she guessed. She says everything's fine. She says the man from the printer's isn't coming in till Monday now. Doesn't that sound like good news? So pour yourself a cup of coffee and stop panicking. Look at the lovely freesias Fritz left for you."

In the middle of the table, leaning lopsided in a tall glass, was a bunch of freesias. Bells of scarlet and purple nodded on the skinny stems, and they breathed out the scent of spring.

"He got them from that stall beside the station, when he went out to fetch the papers."

Mentally, I searched the smoking rubble of my memory. "Were there any reviews? Was he mentioned?"

"Oh yes." Here was another reason for Phoebe's strength and serenity. She was beaming. "There's a picture of him in the *Guardian.* Michael Billington says he has a considerable gift for comedy. Isn't it exciting? He had to go out, to see that agent who wants to take him on. But he left the flowers to cheer you up."

She was not bossy, but she was in charge. I poured myself a mug of coffee and sat down opposite her.

She chuckled softly. "Poor panda eyes."

The dried-up ducts of my panda eyes smarted. I gulped that I was sorry I looked so terrible, sorry that I'd ruined Fritz's first night, sorry that I'd been disgustingly drunk. Phoebe, her face glowing and almost youthful with her warmth for me, made soothing, hurt-knee noises and mildly scolded me for apologizing.

"You've had a nasty shock," she told me. "I must say, I was surprised that a man like Matthew could be so deceitful. But Annabel says I was taken in. She says you can never trust a man with very small earlobes." (You will gather that Phoebe and Annabel were, in many ways, two of a kind.)

"Annabel was here last night, wasn't she?"

"She was staying in the basement," Phoebe said. "She woke up when Fritz brought you in—more dead than alive, you poor sweetheart."

"It's awful," I said, "but I don't remember. I only remember being devastated. Was I still crying?"

"Far from it. I heard you. You were singing."

"Singing?" I never sing. I couldn't carry a tune downstairs. "What was I singing?"

Phoebe's lips twitched. "The theme from *Hong Kong Phooey*."

"What?"

"That's what it sounded like. You kept chanting 'Number One Super-Dog!' over and over again."

"Oh God. I'm so sorry."

"I think you were being defiant."

Some blurred snapshots of memory were coming back to me. I sighed. "I might have been trying to sing 'I Will Survive,' but I don't know the words. Poor Fritz. What an embarrassment. I ruined his first night."

"Nonsense, of course you didn't. Stop blaming yourself."

I wiped my eyes on the sleeve of the dressing gown and drank down a cup of Phoebe's uniquely heartening coffee. I made toast. Phoebe directed me to a packet of painkillers in one of the kitchen drawers. Halfway down the second cup of coffee, I could survey the wreckage calmly.

"Phoebe," I said, "what shall I do?"

"You need to get away from everything," Phoebe said. "I think you should go to see Ruth."

I was startled. I had expected a remedy for a broken heart. At a time like this, I didn't need to be reminded about my poor mother. I didn't want Phoebe to know how distant we had become. With a disagreeable twinge of guilt, I realized that I had not even spoken to Ruth on the phone for nearly three months. I hadn't actually seen her since the previous Boxing Day. The memory of that depressing exchange of bath products pulled me down to new depths. Ruth had retired from the hospital to a small house beside the sea, and I kept finding excuses not to visit her there.

Our relationship had congealed into distant mutual esteem, very much based around rituals of politeness. We avoided all controversial subjects (for instance, my father), and sometimes it was like trying to communicate through a ouija board. Ruth's work was her life, and her life had always been her work. She couldn't seem to stop being a psychiatrist. She planned to spend her retirement writing her book, *The Country Diary of an Edwardian Shrink* (just kidding; it was really about treating the criminally insane).

"You haven't been to the new house," Phoebe said. "Ruth told me she'd love to see you."

Typically, Phoebe was better at keeping up with my mother than I was. She maintained a strange fondness for Ruth, though I felt their friendship seemed rather one-sided.

"Call her now, darling. Tell her you're coming today."

I protested that I didn't have the strength. Phoebe brushed this aside. She was firm. I was to go back to my flat, wash my face, pack some warm clothes and drive down to the coast that very afternoon. In the end, it was easiest to give in.

"I wish I could go with you," she said. "I'll send her a housewarming present, at least. What do you think she'd like?"

"Don't ask me," I said. "What do you get for a person who thinks good taste is a symptom of paranoid schizophrenia?"

"Poor Ruth, you never give her a chance," Phoebe said automatically. She smiled. "Of course. I know the perfect thing. Could you run up to the bedroom and fetch the bluebell quilt?"

Once again, I was startled. "You can't!"

"Why on earth not?"

"Your mother made it!" I couldn't understand why she considered Ruth worthy of the precious bluebell quilt. This had lain across the small chaise longue in her bedroom for years without number. "It's too much. The boys won't like you giving it away."

"Ruth asked me about it once, when you were little," Phoebe said. "She loved the story as much as you did. I never forgot that."

I was curious. The story of the bluebell quilt was simple. Phoebe's mother had sewed it while pregnant with her only child. She had lost two babies, and her doctor had ordered her to rest. For nine months she had sewed all her hopes into the quilting frame, until Phoebe had appeared with the stitching of the last little bell. Why had my mother "loved" this? I sensed that something had passed between her and Phoebe, but Phoebe was serenely inscrutable. It was no use asking questions. Phoebe had decided, and mine was not to reason why. I brought the quilt down to her. She held it in her lap, stroking it thoughtfully.

Her mother had stitched it full of hopes for her child, and now that child was dying. I had a bleak sense of the tragedy of human love. Where did it all go? Was love a foretaste of the next world, or did it only linger as a memory, like the scent of lavender in a drawer?

I followed Phoebe's elaborate instructions for folding and wrapping the quilt. Several times, she apologized for working me so hard.

"I know I'm a slave driver, but it's so frustrating when you know how things ought to be done."

She called for the phone, not trusting me to ring Ruth myself, and it was all arranged.

Three hours later I was on the motorway, with the bluebell quilt on the seat beside me.

The drive into my mother's town filled me with depression. I passed rows of modern bungalows and parades of low-rent shops. The sky was a sheet of lead. Drops of rain flecked the windscreen. A slab of gray sea was visible between wet gray roofs, disappearing into the gray horizon. There were few things more deathly, I thought, than a British resort that hasn't been popular since the 1930s. Huddled figures fought the howling gale on the high street. The windows of the red-brick town hall were boarded up, and there was a FOR SALE sign rotting on the front door. Dirty posters for last year's pantomime lingered on obscure walls. The window of the single clothes shop displayed, on mannequins in lopsided wigs, old-lady dresses of amazing awfulness.

What a dump, I thought.

I followed a dented sign that said ESPLANADE, and nosed my car through narrow streets to a small bay. A single row of beach shops and chippies faced a sullen sea. The only signs of life were the figures of an old man and his dog, struggling past the amusement arcade. How on earth was I meant to stand a whole weekend in this benighted place? Why did Phoebe think being here would help my broken heart?

There was a straggling row of houses beyond the shops, climbing up the hill to the cliff top. I tried (and failed) to picture these in sunny weather, with sandy towels and damp swimming costumes festooned across the wooden balconies. Ruth lived along here, and I counted the house numbers anxiously (please God, let it not be that one with the hideous net curtains). It was difficult, because most of the houses also had names—"Sea Breezes," "Ocean Spray," and other things that sounded like air fresheners.

At the very end of the Esplanade, perched on top of the cliff beside a car park, was a terrace of old flint cottages.

And there was my mother, standing in the road hugging herself, with her straight gray hair all over the place in the wind. I was surprised—I suppose because I had expected her to be wearing the stiff and frumpy maroon suit she kept for work. I had to remind myself that she wasn't working any more. The retired Ruth was absolutely shapeless in men's cords and a thick gray jersey. Oddly enough, she looked nice. She was smiling.

I smiled back. It was one of those determined smiles that have to be removed by surgery, and it continued to distort my face while I parked and unloaded my luggage.

"Well!" I said.

Ruth's face was browner and more lined than I remembered. She stood rigid while I kissed her cheek (it was like kissing a totem pole). "Come on in." She took the large, squashy parcel from my arms.

"That's from Phoebe," I said. "Housewarming present."

"Another one? She sent me one when I moved in. A salad bowl."

"Maybe she forgot," I said.

Ruth's bright, curranty-dark eyes (mine exactly) screwed up thoughtfully. "How is she?"

"Pretty good, actually."

"I mean really."

My smile faded. "It can't be long now. Months, if we're lucky."

Ruth nodded. "Thanks. And I won't ask again."

I found that I appreciated this. I began to feel that I could stop being so terminally polite. I followed my biological mother into the house. It was warm, and startlingly quiet, once the front door had shut out the wind.

And it was really rather nice. Amazingly, Ruth had made herself a setting that was not untidy and depressing. The heavy wooden street door of the cottage opened directly into a small white-painted sitting room. There were armchairs, and a modest coal fire burned in the grate. Ruth had brought the watercolors from her office, and they looked far less dim here. She had added a couple of paintings I had never seen, vivid oils of boats and cliffs. The thick old walls muffled the steady roar of the sea. I always feel calm in places where I can hear the sea.

"This is lovely," I said. "Good grief, you've bought furniture!"

Ruth smiled, less grimly than usual. "Oh yes. I've branched out into interior design in my old age. I didn't bring much from the flat—everything was on its last legs."

"You've bought new pictures, too."

"Hmm." Ruth eyed me cautiously for a moment. "They were gifts. From the artist. His name's George Denny."

"Oh."

"You'll meet him later. He pops in most nights."

I squeaked, "Oh," hardly able to believe my ears. Was Ruth telling me she had a follower, after all these barren and defeated years? And if so, how did this make me feel?

Intrigued. In a very good way. "I'll look forward to it," I replied in the same code. "His paintings look terrific here."

"It's the first place I've ever made that's just for myself," Ruth said. "Your father arranged the Hampstead house, and the Gospel Oak flat was always a symbol of unhappiness for me. Starting again has been very therapeutic."

"It's cozy. I never thought you could do cozy."

Ruth said, "Sit down."

It was evening. I watched her switching on lamps, and drawing curtains across the darkening window. We drank tea beside the fire. My breathing fell into the rhythm of the sea, and for the first time in God knew how long, I felt myself truly calm. The details of my life still seemed horrible, but they were distant. The tea drove away the last remnants of the hangover. I began to see that Phoebe had been right. This was as good a place as any to hide a broken heart.

I told Ruth about the whole Matthew business. I did it without emotion, deliberately dry as a response to her dryness.

"You wanted to marry him," Ruth said.

"Yes. I wanted a life with him. But I can see now that it wasn't working."

"Obviously not."

You had to be very articulate with Ruth, or she'd have you sectioned in a flash. "I mean, I can see that too much of the relationship depended on me. I was the one making all the effort."

"It's very easy to get meshed in that kind of power balance," Ruth said. "One person demands, the other seeks to please. The demands are sometimes a direct response to the other person's need to please."

"Like you and Derek." (My father.) This was bold of me, but I wanted to see how far Ruth's new communicativeness went.

"A little," she said coolly. "How is he, by the way? Have you heard from him?"

"Not recently. He's in California. He got a professorship at Berkeley."

"Full circle," Ruth said. I knew what she meant. She'd been Derek's student when they fell in love.

"I don't speak to him much," I said. "He calls on my birthday. Sometimes at Christmas."

"This is the life he designed for himself," Ruth said. "It was always extremely difficult to ascertain exactly what he wanted. He didn't really know himself. Shall I open a bottle of wine?"

"Wine?" She'd caught me off-guard. I wasn't used to Ruth opening wine. Her usual tipple was a medicinal slug of whiskey. It was becoming clear why Phoebe had sent me here. She wanted me to see for myself that Ruth had—well, how should I describe it?—mellowed.

"I keep a bottle on the go for George," Ruth said.

So George was already a fixture in my mother's house. For the first time, I minded that I was not a fixture. I sensed in Ruth a cautious desire to reach out to me, to comfort me, to protect me from mourning.

"I drank far too much last night," I said. "I'm only just getting over the hangover from hell."

"Try a little." Ruth held up the bottle. "It might be just what you need. A hair of the dog that bit you."

This made me laugh. "A scale of the dinosaur that bit me, you mean. All right, I will try a drop."

The small glass of red wine she gave me went down very well. The surrounding calm was starting to seep into my skin. I began to see that this quiet place had a healing quality, very faintly antiseptic but very beneficial. The two of us had found a level where we could converse comfortably. By the second glass of wine, I had remembered that Ruth could be fascinating to talk to. I thought that her relaxed mood could be due to George Denny, who walked in through the unlocked front door just as the pie was coming out of the oven.

He turned out to be a hale, white-haired widower in his sixties, dressed in yachting slops. He was as undemonstrative as Ruth, but there was no mistaking the strong, calm friendship between them. Ruth was relaxed in his company, as she had never been relaxed during her awful marriage and its aftermath. They even shared jokes, though of a dry sort. George had a subscription to *The Cavendish Quarterly,* and criticized a piece I had written about John Galsworthy, in a flattering way that showed me he had read it in detail.

Against all my expectation, the three of us had a very pleasant evening. I drank wine and ate shepherd's pie. I went to bed at half past ten (my old bed, from the flat; I knew the mattress intimately) and slept without dreaming.

This friendly politeness carried on through Saturday. We walked on the cliff top, we visited George's boat in the little harbor, we ate lunch at a fisherman's pub by the harbor wall.

In the evening (sipping yet another drink and a little wearied by good behavior) I remembered Phoebe's present. Ruth had forgotten, and it was still in its paper.

When Ruth unwrapped the bluebell quilt and gently unfolded it across her knees, her face betrayed nothing and she was silent for a long time.

"How very like Phoebe," she said at last, "to be so shamelessly transparent." She glanced up at me. "I'll phone, and all that. But please tell her . . ." she was touchingly hesitant, "it's probably the most beautiful thing anyone has ever given me."

"She said you loved the story."

"Oh yes. Phoebe knows it has a resonance for me."

"Why?"

Now Ruth was cautious. "The image of the solitary mother, waiting for her unborn child. The loneliness of pregnancy, and the great hope you have."

"Is pregnancy lonely?"

"Mine was."

"I shouldn't think Derek was much of a support," I offered.

Ruth said, "No. He wasn't. I spent hours and hours alone. Just like Phoebe's mother, whose husband was away at sea, except that I didn't pass the time making a quilt. I was writing my doctoral thesis." She looked amused. "You kicked like mad."

"Sorry."

"No, I liked it. I liked feeling you were really there. It was companionable."

I didn't know how to reply to this. I had never been a companion to my mother.

Ruth's hands rested on the padded folds of the bluebell quilt. "Derek didn't want children. I didn't think I did, either. I got pregnant by mistake."

"I guessed I was a mistake," I said.

"Oh, there was no mistake about you." Ruth took a sip of her wine. "The agreement was that I would have a termination—it never occurred to either of us to do anything different."

I was fascinated. This subject had never featured before. "So why didn't you?"

154

"I did," Ruth said. "I had an abortion, and that should have been that." She looked at me. "But I'd made the promise before I knew what it was like to be pregnant. I didn't realize how unhappy the abortion would make me afterward. I felt empty. I grieved for my child. The only cure for the grief was to get pregnant again."

"How on earth did you persuade Derek?"

"Derek didn't know," Ruth said. "You exist because I slipped one past him." Another grim smile. "My sole act of rebellion."

This was extraordinary. I sat very still, afraid she would stop.

"It was fairly easy," she said. "I got pregnant again after about two months. But this time it was different. I didn't tell him."

"But didn't he notice?"

"He's not a noticing man. He only criticized me occasionally for getting fat. I managed to hold on to you until it was too late to get rid of you."

I began to see the bravery and the loneliness of Ruth's deception. In her way, she had fought to bring me into the world. I owed my existence to her stubborn, primitive courage.

"Was he angry?"

"You know him, Cassie. He didn't express anger, but it rotted the marriage anyway."

"I always guessed the divorce was sort of my fault," I said.

"Oh no," Ruth said decisively. "That's quite wrong. It was entirely my fault. I had my baby in utter misery, against his every wish—but I did it. The decision was mine."

I was filled with a new respect for her, and a kind of softened feeling—not love, exactly, but compassion for what she must have been through. "I bet he made you suffer for it."

"Yes. He was angry for at least ten years. So angry that he had to stay with us to punish me. I blurted the whole thing out to Phoebe, after that mix-up when we left you alone. I'll never forget how kind she was."

"That's why she gave you the quilt."

"Of course. She understood perfectly."

I saw it all now—why Phoebe had insisted, against all the evidence, that my mother deserved to be loved. I wanted to tell her, at least, that I was sorry I hadn't been more of a comfort to her.

She went to her little back kitchen to see to supper, leaving me to mull over what I had learned. I thought I knew why she hadn't told me before. At the age of thirty-one, with my own ill-fated love affair behind me, I was finally old enough to understand.

As soon as I arrived home on Sunday evening, I rang Phoebe and gave her Ruth's message. "She says it's the most beautiful gift she's ever had."

"I'm so glad," Phoebe said. "I felt I owed her something special—because what I really owe her is a daughter."

CHAPTER TWELVE

It wasn't quite over with Matthew yet. He is a methodical person, and there was no question of the fat lady singing until he had tied up all the ends. Through the usual chilly medium of e-mail, he booked me for a postmortem the following Saturday evening. I was determined to approach this in a kind of holiday mood. For once, after all, I could be as slipshod as I liked.

"I refused to go to L'Etoile," I told Annabel, on the Saturday morning. "I'm not intending to make a scene, but I have to be able to make one if I want. He's coming round to my place, and I'm making a special point of not cleaning."

"Quite right," Annabel said. "This shouldn't be too easy for him."

The two of us were in a shop near Oxford Circus, in search of baby gifts. Claudette had just given birth to a fine little daughter—the first child to appear in our circle. Annabel and I agreed that we found the whole event thrilling, mysterious and oddly heartbreaking.

"I heard it—I mean her—squawking over the phone," Annabel told me. "Claudette sounded absolutely knackered. She said it hurt like hell. She still has to sit on a bag of frozen peas—can you imagine?"

"I suppose the baby makes up for all that," I suggested doubtfully.

"Hmm, I suppose. I'm sure I'll have one eventually, but I'm putting it off as long as possible. She says she has more stitches than the Bayeux Tapestry." Annabel picked up a tiny yellow cardigan, and we both broke into oohs and aaahs. "Oh, isn't this darling? And there's the sweetest little hat to go with it."

I laughed. "Admit it—you're broody."

"I am not!"

"Spare a kipper for the baby, guv!"

"Piss off."

I said I didn't think we could help it—women seemed to be pro-grammed to turn to marshmallow whenever we saw a teeny-weeny hat or a pair of adorable little socks.

"Perhaps you'll have a baby with Fritz." I really couldn't help sound-ing wistful here.

Annabel giggled. "That would be a bit of a miracle at the moment. We haven't managed sex for over a week."

(She was already living with Fritz—or as good as; he had to stay in the house for Phoebe's sake, so Annabel simply started joining him there af-ter work, and now kept cosmetics there, which any woman will tell you is serious.)

"That doesn't sound like Fritz," I said. "Is he in a decline or some-thing?"

"No, it's mostly my fault." Annabel (awash with money owing to her ridiculous salary) gathered up the cardigan, the matching hat and a pair of exquisite yellow kid shoes. "Work's frantic at the moment, and I get so tired that I have to crash into bed at about ten. Fritz doesn't get home till after midnight. He's still fast asleep when I get up. When I finish work, he's already at the theater. We only see each other at weekends."

"Where is he now? I hope you're not missing a chance for sex on my account."

"He'll still be asleep—this play does make him awfully tired. I thought I'd wake him up with a blow job, then take him out for lunch." Annabel said this casually, and clearly in the hearing of the woman at the till. Not in the least embarrassed, she gave the woman a charming smile. "Could you gift wrap these, please?"

While the woman was wrapping Annabel's purchases, and my Merry-thought Heritage Teddy Bear, I considered what Annabel had told me. Something about it struck me as odd. Fritz had never let a little thing like sleep stand in the way of sex. In the first careless rapture of their romance, he had set his alarm clock so that he would see Annabel before she left for work in the morning. And Annabel had cheerfully stayed up late to see

Fritz when he came off stage. I wondered what was going on, but I didn't have the heart to probe any further when Annabel was so radiant. I told myself that I was probably picking holes because I was jealous. Happiness shone out of her. She was the very embodiment of a woman in love. My love life, in stark contrast, was a blasted heath. I was in absolutely no position to judge.

"Where to now?" I asked, when we were back on Regent Street with our expensive parcels. "Have we earned a cup of coffee yet? Or do you need yet more saucy underwear?"

Annabel had already spent a small fortune in the lingerie department at Dickins and Jones, on a selection of cantilevered bras and filmy silk knickers.

She considered. "Well, I suppose we could have some coffee—but do you mind if we walk toward Wigmore Street? I'd like to pop in on Ben and Neil. Poor Ben had to rush out without any breakfast this morning."

I was touched by her thoughtfulness for her lover's brother. Ben and Neil were rehearsing at the Wigmore Hall for a concert of songs by Hugo Wolf. I was constantly amazed to remember that Ben was earning money these days, and that Fritz was about to (the West End transfer of *Rookery Nook* was to happen the following week). The Darlings certainly had a talent for falling on their feet. They were looking distinctly marriageable. I felt a familiar pang of guilt that I'd done nothing more about finding a match for Ben. I was still sure that Hazel Flynn would be ideal for him, but there was no question of arranging a meeting yet. Poor Hazel's father had died, very suddenly and unexpectedly, and she had taken herself back home in a state of near collapse. Heaven knew when she would be up for romance again. The hurried message she had left for me had contained actual sobbing. Annabel and I had already spent part of the previous evening and the first half of this morning wondering how to offer support. We knew that this wound went too deep for the usual poultice of an available man.

Annabel and I filled two paper bags with coffee and Ben's favorite almond croissants, and threaded through the crowds to Wigmore Street. I only knew the Wigmore Hall (which had always reminded me of a tiled Edwardian swimming bath) as a member of the audience. It also contained a number of rehearsal rooms. I climbed the dark staircase feeling like a person in an old film—artistic endeavor was all around us. You could hear warbling voices, sawing strings or hammering pianos behind every door.

Annabel had been here before. She followed the sound of Neil's gorgeous tenor (stuck on one phrase, like a faulty CD), knocked briskly, and led me into a dusty room. It was furnished with a shabby grand piano, stacks of chairs, and a spindly crowd of metal music stands.

Ben was at the piano, unshaven and a little sullen. His face lit up into a broad smile when he saw us. "You angels—you've brought food!"

"You'll be the ruin of me," Neil said cheerfully, diving into the bag of croissants. "Elspeth's trying to put me on a diet." (Oh yes, he and the Wicked Queen were still an item—I could apparently make wonderful matches when I wasn't trying.)

"She's got a point, mate," Ben said kindly. "Fat opera stars are out of style. I saw Pavarotti at La Scala, and all I could think of was how much leather it took to make his tunic. You could've held a meeting in it."

Annabel chuckled. "La Scala! What poor dear paid for that?"

Ben looked a little hangdog, but he also laughed. How interesting, I thought, that Annabel was allowed to tease him about the Foolish Virgins. When Fritz or I did it, he sulked for ages.

Neil said, "I hope you had the decency to sleep with her afterward."

"Having a girlfriend has made you very smug," Ben told him.

"Don't worry," Annabel said. "We'll find someone for you. Someone very musical and sensitive. Won't we, Cassie?"

I hadn't a clue what to say to this—wasn't it supposed to be my job? Annabel might have bagged Fritz, but I was damned if I was letting her muscle in on my matchmaking. I had made a promise to Phoebe. Any triumphs would be mine and mine alone.

"Two cappuccinos and two lattes," I said. "Plus two plain croissants and two almond. You boys can have first choice because you're working."

"Almond, please," Neil said promptly. "Sod it—I can't hit that b-flat on an empty stomach."

The four of us drank coffee and ate croissants. I was touched to see how Ben and Annabel had rediscovered their ancient friendship, as if they had only just climbed out of the sandpit. They chatted and laughed and carried on a conversation they had obviously been having for ages. They had tons to say to each other. While I talked to Neil about the songs, Ben and Annabel retreated to the window to talk about some household arrangement. I couldn't hear, but there were frequent bursts of laughter. It occurred to me that I'd never seen either of them this relaxed with a member of the opposite sex. I told myself that I had to stop feeling jealous and dog-in-the-mangerish about Annabel and Fritz, since their romance had apparently shed blessings on the entire family.

Ben wanted to know what we had bought. We described our baby presents, and Annabel showed off her underwear.

"Now, be honest," she said, holding up a transparent, underwire bra with embroidery over the nipples. "Will Fritz fancy me in this?"

"Bloody hell," Neil said, reddening and laughing. "If he doesn't, there's something seriously wrong with him."

"You look lovely anyway," Ben said, with a touch of severity. "You don't need to truss yourself up in stuff like this. Does she, Cass? I like that shirt thing you sometimes wear in the mornings."

"Oh, Ben, don't be silly. I just pull that on so I can make tea without you seeing my bum."

"It looks great."

"Yes, but it won't inflame Fritz."

"That bra is too obvious."

I had been listening to this exchange in some surprise. Was Annabel really in the habit of flaunting herself around the Darlings' basement half naked? And since when had she been Ben's most intimate friend? There was an air of familiarity between them, faintly spiked with something else that I couldn't quite identify.

"I want to be as obvious as possible," Annabel explained seriously. "Obvious enough to make Fritz come right home after the theater, instead of carousing with the rest of the company."

"You should join in the carousing," I suggested.

Annabel sighed. "To tell the truth, I don't much like hanging out with the other actors. And Fritz says he doesn't like mixing business with pleasure. He's stopped asking me."

I might have let this one past, if I hadn't seen the expression on Ben's face. He looked annoyed—though not with Annabel—and rather suspicious. He knew his brother better than anyone, and if he was suspicious, there had to be something amiss.

But then again, he was a bit funny about Annabel. And she laughed off his suspicions with such confidence that nobody could doubt her happiness. Perhaps Ben, like me, was a little jealous of the two of them. It must have been difficult, I thought, actually sharing a small basement with Love's Young Dream.

Before we left them to their work, Neil mentioned that he and Elspeth had a spare ticket for that evening's Prom at the Albert Hall. The Proms were in their last week, and this was a very good one—the Berlin Phil and Beethoven's Ninth. Elspeth had probably sold her body and killed several people to obtain her four priceless seats.

I explained that I would be heavily engaged in burying my exploded romance.

"Annabel, why don't you come?" Ben asked eagerly. "After all, you're not doing anything else, and Fritz is working." He was going, of course. Earning money had not dimmed Ben's passion for free concert tickets.

"I'd love to," Annabel said. "Being a theater widow is almost as bad as being single."

"Crap," I put in gloomily. "Nothing's as bad as being single."

I devoted the rest of my day to the business of severance from Matthew. I had decided to cook goulash, with lashings of paprika. He had once complained that it gave him "indigestion"—by which he meant that it made him fart. Ha! Honor could enjoy the subsequent trombone solo under his duvet. I didn't have to worry about this sort of thing any more. I didn't have to vacuum, clean the bath or wear something feminine. I must be positive about this. I would receive him in ancient comfy jeans and cook him farty food, and he would see that I was free.

Matthew arrived on the stroke of eight. He was carrying a bottle of wine, and looking so subdued that I found it hard to keep up my indignation. I poured us both glasses of wine, and we sat ourselves down on opposite sides of the sitting room. This was the first time I had seen him since catching him at it. I swallowed a mad impulse to giggle.

"Cassie," he said. He raised his hanging head, and fixed me with his mournful gaze. "Cassie, darling."

"You told me you didn't like oral sex," I said.

I admit this was a cruel blow. I had the barbed satisfaction of watching Matthew's face turn that dull shade of red. He blushed so hard that his eyes watered. As I had guessed, the loss of dignity was agony for him. He wasn't used to being in the wrong. When a person is accustomed to the high moral ground, they can hardly breathe in an atmosphere of wrongness.

"Cassie, before we say anything else, I'm so desperately sorry. I've behaved like an idiot. I despise myself. I—I don't know what got into me. I've treated you appallingly, and you're the last person in the world—I mean, I have such fondness—we've been so much to each other."

I couldn't let him go on. For one thing, I couldn't stand the clichés. For another, he looked so genuinely miserable that I was softened. Suddenly, a scene was the last thing I wanted. What would be the point? The gulf between us had widened to a chasm. Matthew and I were already history.

"I owe you an apology," I said. "I shouldn't have burst in on you like that. I'd gladly give back your keys, but I'm afraid I threw them out of a taxi window."

He gave a dismal laugh. "That's okay. I don't blame you for being furious. God, I've never been so embarrassed in my life. I suppose—er—I suppose you've told everyone about it?"

"Don't be silly, Matthew. Of course I have."

"Well, of course." He was silent for a moment. "I meant to tell you. I certainly didn't intend you to find out like that. I hate myself."

"Stop hating yourself," I said. "Let's have dinner. I made goulash."

"Oh. Delicious."

We sat down. I served my goulash, oozing scarlet juices, onto plates that did not match. I poured more wine into glasses that had not been buffed with dry linen.

"I do—I did—I mean, I do love you," Matthew said. "I thought I'd made a life with you. I think I loved you because you seemed so right for me. But it was all too—does any of this make sense? I lost my head."

"With Honor Chappell," I said. "And I introduced you."

The sound of her name made him twitch. "Yes. It started that night, when we went out with Phoebe. Part of me thought she looked a mess. And part of me wanted to—to—"

"Jump on her bones," I prompted helpfully.

He made his bad-smell face. "It was extraordinary. You talked about her as if she were some old spinster—and I saw this incredible beauty. I couldn't stop staring at her. I was sure you'd notice."

"How did you get together?" (I figured I might as well satisfy my curiosity.) "Did you exchange numbers then and there?"

Matthew was shocked. "No! Look, do you think I wanted to get myself into this mess?"

"So it happened by accident?"

"Well, no. Not exactly. I tried to forget her, and it was no use. I couldn't get her out of my mind. She haunted me. I had to see her again—just see her. She'd mentioned that she was working at the British Library. So I went there."

"What—you went all the way to King's Cross and got yourself a reader's ticket?"

"No. I waited in the coffee shop. I told the office I was visiting a client."

I began to be sorry I'd asked for details. Now I had to hear all about it—how Matthew and Honor had been helpless in the grip of a mighty urge; how they had fought and struggled against it, hating themselves for their disloyalty to me; how in between bouts of penitence they had been at it like a pair of stoats. The melancholy fact was that Matthew had discovered passion—but not with me.

I read somewhere recently that emotional wounds have been shown to cause actual physical pain. The pain of rejection is, apparently, the equivalent of a broken leg. Maybe this was why I ached in every limb, as if I'd been attacked with a mallet. I was an invalid. I needed rest. I certainly didn't need to hear how Honor and Matthew had wept through a concert at the Queen Elizabeth Hall, because their love could never be. Whether or not one is emotionally involved, there is something basically irritating about other's people's grand passions.

I wasn't angry or vengeful. I didn't care enough. A great wash of sadness lay over my life. I had worked out by now that I wouldn't miss Matthew. Honor was welcome to him. I could even see that they went together rather well.

"You're being great about this," Matthew said.

"Am I? Well, thanks."

"I know everyone says this—but can we stay friends?"

"Oh, of course." Whatever.

"Honor's terrifically fond of you. She feels awful about making you unhappy."

"Tell her not to feel awful, will you?"

"Cassie, you're—"

"Wonderful," I finished for him.

We parted politely. I was left alone, to contemplate my loneliness and admit that I had only wanted Matthew as protection against change and decay. The sad reality was that an army of Matthews couldn't keep those two at bay.

"I've lost a skin," Hazel said. "I feel so small and shivery. I can't stand the loneliness." She hovered at the zebra crossing. "I can't even cope with traffic any more."

She was back in London, reeling from her father's funeral, unable to return to work. I had found her cowering in her small garden flat, in a road leading off Parliament Hill Fields. If emotional injuries really were the same as the physical kind, Hazel was recovering from the equivalent of a gunshot wound. My emotional broken leg was nothing to this. Her face was tallow with the shock of grief. She wore battered trainers and a bulky, unflattering cardigan. I had to hold her arm when we crossed the road.

I had taken the afternoon off work to see her, and decided I had to get her out into the fresh air. The smooth green mound of Parliament Hill was before us, with the usual pair of kites fluttering at its summit. I didn't think Hazel was strong enough to climb it. I led her gently along the path beside the ponds. We walked very slowly. Joggers pounded past us. Mothers fed the ducks with their preschool children, on the muddy banks under the tasselled willows. I had often come here with the boys and Phoebe. Nothing had changed. The innocent mothers at the water's edge did not know they were mortal, or that their stout toddlers would grow into sad adults. It made me sad to think that I was observing the happiest times of their lives, and they were too busy to know it.

"Let's sit down for a minute," Hazel said.

There was a bench nearby. It had an inscription carved into it, in memory of Clive and his dog Zipper, who loved this spot. We couldn't get away from death, wherever we looked. It was even in Arcadia.

"You're doing very well." I tugged Hazel over to the bench. We sat down.

Hazel folded her hands in her lap, gazing out across the pond. "I don't understand it. I can't be tired. I do nothing but sleep."

"We'll rest here as long as you like," I said. "There's no hurry."

"You shouldn't have taken time off work."

"Hazel, kindly shut up about work—yours or mine. Or anyone's."

"Sorry. Can't help it."

I knew what Phoebe would have said to her. "I wish you'd eat something," I heard myself saying. "You didn't touch your lunch."

"Oh, I'm sorry, Cassie. It was sweet of you to bring me lunch. But I've forgotten how to eat since it happened."

"You're still in shock."

"Mum rang me at work," Hazel said. "I took the call in the middle of a conference. He—he just keeled over in the garden, while he was looking at the currant bushes. And I couldn't make myself believe it. We'd been talking on the phone two nights before. He sounded fine then."

"What did you talk about?"

"It was all right. It was nice, even. We were having a good laugh about my Uncle Mark."

"I'm glad you parted friends," I said. "That must help a bit?"

"But the argument wasn't over," Hazel said. "We hadn't *finished*." She wrung her hands. I'd never seen anyone doing this outside a novel, but recognized it now as an authentic gesture of despair. "I want to be angry with him," she said. "Then I suddenly remember riding on his shoulders when I was little. Or when he used to dress up as Father Christmas."

Her face contracted painfully. She began to cry, with an air of returning to her full-time job. Great racking, wheezy sobs shook her. What could I say? There is no comfort you can give to the inconsolable. But I heard Phoebe's voice again, telling me how she had felt when Jimmy died—"It's not comfort you want, it's patience. You need someone to just hold you and be sorry, no matter how long it takes."

I pushed a tissue into the wringing hands, and put my arm around Hazel.

She wept, and I looked out across the pond, listening to the cries of the children and the honking of the ducks. People walked past us. Some glanced at us curiously, or sympathetically. A breeze whipped at us.

A park-keeper drove past, in one of those white electric carts that trundle across the 900-odd acres of the Heath, their open backs laden with leaves and branches. It halted in front of us. The parkie jumped down, and said, "Cassie? I thought it was you."

I looked under the terrible brown felt hat they make the parkies wear, and recognized the thin face and straggling beard of Betsy's Jonah.

"Is your friend okay? Can I do anything?"

He was so gentle and friendly that I was, suddenly, very happy to see him. "Hi, Jonah," I said. "This is my friend Hazel. Her father died last week."

Tender sympathy suffused his (somewhat rabitty) features. "That's heavy." He crouched down toward Hazel. "Hi, I'm Jonah Salmon. Cassie was at school with my sisters. I think you need a cup of tea."

Hazel had stopped sobbing. Dazedly, she blew her raw nose. "I—no, I'm fine," she mumbled.

"You shouldn't be out in this wind. My hut's just over there." He pointed to the farther of two wooden huts, perched on the green bank of the pond. "Come on in, and let me make you both a cup of tea. I've got enough mugs."

"Oh, yes please," I said. It was growing chilly, and I had wanted to see the inside of one of those huts all my life.

Jonah and I helped Hazel to her feet. The fit of crying had passed like a storm. She and I walked slowly to the hut. Jonah went ahead, to park his cart. By the time we arrived, the door to the hut stood open.

It was furnished with a small table, a shelf of books, a very old squashy armchair, a noticeboard and several hundred stacked chairs. The remaining floor space was cramped. Jonah sat Hazel down in the armchair, and

167

unstacked two chairs for us. The kettle that Betsy had given him hissed on the table. He made three mugs of delicious, russet-tinged tea, and opened a packet of chocolate digestives.

"This is cozy," I said.

Jonah grinned. "Fabulous, isn't it? Admit you've always wanted to see inside." He held out the plate of biscuits. "Go on, Hazel. You haven't had one."

To my surprise, Hazel took one and started eating it. She managed a watery smile. "Thanks," she said with her mouth full. "You're ever so kind."

"I can see you're having a really hard time. You can talk about it, if you like. I'm not one of those spooky types who thinks you don't die if you eat enough spinach."

This looks a bit tactless written down—but Jonah said it with such genuine warmth that Hazel laughed. "Oh, don't! You can't imagine how many people have interrogated me about Dad's lifestyle—did he smoke? Did he drink? They want it to be his fault, so they don't have to think it might happen to them."

"It's fear, that's all," Jonah said. "But you've moved on. Your eyes have looked at death."

Hazel nodded. "And now I have, I see it everywhere. People don't realize. Life is so fragile." Dipping her biscuit mechanically into her tea, she told Jonah the story of her father's death. Jonah listened seriously, leaning forward with his elbows on his knees.

"The worst thing," Hazel said, "is waking up in the morning, and finding—emptiness. He's slipping away from me, as if he'd never been alive."

"But you'll hear his voice," Jonah said. "You'll hear it when you least expect it. It's a question of knowing how to listen."

"Listen to what? Where? How will I know?"

Very softly, almost conversationally, Jonah began to recite:

Thy voice is on the rolling air;
I hear thee where the waters run;
Thou standest in the rising sun,
And in the setting thou art fair.

What art thou then? I cannot guess;
But though I seem in star and flower
To feel thee some diffusive power,
I do not therefore love thee less:

My love involves the love before;
My love is vaster passion now;
Though mixed with God and Nature thou,
I seem to love thee more and more.

Far off thou art, but ever nigh;
I have thee still, and I rejoice;
I prosper, circled with thy voice;
I shall not lose thee though I die.

She was spellbound, her damp eyes pinned to his face. I remembered that one of Jonah's degrees was in English literature. He spoke the words beautifully, in absolute belief. I'd never imagined that old Jonah Salmon could be so charming and kind, even gallant. It occurred to me that I must tell Betsy about this. I began to see why she was so proud of him. I remembered Phoebe saying, "Most mothers don't care about their sons being rich or successful—they just want them to grow into men with good hearts."

"Tennyson," Jonah said. "*In Memoriam.* The ultimate newsletter from the planet of the bereaved." He took one of the books from the shelf. It was a complete Tennyson—they were all, I saw now, books of poetry. He gave it to Hazel. "Keep it as long as you want."

Hazel smiled. She murmured, "Thanks. But I wish you'd read it to me. You do it so well."

"Oh, I know reams of it by heart," Jonah said. "Look, you've finished your tea. If you're ready for alcohol, the pub by the crossing's really nice—and I'm just coming off shift."

I'd done it again. I'd made a match without trying. There was that look of frozen wonder on their two faces, like rabbits caught in headlights. Hazel's hand brushed Jonah's, and a little color crept back into her gray

169

lips. I left them together in the pub, passing the book between them, murmuring Tennyson at each other. Though they both begged me to stay, my every instinct told me that three had suddenly become a crowd. I was alone again, marveling at my own unconscious powers, and wondering if I'd ever find someone for myself.

CHAPTER THIRTEEN

Now, as the song says, we come to the tragic bit. I was in the outer office, arguing about something or other with Shay, when Betsy put her head round the door.

"Phoebe's on the phone. She says it's urgent."

I should have seen it coming, but Phoebe regarded all kinds of non-urgent things (thank-you cards, fresh nutmeg) as urgent, and I didn't rush to take the call.

"Hi, Phoebe."

"Cassie, something awful's happened." Her voice was a shadow of itself, and full of wretchedness. "Fritz and Annabel have split up."

"Oh shit." I sat down heavily. "When? Why?"

"To tell the truth, Fritz dumped her. He's taken up with that woman you tried to kill when you were at school. He's been very naughty indeed, and I'm extremely cross with him. You have to come over."

"Me? What can I do?"

"I'm longing to talk to someone who isn't one of my sons, and Sue doesn't come in today." (Sue was her Macmillan nurse; Phoebe needed more care lately.) "I thought everything was going so well—and now our plans are in ruins."

"I can't get away till about eight this evening," I said. "But I'll come as soon as I've finished. I'll take a taxi."

Naturally, I called Annabel at once (with Betsy, Shay and Puffin crowded round me, listening intently). She was not at work—I got a strange, rude man, who told me she wasn't coming in today. I tried her home, and got her answering service.

This was ominous. When a breakup was bad, Annabel couldn't talk to anyone for days. I would have to wait until she called me in floods of tears. Poor thing—she'd only just shelled out for all that kipper-begging underwear.

I can honestly say, with my hand on my heart, that I was deeply and sincerely sorry for her. Forget my little canker of jealousy for a moment. My main emotion was indignation. Phoebe loved Annabel, and had been so happy to think of her as a daughter-in-law. How could Fritz do this to either of them? Nasty, selfish, callous Fritz. He had broken the hearts of the two women I loved best in all the world. I pictured him in bed with Peason, and sincerely wished his cock would fall off.

I didn't get to Phoebe's until after nine. Ben opened the door. He was somber, and he clung to me when I kissed him.

"Thanks for coming—but Mum's asleep. She got so tired, I thought I'd better take her up to bed."

"She's okay, though, isn't she?"

"More or less. Have you eaten yet?"

"No. I'm starving."

"Good, because I made my first cauliflower cheese this afternoon." Ben headed for the door to the basement. "I need someone to appreciate it—and I'm not giving any to that cheating Don Quixote brother of mine."

"I think you might mean Don Juan," I hinted.

"Whatever." Ben was on his dignity. "He's done shitty things before—but this stinks. I can't believe he could do this to a girl like Annabel."

The basement was still fairly clean, but beginning to slide back into a state of untidiness. There was an overflowing laundry basket on the sofa, and a large backlog of dirty pans in the sink. Ben took a heap of old newspapers off the table and threw them on top of the laundry. He opened the oven and carefully, almost reverently, took out a very decent-looking dish of cauliflower cheese.

"That smells lovely." I tried not to sound too surprised that the hapless Ben had managed to cook something edible.

"Mum's giving me cooking lessons," Ben said.

"Really? I didn't know she was still—I mean, isn't she too tired for cooking?"

"I move the sofa to the kitchen," he explained. "Mum lies there watching me, and talks me through it step by step. She teaches me something new every day. She's worried that I won't be able to look after myself."

"Oh God." At a time like this, I didn't need to be reminded about Phoebe's fears for her boys. "She must've been gutted about Fritz and Annabel."

"Yes, she is—but she won't hear a word against that lying shit. She keeps making excuses for him."

I opened a bottle of wine and poured us both glasses. We sat down. Ben glowered Byronically, and forked in cauliflower cheese as if it had done him an injury.

I asked, "When did it happen?"

"Last night. I wasn't there, unfortunately. Or I would've chinned him."

"Oh Ben—what's got into him?"

"I don't know."

"He's been so nice lately!"

"The strain was too much for him," Ben said. "I think he's scared of getting too close to a woman. I sometimes think he deliberately goes for bitches, in case he finds himself accidentally falling for someone nice."

"I could have sworn he was in love with Annabel," I said forlornly. "So what happened, exactly? Take me through it."

Ben wiped his plate with a piece of bread. "Before he went to work last night, he told Annabel to wait up for him. I was there for that bit. Then I went out—Elspeth was working late, and Neil had a spare seat for the LSO at the Barbican."

"And?"

"It was absolutely superb. I've never heard Brahms done better."

"Stick to the plot, Ben."

"Sorry. When I got back, Annabel was here on her own, taking her things out of the bathroom. She wasn't crying, or making a fuss—or screeching and breaking stuff, like the normal sort of Fritz-girlfriend. I asked her what was up, and she said Fritz had told her it was over. That was all. I told Mum this morning."

"What did Fritz say?"

"Haven't seen him. I expect he stayed with that Peason woman."

"Oh God. She's such a cow."

"I tried to tell Annabel she was better off without him," Ben said darkly, "but she didn't seem to be listening. She wasn't ready to hear it."

Poor, poor Annabel. I couldn't help blaming myself. I should have warned her about Fritz. But we had all wanted to believe he had changed.

Ben and I spent the rest of the evening going over the same ground. Because I felt responsible, I made us tea and tackled some of the washing-up. At around eleven, when I was thinking of going home, the basement door slammed and Fritz came in.

He smiled ferociously when he saw our disapproving faces.

"Well, Grimble. What a nice surprise. I take it you've heard about the slight upheaval in my sex life?"

"Yes," I said.

"Spare me the comments, there's a good girl. Just put the key words on a postcard."

Ben scowled. "What are you doing here, anyway?"

"I live here, Ben. I popped back to fetch a few of my things."

"You're going back to that woman, I suppose."

"You suppose exactly right. She has a very comfortable flat in St. John's Wood." Fritz vanished into his bedroom, emerging a moment later with an armful of clothes. "I'm assuming she won't be welcome here."

"Too right she won't," Ben said. "She's a cow."

Fritz's grin became wolfish. "I wouldn't know about that."

"You shit," I blurted out. "How could you do this to Annabel?"

For a fraction of a second, he looked uncomfortable. "There isn't a kind way to send someone to Potters Bar. I was trying to make it quick and clean."

Ben stood up. "She was devastated."

"She'll get over me."

"So was Mum."

"Sorry," Fritz said. "I can't regulate my sex life to please my mother. You'll understand when you go through puberty."

Ben was breathing hard. "You couldn't keep it in your trousers for a second, could you?"

Fritz looked him up and down, chuckling scornfully. Ben's scowl deepened. His hands contracted into fists.

"Well, there you have it," Fritz said. "Alas, the still small voice of my conscience can't make itself heard above the deafening roar of my penis."

"This isn't funny," Ben said. "Annabel's feelings aren't a joke. She's in love with you, you bastard."

"I told you, she'll get over me," Fritz said. "They always do."

"Yes, but she's not one of your usual tarts—she's about a million times better."

"Well, you go out with her yourself, then," Fritz said. "You're obviously gagging to."

Ben let out a strangled bellow and punched Fritz on the chin.

It wasn't a good punch—Fritz moved his head, and it ended up as a bungled slap. But it astonished us all. Ben had never got as far as punching his brother. He stared at Fritz, and at his reddening knuckles, in awed disbelief.

Fritz said, "Don't do that again."

For a moment I was frightened. They stood at bay with their teeth bared. The whole room was electric with hostility.

Ben muttered something and bolted. I heard the slam of the front door, followed by the roar of the car starting.

"Oh shit," Fritz said. He suddenly looked very tired. "He's taken the car. I'll have to call a taxi."

He was exhausted and wretched. Superficially, he seemed suddenly older, with gray hairs at his temples and lines around his eyes. And yet I found myself thinking how young he was, and feeling nothing but tenderness for him. "Fritz, what on earth is going on? You seemed so— everything was going so fantastically!"

He dropped the pile of clothes on to a chair. The aggression had died right out of him. He was resigned and weary. "Grimble, do me a big favor. Just for a minute, stop treating me like the enemy. I know I'm a fuck-up, okay? Let's take it as read and have a cup of tea."

He switched on the kettle and made us tea. I sat down and drank it with him. I found, as I had found with Matthew, that I couldn't sustain my indignation. Fritz wasn't behaving like a heartless Casanova. He wasn't swaggering. He had lines and gray hairs. For the first time in our lives, he made me feel shy.

I asked, "Are you keeping Peason waiting?"

"She'll survive," he said shortly. "Have you spoken to Annabel?"

"No. I can't get hold of her."

He let out a long sigh, not at all like a triumphant lover. "Look, I didn't want to hurt her. She's a darling."

"I thought you were so happy. Both of you."

"We made a perfect picture," Fritz said. "I knew we would. It was just—too easy."

"It looked like a happy ending," I said.

"I know. That was the problem. All the way through, I was thinking of how pleased Mum would be. You made that stupid promise to find us nice comfy wives, and I couldn't help seeing that Annabel was perfect for the role. But I couldn't make it work. I'm deeply sorry, Cass—but she's just not the right woman. I couldn't do it. I was at war with myself."

"Is Peason the right woman?"

There was a brief spark of humor in his eye. "Probably not."

"You do know she's the embodiment of evil, don't you?"

"I know she's not a nice woman. I don't even particularly like her."

"You've lost me. I simply don't understand."

"You would if you were male," Fritz said. "Even when I thought Felicity was a complete pain, I couldn't stop her getting under my skin and into my bloodstream. She's so sensationally beautiful that my brain turns to mush when I look at her. It's like being possessed. There's no point in struggling. I just have to surrender, body and soul."

I said, "It's a shame you can't feel that way about someone nice."

"Isn't it?" Fritz meant this. He wasn't being sarcastic. "God knows I tried."

I was puzzled. I had intended to be so angry with Fritz, and now I was struggling not to feel sorry for him. Suddenly, the heartless, dashing Alpha Male seemed scared and lost and sad.

He must have noticed my unwilling softening. His tense shoulders sagged. "You're furious with me. To tell the truth, I'm rather furious with myself. I absolutely hate myself for making Annabel cry. The poor little thing thought I'd come home early to have sex with her."

"Oh no."

"She was wearing a see-through bra."

"Oh Fritz, no!" This detail broke my heart.

"When I—you know, when I told her, she looked about six years old. Her face crumpled. And at that moment . . ." his black eyes burning into me, he squeezed both my hands across the table, "at that moment, I wanted to run and run and never see either of them again. I wanted to run until I dropped dead. I went back to Felicity's because I reckoned she deserved a shit like me."

"You're not a shit," I said. "You hate behaving like this—so why are you doing it?"

"Entirely for the sex." He was grim.

"Come on!"

Fritz said, "I need unromantic, dangerous, smutty sex because it's the opposite of death. The kind of sex I have with Felicity is like oxygen to me at the moment. She's life to me. Maybe that's why I can't stop fucking her. It's not a question of the sex being good—it's *essential*."

I was angry with myself for failing to see the real and obvious reason behind Fritz's behavior. All roads led back to the awfulness of Phoebe dying.

"Mum's upset with me," Fritz said. "That's the worst thing. I couldn't even stay with Annabel to make her happy."

"For God's sake, nobody expects you to do that."

"And I've never seen Ben so angry. He thinks I'm scum."

"He'll calm down eventually."

"Mum's afraid I won't look after him," Fritz said, tender and exasperated. "She's teaching him to cook, for instance."

"I know. I ate today's lesson."

"She had it all worked out, you see. I was to marry Annabel and live in the top part of the house. Ben was to live in the basement with his grand piano."

"Poor Phoebe."

"She has all these dreams for us, and it hurts to know they'll never come true."

I didn't know what he meant.

Fritz said, "For a start, we won't be living in this house after she's gone."

This came as a sickening shock. It was hard enough to imagine a world without Phoebe. Now I had to hear that her beautiful and bounteous home would die with her.

"I took over Mum's finances about a month ago," Fritz said. "And I found everything in a total mess. She's leaving us with a whacking great overdraft."

"But what about the money Jimmy left?"

"It wasn't as much as she thought. She always was hopeless with money—never read a bank statement in her life."

"Does she know about this?"

"No. Why does she need to know? The bank is letting us run up the debt, on the understanding that the house goes on the market before she's cold in her grave."

"That's appalling!"

Fritz reached across the table to take my hand. "It's not such a disaster. The house is worth a fortune. Ben and I will take away plenty of change. Let Mum think whatever makes her happiest."

"I suppose so."

"My West End wages are keeping us in food at the moment, but I need more paid work. I've told my agent I'll consider anything." I must have looked skeptical. He added, more forcefully, "This isn't the time to worry about my dignity. If there's money involved, I'll dress up as a chicken and hand out leaflets in Oxford Street."

"It's not that bad, is it?"

He smiled. "Actually, I've just been called back for a car commercial. If I get that, I'll be able to send Phoebe out in the lap of luxury."

His hand was warm around mine. We both sat looking over the edge of the chasm. Fritz had decided that Phoebe was to know nothing about the financial mess. He knew how important it was for her to die thinking she had provided for her useless sons. I respected him for fooling her, and I loved him for it. I'd forgotten all about my anger. Talking about Phoebe's death was like climbing out of the world, into a bubble of numb unreality.

He said, "It's not going to be long."

"Is she—is she a lot worse?" My mouth was dry.

"Not exactly. But something's changed in the way she talks. That's all. She told me she dreams about Dad a lot. I can't help feeling—knowing— she's drifting away." I saw that his eyes were brimming. "I don't think Ben has noticed anything. Well, she doesn't want him to."

"She thinks you can handle more."

"She thinks I'm brave," Fritz said. "And I am. I can handle anything."

I had never seen him crying—not even when Jimmy died. He sat gravely looking down at my hand, and the tears slid down his cheeks. Neither of us mentioned them. I ached with sympathy, but knew that Fritz didn't want to be comforted. My anger was forgotten. It came from the other world, where there was no death. But I was dismayed by the way everything around us seemed to be sliding into chaos and ruin. My promise to Phoebe had only made things worse. Her beloved boys were not only not engaged, but not speaking to each other. I was mortally afraid that thanks to me, her death would shatter what was left of her family.

CHAPTER FOURTEEN

It was my duty, as the best friend of Annabel, to hold myself in readiness for the inevitable postmortem. The ends of Annabel's affairs usually fell into a certain routine. First came the solo grieving, which involved sobbing, daytime television and biscuits. After this, there would be a couple of evenings at my flat, combing over the details of what had gone wrong—which involved tissues, takeaway pizza and self-reproach. And then (give or take the odd session with a bottle of wine) we'd be more or less back to normal.

I waited for the summoning phone call. And at first I was rather relieved when the days passed and it didn't come. This latest debacle was rather my fault, after all. But the silence went on for such a long time that I started to worry. Though Annabel was back at work, she apparently took no notice of her voice mail. It was the same story at her flat. I sent message after message into the void, and continued to hear nothing.

Eventually, she sent me an e-mail at work.

> Bum—I've lost my job. I feel so utterly bum about this that I can't face anyone, not even you. Sorry I haven't been in touch. I'm going to Scotland to stay with Mummy and Trevor. Promise to call you when I get back.

Bum indeed. Now I really felt terrible. Poor Annabel had lost both her lover and her arbitraging, and the fact that she had chosen to stay with her daft mother and dafter stepfather in Aberdeen spoke volumes about the state of her mind.

At least I didn't have to worry about Hazel. Her e-mails were little bulletins from paradise.

Jonah stayed over again—it gets better and better!!! He's so sensitive and gentle and thoughtful, and the best part is that my dad would have been horrified. At last I've managed to fall for someone he wouldn't approve of, who also happens to be one of the kindest, nicest men in the world!!!!

"Hazel's fabulous," Betsy said, knitting away in a fury of satisfaction. "I can't thank you enough."

"Don't mention it," I said.

"The girls think she must be crazy, but I always knew Jonah would find someone who really appreciated his qualities. I think he might be moving in with her—wouldn't that be wonderful?"

"Yes, you'll be able to use your attic again. Whatever will you do with it?"

Dear old Betsy, she only laughed at my sarcasm and offered me another piece of cake. Jonah was off her hands at last, and in her joy she bombarded us with cake. Puffin ate so much of it that he had to have his cavalry twills altered. I quickly learned to loathe the sight of hundreds-and-thousands, which she shook over her icing in industrial quantities.

Frankly, this cake had a bitter taste to me. I had intended Hazel for Ben Darling, and her falling in love with Jonah seemed to underline my ineptitude as a matchmaker. I had let Phoebe down. Ben was still single and Fritz was still entangled with old Poison.

Because they loved Phoebe, Fritz and Ben were officially speaking again. But they avoided each other as much as possible, and the strain between them was only too obvious. Ben could not forgive Fritz for his caddish treatment of Annabel. Since the split, he had been intensely moody. Fritz was spending more and more time at Peason's mansion flat in St. John's Wood. Ben spent all his time sulking and seething in the basement. When Fritz called round for his belongings, he put huge effort into not speaking to him.

They couldn't totally avoid each other, however, because one of them had to be with Phoebe. The two of them now took turns living with her in the upper part of the house. One of them always slept in the room next to hers. They never left her alone for a moment.

I found this out when Fritz called me at work. "We need a large favor, Grimble. It's for Phoebe."

"Of course."

"Can you come and stay a night with her next week?"

He explained their arrangement. I was alarmed that it had become necessary, and ashamed of myself for not knowing.

"I'll be shooting all day and going to the theater in the evening," Fritz said. "And Ben and Neil have a concert in Swansea." (Fritz had got his car commercial; you may remember him flaring his nostrils in the wing mirror, to the strains of Vivaldi.) "We can't leave Mum on her own. She's by no means high maintenance, but she needs to have someone with her."

I was brisk and practical. I said I'd be delighted to stay, and asked all kinds of intelligent questions about nursing. Fritz took just the same tone. He didn't need to spell out the fact that Phoebe was getting worse. But we were horribly aware of it. I felt slightly sick, and slightly afraid I'd show myself up by being squeamish.

Fritz seemed to sense my fearfulness. His voice became kind. "Tell you what, come round to the theater. Then I can give you a set of keys and full instructions about the drugs—I know you like to have things written down. Come tonight, if you can bear to sit through it again. I'll even buy you dinner."

"I'd love to see the show again, but I refuse to break bread with Peason."

He laughed. "Fear not. She's doing something else."

"In that case, yes please. I haven't been anywhere for ages. Does it matter that I'm wearing rather awful clothes?"

"You never look awful. I'll leave a ticket at the box office, and book a restaurant that Felicity doesn't like. I'm glad you're coming, Grimble. I want to make the most of my night off."

I felt cheerful after this phone call, and somehow strengthened. Caring for Phoebe—loving Phoebe—had moved us to a new level of intimacy. I was honored to be treated like a real member of her family.

I found *Rookery Nook* even more entertaining the second time. It looked faster and smarter in its West End setting, and I didn't have

Matthew fidgeting beside me. Fritz was as good as ever. He looked wonderful under the lights. God, how I fancied him. And what on earth could I do about it? Here was another reminder of my uselessness. Bloody Peason also looked wonderful. There was no question of competing with her. If I'd ever had a chance with him, I'd missed it. And none of it mattered anyway. Nothing mattered now except Phoebe.

Afterward, I wove through the crowd of well-fed, well-dressed middle-aged theater-goers to the stage door. It opened on to a narrow corridor and a flight of stone stairs, pitilessly lit and packed with shouting strangers. I must admit, I find these places intimidating. I spent some time wedged against a fire extinguisher, being ignored. One of the actors (no doubt remembering my blush-making contribution to the first night party) kindly directed me up three flights of stone stairs to Fritz's dressing room.

I knocked at the door, and Peason's voice said, "Yes?"

I found her sitting in her coat, her face still vividly made up. "Hi," I said.

She was examining herself in the big mirror over the dressing table. "Hi, Cassie—oh, lucky thing, you look so comfy in those jeans. I always have to dress myself up to the nines, and it's such hard work. Fritz won't be long, by the way. He said to sit and wait."

There were two chairs in the small room. One contained Peason, the other was freighted with her handbag. I tried to look as if I didn't mind standing.

"That was marvelous," I said, making my formal obeisance.

"Thanks. People think a West End transfer is easy, but they haven't a clue about the extra work involved."

"It's looking superb." I was having a struggle with my adjectives. "Polished," I added.

"Fritz says you're taking a share of the mother duty," Peason said. She addressed me through the mirror, with a brilliant smile. "I can't tell you how grateful I am. It's so nice of you."

"It's a pleasure, actually."

"The house is gorgeous, of course. I can see why you enjoy being there. It must be worth several million by now. I'd so love to live there, wouldn't you?"

I thought that she looked particularly beautiful, and particularly nasty, when she talked about money.

"Yes," I said. "It's a shame they'll have to sell it."

"I'm so glad you see it like that," Peason said, with a disagreeable rush of intimacy. "It's so hard to get Fritz to see sense. The fact is, there's no real need to sell the place at all. I don't see why he shouldn't live there after—well, you know, after—if only the eternal Ben could be got out of the way."

I hated her. She couldn't wait to get rid of Phoebe and poor Ben. "The house belongs to him too," I said.

"Obviously. Someone would need to buy him out."

Did Peason have enough money to do this? I felt sick again. I didn't want to save the house if it meant she had to live there. Seriously, how could Fritz bear even hearing about such a violation?

"Hi, Grimble." Fritz came in, wearing his street clothes.

"I'll be off then," Peason said. I was no threat to her. She smiled at me, and planted a scorching kiss on Fritz's mouth—the sort of long kiss where you make an "mmmmm" noise. "Have a lovely evening."

She left, and Fritz seemed as relieved as I was. "I've booked us into Joe Allen's," he said cheerfully. "Just let me take off my makeup—I don't want to go in looking like some old queen."

The restaurant was busy and noisy. Fritz said he was starving. He encouraged me to order a large hamburger. We drank very good red wine. There were lights and people and a great babble of talk. Every few minutes Fritz would break off our conversation to wave to acquaintances or exchange kisses with friends. I felt dowdy and countrified. Since the split with Matthew, my world had narrowed down to a shabby flat in Chalk Farm and a shabby office in Dover Street. I was bewildered by the glitter and the noise, and the unreality of being out late.

How long was it since I'd been out to dinner with Fritz? In fact, had we ever been out together? Despite fancying him (which I was used to), I found him excellent company that night. The shared business of Phoebe sealed us in our own world. We were relaxed and unguarded. The relief of being able to talk about her, with someone who felt the same, was like taking off tight shoes.

He had typed me a page of instructions—contact numbers, times of medication, approved foods.

"I'm so glad you can do this," he said. "I hate the idea of leaving her with someone who doesn't belong to her."

I asked him how long he and Ben had been working in shifts upstairs.

Fritz said, "Since the transfer, more or less. Ben's there more than I am. He's wonderful with Mum—knows what she wants before she does." He smiled. "What she really wants is for poor old Ben to get a girlfriend. I'd like it too. If he's getting laid, maybe he'll stop treating me like Jack the Ripper."

"He'll forgive you eventually. He always does."

"This time is different, Grimble. Something's got to give, before he hits me again. Next time I might not be able to stop myself hitting him back. The strain of pretending everything's fine in front of Mum is beginning to tell on us. So do us all a favor and bring some of your eligible names."

I said I'd do my best, and started thinking through my mental card index of suitable brides. The plot, however, was about to confound us all.

Over the next few weeks, summer turned slowly to autumn, and I kept up my hamster-wheel routine of work and home. The days seemed endless, but time was passing faster than I could bear. Once a week, sometimes twice, I spent the night with Phoebe when the boys were otherwise engaged. I got used to the responsibility surprisingly quickly, and it soon became if not a pleasure, then a welcome break in the routine.

Phoebe's physical frailty was frightening, but though the setting had crumbled, the pearl of her personality was as perfect as ever. I don't know how any of us would have coped if the essential Phoebe had changed—she herself had said she'd put up with anything if she could keep her marbles.

The strain between her sons did not bother her as much as I'd feared. She said they were both "hot-headed," just like their father. "You remember the terrible fights Jimmy used to get into. Sometimes it was absolutely mortifying—for instance, when he had that shouting match at parents' evening with Fritz's biology teacher. But his rages never lasted long."

I said, "I think Fritz knows he was in the wrong."

Phoebe said, "He'll see sense one of these days. He's not remotely in love with that frightful woman."

Fritz had (reluctantly) brought Peason to meet Phoebe. And though Peason had shown a flattering interest in the house, the visit had not been a success. Phoebe pronounced her "shallow" and "vulgar," and warned Fritz that her famous bum would be "enormous" by the time she hit forty. Phoebe did not often take dislikes, but when she did she was implacable.

According to Phoebe, Fritz was in love with someone else.

"He doesn't realize it himself yet," she told me, with an air of mystery, "but it's eating away at him. All he knows at the moment is that he's in the wrong place."

Sue, the Macmillan nurse, asked, "Who is this secret someone else, then? Who's he really in love with?" (Sue knew everything about us, and often chimed in with advice. She was a vigorous, dry-witted woman in her forties. Phoebe loved her.)

"She means me," I said. "No matter how many times I assure her that Fritz is not secretly pining for my charms. He's not, Phoebe. Whether we like it or not, Fritz is in love with Felicity Peason. End of story."

I was sitting on the edge of the bed at the time, and I have a clear memory of Phoebe's wasted face on the pillow, creasing into a mischievous smile. "Oh, the story isn't anywhere near the end," she said. "It hasn't even begun."

"I'm back," Annabel said down the phone, "and I need to talk to you."

It was a Friday. We met after work (my work, that is) at the usual wine bar. I hadn't seen or spoken to my best friend for weeks and weeks. It felt like months, or years. We had never been apart for such a long time; not since the day we met in Mrs. Collins's class at school. I'd missed her terribly. Life without her e-mails and phone calls was both lonely and boring. Laying into the Chianti, I wondered why we hadn't fallen into the usual welter of gossip.

Annabel sipped fizzy water. She looked terrible. Her hair was everywhere, and her white face was unbecomingly puffy around the eyes and chin. It didn't take her long to get to the headlines.

Very quietly she said, "I'm pregnant."

Oh shit. Oh hell and damnation. I found myself thinking, how dreadful for Fritz. I then despised myself for thinking of him first, when it was obviously far more dreadful for Annabel.

I managed to stutter out something like, "How long have you known?"

"I found out last weekend."

"Oh, Annabel, you poor thing—what will you do?"

Her chin quivered. "I was hoping you'd know. I haven't told anyone else. Perhaps I should drown myself."

I was frantically trying to collect my wits. Annabel had come to me before telling any of the grown-ups. She trusted me to hew a path through a forest of incredible complications, and I couldn't let her down.

"I wish you'd told me sooner," I said, filling my voice with a confidence I didn't feel. "Come back to my place tonight—you shouldn't be alone right now. And listen, leave Fritz to me. He might be a bit annoyed at first, but there's a heart of gold under all that testosterone."

Tears clouded Annabel's blue eyes. She let out a sob and clutched at my hand under the table.

"Really and truly," I assured her. "He's actually a very kind man. He'd never turn his back on you at a time like this."

She pulled her hand away and blew her nose on a napkin. In a very small voice she said, "It's not Fritz's."

"Wh—what?"

She didn't need to say it again. She gazed at me woefully, waiting for the enormity to sink in.

I took a long breath. "Annabel, are you sure about this?"

"Of course I'm sure!"

"What I mean is, you've never really got to grips with the reproductive cycle, have you? And you've made mistakes before." (There had been a famous scare at college, due to Annabel's vagueness over dates and her belief that you could get pregnant if a man dropped his used condom on your knickers.)

She was firm. "I've worked it out, Cassie. It couldn't be Fritz's. By the end of it all we hadn't had sex for weeks. I'd had a period and everything."

"Well, whose is it, then?"

Another sob burst out of her. "Ben's."

"*What?*"

I had one of those moments when the brain refuses to process information that is too gobsmacking. Astonishment is too weak a word for what I felt. I gaped across the table at Annabel, my mouth and eyes hanging open. My beautiful, daffy friend, the very picture of guilelessness, was telling me that she had managed to get pregnant by her ex-lover's brother.

"Okay," I said. "Take me through it slowly. I need more alcohol. Are you ready for a glass of wine yet?"

"No thanks. What I'd really like is a cup of tea."

I looked at her closely, suddenly fascinated to think of a new life growing inside her. "Do you need something to eat?" I dimly remembered Claudette in the early stages of her pregnancy, complaining of constant sickness while eating her own weight in salted almonds.

Annabel mopped at her eyes once more. "I wouldn't mind a bowl of soup. And some bread. And maybe a small tuna salad. And some cheese. Sorry, but I'm constantly ravenous."

I called over a waiter and ordered food and tea. I was absolutely sizzling with curiosity, but didn't want to interrogate her until the tea arrived in case she fainted or something. Wasn't that what people did when they were pregnant?

Annabel was solemn. "Cassie, my life's a disaster."

"Oh no—"

"Come on. I'm unemployed, I fell in love with the wrong brother and I'm pregnant. How much more disastrous can it get?"

The waiter brought us our pot of tea. Annabel slurped it thirstily. The food arrived, and she crammed in bread, soup and salad as if she hadn't eaten for a month. I decided she was starting to look less terrible. A touch of color crept into her bleached, swollen face.

She said, "It was the night after Fritz dumped me. The night after Ben came in and found me packing my stuff."

"He told me about that."

"I felt—it was so appalling that I was almost numb. I wanted to cry and cry, but nothing would come out. I just sat on my sofa, staring at the wall, for more or less two whole days. I couldn't eat. I was living on chamomile tea. The phone kept ringing."

"I tried to call you," I said.

"I know, and I'm sorry I couldn't answer. I was in shock, I think. I needed time to get used to having a broken heart. This is all so confusing, Cass—but I loved Fritz so much, or I thought I did. I mean, I had a certain idea of what love *was*. And I was wrong, I was missing the whole point." She smiled sadly. "Isn't that exactly what you've been telling me for years? Anyway, then my doorbell rang. I didn't know who it was—I thought it might have been you—but I couldn't face anyone. And then I heard knocking, and Ben's voice shouting through the letterbox. He threatened to carry on shouting till I opened the door. So I did."

"But . . ." This kind of decisiveness was not at all like Ben. "What did he want?"

"He said he couldn't bear to think of me being unhappy. He'd brought me a bunch of flowers, from a garage. I started crying as soon as I saw him. I absolutely howled. But I was tremendously glad to see him. Oh, I can't describe how lovely he was." Her face regained its upward curves, and became beautiful. "He found some wine in my fridge and poured me a glass. He made me sit down like an invalid. He sat down beside me and took me in his arms. He put his coat over both of us."

I said, "He made you a Cotton House."

"Yes!" She was eager. "That's exactly what he—you haven't had an affair with him, have you?"

"Don't be silly. It's from when we were little. So go on—how did sperm get involved?"

"It didn't start off as sex. At first it was just comforting. He made me feel so warm and cherished, and I thought how much I'd come to love him when I was going out with Fritz—and how much I'd miss him now it was over. And suddenly we were kissing, and I wanted him inside me. I suppose I should have thought about contraception and my last period and all that. But there wasn't time. What's the matter?"

"I feel so stupid," I said. I couldn't believe my own blindness. "It's so bloody obvious—Ben's been totally desperate to get you into bed. Oh my God, Annabel, he adores you! He's been pining for you! It's enormously romantic."

"No. You're wrong."

189

"He punched Fritz, for God's sake. He's been too silly to work out that when a dear friend gives you a constant erection, it usually means you're in love with them."

For the first time, Annabel smiled. Her tear-bloated face was absolutely (no other word will do) radiant. "It was—he was—the sex was wonderful. But he kept saying sorry afterward. He doesn't think he can possibly be as good in bed as Fritz. And as a matter of fact, in many ways he's better."

"Really?" (Forgive me, I was dying of curiosity.)

"He's more patient and encouraging. He wouldn't let me hurry my second orgasm."

"Your second?" Good grief. But I had to know it all now. This is the whole point of being a best friend.

"Well, yes," Annabel said. "After the first time—which was inevitably a bit hurried—we took our clothes off and did it properly. It was so amazing, I can't even describe it. But he hasn't been in touch since."

"That's simply because he's an even bigger ninny than you are."

"What do you mean?"

I reached across the table to caress her hand. "Darling Annabel, you and Ben have fallen in love, but you're both too daft to see it. This is like one of those irritating musical comedies where the lovers have a completely pointless misunderstanding till the end of Act Three. Forgive me if I'm being obtuse—but why does this have to be a tragedy? I mean, how do you feel about Ben?"

"I don't deserve to have feelings."

"Your feelings are all we have to go on. Do you love him?"

"I shouldn't—not when I'm supposed to be in love with Fritz."

"Annabel, do you love Ben?" I tightened my grip on her hand. "Because I know he loves you. Please say yes!"

"Yes. He's the one I really miss now. It's more than a boyfriend thing." She smiled rather lopsidedly. "I've never been so—so *intimate* with a man. And I don't mean in a sex way. Ben's my soul mate."

"Well, don't you think your soul mate deserves to know about you being pregnant?"

Annabel said, "He's only just getting his career together. I don't want to ruin everything for him."

"But he's in love with you—I'd put money on it. God, it explains so much. Now, doesn't that change things?"

"I don't know."

"I need to ask you one more thing," I said. It had occurred to me, as I'm sure it has to you, that in the right circumstances this entire, muddled situation could fill Phoebe with untold, unbounded joy. "What about the—the pregnancy?" (I rejected "baby" as too emotive.)

Though I was doing my best to be gentle, I wasn't gentle enough. Once again, poor Annabel's eyes flooded with tears.

I said, "You want it." I knew her. And I was right.

"Oh yes." Her whole heart was in her voice.

There was a lump in my throat. Suddenly, the idea of a baby that belonged to my dearest friend and my adopted brother was piercingly moving.

Annabel said, "I want this baby more than I've ever wanted anything."

"Then you're going to have it," I said. "If Ben won't support you through it, I will. I'll go to all the classes with you, and I'll help you to bring it up. But I have a very strong feeling that Ben won't let me do anything of the kind. You must tell him—you don't know how miserable he is without you!"

Impulsively, absolutely knowing it was the right thing to do, I dived into my bag for my mobile and punched in Phoebe's number. (I knew it was Ben's turn upstairs—this couldn't have happened on a better night.)

"Hello?"

"Ben, hi, it's Cassie. Are you available for a visit?"

"Mum's gone to bed," Ben said.

"It's you I want to see."

Across the table, Annabel looked stricken. She shook her head and mouthed, "No!"

I ignored her. "I can be round in about half an hour."

Ben said, "Okay."

"Put the kettle on—we're going to need tea."

"I can't do it!" Annabel pleaded, as soon as the call ended. "I can't just march in, as if I were demanding a shotgun wedding or something. Oh God, what will Fritz think of me? And Phoebe? Oh God! I've crashed into their family and torn them apart!"

"Annabel, get a grip. You're such a one for making a drama out of a crisis."

I paid the bill and marched her out of the wine bar. I hailed a taxi and pushed her into it. She wasn't protesting seriously. I thought I saw signs of relief. I refused, however, to let her talk about Ben or the baby. On the journey up to Hampstead I made her tell me about her job. This was an effort for her, mainly because it all seemed laughably irrelevant now, and a long time ago.

"It wasn't anything personal," Annabel said. "The bank lost a huge amount of money, and they economized by getting rid of half the staff. We were streaming out of that building like those animals that hurl themselves over cliffs."

"Surely they gave you some notice?"

"Oh Cassie, you're such an innocent." Annabel was almost cheerful—she loved a chance to patronize me. "They don't have to give notice in my world. We were all worried, but none of us had a clue when the sword was going to fall. I walked into work as usual—and ten minutes later I found myself walking out again, with all the stuff from my desk in a binbag."

"But that's awful!"

"That's just life in the Square Mile. Why do you think they pay us so much?"

"Did you manage to hang on to any of it?"

"Not much. Thank God I paid off my mortgage with my last bonus."

Our taxi was drawing up in front of Phoebe's house. I got out and paid the driver. Once she was on the pavement, Annabel got nervous again.

"Cassie, please. I'm not ready. He'll be so shocked—we only did it once!"

"Twice, you mean." I pulled her up the steps and rang the bell.

Ben opened the door. His sullen face opened out when he saw Annabel. They both turned beetroot—which was so romantic that for a moment I was almost tearful. They were so in love that I could feel it in the air between them. I could practically see it.

"It's all right," Ben said. "You don't have to creep or whisper. Mum won't wake up till about three in the morning."

The mention of Phoebe eased the tension between them. Annabel touched his arm gently. "How is she?"

"She sat out in the garden this morning," Ben said. "She wanted to see the trees before the leaves fall."

"That's nice. They do look so lovely."

I led the way into the kitchen. There was enough suffering in this world, I thought; these two could stop suffering now, at least as far as love was concerned. I switched on the kettle to make three cups of tea.

Ben had been working at the big table. It was strewn with musical scores, upon which he had been penciling detailed notes. While I made the tea, he stood with his hands in his pockets, staring—glowering, actually—at Annabel.

I picked up my tea. "I'm going upstairs, just to peep at Phoebe," I said. "I promise not to wake her. I won't be back for ages."

"Cassie, wait—" Annabel made a grab at my arm, slopping tea on the wooden floor.

"Annabel wants to talk to you." I longed to stay. I longed to bang their heads together and force them to cut to the chase. Unfortunately, there are some things you have to let people do for themselves. Shutting the door behind me, I took my tea up to Phoebe's bedroom.

Upstairs, the house was hushed in heavy sleep. The door to Phoebe's room stood slightly open. I stole to the side of her bed and stared down at her still figure, propped on a cairn of pillows and scarcely breathing. I had last spent a night here two days before, and couldn't help checking her for visible signs of decline. I was aware of a mighty surge of protectiveness. It hurt me with a physical pain that cold winds could blow on her. I could see the delicate bones of her skull under the pale mist of flesh. When she slept, the real essence of Phoebe seemed horribly far away. I had to fight a primitive instinct to wake her, to bring her back to us. Oh help me, whatever powers there are that help the despairing.

I don't know how long I stood there. I looked at nothing but Phoebe's still profile, but was aware of the room around me, puzzlingly unchanged. She used to let us lie on her bed when we felt ill. I knew every curl of every rose petal on the faded chintz curtains. I could still find the particular pink rose that slightly resembled Hitler if you half closed your eyes. I remembered, as powerfully as if I'd been lying in her place, the coolness of the fat red eiderdown against a feverish cheek. This was the bed she had shared with Jimmy, and it still looked misshapen without him.

For a moment, death amazed me. How could vivid, breathing, laughing, loving people vanish so completely? There had to be some mistake.

Suddenly, I couldn't stand not being with warm, problematical living people. I crept out of Phoebe's bedroom and finished my mug of tea sitting on the stairs. The big kitchen and sitting room were very quiet. I had been nosy enough, I decided. I would wait until I was summoned.

The door opened. Ben came out into the hall. He looked absolutely dazed (Fritz would later say he looked as if he had electrodes fixed to his balls). His stunned eyes took me in. His face cleared a little.

"Oh, Cass," he said. "There you are." He smiled (another few thousand volts charging through the electrodes). "D'you happen to know where Mum put that bottle of champagne?"

Phoebe rang me at work the next day, bubbling over with joy. It was beautiful to hear.

"Don't mind me if I witter—I'm quite mad with happiness. Poor Annabel was afraid I'd think she was a slut—well, I suppose she is a bit of a slut, but sometimes it's just necessary. I'm glad my lovely future daughter-in-law is a bit of a slut. If she'd behaved like a perfect lady, none of these nice things would be happening."

"It seems so natural," I said. "So expected. I don't know why I was surprised."

"I know, right under our noses," Phoebe said. "A couple of times, when I've been talking to Annabel, I've wondered who she reminded me of. And of course, it's Ben. The two of them are just as sweet and silly as each other. I'm so happy that he's got Annabel to take care of him now. Oh, he's going to be a wonderful father—you should hear him talking about the baby. You'd think he'd planned it." Her voice was faint and breathless, but her giggle was as youthful as ever. "He went out and bought a magazine. Suddenly he has all sorts of opinions about night feeds and weaning—wouldn't Jimmy have howled?"

I asked, "Does Fritz know?"

"Not yet," Phoebe said, "but my guess is that he'll be as happy as I am."

Two nights later, when I went to do one of my stints with Phoebe, Fritz himself assured me that her guess had been right.

"Come on, what do you think? I'm deliriously happy. I thought I'd be looking after Ben till the crack of doom."

"Seriously."

"Never been more serious in my life, Grimble. Apart from anything else, the release from guilt is wonderful."

Peason asked, "What on earth did you have to feel guilty about?" She was irritable—I sensed that something had activated an old disagreement between them.

A spark of anger snapped in Fritz's dark eyes. "If you have to smoke," he said shortly, "open the window."

She sighed, took one pace toward the kitchen window and flicked ash into the sink. Fritz marched across to the window, opening it violently and loudly. Cold autumn air blasted into the warm room.

He turned back to me, as if Peason had become invisible. "I felt terrible about Annabel. That was a mistake I shouldn't have made—not with someone who can't fight back."

"You're right," I said (trying not to be intimidated by the magnificent sulkiness of Peason). "She's not a fighter."

"Neither is Ben. Imagine the harmony of their home."

"And Ben's forgiven you properly now?"

Fritz grinned. "God, yes. All is sweetness and light in our humble basement. I just wish he wouldn't keep hugging me."

It was early on a Sunday evening. Peason was dragging Fritz off to dinner somewhere in the country. Fritz couldn't leave until he had finished his detailed page of instructions. I could never persuade him to leave everything to me. It wasn't that he didn't trust me. He was superbly calm and confident, and a rock for us all to lean upon, but only when he felt he was in absolute control.

Peason, still in her coat, sighed and smoked beside the sink. She looked at her watch. "Are we ever going?"

"Please go," I said. "I know what to do. We'll be fine."

Fritz dropped his pen and leaned over to give me a quick kiss. "Okay, I've written down the new times for the drugs. You won't forget that the white pills are the really important ones?"

"I won't forget."

"And you'll call me if anything happens? Anything at all?"

"I swear."

"Okay, we'll get out. I'll just tell her we're leaving."

He ran upstairs. Peason and I were left alone together. I couldn't help arranging my face into a polite smile, but Peason stayed sullen. At some point, I had obviously fallen off her politeness list.

She said, "Fritz gave you his mobile number, didn't he?"

"Yes, of course."

"Look, will you do me a favor? Don't ring the number unless it's a real emergency. Bloody Ben's been ringing every five minutes."

I assured her that she could trust me not to bother her unnecessarily.

She sighed fretfully. "Frankly, I don't see why Ben has to be in our hair all the time. And now he's adding a wife and baby to the population downstairs. As it is, we're living in an absolute crowd. Why can't he stay with Annabel in her flat?"

"Because of Phoebe," I suggested, putting my hand behind my back so I didn't smack her.

"Oh. Yes. I see what you mean," Peason said. "Well, as long as they realize it can't carry on like this after she's gone."

Fritz came back into the room to collect this loathsome creature. His face was closed and slightly angry. He wasn't in love with her, of that I was sure. If he loved Peason we had lost him.

CHAPTER FIFTEEN

It was a beautiful wedding, all the more so because our joy was heavily spiked with sadness. Nobody said anything, but denial was no longer a possibility. Phoebe was fading before our eyes. Every day, her mooring among us became a little less secure. She was very happy, but she was floating away from us into the air.

As she grew lighter, the task of caring for her became heavier. She spent most of her days lying serenely in bed, her eyes half closed, but she needed constant watching. It hurt me to see my beloved lying helpless, and it hurt me that her boys had to see it. I have to record here—I wish it could be engraved on stone for all time—that Fritz and Ben were heroes. I have come to believe that caring for the helpless is the truest heroism on this earth, and their care of Phoebe was magnificent. Her pride in them took the sting out of her dependence.

When she couldn't sleep, Ben used to leave all the doors open and play the piano to her, sometimes far into the night. In the past, the rather scary people next door had complained about his nocturnal recitals. They never complained now. The scary woman only asked after Phoebe, and her husband left a bottle of wine on the doorstep for the boys. I learned that death, like birth, brings out amazing kindness in the most unexpected people.

Fritz was the rock of the household. In this situation someone has to be in charge, and we all automatically turned to Fritz. I can't imagine when he found time to sleep. *Rookery Nook* was still running in the West End. He had bagged himself another commercial (you'll definitely remember this one—he played the slob who magically transforms into Beau Brummel when his wife makes microwaveable coq au vin). Felicity continued to hold him in sexual thrall, but he somehow found the time to read aloud to Phoebe for hours, or to make her laugh with stories of the past. The past and the present were curiously mingled these days. We lived in both places.

The days chilled and shortened. Weeks slipped past, without any real sense of time passing. We were living in another dimension of reality. I found I couldn't settle to anything unless I was with Phoebe. I made stupid mistakes at work, and didn't give a damn (good old Betsy picked up the pieces). The only person I felt comfortable with, apart from Phoebe and the boys, was Annabel.

Darling Annabel, her kipper-begging days were over. She and Ben lived in a state of mutual worship—which could, if I'm honest, be a little cloying at times. On the whole, however, their love was sunshine in this sad house. One evening, when Phoebe lay sleeping upstairs, and the four of us sat around the table in the kitchen, Fritz said, "You two are serious about getting married, aren't you?"

"Of course!" Annabel cried, her mouth full of fruit cake.

"Well, you ought to do it as soon as possible, don't you think?"

He looked across the table at Ben. Their gazes locked. Ben was tense.

"What, you mean because she's pregnant?"

Fritz was gentle. "I mean, if you want Mum to be there."

Ben said, "Oh," breathlessly, as if Fritz had punched him.

"Is it going to be soon, do you think?" Annabel asked. Her great blue eyes filled.

"There's no way of knowing for sure," Fritz said. "But don't you think we should give her a wedding while she has the energy to enjoy it?"

Ben's eyes were also wet. "I'd marry Annabel tomorrow."

"I thought next week," Fritz said. "We can't do anything elaborate, but we'll make it as perfect as we can, on a small scale. You know what a traditionalist she is."

"Oh yes," I said. "Phoebe will want a church and a white meringue and the whole shooting match. But Fritz, we can't get all that together in a week!"

"Nonsense. Of course we can. And I particularly need your feminine input."

"I'll do anything I can, but I don't know any more about weddings than you do. You should ask Poison."

His smile became bitter. "Dear old Poisony—I did ask her, and she said she didn't want anything to do with it. I spend far too much time with my family, apparently."

I could hardly believe that anyone could be this self-centered. "She does know about Phoebe, doesn't she?"

"She can't understand anyone caring this much about a mere mother," Fritz said. "It's sad, really. And the saddest thing is that I can't make her see how sad it is." He smiled at me. "Anyway, I'd rather do the wedding with you."

"Great," I said. "I'd love to arrange a wedding—it might be my only chance."

Annabel reached out and squeezed my hand. "I won't let you say that. I said things like that till only recently, and look what happened to me, for goodness' sake."

"Cheer up, Grimble," Fritz said. "Winter is coming. Soon the moose will return to the plains to breed."

"Fritz, please. No more moose routines."

He smiled—one of his blazing smiles that warmed the whole room. "I have to be sure you're over him."

"Oh yes," Annabel assured him. "She doesn't even think about him."

"I was asking Cassie."

"I'm totally and utterly over him," I said. "Even to the point of being rather pleased for Honor."

"I told you the crew cut was another moose, darling. It's lovely for her, because she could do a lot worse. And she certainly won't do any better."

"Fritz!"

"Those two belong together. You're different."

"How?"

"You're prettier."

"Am I?"

Fritz fluttered his eyes girlishly and echoed, "Am I?"

"Okay, okay." I might have known I wouldn't get any more. Fritz didn't feel too many compliments were good for my character. But this one would do to be going on with.

The following day, Fritz and I met for a chilly sandwich lunch (we were both skint again) on a bench in Green Park to draw up our plans. Fritz had already spoken to the local vicar. This vicar, who knew Phoebe, was sympathetic. He arranged to do all sorts of complicated and archaic things (I think some kind of special license from the bishop was involved) so that we could have our traditional church wedding the following Friday.

Not to be outdone, I had consulted Betsy. Betsy had married three daughters and there was nothing you could tell her about arranging a reasonably priced yet tasteful wedding. With her help, I had made a list of essentials.

"There isn't an engagement ring," I said. "Can Ben afford one?"

"No," Fritz said, his mouth full of ham baguette. "But he doesn't have to. Mum wants him to give Annabel one of Granny's rings."

Jimmy's mother had left some lovely pieces of jewelry, which I had often played with on rainy afternoons when we were all little. I cried, "Oh yes—the one with the sapphire forget-me-nots! It'll look lovely on her."

"Nope. It's the emerald with diamond bits."

"Whatever." I crossed it off my list. "Thank God we don't have to pay for it."

"Yes, thank God," Fritz said, wincing at the mention of money. "But I'm not doing this on the cheap either. It means everything to Mum, and it's got to be perfect."

I couldn't have agreed more. For once, Fritz and I wanted exactly the same things and were in perfect accord. It felt wonderful. It sent me back to the office with a little pilot light of hope inside me.

That afternoon, Betsy, Shay and Puffin confronted me at my desk. They were solemn. For a moment I thought they were all going to resign, or file an official complaint against my editorship (they were spending a lot of time covering for me nowadays). But it turned out that they wanted to pay for the flowers, as a wedding gift. They all knew that I'd be paying for some of it—we were pooling our overdrafts because this was an emergency. I was deeply grateful to have something crossed off the final bill, and so moved by their kindness that I had to swallow several times before I could thank them.

"A bouquet for the bride, white buttonholes all round and an arrangement for the table," Betsy said. "With our love."

I didn't deserve to be loved by my colleagues. I took my body into work that week, but my mind was everywhere else. The truth was, I had absolutely set my heart on seeing Annabel married in a real bride's dress—a gorgeous great snow-white dress that would make her look like a plump orchid. This became an obsession. Annabel didn't care about anything except making love and eating, but I made her try on about a hundred bridal gowns. It is surprisingly difficult to find one of these in a hurry. They were all too pricey, too silly, too tacky or (most often) too small. Annabel's willowy blond form was, in every sense of the word, blooming. Her breasts had bloomed into Page Threes. Her bum had bloomed into a size I can't reveal because she'd never speak to me again. Why couldn't I find her a simple white dress with a plain bodice and full skirt? I spent hours on the phone and on the Net, searching in theatrical costumiers and antique clothes shops. I tried to find a Charles Dickens–cruel dressmaker, who would make forty fainting girls run up a frock in a ludicrously short time. I found nothing. Worse than nothing—dress after dress so terrible that we ended up in fits of laughter.

And then, when I was beginning to be desperate, the miracle happened. I really think it was a miracle. I was in a taxi, inching along a traffic jam on Kentish Town Road. We drew level with the Help the Aged shop—and I saw it.

It was hanging clumsily on a plastic model in the window, beside a blouson jacket in tan leather and a foot spa. And it was exactly what I'd had in my mind's eye—white fitted bodice, long, full white skirt, both perfect in their chaste simplicity. Great heaven, the Bluebird of Happiness had been in our own backyard all along, I had searched far and wide for Annabel's perfect dress, and here it was in the window of a local charity shop.

I got out of the taxi, my heart thudding—all my senses were, for some reason, in panic mode. I made myself walk right up to the window. The dress was even lovelier up close. And the size was generous. Please, let it not be sold.

It was not sold. It had only arrived that morning. According to the lady at the till, it had been brought in by a woman with a baby, who didn't like to be reminded how fat she'd become. I was glad to hear that the donor of the dress was still married—I wouldn't have liked Annabel to wear a Dress of Doom. And the detail of the baby felt promising, like some kind of fertility symbol.

The lady at the till said she couldn't take less than fifty pounds. I gave her a hundred, which was a fragment of my dress budget. And while she hunted for a large enough bag, I cradled the great bale of rustling white silk in my arms. There was no veil, but I remembered a rather fabulous white taffeta stole I'd seen in some bridal shop or other, which I could now afford. I had done it. Annabel was going to be a real bride.

I couldn't resist rushing it round to Annabel at once. She'd had a hospital appointment that afternoon, and was staying in the basement. When she opened the door to me we both spoke at the same time.

I said, "I've got the dress!"

And Annabel said, "It's twins!"

Yes, there were two of the little Darlings. Phoebe received the news like a gift. Her delight injected her with energy. On the magical, miraculous day of the scan and the dress, she felt well enough to sit downstairs for two hours. It was one of those happy evenings when time stopped.

That's all. Not much happened, except that we told funny stories about the past. We wanted to remember ordinariness. We wanted to pretend things were still ordinary. Phoebe spoke of Jimmy in a teasing way, as if he were listening in the next room. It was very strange, but not as sad as you might think. Not sad at all.

You know, even while they are happening, that the memories of these moments will be jewels to you afterward. You know you'll spend the rest of your life wishing you could climb back inside them.

We were to be a very small party. Annabel had decided to keep her turbulent parents out of the picture. "The two of them can't be in the same room, even after all these years," she reminded me. "Ben and I can visit them later."

I was sorry they would miss it, but only mildly. The antics of her parents had, over the years, caused Annabel a great deal of grief.

"All they cared about was having affairs," she said. "They made a big fuss of me, but they grabbed any excuse to fob me off on someone else. I'm sure everyone says this—but I'm going to do it differently. When my babies come, I'll never leave them for a single minute."

Ouch. Emotion. The revelation of Annabel as a mother, fondly patting her rounded stomach, was oddly moving. It occurred to me that all her kipper-begging propensities had found an outlet at last—but I couldn't think about it too long, because imagining a world with Annabel's babies also meant imagining one without Phoebe. We were all surviving by digging our heels into the present.

The only outsiders present at the wedding would be me, Neil (best man and maker of the cake) and Peason. We all thought it a pity that we had to have Peason, but Phoebe wouldn't hear of excluding Fritz's girlfriend.

"I know she's horrid," she said calmly, "but Fritz always has horrid girlfriends. We'll all have to make an extra effort to be nice to her."

She looked at me when she said this, and I hastily promised to be charm itself. I made a private vow, however, that if Peason said or did one thing to spoil Annabel's wedding, I'd break something over her head.

The weather gods were on Phoebe's side from the start. That Friday morning was hazy and smoke-scented, in golden autumn sunlight, rich but waning. I arrived at the house early, with my new pale gray suit sheathed in plastic. I found myself thinking, as I parked my car, how similar this felt to a funeral. Here was the same sense of dislocation from the real world, the same invisible wall between the ordinary and us.

I found Annabel in the basement, eating her way through a pile of toast. The hairdresser had called, and her blonde hair had been arranged around a wreath of pale pink roses. She was wearing nothing but an old plaid shirt of Ben's and a pair of old blue knickers, and looked as if her head belonged to someone else.

"Here's my matchmaker," said Phoebe. "Happy wedding day."

She sat in the wheelchair lent by the hospital, already wearing her dress of soft blue wool and her white corsage.

I bent to kiss her, suddenly giddy with happiness because—despite the obvious frailty of her wasted body—Phoebe looked so like herself. "What's going on? I thought you were supposed to stay in bed till the last minute."

"I was, but I felt extraordinarily brisk this morning. I decided to lend Annabel a little moral support."

Annabel giggled, and said, "I need all the support I can get—I'm sure my boobs have grown overnight."

I told her not to expect any sympathy from me. I was losing weight again, and I only ever took it off in one place.

Phoebe said, "My boobs vanished after I'd weaned Ben. I went to my cousin's wedding with a bra stuffed full of old tights. And of course one of my bosoms fell out during the speeches."

We all laughed. There was a sense of happiness that nothing could harm, a warm window overlooking desolation.

We had plenty of time. I made a pot of very strong coffee and took two cups upstairs, where Ben and Neil were waiting for Fritz to arrive with the suits.

"They're late." Ben was tense. "I bet it's Felicity's fault. Or maybe the hire shop was shut. Or maybe they had an accident."

I urged the poor agitated man to calm down. "Fritz has worked hard for this wedding," I reminded him. "He wouldn't dream of missing it."

"Don't take any notice," Neil said comfortably. "He does this before concerts."

Ben grinned suddenly. "Funny to hear you sticking up for Fritz. It's normally my job."

I thought about this as I went back downstairs. I wondered when I had turned into Fritz's cheerleader, after nearly a lifetime of criticizing him. These days, I realized, it wasn't really possible to criticize Fritz. Apart from his regrettable entanglement with Peason, he wasn't doing anything objectionable.

Downstairs, Phoebe was watching intently as Annabel carefully uncovered the white billows of her wedding dress. "Mind your hair—don't try to put it on without Cassie—"

The street door of the basement slammed. Fritz strode in. He had three gray top hats stacked on his head, and three suit bags over one arm.

Phoebe beamed at him. "Hello, darling. Where's Felicity?"

He was smiling, but wolfishly. "Unfortunately, she was called away at the last minute. She had to take a very fast train to Potters Bar."

Annabel and I telegraphed looks of astonished joy—Mother of Mercy, was this the end of Peason?

"What a pity," Phoebe said, full of compassion. "But you know, Fritz, you'll get over her awfully quickly. Because she isn't at all nice."

The anger left Fritz's face. He smiled down at her. "I'd noticed, thanks. Sorry if I'm a little late, but we were having a very important row—the one that ends with one of you storming out, while the other one shouts things that can't be taken back." He glanced over at me. "I'm not going to talk about it today. Don't even mention her. This is meant to be a celebration."

As far as I was concerned, the celebration was in full swing. Peason had exited stage left, the house lights were up and the drama was over. I was very curious to know exactly what the woman had done. It had to be something pretty dire—I couldn't remember ever seeing Fritz this angry.

"There's still plenty of time," I said. "Would you like some coffee?"

From the top of the basement stairs, Ben's voice yelled, "Fritz! Where've you been, you fucker?"

Fritz gave me a fleeting look of gratitude, for not going on about Peason. "I think I'd better go upstairs and put on my costume," he said.

He left us. We heard shouts overhead, and thundering footsteps.

Phoebe's rapturous eyes were huge in her wasted face. "It's time," she said. "Put the dress on, my darling. It's time to be a bride."

Annabel and I were both solemn and slightly self-conscious, as if this moment had been part of the ceremony. I lifted the dress down in my arms. Annabel held my hand to steady herself as she stepped into the skirt. I had let the waist out slightly, to accommodate the bump. When the hooks at the back were all fastened, it fitted Annabel's curves amazingly well. The white stole (upon which I had spent my remaining dress budget and then some) lay in a big gilded box on the table. I opened the box, parting the layers of tissue paper. Reverently, I shook out the gleaming folds of white silk taffeta. I draped it across Annabel's shoulders and stood back beside Phoebe to study the effect.

Annabel was perfect: a Juno in spun sugar; a mass of white with roses of the palest pink blushing in her fair hair.

Phoebe clasped her hands. "Oh, I've never seen anything lovelier! You look like a bride in a story!"

I set this apart as one of the most purely satisfactory moments of my life. I had found a bride for Phoebe's younger (and most worrying) son. True, I couldn't really take any credit as matchmaker, but this was Phoebe's dream coming true. I had helped to write her a happy ending.

She held out her hands. Annabel sprang forward to clasp them. She sank to her knees beside Phoebe's wheelchair, her skirts billowing around them both. Annabel kissed her, all blushing and in full bloom beside Phoebe's paleness.

I never will forget the sight of the two of them together. I thought how odd it was, that the happiest moments of one's life should feel so painful.

We made a surreal, sweet, melancholy procession along the street to the church. Ben and Neil, both immaculate in their hired morning suits, went first. Then Fritz, also immaculate, pushing Phoebe's chair. I walked beside Annabel, on a dry carpet of fallen leaves that stirred around the hem of her long dress. The trees in the street had turned the most glorious colors—copper, scarlet, ochre, orange. We moved slowly, and the leaves drifted slowly down around us in the still air, and it was all so strange.

After the ceremony, we were a different procession—euphoric and dazzled, gibbering with relief that the solemn part was over. Several of the neighbors called to us from their front doors. We sat down to the lunch I had prepared—three plump roasted pheasants, wrapped in parma ham, washed down with the finest wines that could be got on Fritz's overdraft. Neil made a speech, and sang "Annie Laurie," which made us all cry. We drank to the bride and groom, to their unborn, unimaginable twins, and to Phoebe. Ben proposed a toast to Fritz and me, thanking us for our hard labor.

Through all this, I watched Fritz as closely as I dared. He did not look like a man with a broken heart. He had elected himself Master of Ceremonies. He bullied us all into having a wonderful time. He made us laugh. He got us all slightly drunk. But there were moments in between when he looked older, and harder all over.

In the pearly light of the afternoon, I unpinned Annabel's dress and helped her into her "going away" ensemble of jeans and jersey.

She pushed her bouquet of pale pink roses into my hand. "This is for you, Cassie. I can't thank you enough. You've given me the happiest day of my life. I mean—despite Phoebe being so ill. I love Ben so much."

"You're supposed to throw the bouquet," I said.

She was serious. "I'd rather just give it to you. That way, I can be sure you'll be next."

I didn't think it likely, but this wasn't the time to protest about the bleakness of my romantic prospects. The newlyweds were going straight to Annabel's mother and stepfather in Aberdeen. Fritz pushed Phoebe's wheelchair to the front door, so that she could throw an old trainer after their taxi, for luck.

The moment they had gone, Phoebe collapsed. She was exhausted, barely able to hold up her head. Fritz carried her upstairs, and I helped her out of her blue dress. She was too tired even to apologize for her helplessness. Like a small child after a party, however, she wanted me to put her wedding corsage in a glass of water beside her bed.

"To remind me," she murmured, "what a lovely day it's been."

I left her in a state of beatific serenity, lying with her face turned toward the flowers.

Downstairs, I found Neil doing the washing-up, back in his normal clothes. He wouldn't allow me to help him. He poured me a glass of brandy with his soapy hands, and told me to take a glass to Fritz.

Fritz was outside, at the very end of the garden, beside the old climbing frame. Nobody had climbed on this for years. Weeds wound around the lower rungs, lashing it to the ground. There couldn't have been a sadder symbol of our growing up.

I gave him the brandy. He smiled. "Thanks. We deserve this, don't you think?"

"I'll say. We worked our tits off—literally, in my case."

"Come now, Grimble. I like your bonsai tits."

"Thanks."

"How has Mum survived, do you think?"

"She's dreadfully tired, but so happy she's practically radioactive."

207

Fritz said, "Mission accomplished, then." He gulped back the brandy. I noticed that he had not been drinking much today.

"It was a howling success," I said. "And I get paid today, thank God. So my overdraft lives to fight another day."

"So does mine—but only just," Fritz said.

"Are things really bad?"

He grinned ruefully. "Until we've sold this place, we're totally and absolutely fucked."

"Oh—fuck."

"I don't know how we're going to eat when the play finishes. I told my agent to send me up for any part that'll bring in some money. I might even ask Jonah if there's a hut going on the Heath."

"Can't I help out a bit?"

His smile became warm, and warmed me. "You're very sweet, but you know I'll manage. My agent says there's plenty around for me—if I really will do anything. Apparently, I have an ideal face for commercials. I might get another one."

"Won't you hate it?"

He shrugged, irritated. "So what? One job's pretty much like another."

"That's not what you used to say."

"My dear Grimble, one used to say all manner of fanciful things. You used to say you were going to marry the moose."

"Okay. Point taken."

Fritz absently tugged at the rope of weeds around the climbing frame. "The thing is, I don't really care any more. I don't give a fuck about anything except my mother. That was the main thrust of Felicity's gripe against me."

"Sorry," I said. "It's been a shit day for you."

"Not at all. I should've got rid of her ages ago."

I had to ask. "What happened this morning, exactly?"

"I told you. We had a row."

"About anything in particular?"

Fritz said, "She wanted to hire two professional nurses, so I wouldn't have to spend so much time looking after Phoebe. She offered to pay for them. When I explained I actually wanted to spend a lot of time with Phoebe, she went berserk. Said I was selfish."

"God almighty—this, from the Queen of Selfish!"

He took my hand. "It's all right. I wasn't in love with her, and sex isn't everything. I was beginning to think we'd done all the positions. And I turn out to have only a limited appetite for that kind of sex anyway. I'm tired of screwing someone I don't love."

"You're too good for her. She doesn't deserve you."

Fritz put his arms around me. He stared down at me for what seemed ages. Tears slid down his cheeks.

He said, "She's asked to go into the hospice."

It was extraordinary how quickly the world could darken and freeze around us. I whispered, "Why? Is she feeling worse?"

"I don't think so. This is just the way she wants to do it. She insists that we mustn't make a fuss."

"Well, we won't," I said, as staunchly as I could. "And it will be easier, Fritz. You and Ben won't have to worry that she's not getting the right care. And you won't need me so much."

He unwound his arms, but kept hold of my hand. "No, you're wrong," he said. "I can't go into the twilight zone without you, Cassie. I'm going to need you even more."

CHAPTER SIXTEEN

The world was contracting around us, until it was no bigger than a walnut shell and contained nothing but Phoebe. Two days after the wedding, she moved into the hospice. I'm not sure how this made me feel. I know I was afraid, but I didn't think about the future. It seemed irrelevant while Phoebe was still so very present among us. My life fell into a new routine, and I thought and behaved as if it would last indefinitely.

I would leave the office a little earlier than usual and take the tube up to Belsize Park. There was a flower stall outside the station. I often bought something I knew Phoebe would like—velvety red roses, chrysanthemums with big russet heads, lilies of the valley that filled a whole room with their soapy scent. I walked up Haverstock Hill, marveling at the ordinary evenings ahead of everyone else in the hurrying crowds. I didn't envy them, exactly. I think I felt slightly afraid of them and their glorious ignorance of life's fragility.

The hospice was a large modern building on a quiet street. Inside, there were smiles and silences, and an atmosphere of drugged calm. The nurses and doctors here were in the business of easing people through their last breaths, ensuring that their eyes closed on this world gently, and without pain. They were, I suppose, midwives in reverse.

Phoebe was in a small single room, which overlooked a car park and a row of back gardens. Plastic tubes snaked out of her shrunken body. She was very weak. Her soft voice had worn to a whisper. If I found her alone, she would be lying with her eyes half closed, in a sleep that was like a trance. And I would murmur her name as if calling her back. Whenever she slept, she traveled a little further. Returning became more of a struggle. But the old Phoebe still smiled out of her eyes at me when she woke. She was still interested in the coarse bustle of the mortal world, and wanted to know about my concerns. Phoebe herself was my only concern, but I gamely fed her snippets of gossip from work, and friendly messages from Betsy.

I didn't often find Phoebe alone. One of the boys was usually with her. Annabel and Ben had returned from Scotland after a couple of days, so that Ben could sit beside her. He and Fritz took turns to stay the night. A steady stream of friends called, bringing such bales of flowers that we were constantly fretting over what to do with them all. There was a kind of elation in the room with her, not unlike hope, though it was hope's exact opposite. We none of us found it difficult to be cheerful.

On two occasions, Betsy came with me after work. She didn't say much, but sat beside Phoebe's bed, knitting briskly, smiling in a motherly way when anyone turned toward her.

At the end of her last visit, she kissed Phoebe, and said, "I owe you a debt of gratitude. If you hadn't put marriage into Cassie's head, she'd never have introduced my Jonah to Hazel." (Completely illogical, but it's the thought that counts.)

One afternoon, I was touched to find Matthew and Honor in Phoebe's room. Honor was embarrassed to see me, but the whole episode of the oral sex was ancient history now. Phoebe was highly pleased to see them both, and that was what mattered. If she'd been stronger, she would have laughed. As it was, her eyes were laughing. This made me feel terrifically fond of both Matthew and Honor.

Outside the room I kissed them warmly. "Thanks so much for coming. Phoebe loved seeing you."

Matthew said, "I loved knowing her. And this must be very—" He broke off, to sift his brain for the right word. "*Tough* for you. Are you okay?"

The expression in his eyes was genuinely tender. I felt the familiar, painful stab of tears in my throat. "Oh, I'm fine."

"Do call, any time," Honor said. "I'm—I'm not at the old number any more. I've moved in with Matthew."

Poor thing, her huge gray eyes were radiant with happiness, pleading for my approval. I was fond of her, and I couldn't help being pleased that she had found her true love. And I didn't want him, did I? I kissed her again, to show that there were no hard feelings, and promised to go to dinner with them. Fritz made moose faces at me for the rest of the day.

Far more surprisingly, my mother called, to announce that she and George would be visiting the following day. I can't explain why I was surprised. There wasn't an ounce of sentimentality in Ruth, and I suppose I didn't expect her to want a formal good-bye. But of course, I realized suddenly, she wanted Phoebe to meet George. She needed Phoebe to see the story's happy end.

I took yet another afternoon off work, to meet them at the station. Ruth kissed me firmly, holding my face between her hands.

She said, "This is very hard for you."

Her sympathy was not the demonstrative sort, but I felt its strength and depth. I felt that she knew a lot about death. I felt she was reminding me that she belonged to me. I'd been dreading her visit, and in the end found it sustaining. I took them both out for an early supper before their train back to the coast, and what had started as a chore turned into a pleasure (I date my respect and liking for George back to that supper).

Ruth said, "I hope you'll come to me for Christmas. If you're there, I'll have an excuse to do it properly."

I hadn't thought about Christmas. It was Phoebe's time of year. The sound of the word flashed a series of archetypal images through my head, all centered around Phoebe—kissing Jimmy under the mistletoe in the hall, hanging up a stocking for me over the fireplace, making the whole house smell of warm gingerbread and spices. Surely the world would end before Christmas could happen without Phoebe. I pushed the whole idea away.

"You mustn't stay here," Ruth said. "It's never good to spend these festivals alone after a bereavement. You'll be too sad."

Possibly—but we were not sad now. There was to be no more sadness at the end of Phoebe's life than there had been at its beginning. We were all determined to inhabit every second as fully as possible while the circle was closing. The old friends kept on coming. The boys handed round cups of tea and glasses of champagne, as if hosting a cocktail party. I couldn't sleep, and took to making biscuits in the middle of the night, while listening to the World Service. I pressed these upon Phoebe's visitors, and left them out in the communal kitchen for the friends and relations of the other patients. I made those bloody biscuits as if the hospice depended on them. I had to be doing something, to keep my thoughts on small things—flour, cocoa powder, sultanas. If I absolutely refused to contemplate the future, I was almost happy.

I could see now that it had been right to bring Phoebe here. She was more comfortable than she had been at home. The everyday cares of the household fell away from her. She had stopped living in real time, and existed in a kind of remote bubble of serenity, halfway between the two worlds. The breathless atmosphere among us, as if waiting for a birth, quickly overwhelmed my life. I felt I had been living in this routine forever.

One particularly happy afternoon, we were all gathered in Phoebe's room—Ben, Fritz, Annabel and me. Phoebe smiled on her bank of pillows. She didn't really want to join in our conversation. Sensing that she liked listening to us, we talked among ourselves, looking at her often, to show that we were including her.

Annabel had brought a photograph of her most recent scan. It looked like a satellite picture of the weather.

Ben tenderly pointed out two fuzzy blobs. "Aren't they sweet?"

Annabel crunched one of my biscuits and reached out for another one. "I can't believe how much they're making me eat. I'm never not hungry."

"That's a good sign, darling," Phoebe whispered. "I like to see you eating."

Annabel giggled. She pulled up her baggy shirt to show the gaping zip of her jeans, insecurely held together with Ben's tie. "It's a good thing Ben likes fat girls."

"I don't," Ben corrected her. "I like *you*. Fat or thin."

He snatched her hand and kissed it. The two of them were still high on their honeymoon bliss. I know Phoebe loved to observe it. She could see that Annabel would protect her boy from the worst of the coming sorrow. I knew that Fritz was also aware of this. It was family policy to protect Ben, officially the Sensitive One. Fritz didn't have any such insulation himself, but he didn't act as if he needed it—I might as well have dreamed the tears. He was tough and cheerful. He ransacked his old medical textbooks, so that he could assault nurses and doctors with his professional knowledge and make sure Phoebe got the very best of everything. He was her voice and her armor, and her joy.

Phoebe said, "Cassie hasn't heard your news."

I looked at Fritz. "News?"

He smiled at me. "She means my fantastic new job."

I knew, because I was the one Fritz confided in, that the money situation was dreadful. His West End run had finished, and he desperately needed some kind of income to service the huge family debt.

"Congratulations," I said lightly. "What is it—the dog food commercial or the year in *The Mousetrap*?"

"Even better. My dear old agent found me a sudden vacancy in a pantomime."

"Seriously?"

Phoebe's eyes were candles of pride. "Isn't it wonderful? I do so wish I could see him. You know how I love a pantomime."

I did indeed. When we were little, Phoebe had taken us to a pantomime every Christmas. We'd enjoyed the shows, but the real pleasure had been watching Phoebe's passionate involvement. She would cry, "Oh no he doesn't!" and "Behind you!" with her whole heart. She would boo and hiss the villain with real indignation.

But it seemed, to say the least, an odd career move for Fritz.

He raised his eyebrows at me, as a warning not to communicate any doubts to Phoebe. "I need your mother's phone number," he said.

"Ruth's?"

"The panto's in her town. Phoebe said she might take me as a lodger."

The idea of this was simply too bizarre to take in properly—Fritz in a pantomime! Lodging with Ruth! "I suppose she might." My thoughts were racing. This could mean that Fritz and I would spend Christmas under the same roof. My whole body went hot, with mingled desire and embarrassment.

"He's playing Wishee-Washee," Phoebe whispered.

"It's *Aladdin*, then," I said. "Your favorite."

She smiled approval. "Good girl. I've trained you well."

"I'm not following," Annabel complained. "Who's Wishee-Washee?"

"Wishee-Washee is Aladdin's less sexy brother," Fritz said. "Rather like poor Ben here."

"Fuck off," Ben said serenely. He laid his head down on the bed, beside Phoebe's hand.

Slowly, Phoebe raised her shaking hand to stroke his hair. "Tell Cassie who's playing the Widow Twanky. "

Fritz grinned at me. "Len Batty."

"What—as in 'Ay-up Mother?' "

"The same."

Despite the absurdity of Fritz appearing in a seaside panto, I was rather impressed. This was *the* Len Batty, the northern comic who had been a television fixture since the year dot. "Ay-up Mother" was his rallying call and catchphrase, and I should think even the Queen knew it. For the first time in his dismal acting career, Fritz would be playing alongside a legend. No wonder Phoebe was thrilled. I had a suspicion that he was partly doing it to please her, never mind the money. She would never see his Wishee-Washee, but this didn't seem to bother her. The whole world of the Christmas pantomime belonged to the happy dream of the past. Jimmy had loved pantos too. He had once (the boys and I nearly died of shame) performed the Chicken Dance onstage with Danny La Rue. You can just imagine the merriment that ensued when Mr. La Rue found out what Jimmy did for a living.

"I think it's fab," Annabel said. "At long last Fritz is in something that isn't either very weird or very boring. I don't have to live in dread of seeing it."

We all—including Phoebe—laughed at this.

"I think we should celebrate," I said. "I happen to have a bottle of champagne in the fridge. Why don't I open it?"

We drank a lot of champagne at the hospice. This was not, however, because we were foolishly extravagant. We'd found that Phoebe still enjoyed tasting a few drops of the stuff. I was going bankrupt buying it, and I didn't care.

"I'll come with you," Fritz said.

I had left my bottle of Oddbins Special Offer Premier Cru in the fridge of the communal kitchen at the end of Phoebe's corridor. In this kitchen we would often meet other watchers from other rooms, headed for the same shipwreck. We passed each other around the kettle, exchanging pale smiles like dazed spirits newly arrived in the underworld.

Today, however, the kitchen was empty. Fritz began to search the cupboards for wine glasses.

"This job," I said. "Is it for real?"

"I'm afraid so. I got it at the last minute. The original Wishee-Washee's gone down with shingles."

"Well, I hope the money's okay."

Fritz leaned against the white Formica counter. "Not bad."

"It all helps," I offered.

He smiled at me—one of his rare, intimate smiles. "I know it's ridiculous. But I honestly don't mind making a dick of myself. All I care about is getting by until we sell the house."

"Shouldn't I be helping a bit more? I don't feel as if I'm doing enough."

"Oh, Cassie. You have no idea how much you're helping." He surprised me by putting his arms around me. "It helps me to see you, to hear you—" He bent his head down to kiss me. We kissed for a long time. We drank at each other's mouths, gulping thirstily at life. I wanted to press every cell of his body into mine. I wanted to climb inside him. When he pulled his face away, my entire being was blushing, from the core outward.

He held my shoulders. "Cassie," he said breathlessly, "I'm going to ask you the most enormous favor. I won't hold it against you if you say no, but it's for Phoebe."

I said, "You know I'll do anything."

"She's still fretting about me, and I can't bear it." His grip tightened. "This is the favor. Would you let me tell her we're engaged?"

I had just breath enough to squeak, "Sorry?"

"We don't have to go through with it—just tell her."

"You want me to pretend to be engaged to you? You want to lie to Phoebe?" I was hurt that Fritz obviously didn't truly want me, but found myself struggling with a perverse desire to laugh. "We can't!"

"Why not? Think how happy it would make her!"

"I can't lie to her, Fritz." This was true. I didn't mean it in the honorable, George Washington sense, either. I meant that I really couldn't lie to

Phoebe—even when dying, she'd see through me in a second. "We'd never get away with it."

"But Cassie, if we could convince her, it would remove her one final worry—she wouldn't have a single care left in the world." He lowered his voice. It became dangerously caressing. "I'd find it a very easy part to play. It would be a very convincing portrayal of a man in love." He went on staring down into my face, holding my shoulders. "You're very lovely, Cass. She knows I fancy you."

"You fancy lots of people."

He laughed softly, not at all shamefaced. "All right—she knows you fancy me."

"Oh, really?"

"Don't try to deny it. Here we both are, Grimble—young and strong and extremely attractive. Of course we fancy each other. We wouldn't be natural if we didn't. Now, where's the harm in playing it up a little?"

When he put it this way, it was hard to see the harm. And I had to admit, seeing Fritz and me together would send Phoebe into the next world on a cloud of bliss.

"All right," I said. "Let's go for it. Let's finish the job in style."

"Thanks, you won't regret it." He planted one solemn kiss on my forehead. "Try not to contradict my account of our courtship."

"Oh, I can't wait. I bet it's romantic."

He said, "Seriously, thanks."

I said, "Seriously, you know I'd do anything to make her happy."

"Don't say anything to Ben and Annabel, by the way. I'll fill them in later."

"Okay."

Without another word, we took the champagne and the glasses back to Phoebe's room.

We drank the champagne. I fed Phoebe her usual tiny sip, which she rolled slowly round her tongue. Ben and Annabel left soon afterward. Ben had a concert with Neil. He said he would come back when it was over. He leaned over the bed to kiss Phoebe.

She whispered, "I hope the concert goes well."

"I'm coming back later. I'll tell you all about it—don't I always?" He blew her another kiss at the door.

Phoebe's eyes followed Ben out of the room. She smiled to herself, and her lips moved.

Fritz asked, "What?"

She hadn't been talking to us. Her clouded eyes cleared. She drew Fritz into focus.

He flicked a look at me and took my hand. This was our moment. When it came to the point, I was ridiculously nervous.

"Mum," Fritz said. "Darling, Cassie and I have something to tell you. We've discovered that we absolutely adore each other. We're getting married."

I think of this as the single most rewarding moment of my life. As I watched, joy poured into her wrecked body, filling her dim eyes with light.

She whispered, "Wonderful." Her eyes turned toward me. "You're just the right girl for him. I always knew it."

Fritz said, "Yes, you were right all along. Now you can stop fretting that Cassie won't have anyone to look after her. Because I'll be doing it."

Phoebe's lips, faintly curved into a beatific smile, moved.

"Sorry, darling—can't hear." Fritz put his ear close to her mouth. "What is it?"

"Granny's ring."

"Oh, you mean the one with the sapphires. You want me to give it to Cass."

Phoebe whispered, "It will look so sweet on her little paw."

"You're right," Fritz said, smiling at me. "It could've been made for her."

"And the pearl necklace is in the top drawer. I've been saving it for your bride."

There was so much I wanted to say, and I didn't need to say it. Phoebe and I gazed our love into each other's eyes, straight through the vein and into the heart. I bent over the bed and planted a kiss on her thin cheek. The texture of her skin felt different—tepid, and a little clammy.

"Darling Cassie." Phoebe gave me a sleepy smile. "My little brown bear. How happy you've made me."

I had made her happy. What else mattered? I gave her another longer kiss. The backs of my eyes were hurting, and I left the room before anyone saw.

Fritz followed me out into the corridor. He held my arm. "Cass, wait. Are you okay?"

"Of course." I had to go home to cry. Tears were wrong in this place, because they belonged to the world.

He wouldn't let me go. "Are you sure?"

"Yes. Absolutely sure. For God's sake, don't worry about me."

"You saw her. We made her happy."

"We mustn't spoil the effect now," I said. "I'll wear the ring for a bit, if you want."

Fritz said, "Good idea—she'll adore that. I'll fetch it when I go home for a shower."

But he didn't go home, and the blue forget-me-not ring stayed in the drawer.

The call came when I was at work, at about three o'clock the following afternoon.

It was Fritz, and he simply said, "She's gone."

CHAPTER SEVENTEEN

Wherever I seek for her now in this world, she cannot be found; no more than a flower or a leaf which withered twenty years ago.

That's not me. Poor Charlotte Brontë, high priestess of bereavement, wrote those words, but they express my despair at the finality of it all. How did I feel? Be patient with me. Remembering means going back into that peculiar emotional soup of dread, relief, horror, elation and sheer unreality.

At the exact moment of the phone call, all I could think about was Fritz. He was as calm as ever, but I knew there was a world of desolation waiting to claim him.

"Are you all right? And Ben?" I ached for both of them, still trying to bury my own anguish under a show of efficiency. "Where are you? Tell me what I can do to help."

"Come to the house," he said. "We need you."

"I'll be right there."

I put the phone down.

My three colleagues were standing in a mournful cluster behind me—they had sensed the bad news like a hive of bees.

I said, "Phoebe's gone. Apparently she slipped into a coma last night. It happened about half an hour ago. Fritz says it was very peaceful. Both the boys were with her."

I was calm, and I thought I was very collected. But I blundered around the office in a glassy-eyed daze, finding all kinds of pointless things that had to be done before I could leave. I had to be pulled together and pushed out of the door by my dear old colleagues.

Betsy, her eyes leaking tears, put motherly arms around me and made me a cup of tea. Shay put in a slug of something from the flask in his pocket. Puffin ran downstairs to fetch me a cab. All three of them had a whip-round when I remembered I had no cash. In the middle of that dark afternoon, I rode through town in a taxi, watching all the thick-skinned immortals milling around me. I had imagined I would be inconsolable when it happened, yet I didn't break down. It didn't seem real. There had to be another development. The drama couldn't be over.

Annabel opened the door to me. We clasped each other wordlessly. I followed her into Phoebe's kitchen. The fact that it didn't look at all strange was immensely strange. She could so easily have been asleep upstairs.

I don't remember much fine detail for ages after that. I do remember an atmosphere of excitement and elation, of bustle and urgency and domestic catastrophe, of us all milling about thanking each other—God knows for what.

I remember Ben sobbing on Fritz's shoulder, and Fritz's arms clasped protectively around him. I remember Annabel, with such gentleness, making us all cups of tea, her mouth and her eyes full. I remember no fewer than seven inconsolable neighbors calling round with bottles of red wine. I don't know why mourning and red wine should go together, but this was what people assumed we would need. I remember that we knocked it back like medicine, without getting remotely drunk.

We sat at the table, talking and drinking furiously. At most points, one or other of us would be in tears. Sometimes we were all in tears. And then we'd all be shrieking with laughter. Grief, when it is this pure, puts you in a curiously elevated place. We had traveled with Phoebe this far into the light, and not yet accepted that we could go no further.

At midnight, Annabel (who needed to sleep as much as she ate) told Ben it was time to go downstairs to the basement and to bed.

Poor Ben was exhausted. Neither he nor Fritz had had a proper night's sleep in days. I was deeply thankful that he had Annabel to lean on now. Her love wrapped and wadded him like a warm cocoon—a spiritual Cotton House.

Ben said, "But I can't—shouldn't I—" He stopped, and looked bewildered. "I keep forgetting, there's nothing to do. I keep getting worried because we're not listening for her."

Annabel murmured, "Oh sweetheart! But you can rest now. You can let me take care of you."

Ben said, "Okay, precious one."

The minute the basement door closed behind this pair of turtledoves, Fritz assumed a mournful, faintly gormless expression, and echoed, "Okay, precious one."

"Stop it." I was laughing.

"Sorry, Grimble. But even in these tragic circumstances, I can't help noticing that my brother is a great big wendy."

"You're awful."

"Why? I'm just as bereaved as he is."

This was true. Though Fritz didn't show his feelings in the way that Ben did, I knew he was struggling angrily with sorrow.

I poured him more red wine.

"Thanks," he said. "And Cassie—thanks for doing the engagement thing. She went out without a care in the world, and it's entirely due to you. We can break off our betrothal now."

"I won't sue you for breach of promise," I said. We smiled painfully. Our false engagement looked faintly comic now. We both wondered how much we had really meant to each other during our charade, but this was not the right time to ask.

Fritz said he wasn't hungry, but I made him cheese and onion on toast anyway, from Phoebe's recipe. While I prepared the food, he gradually sank into a dark, weary silence.

We were both starving, and both of us were full after a few mouthfuls. Yet more red wine was consumed, and no amount of it could make us drunk. And then Fritz told me the story of Phoebe's last hours. It poured out of him like the confession of a man who has witnessed a cross between a car smash and an apparition of the Blessed Virgin.

The details of a death are as intimate (and as universal) as the details of sex. That is to say, it was the usual sort of death, and it would be wrong to reveal any more. All anyone needs to know, to put the last stitches into the sampler of Phoebe's life on earth, is that she died as gracefully as she had done everything.

I had expected to hear Phoebe's voice inside my head, and there was nothing. When I needed her most, and sent out the most desperate calls for some sign that she was still among us, the silence was as endless as the universe.

I dressed for the funeral with an angry sense that I'd been conned. Life was shit. What was the point of it, when death came along and ruined everything? And knowing about death, how could the world go on?

I didn't want to wear black. Somehow, black was too somber to be associated with Phoebe, and too theatrical, like dressing up. I wore the gray suit I'd bought for the wedding, mainly because it was clean. I dithered over tights and shoes. Would fishnets make my grieving seem insincere? How long could I bear to stand around on high heels? As for the vexed question of lipstick—well, my Brownie Book of Poise contained nothing about suitable makeup for a funeral. But I had to smear something on my ghastly white lips, and I dithered further over which color made me look least tubercular. I was nauseous and giddy from lack of sleep.

In the end I had to hurry, because George wanted to get into the bathroom. Yes, Ruth and George were staying with me for two nights. I'd dreaded this, and it turned out to be comforting. Sometimes, when the void was blackest, the contemplation of my own loneliness drove me to despair. Ruth knew this, and made me aware of belonging to her. Perhaps because of dear old George, who couldn't help being cheerful (he hummed and pom-pommed round the flat all day), my mother and I talked with less caution than usual.

"You should make an effort to go out more, you know," Ruth had said, on the night before the funeral. "You have a gregarious nature. You can't spend all your time shuttling between here and the office. This isn't a good time to be solitary."

"I don't want to be solitary," I said. "But all my friends are deep in coupledom, and madly happy—and when I go round to their houses, I feel like Banquo. And I don't have the energy for polite conversation. What I crave is intimacy, and there's nobody I can be intimate with."

Ruth said, "Careful. In that state, you'll marry the first man who asks."

I assured her that I would be cautious. I had not told her about my short, ghostly engagement to Fritz. Neither of us had mentioned this again. Yet it had left me with an aching awareness of how much I loved him.

Oh Phoebe, where are you? You left before it was over.

Phoebe's funeral was held in the biggest chapel at the Golders Green Crematorium; a hangar of varnished wood, unctuous hush and sterile flowers. I remember a large courtyard, crammed with lively people, and undertakers chatting amiably beside an empty hearse. Fritz and Ben, resplendently handsome in their dinner party suits, were being accosted by practically everyone they had ever met—from Dr. Nboki (father of Claudette) who had delivered them, to their teachers, schoolmates, colleagues, friends and neighbors. We were all here because we had loved Phoebe, and lost her.

I was frozen with disappointment. Somehow, deep in my subconscious, I had hoped that Phoebe—something of Phoebe, at least—would be here to say a proper good-bye. And she was more absent than ever. Her voice was not on the rolling air, nor where the waters run, nor bloody anywhere. The reality of never seeing her again began to bite.

Once again, I'm remembering a lot of it in a series of snapshots—faces and voices, scraps of impressions. The day was cold. My smart suit was thin. I couldn't stop shivering. I had intended to sit with Ruth and George. At the last minute, however, when the great crowd began to move toward the wooden seats, an arm went round my waist.

Fritz said, "Come and sit with us. She was yours too."

I was immensely, humbly grateful for this recognition. I joined Ben and Annabel at the front. Annabel took my chilled hand.

Ben whispered, "Hi, Cassie."

"Hi, Ben. How are you?"

"I don't know. How're you?"

I didn't know either. How were any of us? At this moment, I didn't think I would ever feel like shedding tears. I could only stare at the pale wood of the coffin, and the smooth edges of its brass handles, and wonder idly who had ordered the heap of white roses on the lid. I could not connect it with Phoebe—except when suddenly assaulted by a lightning vision of her body lying inside it, which would make me momentarily giddy. I looked in my bag for the packet of tissues I had bought at the newsagent's, placed it on the little ledge in front of me and immediately felt stupid. They looked melodramatic, as if I were claiming too high a place in the order of grieving. I dropped them back in my bag.

It was a good funeral. We had hymns—"The Day Thou Gavest, Lord, Has Ended," and "Jerusalem." Neil sang "The Land of the Leal," raising an aching lump in my throat. Ben stood up to read his mother's best-beloved poem, Keats's "Ode to a Nightingale." He read it very well, inviting us to hear Phoebe herself as Philomel, her sweet voice fading over the glades into the next valley.

And all this time the coffin lay a few feet in front of us, terrible and undeniable.

The kind vicar who had married Ben and Annabel made a little speech about a character called Phoebe, who seemed to bear only the vaguest resemblance to the Phoebe I had loved. I drew a breath that came out as a sob.

Fritz whispered, "Chin up, Grimble," and passed me a tissue.

The vicar nodded to him. Fritz stood up. The packed chapel fell eerily silent as he took his place at the lectern, beside the ghastly coffin. I thought how strong he looked, and how beautiful, and how incredibly, ridiculously proud of him Phoebe would have been.

Fritz suddenly smiled. The smile cut through the atmosphere like a blade of light.

He said, "I'm supposed to be telling you what Phoebe was like—but you all knew her. And you know she wouldn't want to be remembered in a funereal sort of way. That wasn't her at all. So I don't think we should say good-bye to her like this, because our grief is our problem—it shouldn't have anything to do with the essence of Phoebe. Father David did all the stuff about her being a perfect mother. Now I want everyone to think about what it was like to know her."

He spoke—with a gentle humor, full of affection—about her sense of fun, her soft heart and her innocent love of interference. He reminded us that Phoebe had been a leading Nosy Parker, and that knowing her had often involved maddening amounts of trouble. He told famous stories of her daftness.

"For instance, the Christmas when she had a terrible dream about burglars stealing all our presents. She was so convinced this would happen that she slept under the tree on Christmas Eve, clutching the poker. Dad was absolutely furious to find her there in the morning."

The lump in my throat had begun to soften. I found that I was smiling. Yes, I remembered that particular Christmas. I'd gone round for lunch (I was always included), and Jimmy had met me in a state of boiling indignation. "I tell you, Cassie, if that daft woman so much as mentions ever again that she's had a prophetic dream, I'll divorce her." I'd already heard the shouting through the wall, and wondered what was up.

"It wasn't a famous life, or a distinguished life," Fritz said. "But it was full of achievement because it was a happy and satisfied life—and because she had such a gift for sharing the happiness. The fact of knowing Phoebe made people's lives better, and I can't think of a greater achievement than that. Wherever Phoebe was, there was light and laughter—and hospitality. If she could, she'd have sat the whole world at her table, and fed them until they begged for mercy."

More people were smiling now. There was a kind of collective breath, like a sigh of relief.

Fritz said, "I think we should all remember the dishes we loved, that Phoebe loved to make for us. Personally, I couldn't get enough of her beef stew with Guinness. My brother would still do anything for her chocolate cream pie. Little Cassie from next door was addicted to her Bakewell tart." (Oh yes—the smells of warm raspberry jam and almonds waft around me now.) Fritz gave me a special, intimate smile. He then smiled round at us all, taking in the people crammed into the gallery. "Come on," he said. "Think about food. Let's have more nominations."

There was a silence, rather tense and awkward.

A female voice, from somewhere in the middle of the congregation, timidly offered, "Damson chutney."

"Thank you," Fritz said. "Come on—get your memories and your salivary glands working."

It was like an auction. There was a general stirring of interest, and more silence. Fritz waited patiently.

Someone called, "Pheasant bordelaise!"

After that, they came in thick and fast.

"Ginger pudding!"

"Plum duff!"

"Ham and lentil soup!"

Then, the loud voice of the boys' old headmaster—"Spotted dick!"

And the whole chapel dissolved into a warm hum of laughter.

Someone else shouted, "Marmalade!"

More laughter—and a round of applause, starting cautiously, then rolling on and on. The mood lifted. At last we had evoked the spirit of Phoebe. She hovered over us and scattered herself among us like a summer breeze. We applauded thunderously. Now we were clapping the entire performance and wishing we could call for an encore.

"I was waiting for someone to mention the marmalade," Fritz said. "It was deservedly celebrated. When you all leave this chapel, you'll be handed a piece of paper containing the recipe. Ben and I want you to make Phoebe's marmalade for yourselves, because we think it's exactly how she'd want to be remembered."

And in fact, that is what I remember most distinctly about Phoebe's funeral—not the blur of the coffin sliding away behind the curtains, leaving behind a horrible polished void, but the undertakers handing out copies of Phoebe's most famous recipe. Everybody took one, and I saw more than one person reading it while we were all milling about outside, looking at the flowers (incidentally, what an awful part of a funeral this is—all flowers are hideous at funerals, I think because they look so dead). I saw a couple of women I knew to be good cooks murmuring to each other, nodding approval.

"So *that's* how she did it," one of them said.

I can testify that there wasn't a Seville orange to be had next day, in the whole of northwest London.

Fritz had ended his funeral oration with an invitation and a request. The invitation was to an informal wake back at the house. The request was for alcohol, which the Darlings couldn't afford. And I have to say, the friends and neighbors came down handsomely. George and Ruth brought four bottles of malt whiskey. The slightly scary couple next door produced a whole case of champagne. Betsy, her daughter Sally, Jonah and my dear old friend Hazel each dragged in a clinking bag of red wine.

There is something about a funeral that inspires an almost pagan jollity. Barely an hour after the velvet curtains closed on Phoebe's coffin, we were all as sozzled and merry as Christmas puddings. I think that once the emotional part of a funeral is over, people are giddy with the sheer relief of being alive and belonging to the world.

We didn't mind the party atmosphere. Not at all. Fritz absolutely revelled in it. He and Ben poured wine. Annabel and I made vats and vats of spaghetti. The sitting room and kitchen were crowded with animated people, all talking, drinking, eating and even laughing. Phoebe's last party was going with a real swing.

I lost all track of time, but I think it was dark when I registered that I hadn't seen Fritz for ages. The party had reached a stage where everyone was full of food, and happily helping themselves to booze. Nobody appeared to need looking after. The friends were lapsing back into sociability, and the relatives were avidly exchanging news. I climbed upstairs, above the noise.

The door to Phoebe's bedroom stood slightly open. There was lamplight inside, for all the world as if Phoebe herself were still propped up in bed, with her blue cardigan round her shoulders, her reading glasses pushed up on her forehead, turning the pages of a magazine—see how easy it is to slip back? Remembering was a constant effort.

I pushed open the door. The room still smelt of her; of roses and sponge cake. The scent lingered deep in the drawers, and inside the white-painted cupboards.

Fritz was sitting on the bed, crying. He didn't stop when I sat down beside him. I gave him a tissue, from the emergency supply inside my bra.

He said, "Thanks."

I didn't put my arms round him. We sat for a few minutes in silence, listening to the chatter downstairs.

I asked if I could fetch him anything. "A glass of wine, some tea? Something to eat?"

"No, no. You don't have to ply me with things. Just stay here for a bit."

"Okay."

He blew his nose. "Phoebe loved you a lot, you know."

"I know."

"A few months ago, when she heard that I was going out with Poison, she told me that I had to take care of you—no matter who I married."

"Did she?" I wanted to laugh at the idea of anyone taking care of me. But I remembered that Phoebe had always thought me "delicate" or "peaky," and in need of special care, and almost cried.

"She told me not to let you marry anyone whose head belongs on a taxidermist's wall."

"She did not!"

"Okay, I made that bit up." Fritz blew his nose. He smiled thinly. "I'm trying very hard not to be an arsehole at the moment. But the old Adam will keep breaking out."

I told him, in that sacred room, how much I had admired him—looked up to him, relied upon him—while Phoebe lay dying.

I said, "You don't have to be brave and virtuous any more. Give yourself a rest."

"Hmmm." He frowned slightly, to himself. We sat for a moment longer, then he kissed my cheek and stood up. "I think I need to be on my own for a while."

My doorbell was ringing. It ripped me out of a deep, dreamless sleep at half past two in the morning. I pulled on my dressing gown (I wonder why dressing gowns are always inside out when you need them in a hurry) and stumbled downstairs.

On the doorstep I found Fritz, and a rather spotty young policeman.

"Cassie, darling," Fritz said. "This is Chris. Tell him you know me, then you can make us both a nice cup of tea."

Chris, the policeman, asked, "Are you Cassie Grimble?"

I was, by now, awake enough to see that Fritz was splendidly drunk.

"Actually, it's Cassie Shaw," I said, "but I do know him. What's wrong?"

"I've been told off for making a nuisance of myself," Fritz said. "Chris was summoned, and when I explained that I'd just buried my mother, he couldn't have been sweeter. I'm beginning to feel that our police are wonderful."

Chris raised his eyebrows at me. "He asked me to bring him here. Can I leave him with you?"

"My dear Chris, of course you can," Fritz loudly declared. "Cassie is my sanctuary."

"Do come in," I said. I drew my inside-out dressing gown around me, wishing my hair did not look crazy. "Would you like a cup of tea?"

"I'd absolutely love one," Fritz said. "And something to eat. And I'm dying for a pee."

"I wasn't asking you."

Chris said, "No thank you, madam. If you're sure everything's all right . . ."

I assured him that it was. Fritz, highly amused to be handed over in this formal manner, embraced Chris, who turned scarlet.

I shut the door and pulled Fritz up the stairs to my flat. "Keep quiet— the woman downstairs goes crazy if I make a noise at night."

"You poor little shrimp, we got you out of bed!"

"Fritz, shut up." I closed my door. "What on earth has been going on?"

"Tell you in a minute." He dived into my bathroom.

The bathroom was in a bit of a state, but I didn't think Fritz would notice. He didn't have Matthew's eye for an unwashed tub. I put the kettle on, took out the plastic box containing my latest batch of biscuits, turned my dressing gown the right way out, and tugged a comb through my hair.

Fritz was in the bathroom for a long time. He emerged smiling. I saw that he was not as drunk as I'd thought. "Biscuits? How wizard. You're a goddess."

"I'm curious, Fritz. The last I heard, you were wandering off to be alone with your emotions. How on earth did the police get involved?"

"Oh, Grimble, don't call poor Chris 'The Police' like that—it sounds so mean."

I was laughing. "Come on, you've dragged me out of bed for this. Make it good."

Fritz sat himself down at my tiny kitchen table with a mug of tea and all the biscuits. "You were right, being extremely virtuous has been a strain. I was following your advice and giving the old virtue a rest."

I said, "I didn't advise you to get arrested."

"I needed to stop being a tower of strength," Fritz said. "When I walked out of the wake, I had an overwhelming urge to be a tower of terrible weakness. I went to three pubs, intending to drink myself into oblivion. I was as drunk as a fart but I couldn't pass out—it was like a witch's curse. The pubs closed, and I was still full of this horrible energy. I found a whole pile of spare marmalade recipes, so I thought I'd post a few of them through people's doors."

I said I didn't think giving away recipes for marmalade was a criminal offense.

"Oh well," he said. "You had to be there."

"What else did you do?"

"I was making a nuisance of myself at the traffic lights."

"Sorry?"

"There was some singing, apparently," Fritz said, as if he had not been present. "Also some shouting. Chris apprehended me in Flask Walk, and insisted on escorting me home."

He was quiet. The anger around him subsided. He was very tired.

"You didn't go home," I said.

"I couldn't face it. Ben and Annabel were asleep downstairs. The rest of the house was too empty. I saw what was wrong about it. It didn't have you in it. I wanted to be with you. Seriously, do you mind?"

"Of course not. Stay here as long as you like."

He smiled suddenly. "You've turned your dressing gown the right way out. That's terribly sweet. Are you naked underneath?"

"Sorry, I'm wearing a voluminous Edwardian bathing costume."

"Don't. That's even more arousing."

"Would you like some toast?"

"No. It would interfere with the purple riot of my thoughts."

I made toast and more tea—mainly to avoid looking Fritz in the eye. He lounged magnificently on one of my small folding chairs. I had to keep stepping over his legs.

"People ask me if I'm all right," Fritz said. "But what a stupid question. No, I'm not all right. I can't stand the way life looks without her. And I failed to save her."

"Did you think you could save her?"

He frowned. "I was giving one last chance to the gods of medicine.

231

They couldn't save Dad. Now they've let me down again. It's all a total waste of time."

I said, "Don't—you know that's not true."

"There are no cures for anything that matters," he said. "And no real illnesses, except for the one that kills you. What a waste of time."

I wanted to protest. I wanted to say all kinds of encouraging and invigorating things. But Fritz looked at me with such black-eyed intensity that I couldn't assemble the words. The comforting clichés only seemed to work for other people.

He said, "God had better not exist, that's all. Because if he does, I'll chin the bastard."

I ate a biscuit. I wasn't hungry, but once again I needed something in my mouth to block out the platitudes. All I could do was watch him and listen to him, hoping he could sense how much I loved him.

Fritz stood up, making the room far too small. There was a phone attached to the wall. He snatched the receiver and began punching out a number.

"What are you doing?" I tried to snatch it back. "It's nearly three in the morning—you can't phone anyone now—"

He was strong, and held me off as if I'd been a mosquito. I heard the phone ringing at the other end. Fritz suddenly pulled me close to him and placed the receiver between our two heads.

A voice on the other end of the line, fresh and sweet as the dew on a rose, said, "Hello—is this really on?—oh yes. Hello. You've reached the residence of Phoebe Darling. I'm obviously not available at the moment, but please leave a message after the beep, and I promise I'll get back to you as soon as possible."

Hearing her voice, so full of warmth and life, hurt like knives. When the beep went, I wanted to blurt out, "Come back—I want you!"

Instead I took the phone out of Fritz's hand and put my arms around him. Inside his chest, I felt the force of his exploding sobs. He cried as I had never seen him cry. I was crying too, but Fritz's grief blew mine away like a leaf in a gale. I held him as hard as I could, as if I could press him into my body and my heart.

I was in love with him. I ached for him. I could not untangle a desire to comfort from plain desire. And Fritz needed love with his body as well as his heart. I'm saying this to make the inevitable consequences sound more elevated—because what we did was more than sex. I can't pinpoint exactly when it started, but we were suddenly kissing as if gulping at life. We made love with breathless urgency, in silence. Fritz was hard and savage, and out of control. I heard, with amazement, my own voice crying out as I came. Dear God, it was wonderful.

We were both crying, all the way through. Afterward, Fritz plummeted heavily into sleep. We lay on my bed in a tangle of duvet. I stayed awake for a long time after he had fallen asleep, clutching his hot, heavy head against my chest. I didn't realize I was also asleep until the doorbell woke me again.

Crumpled and reeling, I stumbled downstairs. I registered that it was gray daylight, and raining, but had no idea of the time.

Ben was at the door. "Hi, Cass. He's here, isn't he?"

"Yes."

"Oh God, sorry if I woke you."

"That's okay."

"I thought I should fetch him. We should never have left him alone."

I hadn't expected Ben to take care of Fritz. It was usually the other way round. But this was a new Ben, made strong by his love for his brother. I took him upstairs. He went into my bedroom, and I heard him waking Fritz with the gentleness of Phoebe herself. He was also very kind to me, folding me in a long embrace, and making us all tea. With very uncharacteristic tact, he made no mention of the obvious fact that Fritz and I had had sex.

Fritz had a terrible hangover. He drank his tea in silence, and in silence he kissed me good-bye.

"Thanks," Ben said, kissing me with special tenderness as Fritz stumbled away from me into the wet street. He lowered his voice. "Cass, you're not going to mind about this, are you? I mean—the fact that he's acting—you know . . ."

I assured him that I understood, which was true.

Ben nodded. "It's like I told you—he's not as tough as people think. He says he wants to be left alone, but you mustn't listen to him. Keep in touch, won't you? With Fritz, I mean, as well as us. Don't stay away from us now the work's finished. It's not so bad for me. I've got Annabel."

I hugged him. "Give her my love."

In the street, Fritz suddenly turned and looked at me. He strode back up the path, nudging Ben aside, and kissed me on the mouth. Then he charged away to the car, without looking back again.

I was on the doorstep in my dressing gown, and it was raining stair-rods. I shut the door on the Darlings, and trudged back to my flat to begin the dreary business of living without Phoebe.

CHAPTER EIGHTEEN

That glorious October faded into a cold, pale November, and I faded into a listless drone. Fritz did not call me. I saw him a few times, when visiting Ben and Annabel, and tried not to mind too much that he never mentioned the sex. Here was a man engaged in a hand-to-hand struggle with grief. I sensed that it took every ounce of Fritz's strength to ride the worst of it. I loved him too much to spoil it by striking a wrong note.

And though I had not lost a mother, I had an idea of what he was enduring. Living without Phoebe was very dull, and all the sadder because she seemed so far out of reach. I longed to hear her voice in my head. I had counted on hearing it. And still I was met with that endless, fathomless silence. This made me cynical and depressed. I carried on getting up in the mornings, dressing myself in reasonably decent clothes and going to work. But I stopped caring what I looked like, because what was the point?

The next few weeks were the most purely miserable of my entire life. I was endlessly tired. A gray wash of inertia lay over everything. I forgot that I ever had a sense of humor. I was nipped and pinched with cold, and sat bundled in cardigans and shawls like a Victorian invalid. At intervals (and I still don't understand this) I darted out of my self-imposed isolation long enough to buy completely useless things—for example, a quilted jacket in buttercup yellow, a complicated machine for frothing milk and a radio that could withstand extreme temperatures. I took no pleasure from these purchases. I didn't even like them while I was buying them. What was I thinking?

"But this is grief," Ruth said. "This is what it's like. You have to think of it as a physical illness."

I never phoned anyone, but Ruth had got into the habit of phoning me at least twice every week. At first I didn't know what to say to her, and could only breathe at her down the line. She rode my silences with mild patience, never discomposed. And then I began to test her by letting out little snatches of my shell-shocked emotions.

"I assumed I'd be distraught. But it's not like that. I don't howl and sob. I just sit, staring into space or reading the same page over and over again. I can't concentrate. This whole thing sort of squats on me, like a great weight." Good grief, I could hardly form a sentence.

Ruth, however, seemed able to penetrate my gibberish. "It shouldn't last long," she said. "But you won't stop the worst of the mourning until you force yourself back into normal life. I'll say it again, Cassie—you should get out more."

"I like being at home."

"You've never liked being at home. I spent years talking to your back while you bolted out of the door. This really isn't natural, if you want to know."

She was not laying down the law; simply observing. I had a vivid memory of my teenage self, just as she remembered, constantly escaping. Unfortunately, at the moment, I had nowhere to escape to. But they were all on at me to go out.

Betsy said, "You need to be with *people*," as if I'd been hanging out with some other species. She said it when she saw me putting on a third cardigan and lunching on a Toblerone. She had raised four daughters, and could read female eating-patterns like a wise old gypsy reading tea leaves. "Seeing more people will take you out of yourself."

I said, "I can't be bothered. I'm too tired. After a day in this office, all I'm fit for is tinned spaghetti and Inspector Morse."

Betsy handed me a slice of the latest cake. "You'd soon perk up if you had something to do. I'll have a word with Jonah and Hazel." Dear Betsy, how she grabbed at any opportunity to say "Jonah-and-Hazel" in that casual way—she was so delighted that Jonah was out of her attic at last. "I know they'd love to have you round to dinner."

I felt that mean little stab of jealousy when I contemplated Hazel's happy coupledom. Losing Phoebe had not made me nicer. I had inherited none of her kindness. I didn't even try to emulate it. I could only feel small and hard-done-by and overlooked. The same worm of jealousy kept me away from Annabel, with her adoring husband and imminent twins. Annabel was fortunate, and had nothing to do with a loser like me. The monumental unfairness of life was a continual amazement to me. I'd brought Ben 'n' Annabel and Hazel 'n' Jonah together. I'd brought several couples together during my matchmaking career—and I'd forgotten to find anyone for myself. I felt scaly and hideous with self-pity.

"Hazel can't cook," I said.

Betsy picked up her knitting. "Jonah does most of the cooking, actually. He's only part-time on the Heath at the moment, and Hazel's hours are ridiculous. He makes a wonderful lentil stew."

"Yum," I said crossly.

"Well, it would do you good to eat something healthy. How long is it since you've had a cooked meal?"

"Betsy, your concern touches me deeply, but please don't worry—I'm not living on Pot Noodles."

"I don't like to think of you spending so much time on your own. Why aren't you seeing more of the Darling boys?"

"They're busy." I was defensive, because my heart leaped every time the phone rang, and it was never Fritz. "They have to get the house into a decent state, so they can sell it."

"Poor things," Betsy said, instantly sympathetic. "That must be very hard."

The chill fog around me lifted, just enough to make me ashamed of myself. I saw that one symptom of my grieving had been selfishness. I'd been so sorry for myself that I hadn't stopped to think how nasty all this must be for Fritz and Ben. I was staying away from the old house because I couldn't bear it without Phoebe, but they did not have a choice.

And hadn't I promised to keep in touch with Fritz? I waited until Betsy had gone downstairs with the day's post, then I rang his number.

He had replaced Phoebe's phone message with a terse one of his own. I stammered out a few lame words, hoping he was okay and rather grudgingly offering help with the house.

He called back about ten minutes later, while Betsy was making us a pot of tea. The kettle was roaring on the filing cabinet beside me, and I had to ask him to speak up.

He sounded amused. "I said, do you want to come over sometime?"

"Yes. That'd be lovely." He wanted me. My spirits rose a couple of points above zero.

"There's some stuff I want to give you."

"Stuff?"

"I'm not explaining now. Get over here."

Betsy called, "She's free tonight!" (What hypersensitive ears this woman had—I had learned long ago that there was no such thing as a private phone conversation around her.)

"Excellent, so am I," Fritz said briskly. "Come round after work."

It had been decided for me. Grief makes you incapable of deciding anything for yourself. I was deathly tired, I knew I looked awful and I didn't feel like seeing another living soul, but I didn't have the energy to argue. I was yearning, in any case, to see Fritz. I took the tube up to Hampstead. The night was blustery and uncomfortable. I bought a bottle of wine, thinking sadly of all the times I had stopped at this very off-license to buy wine for Phoebe. It hurt so much to approach the old house that I had a physical pain over my heart. I steeled myself to face a dead house; a house whose soul had fled.

The reality, however, was both better and worse. There was no great change. I don't know what I'd expected, but here were the same window boxes, lovingly tended by Phoebe until only weeks ago. Here were the familiar lamps in the window, throwing circles of light against the white blinds. It was easy to imagine I could run up the front steps, hammer on the door and fall into Phoebe's arms.

Fritz opened the door, and gave me a brisk kiss on the cheek. "Hi, Grimble."

I followed him into Phoebe's drawing room, and gasped aloud when I saw the state of it. "Oh God! What's going on?"

The Persian runners and rugs were tightly rolled up and stacked in a corner like sausages. Every other inch of floor was covered with boxes—old and new, all overflowing with stuff. The sofa was heaped with historical linen, right back to some guest towels that had been among Phoebe's wedding gifts. There were piles of old *Lancets* and *British Medical Journals* crowded on top of the grand piano. Two of Fritz's surfboards were propped against the bureau beside the fireplace.

"Thirty years of accumulated rubbish," Fritz said. "Take what you want before I chuck it all out."

"All of it?" A box of mismatched crockery had already caught my attention. I picked up a nice little blue jug. "Won't you want it for your next house?"

"Nope. There's enough here for three houses. Mum never threw anything away, and I refuse to be sentimental about my old finger paintings."

"Well—maybe I will rescue a couple of things . . ." I picked up a small cushion, with the same rose pattern as the bedroom curtains. It smelled a little musty, but beyond the mustiness was the ghost of Phoebe in her bedroom, a jewel in a velvet setting. I would only have to look at it to summon her into my mind's eye.

"Let's open the wine." Fritz took the bottle from me.

Belatedly, I remembered that I had toiled up to Hampstead to be supportive. It seemed odd to be supporting Fritz, and I wasn't sure how to go about it. "How are you, anyway? This must be awful for you. Dismantling your home."

"Not particularly." He was dismissive. "It's not a shrine."

"No, I suppose not." Now that I was here, the dismantling of the home no longer seemed fearsome. The gods of the household, the Lares and Penates in the shapes of Jimmy and Phoebe, had departed. Without them it was just a house.

"Tell me what I can do," I said.

He looked at me narrowly, taking me in for the first time. "If you're really up for it, you can help me with the sorting."

"All right. Just give me your orders." I spoke as briskly as possible, to mask my slight dismay. I'd come here to make sympathetic noises—I wasn't prepared for physical labor.

He gave me a glass of wine. "The heap by the window is everything that'll burn—we're going to have a vast bonfire when Ben gets back from Glossop."

"Where?"

"Glossop, darling. Gateway to the Peaks. He's got a gig up there. Don't we play some smart places? All the stuff on or around the sofas is for the vicar's next jumble sale. The stuff on the table is for keeping or selling. Start sorting."

I found that I was not as exhausted as I had thought. There was something enjoyably practical about sorting through the fallout of the past. In a remarkably short time I was on my third glass of wine, stripped to only one cardigan, energetically sifting through box after box of tatting. I remembered nearly everything that I disinterred—a wobbly plate Ben had made at pottery class, a bundle of Cash's labels with "C. Shaw" in red copperplate, the program from Fritz's dire college production of *Othello*. I couldn't stop smiling over each treasure. Phoebe could never bear to throw stuff away. Jimmy was constantly shouting about "drowning in crap" and threatening to burn it all. I found one or two things he had absolutely hated (a lamp fashioned from a Mateus Rosé bottle; a set of mildly pornographic Roman coasters), and was amused that Phoebe had stubbornly squirreled them away, sure he would change his mind one day. I decided to keep the coasters—I remembered how they had made us giggle.

Fritz laughed at the collection of objects I was putting in my pile to take home. "You don't want this!"

"Yes I do. Put it back."

"Grimble, no man will ever sleep with you if you own a draft excluder in the shape of a snake."

"Piss off. I like it." I snatched back the terrible thing (brown and orange felt, stuffed with beans, made by Phoebe from a kit). "And Ben will kill you if anything happens to Norman."

"Norman? God, you two are so wet."

"You're cold and hard-hearted," I told him. "You're throwing away far too much."

"Fine—take all the shit you like, but if it doesn't leave this house before midnight, you'll never see it again. Why are you sniggering, Grimble? Do you not believe me?"

"You sound just like Jimmy."

"Do I?" He smiled suddenly. "Thanks for coming. It's nice to have some help."

I dropped a dented biscuit tin on top of the rubbish pile. "You should have asked me sooner. Or I should've called."

"No," Fritz said, "I should've called you."

"We could argue about this for ages. What I'm trying to say is, I didn't mean to leave you alone."

"Stop being nice, Cass. You're supposed to be demanding an apology."

"Am I? What for?"

"Come on. I shagged you and then didn't call. I was a drunken lout."

"You had a good excuse," I said.

"You were incredibly kind to me." Fritz turned his back and began bundling old magazines into a black binbag. "Just as you've been incredibly kind for weeks and weeks. Now that it's all over, I've been trying to keep out of your face—but I've missed you. Okay? I want you to know that."

He wouldn't look at me. I wished I knew how to reach him, but beyond a certain level he did not communicate. Phoebe's death had thrown up a shield. Still, I was aware of something very like happiness, simply because he had said he missed me. I was working beside him. We were comfortable together, winnowing through the rubbish. I had never felt this comfortable with a man I was in love with. We made a highly effective team. In a couple of hours half the chaos had been graded and tidied into symmetrical piles.

Fritz flopped down on a sofa space that had just been cleared. "How skint are you?"

"I'm low on cash, but my Switch card is responding nicely at the moment." (Here was another first—telling a man I loved the truth about my finances.)

"Good, we can order an Indian."

We did so, and the meal arrived with another bottle of red wine. It was rather sour, but we were drunk enough not to mind. Fritz ate enormously. So did I. We sat on the sofa, beached and lazy.

"You know," Fritz said, studying me thoughtfully, "I like what's happened to your hair."

"It's grown," I said. Back in another life, when I was in love with Matthew, I had formed the habit of short, neat hair. I tried to remember when I had last managed to get to John Frieda (New Cavendish Street). To me, the uneven, undisciplined growth was as disturbing as a neglected shrubbery. I was surprised that the fastidious Fritz approved.

He was still looking at me solemnly. His face was close to mine. "You're very sexy when you loosen up. It doesn't suit you to be minimalist. You should let out your inner hippy chick."

"None of my inner chicks are hippies."

"Don't fight it. Let your wild hair grow. Show an inch or two of bare flesh. Wear lipstick."

"Now?" I hadn't worn a single smear of makeup since the funeral.

"Don't be silly. I just mean in general. To show the world you're interested in sex."

Sex flickered between us—and then the bloody doorbell rang.

Who knows what might have happened? It doesn't matter. The spark died. Fritz, with fleeting regret, went to answer the door.

I heard a low female voice, and a moment later she was in the room.

"Cassie!" She swooped to kiss me. "MmchWAH!" (A real sink-plunger.)

Felicity Peason. She was as vulgarly beautiful as ever—all lustrous hair and antelope limbs. She was pointedly conveying sympathy. She rattled out a speech about how sad it was, how sorry she was. She accepted a glass of sour wine, and sipped it without making a face. She was on her best behavior. What was she up to?

Fritz was distantly polite, simmering with leftover anger. She placed a hand on his sleeve, and he shrugged it off almost with violence.

"I won't stay long," Peason said. "I can see how busy you are. It's such a huge thing, isn't it, when you're selling a house?"

"I wouldn't know," Fritz said. "I've never done it."

"Oh—" I felt Peason's senses sharpening. "But you are—the house is going on the market, isn't it?"

"Yes."

She relaxed. "That's what I've come about. Cassie, do forgive us for talking business."

Was this a hint for me to leave? If so, up hers.

"Don't mind me," I said. "I love other people's business." I started sorting again.

Fritz said, "What are you talking about, anyway?"

"I'm here about the house," Peason said. "I know this is cheeky of me—but have you had any offers yet?"

Fritz said, "No. It's not on the market yet."

"Oh, how marvelous. I'd like to put in an offer now. I'd like to buy this house." She glanced around the room in (I thought) a proprietorial way. "I've managed to persuade my father to see it as an investment. We'll obviously expect to pay the full asking price—and you can sidestep the estate agents."

I was intensely annoyed. Fritz did not like Peason. But she was still very sexy, and I didn't trust him not to fall back into the void.

"Anyway, please do think about it. Please, Fritz." (She said this in a lick-my-tits voice that set my teeth on edge.) "It could all be so easy and hassle-free if we did it like this, not to mention cheaper. Why not?"

Fritz was listening. "I don't know," he said. "It's not a bad idea, I suppose. Have you really got that much money?"

She smiled and shrugged. "Yes, more or less. And I've been in love with this house since—well, since I was in love with you."

A private signal passed between them—very brief, but as noticeable to me as a scream.

"I can't make any promises," Fritz said. "I have to talk to Ben."

"Of course. Please believe me, Fritz—I'm not trying to get special treatment. I felt free to make my offer because it would work for both of us. That's all."

"It'd be good to save the estate agent's percentage," Fritz said thoughtfully. "They charge a fortune."

"Exactly. And I know you're short of money. Or you wouldn't be doing that pantomime."

He winced slightly. "It's work. How about you? Anything lined up?"

"Oh God, don't talk to me about work!" Peason rolled her eyes. "The RSC made me an offer, but only to understudy—"

They talked, in a stilted, only half-truthful fashion, about the theater.

243

I hefted piles of old vinyl recordings, willing Peason to leave. I was sure she was coming on to Fritz, and he was visibly thawing. He even offered her another glass of wine.

She laughed, and said she was going out to dinner. She kissed us both, and left a cloud of perfume where she had been standing, like a very expensive fart.

"Of all the nerve," I said, after she had gone.

Fritz picked up another box, without seeing it. "I wonder if she's serious?"

"Forget it."

"Certainly not. It's a bloody good offer, if she really has got the cash."

"It's a horrible offer," I said. "Doesn't it make you sick, to think of her living here?"

I thought he looked, for a moment, uneasy. But he said, "Darling, we can't afford to wait until someone virtuous buys this place. There's a chronic shortage of people with silly amounts of money. We might be languishing on the market for months."

"You can't mean you'll do it!" I was aghast. I knew I was jealous and irrational, but the bare idea of Peason in Phoebe's house was appalling. "No!" I dropped a pile of records in a fury. "You can't! You remember what she's like—what a selfish bitch she was about Phoebe!"

"Phoebe's dead," Fritz said. His voice was steady, but his face was suddenly blank and bleached. "Nothing Felicity says or does can hurt her now."

"Think of yourself, then—and Ben. How will you feel, knowing your childhood home has been raped?"

"I told you," Fritz said. "It's not a shrine. Do let's be rational. If it's any consolation, I'm not planning to jump back in bed with her."

"Really? Are you sure about that?"

Fritz snapped, "For God's sake! Of course I'm sure!"

"She looked as if she was planning to jump back into bed with you. She couldn't have made it clearer if she'd whipped her clothes off."

"She'd have been wasting her time."

"Good."

"Grimble, pull yourself together." Fritz moved a heap of books to the pile for the jumble sale. He faced me, planting his hands on his hips. "I thought we were being civilized, but you're as determined as ever to cast me as a bastard. I wonder sometimes if you actually like me better that way. I wonder if it turns you on to see me as a priapic bastard who goes out of his way to fuck the nastiest woman he can find." His voice hardened. "You've been very complimentary about my recent decency—but perhaps you're getting bored with it."

"I'm trying to warn you about getting caught up again, that's all."

"Cassie, is this because we slept together? Have I unwittingly outed you as a jealous harpy?"

"No!" I was stung. "I'm not jealous of Peason. I know you despise her."

"In that case, please keep your nose out of my sex life."

"I wasn't being nosy," I snapped. "I've a perfect right to express my opinion of Peason. I've never made a secret of the fact that I hate her."

"Grow up." To do Fritz justice, I don't think he knew that I had fallen in love with him. "You're too old to use words like 'hate'—get out of the fucking playground. Felicity's bitchy because she grew up in the family from hell. That's why she can't understand someone like Phoebe."

I made my voice as rational as possible. "Yes, but you know what she's up to, don't you?"

"She wants to buy this house."

"Yes," I said. "And she wants to get it half-price."

"What? What the fuck are you talking about?"

"Fritz, wake up. If she moved in with you, she'd only have to buy out Ben."

He looked at me blankly for a moment. "Don't be stupid."

I couldn't stop now. "That's why she kept thrusting her tits at you, and doing that thing with her tongue."

Fritz let out a snort of laughter. "You're demented."

"I'm telling you, she's determined to seduce you. She knows you'll fall for the tongue thing eventually, because she seems to have some sort of electrical path to your gonads, which entirely bypasses both your heart and your brain—"

"You're ranting at me," Fritz said.

I had to rant. I was ranting out a warning. "You don't know how much she cares about money—and she's the world's biggest snob. I'm not denying that she fancies you—"

I had to make him believe that Peason would rob him and break his heart—and probably only let him go when she had ruined him for all other women. Not for nothing was I named Cassandra.

He was laughing at me, not very kindly. "You're hysterical. I ought to slap you."

"I'm only saying that if she happens to beg for your hand in marriage, don't be too flattered—she's got her eye on your double bay windows and original cornicing."

"You obviously didn't hear me the first time," Fritz said, loudly and slowly, as if to an imbecile. "I am not getting back with Felicity. I have no intention of sleeping with Felicity."

"Well—good." My cheeks were hot. I was aware of being absurd and childish. Deep down, I really wanted a weighty declaration of eternal love. I couldn't stay without it. I felt I'd become a fool.

The fact was, I didn't trust him to resist her. I left soon afterward, clutching my box of relics, with a million miles between me and the man I loved.

CHAPTER NINETEEN

I don't feel like going out just at the moment," I explained to Ruth, when she called. "I'm not fit to go out. When I see people, I behave like a nutcase."

Ruth's steady voice gave no indication that she disapproved of terms like "nutcase." "In what way?"

"Well, for instance, I managed to insult Fritz. I practically accused him of having an affair—and I know it's probably because we slept together that time, and I wanted it to be more than it was." These days, I wasn't merely talking to Ruth. I was spilling my guts. She was the only person in the world to hear my loveless ranting and whining. Our conversations were now essential to me. She didn't build me up and cosset my ego, as darling Phoebe had done. But she definitely made me feel less of a loser. She braced me to deal with the world, and would not allow me to slide into despair.

Ruth said, "Try not to obsess about Fritz. It's not really fair to either of you. When you made love, you were both intensely vulnerable—I imagine the whole experience is still mixed up with the experience of the funeral. I still think you should be leaning more on your girlfriends. Make an effort to see them. I mean it, Cassie." Her neutral voice firmed slightly. "This sort of depression overwhelms you, unless you fight it."

I couldn't fail to be impressed by this, for Ruth certainly knew what she was talking about. Hadn't I lived under the shadow of her depression? And now she was warning me not to turn into her—at least, that was how I understood it.

For once, I would take her advice. I decided to organize a girls' night out. I'd done this many times in the past, and not thought twice about it. Now, it felt like a tremendous effort—all that phoning and leaving cheery messages, and pretending I was as busy as they all were.

We met at the usual wine bar—me, Annabel, Hazel and Claudette. I made a special effort with my clothes. I took my sexy Paul Smith shirt from the back of the wardrobe, scrubbed the stains off my smartest skirt and underwent the martyrdom of thin tights. It is always important to dress for your female friends, because they use your clothes to read the state of your mind and I was determined not to appear in the character of a desperate single. I was the only single person at the table.

First, we passed round the latest pictures of Claudette's baby daughter, in various adorable poses. Please don't get me wrong—I considered little Jessica perfectly beautiful, and quite saw why Claudette could think and speak of nothing else. But I did feel the cooing went on for rather a long time.

A few months ago, I would have been able to roll my eyes at Hazel, who never got silly over babies. What had happened to her? This evening, she pored over every photograph with a dreamy, half-witted expression that (I thought) looked odd with her fabulous silk cardigan and Prada handbag.

Claudette laughed, and accused her of being broody.

"Oh yes," Annabel said, "Hazel's definitely fallen under the spell."

"I have not!" Hazel protested. She was smiling, and not protesting (I thought) hard enough. "We've talked about it, that's all. Jonah's always telling me about the kids he sees on the Heath. He says he fancies being a dad."

"As long as someone else earns all the money," I said cattily. I was famous for my catty asides about useless north London males.

Nobody seemed to hear me. Hazel, Claudette and Annabel all exchanged radiant looks—the freemasonry of happy coupledom.

"I don't mind being the breadwinner," Hazel said. "In fact, I like it. Jonah never nags me about the hours I work. He says my mania for work is part of me, and he thinks successful women are sexy."

"Come on, Hazel," I said, "tell us the truth. Isn't he just a tiny bit chippy?"

This was, frankly, scary. Instead of going into her usual barrage of complaints about the latest dreadful boyfriend, Hazel's face was still suffused with that sickening, enviable glow.

"Oh, but Jonah's different. He's been so lovely, so supportive—even my mum likes him. He has such a sense of what's really important. I knew that the very first time I met him, when we spent practically the whole night reading Tennyson and Browning to each other—well, Cassie was there, she caught us at the very moment of falling in love." She looked round at us all, smiling in a new way. "The thing is—"

The thing was that Hazel and Jonah were getting married.

Claudette and Annabel both went, "Ooooh!"

"Congratulations," I said, as heartily as possible. "And please make sure Betsy's sitting down when she hears—she may very well explode with joy."

I ordered a bottle of champagne, hoping this would mask my lack of ooh-ing. We all toasted the happy couple, but it was rather a letdown. Annabel was pregnant and Claudette was breast-feeding, and they only sipped at the champagne. Hazel was too fulfilled and happy to cane the booze in the old way. I drank most of it, and spent the rest of the evening covering the fact that I was plastered. I truly didn't want to be a dog in the manger, but I couldn't help feeling I had fallen off the edge of the world. It was probably a judgment against me, I thought, for being so smug when I was with Matthew.

"Now, Cassie," Claudette said. "How's your love life these days?"

"You should make your play for Fritz Darling," Hazel said. "Quick, while he's still available."

"Oh, I don't know about that," Annabel said. "I think he's spoken for."

I was glad everyone looked at her, and missed the ghastly expression my face went into before I could wrestle it back into polite interest.

Annabel sighed. "It looks as if Poison Peason is back on the scene. Such a shame."

"She was talking about buying the house," I said, in a faint voice. "That's all, surely."

"Oh, she still wants the house—she appeared in the basement yesterday with a tape measure. God knows what she's planning. And she had one of those posh books of paint samples. Ben got annoyed, because she kept dropping hints about us moving out before the babies come."

"Yes, but her buying the house doesn't mean Fritz is sleeping with her," Claudette pointed out.

Annabel giggled. "We heard them at it."

"Doing it?" I tried to look prurient instead of distraught.

"Not half. Right over our heads, while we were having supper." She giggled again. Everyone giggled, except me. "It was sort of like this—" Annabel let out a series of theatrical orgasm noises. "We had to go into the bathroom so they wouldn't hear us laughing."

"You're kidding," Claudette said. "Has the woman no shame?"

"Of course not—come on, you remember her from school. She hasn't changed."

"Neither has Fritz, obviously," Hazel said. "I'd like to meet the woman who could make *him* settle down."

Annabel put her hand on my arm. "You'll laugh at this, Cassie—but me and Ben hoped he'd get together with you."

"Oh well." I should have won an Oscar for my breeziness.

"She can do better for herself," Hazel declared. "We have to find someone for Cassie, girls. She's the only one of us who hasn't found her true love."

I cried in the taxi on the way home. I have since been told that crying in taxis is part of the female condition, but I had never done it before. I was heartbroken and furious. Bloody Fritz. Curse and damn him. Never going to sleep with Peason? Huh. I should have made him put it in writing. He was weak-willed and shallow, and probably deserved her.

Mostly, however, I was heartbroken. I knew Fritz too well to stay furious for long. I had seen his courage and his kindness. I had ached over his tenderness with Phoebe. Through all that sad time, he had been my best friend and right arm, the one thread of sanity connecting me to the world. I knew that love went very deep with him, and I couldn't understand why he was wasting something so rich and rare on Felicity Peason. I mopped up rivers of tears, until my single frayed tissue was a sodden scrap.

The taxi driver was nice to me—apparently, they often are. When I climbed out and paid the fare, he said, "You okay, love?"

"Oh, yes. Fine."

"You take care, then."

"Thanks."

His kindness hurt me by reminding me of my loneliness. By the time I let myself into my flat, I was sobbing. I lay down on the sofa without taking my coat off, and wept as I had never wept over Matthew. It was clear to me now that losing Matthew had damaged nothing more than my pride. Losing Fritz was like having my heart torn up at the roots—until now, I hadn't realized how I'd been banking on winning him in the end.

I longed for Phoebe. I knew exactly what she would have done. She would have let me cry, and said "poor darling," until she judged I was ready for a cup of tea. Then she would have said something about Fritz, and what an idiot he was to choose Peason instead of me. She would have reminded me that I was only young—yes, far too young to be deciding everything was over. It was a great maxim of Phoebe's that true love existed for everyone, and could strike at any time.

"There's nothing wrong with dreaming about falling in love," she told me once. "It's perfectly natural. Wanting love doesn't make you any less of a feminist. Needing it doesn't mean you're weak. We weren't meant to be alone."

She had gone on to remind me (this was just after I split up with Matthew) that I didn't know myself well enough to recognize the right man when I saw him.

"Keep an open mind," she had said. "And don't lose hope. You have to hope that life will change, or you'll never change anything."

Phoebe was a natural optimist, and her stubborn streak gave her optimism an edge of steel. The sun would come up, things would get better, people would see the error of their ways, and faithless lovers would either repent or be forgotten. She was sure the world would come right eventually—and for her, it always did. Phoebe said she was unusually fortunate. I thought she attracted good fortune to herself because she deserved it.

I struggled into a sitting position, feeling a little less hopeless. If

Phoebe had been here with me, I thought, Cousin Molly would have come up by now. Cousin Molly was Phoebe's standard story of hope triumphant. Phoebe loved to sermonize. Her moral stories always followed the same meandering course, and could not be hurried or varied. We heard them over and over again. I loved the repetition, and so did Jimmy and the boys, though they couldn't resist teasing her. I settled more comfortably against the cushions, running the famous example of Phoebe's cousin (on her mother's side) through my memory.

Cousin Molly had fallen in love with a young naval officer, but he had not loved her in return. Instead, he had waltzed off with some showy blonde—"a Diana Dors type," according to Phoebe—and poor Molly's heart had been broken. She knew she would never love again. She resigned herself to a life of dreary spinsterhood, delivering the parish magazine and taking care of old Uncle Angus.

At this point, Phoebe would usually have to stop the story, to ask Jimmy, in a soft and sorrowful voice, why he was laughing. For some reason, the mention of "old Uncle Angus" always sent Jimmy and the boys into hysterics. Dignified and slightly reproachful, Phoebe would address the rest of the story to me. The boys were naughty to laugh, she said, because Molly had a terrible time after her heart was broken. She nearly died in a car accident, and had to have her left leg amputated just below the knee—"Boys! Jimmy! Really! It isn't at all funny, how could you laugh?"

Here, Phoebe's voice would rise slightly. We had plumbed the depths of the valley, but now we were heading up Happy Ending Hill. Two long years passed. Then, quite by chance, Molly ran into her naval officer again—and this time, he fell properly in love with her, despite her injury (perhaps, Phoebe once remarked, because being in the navy made him more used to one-legged people). Two weeks later, on the golf course at Fort William, he had proposed. Which just went to show that you should never lose hope, because thirty-five years later Cousin Molly was still happily married and had three children. ("Oh Ben, don't be silly—of course they all have two legs.")

I couldn't think about Cousin Molly without feeling comforted. I sniffed deeply, limply and almost pleasingly tired. It was possible that I was overreacting about Fritz. All kinds of things were possible—well, look at Cousin Molly. Maybe I should saw a leg off. I stood up, removed my coat and made myself a cup of tea.

I only saw it when I was drinking my tea in front of the television. I had been depressed because I couldn't hear Phoebe's voice. But perhaps remembering the sayings of the dead, and having an instinct for what they would have said in certain circumstances, is what people mean when they say they have "heard" them. It wasn't like having a vision, or seeing a ghost. There was nothing mystical about it. I was simply remembering with particular intensity. But the end result was that I went to bed comforted. So in some sense, Phoebe had been with me, and I had heard her.

A couple of dreary weeks later, toward the end of November, I ran into Fritz in Camden Town. It was a Saturday morning. I had been to the wholefood shop, as part of my resolution to lead a healthier life. I saw Fritz running toward me, on the crossing beside the station.

He smiled when he saw me, and gave me a mighty hug that swept me off my feet. "Cassie, how great to see your shrimp-like form. I was just wishing someone congenial would buy me a cup of coffee."

"Your wish has come true. I'm headed for Costa's."

"Wonderful. Let me take your shopping—good God, what have you got in here? A brick?" He wrenched the recyclable paper bag out of my hand and pulled out a wholemeal loaf. "Are you supposed to eat this? Or are you building a wall in installments?"

"Stop mauling it about." I took back my shopping. "What about you? What are you doing here?"

He laughed, a little wryly. "Costume fitting. I've been in a sort of warehouse down a back street, filled with rack upon rack of pantomime ensembles."

"Oh wow. What do you have to wear?"

"Just the bog-standard Wishee-Washee outfit—Chinese suit, little round hat. Rags for Act One, red satin for after the laundry scene. Please feel free to laugh."

I laughed. "Red satin?"

"Oh yes. I'll be candid with you, Grimble. When I saw myself in the mirror, I was absolutely mortified." He spoke lightly, but he was not joking.

I said, "Still, it's money. And nobody will ever see you."

"Very true. I should even be grateful. The girl who was fitting me got the papers mixed up, and asked me which end of the horse I was doing. It could be worse."

We sat down at one of the tables in the back of the coffee shop. Fritz spooned froth off his cappuccino, looking at me warily. He said, "I expect you've heard about Felicity."

"Yes, Annabel told me."

His color deepened. He had the grace to be embarrassed.

He said, in Peter Lorre's voice, "You despise me, don't you?" (*Casablanca*.)

"It's none of my business," I said.

"I told you I had no intention of sleeping with her again."

"Oh, I remember. That's why I was so surprised."

"You needn't be sarcastic, Grimble. At the time, I wasn't lying. I thought I could resist her. You were right, I'm obviously putty in her hands. She's still a fiend in human form—but what a form."

He was glowing with health, vivid with energy. Evidently getting back in the sack had been good for him.

I said, "If it makes you happy."

"I don't know if happy is the right word," Fritz said. "I'm an orphan, I'm deeply in debt and I have to earn my living dressed in red satin. Great sex only makes these things a shade more bearable."

I had to say what Phoebe would have said. "Yes, but things can change. After your pantomime, when you've sold the house, you'll be able to find something better."

"What, for God's sake? Every job I've ever had has been quite amazingly silly. It's a sobering thing, to reach your early thirties and realize that your entire life is useless." He was calm and conversational, but I didn't doubt that he was serious. Intrigued, I wondered what had suddenly brought Fritz face to face with his uselessness. I'd always assumed he was perfectly well aware of it, and simply didn't mind.

"Earning a living is never useless or silly," I told him bracingly. "You need the money. Pull yourself together."

"This is the worst thing," he said, not smiling. "It hit me in that fitting room. There I was, in front of a mirror, in my Wishee-Washee costume, despising myself. Then that girl has to ask which end of the horse I was doing. And that's exactly what Dad used to say—don't you remember? He said I'd end up playing a horse's arse. It was his standard objection to my acting career."

"But Jimmy couldn't see the point of any career that wasn't medicine."

"God, no—he was on a mission to cure the world." Fritz frowned into his coffee. "It's a pity both his sons disappointed him."

I said, "I don't think he ever expected Ben to be a doctor." Too late, I saw my tactlessness.

"But he expected me to be one," Fritz said.

"He was wrong about you, that's all."

"He told me I'd be good at it."

"Well, you would have been—"

"Cassie," Fritz interrupted me, "can I ask you something?"

"Of course."

"You were on Dad's side, weren't you? You were pissed off when I gave up medicine."

"No, I—"

"Bullshit. I disappointed both of you, didn't I?"

We had never spoken about this. But if he wanted the truth, he could have it. "All right, I was—surprised. I did agree with Jimmy that it was a bit of a waste. Not because you're not a good actor," I hastened to add (buffing the awful truth with a small lie), "but because you'd have been such a terrific doctor. Jimmy thought you'd have a career in surgery."

Fritz groaned softly. "Surgery! The rest of my natural life slicing hernias and replacing hips! He adored it all, and that's why I couldn't make him understand. I needed more challenge, less predictability. I just wasn't ready to be middle-aged. To be brutal, I wasn't ready to turn into a copy of him."

I didn't know what to say. I hadn't seen his dread of routine before.

He smiled at me. "I know you think I'm a terrible actor. You're absolutely right. I don't have much talent." He spoke casually, as if barely interested.

I didn't understand. "Fritz, what is this? Are you having some sort of existential crisis?"

"Don't be silly. I'm not saying I mind about it. One of the many depressing things about acting is that lack of talent doesn't really matter."

"But—are you telling me you want to give it up?"

Fritz was quiet for a long moment. "No," he said eventually. "Not while it brings in a modicum of money." He stood up. "Would you like another coffee?"

"Yes, thanks."

That closed the subject of acting. When Fritz brought our coffees back to the table, the barriers were up again.

He said, "Before I forget, Ruth wants to know when you're coming."

It was so disconcerting to hear him talking about my mother that I was confused. "Sorry? Coming where?"

"To her house, Grimble. You are coming down for Christmas, I take it?"

"I suppose so." I hadn't thought about it. I couldn't bear to.

He reached over to squeeze my hand. "You have to come down. I like Ruth, and I like her dotty old Mr. Pastry boyfriend—but Ben and Annabel are going to Scotland, and I don't want to be alone. Not this year."

I said, "Neither do I." It was very good to know that Fritz and I had the same hopes for our forlorn festivities. "I've been so out of touch—I didn't know you'd arranged everything with Ruth."

"Oh, keep up—I did it ages ago. I'm moving into her spare bedroom on Sunday, just in time to start rehearsals on Monday. The show opens on Boxing Day, so you'll be able to witness my shame. I've promised Ruth seats in the circle."

"But—what about Peason?"

"Oh, fuck no! Do you think I'd let her anywhere near my Wishee-Washee? She'd never want to touch me again, let alone sleep with me." Fritz was chortling, not very kindly. "She's spending Christmas with her mother."

This was excellent news. It nerved me to face the prospect of Christmas without Phoebe. "What a pity Ruth won't get to meet her," I said. "She's fascinated by the workings of the criminal mind."

Frtiz said, "Thank you, that will do."

"No it won't. You were always making cracks about Matthew."

"That's different. I didn't like Matthew."

"Well, I don't like Peason."

He was still smiling, but thoughtful. "You made up your mind about her rather a long time ago. Aren't we due for an update?"

"No."

"Don't be so pig-headed. If she didn't have one or two good points, I wouldn't sleep with her."

"Yes you would."

He laughed. "Okay, yes I would. But the thing is, Grimble—" (serious again), "this time, she's showing a much better side of herself. I hope you'll believe me one day."

I made some sort of throwaway reply, as if I didn't really care. We parted in the high street, casually looking forward to meeting over Christmas.

I went home on the bus, feeling that if my mood fell any further it would drop through the floor.

Christmas is hell for the bereaved. That horrible year declined in a welter of tinsel, booze and constant festivity. I observed it all through my glass wall. Doggedly, I spent a couple of Saturdays buying gifts. There was little relish in it. I worked my way through the merry throng of shoppers, snapping at children and snarling at beggars.

Annabel got silver earrings. Ben got new headphones. Ruth got a jersey (burgundy lambswool). George got a book token, plus my office copy of the new Browning biography. Betsy, Shay and Puffin all got Fortnum's chocolates. Fritz, in equal measure the most important and the most difficult, got a plain silver frame in which I put a photo of Phoebe. I sent Hazel and Jonah a bottle of champagne, via Betsy.

Angelic Betsy, she was overflowing with happiness because Jonah was bringing Hazel to lunch on Christmas Day, but not for a second did she forget that I was in mourning. She was determined to create a happy atmosphere. I nearly disappeared under a mountain of cakes, biscuits and mince pies. She stuck holly on our computers and draped the filing cabinets with tinsel. She warbled carols as she subbed the crossword, and was always looking for excuses to pull crackers. I spent hours sitting gravely at my desk with a tissue paper crown hanging over one eye.

'Twas the season to be jolly, and I tried very hard. But Phoebe was not here, and Fritz seemed to be falling in love with Peason. I was very unhappy. I was the unhappiest I'd ever been in my life.

Fritz was at my mother's house beside the sea. Ruth said she liked having a lodger.

"I hardly see him—he's either rehearsing, or pelting back to London to his girlfriend," she told me, over the phone. "If he sits down to supper here, I'm curiously honored. I catch myself in the very act of being charmed. I find that I'm enjoying having him around. And I used to think he was such a lout."

We had arranged that I would drive down to Ruth's on the day before Christmas Eve. The night before that, we had our office party—cheap and cheerful, at a curry place in Drummond Street. More crackers were pulled. Betsy got uncharacteristically hammered, and Puffin and I had to bundle her (and her hundreds of shopping bags) into a taxi.

Puffin was driving up to the country. He kindly took a small detour to drive me home (I spent a painful twenty minutes squashed against his luggage, which seemed mainly to consist of rods and guns). I kissed him affectionately and wished him a merry Christmas. We said we'd meet "next year," not really believing it.

Then I was alone, and I felt the city closing down around me. London was a mass of snails, retreating into cozy shells. I threw a few clothes into my suitcase, then got bored and went to bed. I didn't think it mattered what I wore at Ruth's.

I had a little more shopping to do the next morning. Ruth entirely lacked Phoebe's genius for hospitality, and I knew that her house was likely to be short of seasonal luxuries. Phoebe, as a matter of course, had provided puddings and chutneys, amazing cheeses that stank out the fridge and chocolate of silken grain and melting texture. I didn't want Fritz to miss things like this on his first Christmas without her.

As Phoebe had always done, I went to the big delicatessen on Rosslyn Hill. It was warm and noisy, thronged with people. A stout security man in a blue uniform guarded the doors. I hadn't bothered with breakfast, and the delicious smells made my light head spin. I filled my basket with the things Phoebe would have bought. I knew exactly what these were. A year ago, I had driven her up here, to help with the carrying. Nothing had changed. It was easy to imagine she was still beside me, laughing over the pictures on the jars of sauerkraut.

"Which shall we take—the fat man in leather shorts, or the fat lady with the mad smile?"

Last year, she had been extravagant. We had heaped our baskets with liqueurs and fine French pâtés, and a flask of (in Phoebe's words) "the rarest balsamic vinegar ever to come out of Modena." She had been very tired, but she had planned weeks of fabulous cooking. I hadn't wanted to think it then, but it occurred to me now that Phoebe had known it would be her last Christmas on earth.

She made a real German Stollen cake, I remembered. Fritz had loved it.

Phoebe used to say, "This is how you catch a man—you bake him something stodgy and sweet, and he'll never leave your side again."

Thanks, I told her shade, I'll take the hint. I decided to bake Fritz the best damn Stollen this side of the Black Forest. My spirits were lifting. What was I thinking? Why was I assuming Ruth would be doing the cooking? Ruth was a very indifferent cook. I was a good one—I'd been taught by Phoebe.

I was going to take charge of the cooking. I was going to spend hours of scented serenity in Ruth's cramped kitchen, mixing cakes while listening to Radio Four. Something shifted in my mind, and I was suddenly looking forward to it. Phoebe had left me her box of cookery books. I hadn't been able to bear looking at these precious volumes, which were penciled all over with her notes and amendments. Now I needed them. If I planned to take Phoebe's place on Christmas Day, I needed all the help she could give me.

I filled two large baskets with every imaginable delicacy.

I halted, on my way to the till, to pick up a large bag of gold and silver chocolate coins.

"Oh. Cassie," said someone beside me. "Hi."

It was Peason, magnificent in scarlet sheepskin.

I wasn't pleased to see her, but thinking of intensive cooking had left me with a genial glow. "Felicity. Hi. How are you?"

"Pretty exhausted, actually." She didn't look exhausted. She was carrying one bottle of Cointreau. "Don't you find this time of year incredibly stressful? Or perhaps it's just me." She glanced down at my heaped baskets. "God, you've bought tons."

"I'll be cooking for four people."

"Cooking!" Peason shuddered. Then she made a sour face. "Oh, of course. You'll be going down to bumfuck-on-sea for Fritz's panto."

I couldn't resist. "Yes, won't it be fun? When are you coming to see it?"

Peason said, "Look, I might as well tell you. I'm not going out with that shit any more."

Oh, joy and rapture and merry Christmas to everyone—I nearly keeled over with the sudden injection of hope.

I said, "I'm sorry," over the Hallelujah Chorus inside my head. Fritz was single again, and I was still in with a chance.

"He just turned out to be totally selfish and unreasonable." Peason pouted, which really beautiful people can do without seeming half-witted. "It was the house that did it in the end."

Again, why should I resist? "Would that be because he refused to let you move in with him?"

A cloud of suspicion crossed her eyes, then passed. She didn't really care what I thought. "Oh, he told you. Well, don't you think he was being rather stupid? I gave him a chance to stay in his gorgeous house."

"And you gave yourself a chance to get a gorgeous house at half-price," I said.

"Precisely. You'd think he'd be grateful. But he actually wants to move out. He actually wants to buy himself a flat in some appalling part of town. Fine—but he can't expect me to go there with him."

She paid for her Cointreau, then stood watching as I unloaded my baskets.

"I simply don't understand him," she said. "I know people thought we made a fantastic team. I wanted us to be a power couple with a house in Hampstead. It would have been brilliant for his career." She sighed. "But he doesn't seem to want a career."

She hung around while I signed away a huge sum on my whited sepulcher of a credit card, and watched, with faint interest, while I stuffed four bags with my purchases. With two bags in each hand, I staggered toward the doors. Peason strolled elegantly beside me, cradling her Cointreau.

"Anyway," she said, "he was getting dull. You should go for him."

Cheeky cow. I refused to answer.

"He doesn't fancy you," she went on, "but there's things you could do about that. He's not in a position to be fussy if he insists on moving to Crouch End."

The security guards had changed shifts. This new man at the door was tall, black and extremely handsome. He was sitting on a camp stool, reading a yellow paperback—good grief, Flaubert in French. It could only be Claudette's brother, the most ornamental security guard in London, and the most useless (you remember—the one who was chucked out of Cambridge for sleeping all day).

I let my bags drop to the floor. "Pierre!"

He looked up. "Cassie—Cassie Shaw!" He jumped to his feet to embrace me, mainly triumphant that he had remembered my name. "Happy Christmas—how are you?"

I had to tilt my head up to look at him. Claudette took after Mrs. Nboki, a plump little hamster of a Frenchwoman. Pierre was a clone of Dr. Nboki, their princely Nigerian father, who used to appear at school events fabulously attired in gold-embroidered robes.

"I thought you were working in a nightclub," I said.

"I was, but it was getting too heavy," Pierre said. "I have a peaceable nature and I don't like aggression. You don't get nearly so much trouble in a Hampstead food shop. And the hours are better." He glanced aside at Peason.

She said, "Hello, do I know you?" She was smiling all over her face— all over her entire body, in fact. Her lustrous eyes gaped an invitation.

Who could have ignored that shrieking signal? Certainly not Pierre Nboki, once the Errol Flynn of University College School.

He switched on his famously seductive smile. "I'm Pierre. I think you might know my sister, Claudette."

"My God," Peason murmured. "*You're* Claudette's brother?" She matched his smile. The two smiles locked and fused, generating a sexual charge you could almost see. "You don't look anything like her."

I had a life to get on with. I had to drive down to the coast. I wished Pierre and Peason good-bye and merry Christmas, and left the two beauties standing together in the doorway, entirely absorbed in one another's infatuated gazes. Yes, I had done it again. It looked as if the Little Match-maker Girl had made another match (I was right; Pierre took up residence in St. John's Wood shortly afterward).

What, I wondered, was I doing for other people that I couldn't do for myself?

CHAPTER TWENTY

In the last gray rags of twilight, Ruth's town was desolate. The only sounds were the sawing of the wind and the constant boom of the waves. The only splashes of color were the posters for *Aladdin* at the Theatre Royal, showing Len Batty in a red wig and striped stockings, his garishly painted face frozen in a rictus of jollity. I wondered how this place could possibly muster the audiences for a pantomime when it didn't seem to have a population.

Driving along the deserted esplanade, where small tufts of seaweed smacked into the windscreen and tangled in the wipers, I fought off depression. It was Christmas, and I was not going home to Phoebe. The entire thing still seemed pointless without her.

I'll admit, I was surprised to feel the sadness lifting when I pulled up outside Ruth's flint cottage. There was a wreath of holly on the door, tied to the knocker with a scarlet ribbon. The door opened and Ruth came out to meet me.

I sprang out of the car—mainly because it was so good to have someone to spring out at—and we hugged, with more warmth than usual. Ruth, looking at me keenly, asked me how I was.

"I'm fine," I said. "When I'm down, I remind myself how much worse it must be for Fritz."

Ruth let out one of her dry cackles. "Oh, I shouldn't worry about him. He's a whirlwind of energy. Made me stop work to help with the decorations."

She shut the front door, muting the roar of the waves, and I thought the little firelit sitting room looked charming. Ruth had added more cushions since my last visit, and there was another of George's paintings—a sunny watercolor of a famous local lighthouse. A Christmas tree twinkled in one corner. There were sprigs of holly in the picture frames. Phoebe had always done this, and I thought I recognized the hand of Fritz. Ruth had no idea about things like Christmas decorations.

George emerged from the kitchen, wearing a striped apron and a yachting cap and clutching a spatula. I kissed him, and he said he was glad I was here, because I could give him some advice about cooking.

Ruth said, "She's only just arrived. Don't put her straight to work."

I followed George into the narrow kitchen. A pallid, deformed and generally inadequate chicken sat in the middle of a large roasting pan. George had been about to shove this into the oven without seasoning, herbs or even a decent burial. Of course I had to intervene. Suddenly, my blood was up. I took the roasting pan into custody and asked George to bring in my boxes and bags of food.

I spent a peaceful couple of hours cooking the chicken, eking it out with roast potatoes and spicy Spanish sausages. Ruth came in. She poured us both glasses of red wine and leaned against the counter, watching me.

"You remind me of Phoebe," she said.

"Do I? How?"

"You associate kitchens with relaxation."

"As opposed to what?"

"Drudgery. Resentment."

"Oh." I wished Ruth would get some idea of small talk. I said, "I suppose I must have picked up at least a few of Phoebe's habits."

"Of course you have. And her system of values."

"I've never found a better system."

"Oh," Ruth said, "don't misunderstand me. I'm not criticizing. Phoebe was, in the most unambiguous sense, what is called 'good.' She brought you up when I couldn't."

We were embarrassed. I busied myself basting the chicken. Ruth was not worried by silence, and sat like a slab, eyes hooded in thought.

At last, in what was for her a lighter voice, she observed, "You're making a lot of food."

"No I'm not." The moment of near-closeness was over, and I relaxed. "There's four of us, don't forget."

Fritz was not expected back until after midnight (George told me this; he was fascinated by the goings-on at the theater, and knew Fritz's callsheet by heart). Fritz erupted among us, however, just as I was carving the chicken. His face was covered with a waxy layer of yellowish-brown foundation. His eyes were outlined in black and turned up at the corners. He had an hour's dinner break, and had run through the town in his makeup to see me.

I was ridiculously happy to see him. He ate a huge supper with great speed, bombarding me with questions about Ben and Annabel, and entrancing George with a vivid account of a disastrous technical rehearsal.

He glanced at the clock. "Cass, are you tired?"

"No."

"Do you fancy taking a walk with me, back to the theater?"

"She'll be blown away," George said, "little thing like her."

As if to illustrate this, the wind keened around the house. But I wanted to talk to Fritz. I put on my thickest coat, and we went out into the cold salt air. I clutched his arm, trotting to keep up with his long strides. We had to shout at each other to be heard above the wind and the waves.

Fritz said, "You were right."

"What?"

"You were RIGHT. About Peason."

"I know I was right," I shouted. "How incredible that you should see it too."

"Don't rub it in."

"Sorry."

"She was after a cut-price house. She wouldn't follow me to the ends of the earth."

"Did you ask?"

He laughed briefly. "She wasn't even ashamed—didn't see any reason why she should be. Ruth says brazen lack of conscience can be a sign of bipolar disorder in its manic phase."

I tried, and failed, to imagine Fritz discussing his love life with Ruth.

"You don't seem very grief-stricken about it," I said. "I knew, anyway. I ran into her this morning."

"It's over, Grimble."

"Sorry?"

"It's OVER. Me and Peason."

"Hurrah!"

"I knew you'd be pleased."

We had been making our way, heads bowed, along the esplanade. We turned into one of the narrow lanes that led up to the high street. The wind was immediately quieter. Fritz halted.

"Seriously, I think I went crazy. You're worth ten of her, if you want to know." He took something out of his pocket. "Better-looking, too. And I wanted to give you something. It's not a Christmas present."

He gave me a little box. I recognized it, and cried out with delight when I opened it. Inside was the forget-me-not ring. The tiny sapphire petals glinted in the orange light of the street lamp above us.

"It's really from Phoebe," Fritz said. "I thought you should have it. After all, we were engaged—only for a couple of hours, but you deserve to get something out of it. You made her so ridiculously happy."

"Thank you. It's wonderful. Thank you."

"Put it on."

I pulled off my gloves. I plucked the ring from its setting of bald velvet. For a fraction of a second, I hesitated over which finger to put it on. It couldn't be my left hand, or he'd think I expected a wedding. I slid it on to the fourth finger of my right hand. It fitted perfectly. It looked exquisite. I loved it.

And there we were—in a side street outside a shuttered tattoo parlor, both a little lower than the angels. I didn't care that it wasn't a proper engagement, or even a declaration of love. I didn't care that I was gazing sentimentally into the painted face of Wishee-Washee. I was happy because I saw and sensed his tenderness. I was wrapped in warmth, light as a summer's day.

"You're cold," he said. "Come into the theater."

"No, I said I'd go straight back."

"Just for a minute. I'd like you to meet Len."

266

I was suddenly shy. "Oh no, not now."

Fritz laughed and grabbed the hand with the ring. "Come on, you can't miss this. Len's the best thing about this wretched job."

He hurried me to the high street. The front of the Theater Royal—emblazoned with more posters of Len Batty—was dark, but light spilled into a shadowy alley that ran down one side. The stage door stood open. Two women were smoking outside. Both were plastered in makeup, and when you got close they looked about sixteen. They giggled when they saw me.

"Evening, ladies," Fritz said. To me he whispered, "Dancers, poor little things," as if this explained everything.

Inside the dirty warmth of the stage door, all was noise and confusion—the inner workings of a theater are baffling to an outsider. I heard disembodied shouts, loud hammering, and the same ten bars of "Search for the Hero Inside Yourself," played over and over on a loudspeaker. More dancers, caked in paint and wearing silver bikinis, were sharing a grease-spotted paper of chips beside a grimy institutional radiator.

It was fascinating to see the nuts and bolts behind the glitter. Fritz knew I would be fascinated. Keeping a tight hold of my hand (we were nearly severed by two stagehands carrying a gaudy painted flat of a Chinese house), he led me through a maze of fire buckets and dangling ropes until we suddenly emerged into a blaze of light. We were in the wings, looking out at the glare of the stage.

Len Batty sat on a low chair nearby. His famous basset-hound face was made up with lipstick and rouge. His thinning hair was covered with a wig-stocking, which made him look as if the top of his head had been sawed off. He wore a yellow bathrobe over a corset and comic bloomers, and he was eating a cheese roll.

"Ay-up, Fred," said the famous voice. "Where did you get to at dinner, then?"

"I went back to my digs," Fritz said. "I brought Cassie back."

Len Batty looked at me, chewing imperturbably. It was a strange feeling, rather like being inspected by a fictional character. "So you're Cassie," he said. "Young Fred here never stops talking about you."

Fritz grinned. "He refuses to call me Fritz."

"My dog's called Fritz, that's why," Len Batty said. "It's no name for a human." Under the paint, his face was tired. "By the way," he said to Fritz, "I got us more time for that change. The horse is set to do a tap dance."

Before I could interpret this, a man's voice shouted, "Okay, people—taking the song from the top—"

The milling about intensified. Len Batty finished his roll with a sigh. "No rest for the wicked. Nice to meet you, Cassie."

Fritz dropped a kiss on my cheek and returned to his dressing room. I ran back to Ruth's through the shuttered town, and found Ruth and George settled comfortably over the fire. In my new, happier mood, I wanted to laugh—they looked such dear old souls. Who would have imagined Ruth turning into such a thing?

George closed his book (O'Brien, *The Wine-Dark Sea*), and stood up, waving me into his chair. "Come and get warm—would you like a hot toddy?"

"I recommend it," Ruth said, glancing over the top of the *New States-man*. "It's mostly whiskey."

"I'd love one," I told him.

George beamed. "Good-oh." He went off to the kitchen, his slippers flapping against the floor tiles. I took the slippers as an emblem of his establishment here.

Reading my mind, Ruth said, "George is living here now."

"I think that's excellent," I said. "I hope it means you're going to marry him."

She shut the magazine and gave me one of her rare, rusty smiles. "I don't know about that. Neither of us is going anywhere. Seriously, you like him, don't you?"

I was touched that she minded what I thought. "I like him very much," I said. "He's lovely. I just wish I could find someone half as lovely for myself."

Ruth smiled, eyeing me curiously. "That's a very pretty ring."

My face was hot. "Fritz gave it to me. It was Phoebe's."

"But it's on your right hand."

"Yes. It's not that sort of ring."

She was still looking at me, with an unaccustomed softness in her face—though this might have been the effect of the firelight. She said,

"You're very pretty at the moment. I think it must mean that you'll be happy again sooner than you think."

"You're happy, aren't you?" I said. "I've never seen you so happy."

Ruth's eyes widened at the boldness of this, the intimacy. But she was pleased. "I am happy, actually. George has a very restful presence, and a capacity for cheerfulness that I find quite amazing. This is why I was keen to introduce him to Phoebe. I wanted to show George that I recognized his species."

I would never have thought of comparing George and Phoebe, but now saw that there was a kind of similarity between them. They shared an outlook; they struck the same chords and created the same trustful atmospheres. George was pom-pomming to himself in the kitchen. Like Phoebe's, his singing was a constant and reassuring lullaby.

Ruth continued to smile. Aging suited her, softening her angles. "George loves having Fritz around. And I must say, so do I. It's rather like standing in a high wind—tiring yet exhilarating. I never imagined he'd mature so well. He was one of the most ghastly teenagers I've ever met."

"You know him better now," I said.

"Hmm, I'm not sure about that." Unconsciously, Ruth echoed the words I'd heard from Peason. "I don't understand him at all."

"How do you mean?"

"The man's an imposter," Ruth said. "I'd like to know why he's masquerading as an actor, when he evidently belongs somewhere else."

"What do you think he should be doing?"

"Good heavens, I don't know. Growing up would be a good start." Before I could open my mouth to protest that Fritz was immensely mature, Ruth said firmly, "There's a perfectly decent, respectable, middle-class man hiding somewhere inside Fritz. He ought to admit it, and let the bugger out before it's too late."

Quite unexpectedly, we managed a decent Christmas. Fritz had the day off. I cooked a spectacular lunch, which kept me busy enough to take the sharpest edge off my longing for Phoebe. Afterward, the four of us ate and yawned and watched the Marx Brothers (*Duck Soup*) on television. Ruth cracked nuts and told fearsome anecdotes about her work.

Fritz was lively and hilarious, but I sensed restlessness in his energy. He wasn't himself, and it was about more than missing Phoebe. Anger gnawed at him, like a piece of grit trapped under his skin. Though he was charming to me, he wouldn't give me the chance to reach him—he used Ruth and George as shields, so we wouldn't be alone together.

Eventually, toward the end of the short afternoon, I cornered him in the kitchen. He was standing beside the open fridge, morosely eating cold turkey straight off the plate.

I said, "Let me make you a sandwich."

"No thanks."

"Or have a piece of Stollen. It came out really well."

"I don't doubt it, but no thanks."

"Fritz, are you okay?"

"Of course not. You've seen where I work."

"The panto? It's not that bad, is it?"

He looked away from me to shut the fridge. "Ten shows a week, for a month."

"Yes, but that's not forever."

"Afterward is even worse," Fritz said gloomily. "I have nothing to look forward to except auditioning for more commercials, and occasionally fucking the plainer casting directors, who might be grateful."

"Maria," I said, "I don't think you were cut out to be a nun."

He laughed. "I knew you'd tell me to give up acting. I wondered how long it would take you."

"Well, if you hate it all so much, aren't you in the wrong career?"

"I wouldn't be here if I had the slightest idea what I wanted to do instead. I envy you and Ben sometimes."

"No, you don't. You think we're wet and prissy, because we like posher books and music than you do."

Fritz said, "You both work at the thing you're very good at."

I considered this. Sometimes I needed to be reminded that I was fortunate. I earned a living doing a job I loved, as part of a career that was my life. Ben was the same. Neither of us minded our meager wages, because that wasn't the point. If nobody had paid us, we would have done it for nothing.

"Look at me," Fritz said. "When I was a student, all I cared about was qualifying. The goal was everything. But when I'd reached it, I found I didn't want the life that went with it."

"It's not too late to change direction," I offered, knowing how lame it sounded. "Keats was a doctor before he became a poet."

Fritz laughed. "That's a crap example. Keats was incredibly unsuccessful as a poet, and by the time he was my age he was dead."

"Well, maybe you should become one of those sexy media doctors, with a nice newspaper column, or a television show. . . ."

"Face it, Grimble," Fritz said. "I'm nearly thirty-two, and I'm making my living in red satin. I might as well be a pole dancer. I can't move on, or be fulfilled, or anything. Whatever my big chance was, I blew it."

CHAPTER TWENTY-ONE

In the evening of Boxing Day, George, Ruth and I went to the theater for the opening night of *Aladdin*. George, like me, was a devotee of pantomime. Together we tried to explain the various traditions to Ruth. She was immune to fun, and kept looking for logic.

"You've lost me again. Who is Abanazer, and why do I have to boo and hiss him?"

George was patient. "Because he's the villain. He's trying to steal Aladdin's wonderful lamp. Just copy me and Cassie. You'll soon get the hang of it. I must say," he added to me, "I'm looking forward to Batty's Widow Twankey. It's bound to be an interesting interpretation."

"Good grief," Ruth said. "You make it sound like King Lear."

"The role is every bit as demanding," George said. "I saw Stanley Baxter's Twankey at the Edinburgh Lyceum. It was one of the high spots of my theater-going career."

The Theatre Royal had sprung to gaudy, swarming life. Crowds of people pushed up the steps and jostled for souvenirs and bags of sweets. There were toddlers shrieking like train whistles, and teenagers trying to look cynical. There were parties of old people, some Sea Scouts and the B&Q staff outing.

George steered Ruth and me through the crowd in the foyer, pausing to buy three glossy programs and a large bag of wine gums. I should mention here that I was getting fonder of George by the hour—he would not let Ruth spoil this blissful experience, for herself or anyone else. And even Ruth couldn't resist his murmurs of delight as we took our seats.

If you've never been to a pantomime, I hardly know how to describe the atmosphere. It is the purest essence of theater. The audience never sits in silence, but constantly stirs and seethes. There is a sense of excitement, not only among the children. A pantomime audience expects broad comedy and noisy glitter. It is supposed to be tawdry—attempts at good taste are always awful. A real pantomime means vulgarity, crass topical references and television stars as familiar as your furniture.

Our seats were in the front row of the dress circle. (Len Batty would address us as "you on the mantelpiece.") It was a fine old auditorium, all red plush and gilt cherubs, just like the little cardboard theater I had glued together as a child.

Wine gums circulated. We studied our programs. I always love the potted biographies of the cast, and these were little gems of understated tragedy. Each artiste's photograph was attached to a list of dreadful jobs they had done in the past—dancing engagements on cruise ships, small parts in obscure television soaps, stints of understudying on post-post-West End tours. Abanazer had been in some films (*Ding-Dong-Dangler, She Likes Them Lusty*) that sounded distinctly dodgy. There could have been no better illustration of the hardships of the professional stage. They should have handed copies of this program to all first-year drama students.

Fritz's photograph was saturnine and brooding. His professional credits were short and to the point—a list of fringe productions no one had ever heard of, a couple of television commercials and *Rookery Nook*. I thought I could see why he had been so depressed the night before. Boiled down to a single paragraph, his career did not look illustrious.

The house lights dimmed. Down in the orchestra pit, a drum rolled (boom-tish!). The Spirit of the Lamp appeared in front of the tabs. The chatter of the audience died down to a murmur. The Spirit wore a long gold robe and carried a wand. She addressed us through a radio mike in deafening rhyming couplets.

Nostalgia pierced me. I started to cry. I wasn't sad, but remembered happiness hurts.

The curtains opened on a village street in old China, dominated by the Widow Twankey's Laundry. Wishee-Washee and Aladdin appeared, in the persons of Fritz and a girl from a minor sitcom.

I have permission from Fritz to reproduce his first speech:

"Hello, boys and girls! Did you have a good Christmas?"

It was huge fun. I realized that I hadn't been in a theater since going out with Matthew. The last time had been a couple of weeks before the oral sex incident. We'd sat through a highly fashionable foreign thing at the Almeida, which I'd pretended to love. It had been very worthy, but this was far more enjoyable.

Len Batty's portrayal of the Widow Twankey was caustic and mournful, full of ironic asides, and in its way as many-sided as a good King Lear. He was so funny that even Ruth chuckled. Hideous red ringlets framed his baggy face. He swirled up his skirts to show his bloomers. He attempted to milk the dancing horse and made satirical remarks about the local council.

I threw myself into it, loving every minute. I booed Abanazer. I yelled "Behind you!" I did a dance that involved standing up and mooing like a cow. I went to war with the stalls over who could make the loudest chicken noises. George was just as enthusiastic. Ruth watched us both with (I suspected) professional interest.

About half an hour before the intermission, the flat of the village street was removed and we were inside old Mrs. Twankey's laundry. Two large tubs of foam were placed center stage. George and I grew more excited, for this was the famous "Slosh" scene, in which Fritz and Len Batty were to soak each other with water, spray each other with foam and bounce huge padded bras into the orchestra. They had been rehearsing it minutely for weeks.

The "Slosh" scene was fast and furious, and immensely wet. Both men were soaked to the skin within minutes. Widow Twankey ordered her useless son to count a row of comedy bloomers on a washing line. He got it wrong and accidentally dunked his old mother in the tub (I'm slightly ashamed to report that I was helpless with laughter; you'd never get Q. D. Leavis laughing at such basic slapstick).

"Look what you've done," Len Batty said. "I'd better take off this wet frock—all you men turn your backs."

274

Fritz said, "You're in no danger, Mum!"

"Why, you cheeky little—" Batty chased Fritz round the stage. He grabbed a bucket of water and upended it on Fritz's head.

I'm not sure how long it took for the audience to realize something was wrong. It seemed ages, but was probably only a couple of minutes. Len Batty suddenly halted, made an unearthly moaning noise no one could mistake for comedy, and crashed to the floor.

Fritz pulled the bucket off his dripping head. People were still laughing, but also beginning to be anxious. Len Batty lay on the wet stage, his flesh livid under the paint.

And then, for a moment, it looked as if Fritz was attacking him. He dived at Len Batty's chest, tugging at the material of his costume until it ripped apart.

He shouted, "Shut the curtains—get an ambulance!"

As the curtains closed, we saw Fritz pumping violently at Len Batty's chest.

Before we could all disintegrate into chaos, a man in a bow tie came out with a microphone. He told us to leave our details at the box office and go home. Everyone was very sorry, but Len Batty had been taken ill. Nobody laughed when he asked, several times, if there was a doctor in the house.

"I'd better go down, I suppose," Ruth said. She stood up. "But it looks as if Wishee-Washee's doing fine by himself."

I asked, "Do you think he's going to be all right?"

Ruth said, "I don't know. He might have been dead when he hit the floor."

"Let's look on the bright side," begged George. "I'm sure Fritz knows what to do."

"I hope so," Ruth said. "I haven't done this sort of doctoring for decades."

We hurried round to the stage door. Ruth, totally impervious to her surroundings, strode into the chaos and announced herself to a frantic man with a clipboard. He shouted something into a radio. Ruth was led away toward the stage.

"No ambulance yet," George said, his optimism wavering for the first time. "Oh dear."

We were on our second hot toddy by the time Ruth came home.

"Well?" I demanded. George and I had been on tenterhooks. At several points George had been on the verge of tears. We had agreed that there was something especially heartrending in the thought of the poor old comedian being struck down in a corset and full makeup.

Ruth, never in a hurry, warmed herself at the fire. "The last I heard, they think he'll be all right."

George asked, "How long did you have to wait for the ambulance?"

"Ages. Please remind me not to have a heart attack in this town. And don't you dare do it either. The nearest decent hospital is miles away."

"I'd say you need a stiff drink. I'll make another round of hot toddies." George stood up and went to the kitchen.

Ruth took his chair. She smiled at me. "Thank God Fritz was there. He saved that man's life."

"Really?"

"Oh yes. He knew exactly what to do, and the great thing is to do it quickly. I helped a bit until the ambulance came, but if it had just been me, I'd have been too late."

"Oh my God." I was deeply impressed. "He's a hero!"

"He was pouring sweat and utterly exhausted—but he wouldn't give up. He was ferocious. He refused to stop until he saw the paramedics and the equipment."

"Where is he? Is he with you?"

"No, he went in the ambulance. Still dressed in that idiotic costume." She lowered herself into the armchair opposite. "It struck me that he's a very fine man these days."

"Phoebe would be so proud," I said.

"Oh yes, but Phoebe was always proud of him, whatever he did. I was thinking that Jimmy would be pleased at the way he'd turned out."

I was touched that she had thought of Jimmy, to whom she had never been close. "I wish you'd tell Fritz. He was always dying for his father's approval."

Ruth sighed. "Father's approval and mother's love. I sometimes think they're the only essential ingredients for happiness in this life. If everyone in the world had those two things, I'd be out of a job."

"I wanted Derek's approval," I said, remembering.

"You had mine, anyway," Ruth said. "I hope you know it. And you had my love—though I couldn't show it in the way that Phoebe did. But I did love you."

"I know," I said. "Really."

"This is why I got so worried about you sliding into depression—because my life was so blighted by it. And yours. I think I owe you an apology for what I went through when you were a child."

Her voice was calm, but there was a longing in it, a fear that what she offered so hesitantly would be thrown back at her, and my eyes filled.

"You mustn't apologize," I said. "I can see now that you were ill."

"Thank you." She settled against the cushions more comfortably. "It went on for ages. But it's fair to say that I'm better these days."

As if to illustrate this, George came in with a glass of hot toddy. Ruth and I exchanged smiles.

"I wonder what will happen now?" George wondered. "I mean, to the pantomime. They can hardly do it without the star."

"Poor Fritz," Ruth said. "Out of a job again."

The emergency had made the three of us very companionable. We sat by the fire, going over every moment. Ruth said she certainly hadn't anticipated giving mouth-to-mouth to Len Batty. She told us that her face had been covered with his makeup afterward, and she hadn't known until one of the dancers gave her a tissue to wipe it off.

We were still waiting for Fritz at eleven. George and Ruth went to bed. I stayed beside the fire. I couldn't possibly go to bed until I had seen him. I made myself a cup of tea and picked up a book, but I could not read. I stared into the flames, thinking about Fritz. I was ashamed of the way I had underestimated him. How could I ever have believed Matthew was a better man?

I'd been blind and snobbish, and though I fancied myself for my insight, I had managed to overlook Fritz's bravery—his strength, his sheer goodness. I had been too far up myself to look beyond the louche north

London layabout. I couldn't trust this layabout with my best friend, but I would trust him with my life.

Just after midnight I heard the drunken scraping of a key in the lock, and a muffled voice at the door—"Oh fuck."

I jumped up to let him in. Fritz was wearing his street clothes. His face was striped with paint. He smelled of spirits, and had that fiery glow of triumphant energy I hadn't seen for months. His dejection had gone. He swept me into his arms and kissed me hard on the mouth.

"Cassie, Cassie my darling—at last I'm fit to look you in the eye."

I begged him to put me down, and to keep quiet. "You'll wake Ruth and George!"

He dropped his voice to an exaggerated whisper. "Whoops, sorry. Can't have that."

"Where have you been? At the hospital?"

"No, I didn't stay there long. I went back to the theater, and my colleagues were kind enough to ply me with strong drink."

"Quite right, you deserve it," I said. "Ruth says you were brilliant."

"No, Grimble, not brilliant. Better than brilliant—I was *there*. That's the main thing. It wasn't wasted. All that medical training did just what it said on the tin. I think I was sent here to be matched with this hour."

"How's Len?"

"Fairly stable. But he won't be doing any more panto for a while." He swept me up again, and danced me round the small room like a rag doll. "Hurrah, I'm unemployed! O frabjous day! Callooh! Callay!"

I gasped, "Put me down!"

"Sorry." He dropped me.

"Would you like something to eat? You must be starving."

"I believe I am, but don't disappear into the kitchen. I want to talk to you."

"Talk to me in the kitchen."

He followed me, and stood at my elbow while I made him a ham and tomato sandwich. He wolfed it down in a few bites, and took George's whiskey bottle into custody. I built up the fire, and we sat together on the hearthrug.

"I couldn't save Phoebe," Fritz said. "And I can just about live with

278

that, because nothing could have saved her. But if I hadn't saved Len, I'd have been gutted. Do you understand?"

"Yes."

"For one thing, I was the one who nearly killed him. I wouldn't have been so rough with him in the Slosh scene, but he had to behave as if he was indestructible. Poor old sod, he tried to say 'Ay-up Mother' for the guys in the ambulance."

"And there's no chance of the show going on without him?"

"Nope. The notices were up by the time I got back to the theater. You can give me a lift home whenever you like."

I said, "You're really happy about this, aren't you?"

Fritz wrapped his arms around me. He spoke into my neck. I felt his warm breath on my skin. "I'm happy that I didn't mess up in front of you. I know you think I'm a waste of food."

I said, "I think you're wonderful."

"What kind of wonderful? Boy Scout wonderful?"

"Better."

"You approve of me, then."

"Totally."

"I don't know why, dear Grimble," Fritz said, "but I've always wanted your approval. Even when you were plain."

"Wow, thanks."

"You were such an incredible smartarse when we were kids—actually, until quite recently. When you were threatening to marry the moose I thought you were turning yourself into a culture bore with bad hair."

"It's all true," I said. "I'm too comfortable to argue."

He brushed his lips against my neck, sending shooting stars through my veins. "But then you got rid of him and stopped trying to look elegant, and I discovered that I was starting to find you seriously sexy. I'd be thinking about you—just in a normal sort of way—and suddenly I'd have a huge erection. What's the matter?"

I was shaking with laughter. "How romantic."

"But it was intensely romantic," Fritz said. "Because at the same time I was liking you more and more, wanting to tell you things, wanting to spend all my time with you. And I made a discovery."

"What?"

"That I'd fallen in love with you. In fact, that I've probably been in love with you since the day we met. And I still feel just the same." He put his mouth very close to my ear. "I like you, and I like your bottom."

CHAPTER TWENTY-TWO

That night, for the first and last time, I dreamed of Phoebe. In my dream, she was standing in her kitchen. The window was open. She was young and full of vitality, not any particular age, but all her ages. And she was stirring and singing, as I had seen her a thousand times. This was all, but it filled me with a strong sense of comfort and serenity. There was no sadness. I felt I had been allowed to glimpse something eternal, and took it (perhaps inevitably) as a Sign.

Next day, Fritz and I drove back to London. To put it mildly, I was happy. Ruth and I had got ourselves to a place in which we could talk without reserve. She could never replace Phoebe, but the sense of her love for me was extremely sustaining. And I was rapturously in love, which had turned the whole world inside out. I was utterly pierced and kebabbed with love. His smile could bring tears to my eyes. One breath of his could make me come.

Fritz, however, was moody. Though perfectly cordial to me, he was distant, wrapped in thought.

I stopped the car outside the Hampstead house. "Here we are. Do you want me to come in?"

"I don't think so."

"Oh."

He smiled and said, "Don't panic, darling—I'm not having second thoughts. Actually, they're more like first thoughts. You may have gathered that I'm going through a small mental crisis."

"Can't I help?"

"Oh, Cassie, you've done far too much already." He leaned over and kissed me on the mouth. "I'll call you, okay? I'm not going back on anything I've said. I just need to get my head sorted out."

I said I never knew what that meant.

Fritz said, "It means I can't ask you to share a life that's a load of shit."

To prove that he would ring me, he called me about five minutes after I'd got home. "There, you believe me now," he said. "You don't have to tell all your girlfriends I shagged you and never called."

I felt that I should have been insulted, but had already started laughing (you will have noticed this often happened in our relationship; perhaps I'm inclined to take myself too seriously).

I asked, "How many calls do I get?"

"One per shag."

"And how many shags?"

I heard him laughing at the other end. "As many as you want."

"Good," I said. "Are you all right?

"Of course. Naturally. Why shouldn't I be all right?"

"Seriously, Fritz—what's the matter?"

"Nothing. I'll both call and shag you tomorrow."

He was gone, and I had to be satisfied with this. But I knew something was the matter, and I was worried. Why was he so angry? What was eating him? I couldn't be entirely happy until he was.

Over the next couple of weeks, I saw Fritz nearly every day. Sometimes he met me after work. Most often, he let himself into my flat, with the key he had coolly filched from my bag after our second night together. Fritz had none of Matthew's caution about moving too fast. He behaved as if he meant to stay for the rest of his life. I used to come home to the smell of cooking, and my heart would lift with happiness to find him in my tiny kitchen. On one occasion I found him naked in my bed, with a magnificent—well, we needn't go into it. Despite Fritz's occasional spells of black-browed silence, he made my life blissful.

"Dear me, you haven't stopped smiling for hours," Betsy said, one afternoon at the end of January. "I wish you would. It's rather eerie. Like a shop mannequin."

"Sorry," I said. "I can't help it."

"I'm surrounded by people in love. Everywhere I look there's some-one canoodling. I blame you, Cassie."

"Me?"

"Well, you started all this matchmaking business. Suddenly you're all in pairs. It's starting to get on my nerves."

I said, "You're just miffed because you're not arranging Jonah's wed-ding."

Betsy sighed. "It seems unfair, that's all. If only she'd listen to a few of my suggestions." ("She" was Hazel's mother.) "To tell the truth, I'm used to being the mother of the bride, and it's a bit of a comedown. The groom's mother is *nobody*—at my girls' weddings, she was always stuck down at the very end of the top table, with Grandma and Auntie Rose-mary. And it ought to be the other way round, because marrying off a son is far harder. I'm formally handing over the greatest responsibility of my life."

I'd been hearing a lot of speeches like this—Betsy was finding the cutting of the cord unexpectedly painful.

"Part of me thought he'd always be living with us. I know it's time he moved out, but I can't help missing him."

I was glad when my phone rang. It was Fritz. He wanted to know if I could make myself free the following day. It was a special occasion, he said. Len Batty was out of hospital, and had invited us both down to his house in Oxfordshire.

On the way down, I found out why Fritz was tense. Len's wife had re-quested this visit because she wanted to meet him, so that she could thank him for saving her husband's life. Fritz dreaded being thanked.

"I knew what to do because I've had several years of expensive train-ing," he said. "If I hadn't done it, I'd just be a disgrace. I hope she's not going to go on about it."

"Do be nice, though," I said. "I mean, don't be tetchy if she wants to weep all over you."

"I'm never tetchy."

I felt bound to say, "Yes you are. You're extremely bad-tempered at the moment. You jump down my throat whenever I try to be complimentary."

Fritz was driving. He glanced aside at me keenly. "Do I?"

"You did something good, Fritz. Take it like a man."

He sighed. "I hate being thanked simply because I didn't behave like an arsehole."

The Battys lived in a farmhouse on the outskirts of Banbury. With the map open on my knee, I navigated us through lanes and villages of fat prosperity. It was the extremely tame and genteel sort of countryside, all gleaming outbuildings and houses with names—"Scrote Farm," "Four-ways," "The Old Rectory."

Len's house was called The Tithe Barn. It didn't look like a barn. It was a red-brick building of glaring newness, set behind a gate made of cartwheels. We parked on a stretch of immaculate gravel, a little awed by the extreme cleanliness of everything.

I whispered, "You wouldn't even need wellies if you lived round here. It's tidier than Hampstead Heath. Do I look okay?" I had dressed for the country, in jeans and a baggy jersey, but these didn't look right here.

"More than okay," Fritz said. "How many more times? You actually look better when you're not trying."

The front door (shining wood between a pair of brass coach lamps) opened. A slim blonde woman appeared, dressed in elegant trousers, a sweater with satin appliqué and abundant gold jewelry. This was Mrs. Batty. She came toward us, smiling, and I saw that she was older than she looked from a distance.

"You're Fred," she said. "I'm afraid I have to give you a kiss." She put her arms around Fritz and kissed him resoundingly. "Len says I mustn't embarrass you, but I don't care—I think you're fantastic." She smiled at me. "And you're Cassie." She released Fritz and kissed me, engulfing me in her perfume. "I bet you're proud of him. And isn't he handsome?"

As her husband had done, she took me for granted as Fritz's girlfriend. I wondered what Fritz had said about me.

Inside, the house smelt strongly of furniture polish. Its shining perfection made me feel a little shy. I had an impression of plump cushions, crowds of photographs in lacquered brass frames and dustless guest lavatories. The snob in me registered that there were no books except photograph albums, and no pictures. Evidently Mrs. Batty (Joyce, as we were instructed to call her) did not like clutter.

Len Batty was in the sitting room, in an armchair beside a large picture window. I had last seen him in full pantomime makeup, and was startled to see how gray he looked now, and how diminished. His eyes were almost invisible behind folds of exhausted flesh. He greeted us in a voice that was a breathy shadow of itself.

"You found us all right, then."

Fritz took both his hands eagerly. It touched me to see his affection for Len. "How are you?"

An elderly Alsatian dog lay on the carpet, resting his gray muzzle on his crossed paws. He rose when he saw strangers, and sniffed us both with distant courtesy.

I stroked his head. "Hi, Fritz."

Len Batty chuckled wheezily. "Yes, that's Fritz. You'll have to start calling Wonderboy here by his real name."

"Oh, nonsense, stop laying down the law," Joyce said. She dived for the cushion at Len's back and smacked it into a more comfortable shape. "You'd be pushing up daisies if not for him. As far as I'm concerned, he can call himself anything he likes."

She had cooked us an amazing lunch—roast beef with all the trimmings and a real, old-fashioned sherry trifle to follow. Len hobbled through to the dining room clutching Fritz's arm. Though he sat with us, he only ate a small bowl of porridge and a few leaves of salad. I noticed that Joyce, busily serving us and bombarding us with questions, watched him beadily.

After lunch, Fritz helped Len back to his invalid's chair. I carried plates and dishes into the kitchen.

"Wow," I exclaimed, stopping short on the threshold. "This is palatial! This is like something out of a magazine!"

Joyce—busily stacking one of two dishwashers—laughed. "I won't deny it. As I said to Len when we put it in, I reckon I deserve a fabulous kitchen. When we first met, we could barely afford a secondhand stove."

I passed her a pile of plates. "How long have you been married?"

"Forty-five years. Can you imagine being married to your Fred that long?"

"No."

"Well, I won't say it's been a picnic. We've had our fair share of ups and downs. When our girls were small, I hardly saw Len from one week to the next. There was still a big club circuit in those days, and he had to work all hours, up and down the country, just to scrape a living. I always say that's what wore his heart out." She shut the dishwasher, shaking her head. "He's a real workaholic. Won't say no to anything—even though he can these days."

"He'll take it easy after this, surely."

She laughed shortly. "I bloody hope so. I've told him, if he's not around for our fiftieth anniversary, I'm never speaking to him again."

I said, "He's had the warning now."

"Oh, we've had plenty of warnings. I've lost count of the doctors who've told him to stop working before he drops dead." She wiped away an invisible speck, and snapped on a brand-new electric kettle. "I wish you'd ask your Fred to have a word. If your Fred told him he had to slow down, he might listen."

I found myself thinking how likeable she was, and how famously she would have got on with Phoebe. "Len thinks a lot of him, doesn't he?"

She laughed, and I could see how pretty she had been when she was young. She was still pretty, despite stripes of glittery mauve blusher. "I've been hearing about Fred since the first day of rehearsals. Len came back to our hotel in a right mood. Said they'd recast Wishee-Washee and he was some useless posh bastard." She broke off to giggle. "After that, there was something new about him every day. First it was the dog's name. Then he comes back and says, Joyce, that boy with the dog's name can speak perfect French!" (True—Fritz seduced my French exchange student, and spent the rest of that summer on her farm in Gascony.)

Joyce began to take cups and saucers out of a cupboard. "When he found out Fred was a doctor, he couldn't get over it." She smiled. "Couldn't believe it. He kept saying, why, Joyce? Why is a qualified doctor working in a seaside panto? We know what hard work it is, you see. Our eldest is a doctor."

She broke off to wheel out a tea trolley. I watched her putting out the tea things, not daring to help in case I broke something. She wheeled it across smooth acres of floor to the sitting room.

Len said, "Cassie, we've been talking about you. I bought a copy of that magazine of yours. Very interesting stuff."

"He read it from cover to cover," Joyce put in. "Even the ads at the back."

"I like reading about writers."

I told him truthfully that my colleagues would be thrilled. Len said he would sign a picture for them (he did, before we left).

He said, "You must have been quite a swot at school, Cassie."

"I'm afraid so."

"No, don't you apologize—why would you be ashamed of working hard?"

"Pipe down, Len," Joyce said. "You're meant to be resting."

He smiled at me. "I was always saying that to our daughters. Be proud of working hard. Get yourself some real qualifications."

I asked, "Did either of them want to follow you on to the stage?"

"No," Len said. "They could see the other side. They could see that I wouldn't have done it if I'd been able to do anything better. I wore out this heart"—he pointed to his chest solemnly—"with years of late nights and cheap digs and too much booze. I wanted the girls to have a choice."

Joyce handed me a cup of tea. "They've never wanted anything to do with the business. Joanne's a doctor, and Susan's a headmistress."

There were photographs of Joanne and Susan and their children on every available surface, displayed at each stage of their lives, from birth, through Brownies and academic robes, to wedding dresses and prosperous matronhood.

Len looked hard at Fritz. "You had a choice," he said. "So what the bloody hell are you doing?"

Fritz was very quiet on the drive home. I thought he had retreated into one of his moods. I was surprised when he parked his car outside my front door.

"Are you coming up?"

"I am," he said. "I want to talk to you. I have something very important to say." He locked his car. He used his own (stolen) key to let us into my flat. Kindly but firmly, he pushed me down on the sofa. "Please don't interrupt. There will be a question-and-answer session later."

"What are you doing?"

"I said, don't interrupt. I want to marry you. Will you marry me?"

"Yes, of course I will." (As the Americans say, "Duh!") "Why are you being so serious?"

"Hang on, we're doing this all wrong. We're not being momentous enough." Fritz went down on one knee beside me. "Cassandra, will you marry me?"

I was laughing. I could see, from the expression in his wondrous dark eyes, that he knew I adored him. "Oh, get up."

"Don't say yes until you know what you're doing. You're agreeing to marry a very bad-tempered actor."

"Your temper isn't that bad."

Fritz took my hand—the one with the forget-me-not ring—in both of his. "You might not feel the same way about a bad-tempered junior doctor."

The End and the Beginning

At the very end of my wedding day (note how casually I slipped that in—*my wedding day*), when most of the guests had reeled off home, Fritz and Ben and Annabel and I were at the bottom of the garden, beside the climbing frame. Annabel sat on the edge of an upturned wheelbarrow, like an elegant Humpty-Dumpty in pale blue silk. I wore a glorious white dress and miles of filmy white veil, neither of which had come from a charity shop. Ben had found one last bottle of champagne, which he was opening. It was very good champagne. The house had been sold, and we were drinking the profits—this was why we got married in such a hurry. We wanted to throw Phoebe's house open one last time, for the greatest party of them all.

In the dark, chilly spring evening, we drank a toast to Phoebe. We had toasted her during the speeches, but this was private.

"She knows we'll be all right now," Ben said, stretching one arm around Annabel's barrel of a stomach. "She found our wives for us."

"God bless your memory, you interfering woman," Fritz said. "Now we've done exactly as you wanted, and married the girls you picked out for us. So you can stop fussing and have a nice rest."

"Oh no," I said. "As long as there's the smallest pulse of Phoebe in the eternal mind, she'll never rest. She'll fuss over you two until the crack of doom."

"And her two new grandsons," Annabel said. We now knew that the twins were boys. "Isn't it sweet to think of Phoebe as a granny?"

Fritz patted her belly. "Dear me, two more north London males, beautiful and useless."

I said I thought north London males were wonderful, when they finally got their acts together. Phoebe had shown me that there were some lovely qualities in our useless males. And they weren't really useless at all. Quite the opposite—the Darling boys were now so useful that Annabel and I couldn't live without them. I said, as I knew Phoebe would have said, that I thought we could do a lot worse.

Kate Saunders, the author of *The Marrying Game,* has also written for the *Sunday Times,* the *Sunday Express,* the *Daily Telegraph,* and *Cosmopolitan.* She lives in London with her son.